house of shadows

Also by The Medieval Murderers

The Tainted Relic
Sword of Shame
The Lost Prophecies

house of shadows

A Historical Mystery

By

The Medieval Murderers

Bernard Knight
Ian Morson
Michael Jecks
Philip Gooden
Susanna Gregory

POCKET
BOOKS

London • Sydney • New York • Toronto

A CBS COMPANY

First published in Great Britain by Simon & Schuster UK Ltd, 2007
This edition first published by Pocket Books, 2008
An imprint of Simon & Schuster UK Ltd
A CBS COMPANY

1 3 5 7 9 10 8 6 4 2

Simon & Schuster UK Ltd
1st Floor
222 Gray's Inn Road
London WC1X 8HB

www.simonandschuster.co.uk

Simon & Schuster Australia
Sydney

A CIP catalogue record for this book is available from the British Library

ISBN: 978-1-84983-551-0

Typeset in New Baskerville by Palimpsest Book Production Limited,
Grangemouth, Stirlingshire
Printed and bound in Great Britain by
CPI Cox & Wyman, Reading, RG1 8EX

'The Medieval Murderers'

A small group of historical mystery writers, all members of the Crime Writers' Association, who promote their work by giving informal talks and discussions at libraries, bookshops and literary festivals.

Bernard Knight is a former Home Office pathologist and professor of forensic medicine who has been publishing novels, non-fiction, radio and television drama and documentaries for more than forty years. He currently writes the highly regarded Crowner John series of historical mysteries, based on the first coroner for Devon in the twelfth century; the twelfth of which, *The Manor of Death*, has recently been published by Simon & Schuster.

Ian Morson is the author of an acclaimed series of historical mysteries featuring the thirteenth-century Oxford-based detective, William Falconer, and a brand-new series featuring Venetian crime-solver, Nick Zuliani.

Michael Jecks was a computer salesman before turning to writing. His immensely popular Templar series, set during the confusion and terror of the reign of Edward II, is translated into most continental languages and is published in America. The most recent novels in the series are *The Malice of Unnatural Death* and *Dispensation of Death*. Michael was chairman of the Crime Writers' Association in 2004–5.

Philip Gooden is the author of the Nick Revill series, a sequence of historical mysteries set in Elizabethan and Jacobean London, during the time of Shakespeare's Globe Theatre. The latest titles are *Mask of Night* and *An Honourable Murder*. He also produces reference books on language, most recently *Faux Pas* and *Name Dropping*. Philip was chairman of the Crime Writers' Association in 2007–8.

Susanna Gregory is the author of the Matthew Bartholomew series of mystery novels, set in fourteenth-century Cambridge, the most recent of which are *To Kill or Cure* and *The Devil's Disciples*. In addition, she writes a series set in Restoration London, featuring Thomas Chaloner; the most recent book is *The Butcher of Smithfield*. She also writes historical mysteries under the name of Simon Beaufort.

Medieval
Murderers

The Programme

Prologue – In which Bernard Knight lays the foundation for the ghoulish tales that follow.

Act One – In which Bernard Knight tells how Crowner John arrives at the priory of Bermondsey to investigate murder most foul.

Act Two – In which Ian Morson's William Falconer uncovers dark deeds during an eclipse of the moon.

Act Three – In which Michael Jecks' Keeper Sir Baldwin and Bailiff Puttock foil a treasonous plot.

Act Four – In which Philip Gooden relates how the poet Chaucer becomes embroiled in the priory's dark history.

Act Five – In which Susanna Gregory's Thomas Chaloner, spy for the Lord Chancellor of England, avenges a violent death.

Epilogue – In which Bernard Knight exposes the final secret.

hISTORICAL NOTE

Bermondsey lies on the south bank of the Thames, near where Tower Bridge now stands. A priory was established there as early as 1089 and became one of the richest in England due to numerous gifts of land and money. Originally founded by four Cluniac monks from France, who built on ground donated by a rich London merchant, the priory became a Benedictine abbey in 1399, surviving until Henry VIII dissolved all monasteries in the sixteenth century. It was then built over repeatedly, though the gatehouse survived until the nineteenth century.

Though this famous monastery had a very real existence for hundreds of years, the stories in this book are works of fiction. In the early years of the twenty-first century, extensive excavations were carried out by archaeologists, prior to a huge commerical complex being built over the site. The events described in the Epilogue are similarly fictitious.

PROLOGUE

December 1114

Grey mist, like wet smoke, slowly rolled over the wall of the priory, seeping in from across the marshes that lined the Thames. Together with the winter twilight, the fog made it almost dark, though the bell for vespers was only now sounding, its doleful tone muffled in the moist air.

A small procession was slowly crossing the outer courtyard towards the west front of the church, the black Cluniac habits adding to the already sombre atmosphere. Of the dozen hooded figures walking in pairs, three were openly sobbing, and the expressions on the remaining grim faces were set in barely contained emotion. Behind them in the inner court-yard was a closed door, which until today had been merely the entrance to the cellarer's storeroom but which now concealed a dreadful secret.

As their sandalled feet padded across the damp earth towards the steps of the new church of St Saviour's, the monks' faces were lit by the flickering yellow light of two pitch-brands set in iron rings on each side of the west door. The light fell first on the prior, Peter de Charité, who at fifty was a strong, hard-faced discipli-narian. The monk alongside him and the two imme-diately behind were Richard, Osbert and Umbold, who had accompanied him from France fifteen years before,

1

sent to establish a new daughter house of Cluny in this fog-ridden swamp that was Bermondsey.

Since then, eight more monks had joined them as the priory flourished, nurtured by gifts of land from various benefactors. There had been nine, and therein lay the cause of their present misery.

'King Henry must never hear the truth of this,' murmured Osbert, his teeth chattering from fright rather than the cold.

'But how are we going to keep it from him?' keened Richard, who was too old to have teeth to chatter.

'Be quiet, brothers!' snapped Peter. 'In fact, keeping very quiet is what we must all do.'

The four founders were sitting around the fireplace in the prior's chamber, the other monks having been left in the church to pray for absolution until it was time for the evening meal. Umbold, a fat man of middle age, had no tonsure like the others, as he was completely bald.

'Count Eustace will be here after Epiphany to confirm the grant,' he moaned. 'What are we to tell him?'

There was silence as they all considered this yet again. The problem had dominated their minds ever since the catastrophe had fallen on them three days ago. Earlier that year, Mary, the wife of Eustace, Count of Boulogne, and sister of Queen Maud, had granted the manor and advowson of Kingweston to the priory. Recently, Eustace had declared his intention of visiting them personally to confirm the grant. Six months earlier, his wife had sent her junior chaplain, Brother Francis, to join them – ostensibly as a gesture of goodwill, though Prior Peter suspected that it was really to make sure that the proceeds of her gift were being spent wisely in the extension of the building.

'We tell the count what we shall tell everyone else, including the king,' growled the prior. 'That they both ran away and now we know nothing of their whereabouts!'

'That will satisfy no one, least of all King Henry,' whimpered Osbert. 'The girl was placed here in our safekeeping.'

This was a greater problem than even that of Count Eustace, as a month after the arrival of Brother Francis the king had sent them Lady Alice, his most recent ward. She was the orphaned daughter of Drogo de Peverel, dispatched to live at the priory until she could be found a suitable husband. Her father had been killed in a skirmish in Normandy and, with her mother already dead, his lands had escheated to the Crown and his daughter became the king's responsibility. At eighteen, Alice had already shown herself to be a wilful girl of independent spirit, and Queen Maud, familiar with the task of dealing with her husband's wards and cast-off mistresses, decided that the isolated location and stern discipline of Bermondsey would be a suitable place in which to keep the girl until she could be used for some political and financial advantage.

Unfortunately, the inevitable happened. Within a month of her arrival, Lady Alice's seductive wiles easily overcame the vows of the immature young chaplain and soon she found herself with child. Even worse, the priest's remorse at the discovery sent him out of his mind, into an explosion of violence.

When the awful results of this secret liaison burst on the small community a few days ago, Peter's authoritarian character, nurtured in the rigid discipline of the Cluniacs' strict interpretation of the Rule of Saint Benedict, overcame his common sense. Instead of admitting their failure to foresee such a catastrophe and delivering the problem to the king and Count

Eustace, the prior decided to deal with the matter himself. Partly from a stubborn desire to regulate the affairs of his own priory, but even more from the fear of losing the lavish patronage of those who offered support to Bermondsey, Peter decided to act as he thought God and the Pope would require and wreaked terrible retribution on the errant chaplain.

Now they were burdened with the consequences of that decision and could do nothing but bow their heads and hope to weather the storm that soon would inevitably burst over them.

ΛCT ONE

February 1196

'We'll get no further, Sir John,' called the shipmaster from his place at the steering oar. 'There's not a breath of wind left and the fog's thickening.'

Straining his eyes, John de Wolfe could just make out a low shore a few hundred yards away on the larboard side of the little cog *Saint Radegund*, but even that view came and went as greyish-yellow fog rolled in intermittent patches up the estuary of the Thames.

'Where in God's name are we, William?' he shouted back to the bandy-legged sailor who commanded the vessel from the high stern.

'Just off Woolwich, Crowner! As far as we'll get on this flood tide with no wind. Unless I anchor now, we'll drift back down with the ebb.'

John's two companions heard the news with mixed feelings. Thomas de Peyne, the small priest who was the coroner's clerk, was murmuring thanks to the Almighty for the flat calm that came with the fog, for this was the first day he had not been trying to turn his stomach inside out on the four-day voyage from Devon.

However, the coroner's officer, Gwyn of Polruan, was irritated by their lack of progress, especially as until now they had had an exceptionally swift passage from Dawlish, a small port not far from Exeter. A brisk westerly wind had raced the ship along the south coast in record time, and when it conveniently changed to a north-easterly after they had rounded the butt end of Kent it pushed them up the estuary as far as Greenwich. Only then had it failed them, as the wind dropped and the fog rolled in. The tide carried them a few more miles, but now even that had deserted them.

Gwyn, a giant of a man with wild red hair and long moustaches of the same hue, looked up at the single sail, hanging damp and motionless from the yardarm.

'If we want to get to Bermondsey by river, we'll have to swim the rest of the bloody way!' he growled. A former fisherman from Polruan in Cornwall, he claimed to be an authority on all things maritime, and he watched critically as one of the four-man crew, a lad of about fourteen, heaved the anchor over the bow – a stone weighing a hundredweight with a hole chiselled through it to take the cable.

Annoyed, his master, John de Wolfe, slapped the wooden rail that ran around the bulwarks. 'We made such good time, compared with flogging up from Exeter by horse,' he complained. 'The justiciar said that time was of the essence and here we are, stuck only a few miles from the priory.'

Thomas stared through the murk at the dimly seen shore. 'Is there no way we can continue by land, Crowner?' he asked hesitantly.

Gwyn turned to look at the curragh lashed upside down on top of the vessel's single hatch. It was a fragile cockleshell of tarred hide stretched over a light wooden frame, like an elongated coracle.

'They could put us ashore in that, I suppose,' he said rather dubiously.

The coroner shrugged and shouted at the master, William Watts. 'How far is it to Bermondsey from here?'

'About six or seven miles, Sir John, as the crow flies.'

'We're not bloody crows!' grumbled Gwyn. 'But I suppose we could get horses in that miserable-looking hamlet over there.' He pointed to where a couple of shacks were fleetingly visible between the walls of yellow fog, then watched his master lope away across the deck to arrange their disembarkation.

The coroner was a forbidding figure in the wreathing mist, dressed in his habitual black and grey. As tall as Gwyn, he was lean and spare, with a slight stoop that gave him the appearance of a large bird of prey, especially with his hooked nose and jet-black hair that was swept back to his collar, unlike the close crops of most Norman knights. Gwyn had been his squire, companion and bodyguard for twenty years, in campaigns from Ireland to the Holy Land, where the Crowner's taste in clothing and the stubble on his lean cheeks had earned him the nickname 'Black John'.

Half an hour later, after a short but perilous voyage in the flimsy curragh, they were landed on a muddy beach and shouted farewell to the shipman who had paddled them ashore. As soon as he had returned to the *Saint Radegund,* the vessel up-anchored and drifted down on the tide to begin its journey to Flanders with a cargo of wool. John had used the voyage to get to London as quickly as possible, as on horseback it would have taken the better part of a week.

As their last link with home vanished into the fog, the three men trudged up the muddy foreshore, thankfully narrow at this state of the tide. At the top, they followed a track to the straggle of huts and a few larger dwellings that was Woolwich, looking even more dismal than usual in the moist gloom of a winter's morning. The largest building was a single-storeyed erection of wattle and daub, the thatched roof tattered and moss-infested. However, over the doorway hung a withered bush, the universal sign of an inn, and after a quart of ale each the coroner negotiated the hire of three horses. Though the tavern-keeper was reluctant to allow his nags to leave the parish, the coroner waved a parchment scroll in front of him. None of them could read it, apart from Thomas de Peyne, but the royal seal dangling from it impressed the man sufficiently to agree to let them have the beasts.

They set off on the underfed rounseys, following a lad on a pony, who would show them the way to Bermondsey and bring the horses back again.

What they could see of the countryside, which was very little in the mist, looked bleak and barren, mud-flats giving way to scrub-covered heath, rather than the forested dales they were used to in the West Country. As they plodded along, at half the speed of a decent horse, de Wolfe asked his clerk what kind of a place they were bound for. Thomas, always eager to share his vast store of knowledge about things religious and historical, was pleased to oblige.

'The priory was founded over a century ago, master. It's a daughter house of a Cluniac abbey, St Mary's at La Charité-sur-Loire. Four monks came over from France to take advantage of a gift of land from a rich London merchant.'

Gwyn, whose blunt views on religion were well known to his companions, said that he didn't give a damn who founded the place, as long as they kept a good kitchen and a comfortable guesthouse. For once, Thomas agreed with him in respect of their accommodation.

'Thank God for a bed that won't roll around for four hellish nights!' he said fervently, crossing himself several times, in recollection of the misery he had suffered on the *Saint Radegund.*

They rode in silence for a while, the coroner contemplating the circumstances which had brought him so far from his home, wife and mistress. A week ago he was minding his own business as coroner in Exeter, dividing his time as usual between his chilly chamber in the gatehouse of Rougemont Castle, his house in Martin's Lane and the taproom of the Bush Inn, where he enjoyed the company of his pretty mistress, Nesta.

Then one freezing morning a herald with the king's insignia on his tabard arrived, guarded by two men-at-arms. He bore a parchment with the impressive seal of Hubert Walter, virtual regent of England now that Richard de Lionheart was permanently in France. As de Wolfe could read little more than his own name, Thomas de Peyne rapidly translated the Latin text, his eyes growing wider as they scanned the lines of manuscript.

'The chief justiciar wants you to go to London, master!' gabbled the little priest. Hubert Walter was not only Archbishop of Canterbury but was also the head of England's legal system and effectively of its government. Impatiently, John de Wolfe waited for his clerk to deliver the rest of the message, with Gwyn peering over Thomas's shoulder as if he could decipher the words himself.

'He requires you to go with all speed to the priory at Bermondsey, to investigate the death of a ward of our lord the king. He gives you this Royal Commission as a temporary Coroner of the Verge, as the former coroner is laid low with the ague and is likely to die.'

John knew that the royal household had its own coroner, the 'Verge' being the area of jurisdiction radiating twelve miles around wherever the perambulating court happened to be.

'Where the hell is Bermondsey?' demanded Gwyn.

De Wolfe shrugged. 'Somewhere in London, as far as I know.'

His clerk looked slightly aggrieved at their ignorance. 'Bermondsey Priory is a famous house, on the south

side of the Thames, just below King William's White
Tower on the opposite bank.'

The coroner was more concerned with his mission
than with the geography. 'Does Hubert not say what
he wishes me to do?' he demanded.

Thomas rapidly read to the end of the short message.
'It seems that the circumstances of the death of this
lady are suspicious, but the justiciar says that you will
have the details when you arrive. He will be absent in
Normandy, but the prior will acquaint you with the situation. The last sentence emphasizes the urgency of your
arrival at the priory, in order to examine the corpse.'

'God's bones, she'll be pretty ripe by the time we
arrive!' grunted the Cornishman. 'That messenger
must have been on the road for almost a week and it
will take us another week to get there!'

As it turned out, the delay was somewhat less, as the
herald had made a forced ride with numerous changes
of horse and had covered the journey from London to
Exeter in four days. Together with the fortunate voyage
of the *Saint Radegund*, it was not much more than a
week before they found themselves jogging into
Bermondsey.

This was even less of a community than Woolwich,
as it consisted mainly of the priory, with a few cottages
sheltering under its walls. The surroundings were
bleak, especially on this icy winter's day, being a waste
of marshes that ran along the Thames, which was about
a quarter of a mile from the priory. The fog was thinner
here and the coroner's trio could see humps of reedy
mud rising above a network of reens and ditches, as
the great river had poorly defined edges that changed
with the tides and the rainfall.

The priory was built on the first solid ground that
rose slightly above the swamp, and as they rode towards
the gatehouse de Wolfe could see that the walls formed

a substantial rectangle of masonry, within which buildings could be seen, one of them a church. Though Gwyn was not impressed by his first sight of their destination, Thomas's eyes lit up as he saw a new ecclesiastical establishment. He crossed himself vigorously and muttered some Latin prayers under his breath.

As far as the coroner was concerned, this was a new challenge to his professional reputation, as he had secretly been proud to have the summons from the justiciar, ahead of all the other county coroners in England. It was true that he had a special relationship with Hubert Walter – and indeed Richard Coeur de Lion himself – as he had been part of the king's bodyguard in the Holy Land and had accompanied him on the ill-fated voyage home when he returned from the Third Crusade.

Still, to have been appointed coroner of the verge, even if only as a locum tenens, was an honour, for this unique post was responsible for the investigation of deaths, assaults, ravishments and fires that might involve the king, his court and anyone associated with that grand if cumbersome entourage.

With these thoughts in mind, he followed the lad on the pony to the gatehouse on the western side of the walls. It had a wide gate under a stone arch to admit wagons and a side gate for pedestrians. As soon as they dismounted and untied their sparse belongings from the saddles, the boy from Woolwich rapidly roped the horses into a line and vanished into the mist without a word, leaving the three men standing outside the forbidding oaken doors like orphans left outside a poorhouse.

De Wolfe strode to the small door and saw that alongside it there was a bell hanging from a bracket, with a cord dangling from the clapper. He rang it vigorously and a moment later a large man with a face like a bulldog appeared. He wore a faded cassock, and John, correctly taking him for a lay brother, dragged Thomas forward to explain who they were. Grudgingly, the porter motioned them in, and without a word slammed the door to the secular world behind them.

They found themselves in a wide outer court, the west end of the church forming the further end, with a cemetery visible over a low wall on their left. A line of buildings formed the right-hand side, and without a word the door-ward pointed to another gate about a third of the way down this stone façade.

The coroner's team made their way to this inner entrance and saw a small wicket-gate in the centre. Stepping through, they entered a long inner court stretching down to the high boundary wall in the distance. On their left were more buildings, with several doors and a row of shuttered windows on the upper floor.

'God be with you, brothers,' came a voice from nearby. Turning, they saw that a small lodge lay inside the gate, from which a tubby monk now emerged. In his element, Thomas de Peyne advanced on him, inevitably making the sign of the cross, and greeted him in fluent Latin.

'Why can't they damned well talk English?' grumbled Gwyn. 'Then we'd know what they're gabbling about!'

Thomas ferreted in his shoulder-bag and produced the scroll that had carried Hubert Walter's commission to Exeter. He displayed the ornate red wax seal of the Archbishop of Canterbury and allowed the guardian of the inner gate to read the text. Suitably impressed, the ruddy-faced monk bobbed his head in deference to the king's coroner and, to be on the safe side, to Gwyn as well. Then he said something to Thomas and trotted off towards a doorway in the nearest building.

'That was Brother Maglo and he's taking us to the

prior, but first of all will show us where we will be accommodated,' explained their clerk, delighted to be within a house of God once again. 'This is the cellarer's building and above it is the guesthouse.'

Inside, the ground floor appeared to be a series of storerooms with several small offices where monks were keeping lists and tallies of all the food, drink and supplies needed for the bodily health of the inhabitants, their spiritual health being dealt with deeper inside the priory. The whole place smelled of damp, mouldy grain and a hint of incense. As they reached the far end of the central corridor, their guide spoke in English for the first time, in a voice with a strong Breton accent.

'Sirs, these are the stairs up to some of the guest-chambers and the dormitory. You will eat here, in this small refectory, as the kitchens are through there.'

Maglo pointed first into a large room at the foot of the staircase, then to a door in the end wall from behind which came a clashing of pots and pans. They climbed the bare stone stairs to the upper floor, where a long dormitory lay above the cellarium below. The first quarter was partitioned into four small rooms, two on each side, the rest of the attic being laid out with a dozen mattresses along the floor. A large crucifix hung over a door at the end.

'That is the way down into the cloister and to the church,' explained Brother Maglo. 'You, Sir John, have this cubicle here. Your assistants will sleep in the first two beds of the common dormitory.'

Having firmly established the statuses of the new arrivals, the rotund Cluniac hurried back to his post, after a final word to explain that someone would soon come to escort them to the prior and afterwards see that they were fed and watered.

De Wolfe entered his cell, which had no door, and

dropped his saddlebag on to the mattress, the only furniture in the room. His luggage contained little apart from two clean tunics, a couple of pairs of hose and several clean undershirts, all packed by his cook-maid Mary, as his surly wife Matilda was utterly bereft of any domestic skills.

A hairbrush and a specially sharpened knife for his weekly shaves completed his belongings – he suspected that Gwyn and Thomas had even less, though his clerk always carried his Vulgate and prayer book, together with writing materials. As a token of respect for a religious house, he unbuckled his sword belt and pulled the supporting baldric from his shoulder, then hung them on one of the pegs fixed to the wall, with his grey wolfskin riding cloak alongside it.

Going out into the main dormitory, he found that his assistants had dumped their meagre possessions into small cupboards that stood against the wall. Gwyn had opened the shutter of the nearest unglazed window and was peering out.

'Bloody cold, Crowner, inside and out,' he observed glumly. 'The fog's clearing but it looks like snow. At least the weather will keep the corpse all the fresher.'

De Wolfe and Thomas moved to his side and looked through the narrow slot in the thick stone wall. Below them was a narrow sloping roof of grey tiles, extending around a large square, with a patch of frosty grass occupying the centre.

'This is the cloister walk, with the garth in the middle,' observed Thomas. 'That must be the chapterhouse and prior's quarters opposite, with the dorter and frater over to the right.' These last were the dormitory and refectory for the monks, the lay brothers and domestic servants eating elsewhere. The lofty church formed the side of the cloister to their left, blocking any view of the marshes and river to the north.

Their inspection was interrupted by a creak as the far door opened and another monk appeared in a long habit of Benedictine black which swept the ground. He was tall and thin, with a ring of sparse grey hair below his shaven pate. A mournful face reinforced John's impression that Bermondsey Priory was not a very joyful establishment. He seemed to glide up the dormitory as if he was on wheels rather than on a pair of feet, and when he reached them he inclined his head in a faint greeting.

'I am Brother Ignatius, the prior's chaplain and secretary. I bid you welcome, though regrettably the reason for your visit is not felicitous.'

He addressed his opening speech to Thomas, whom he saw as a fellow priest, but it was the coroner who answered and gruffly introduced the trio.

Ignatius swivelled around on unseen feet and indicated the door through which he had entered. 'I will conduct you to the prior, who is anxious to speak to you. Then no doubt you will be glad of some refreshment after your long journey.'

The others could almost hear Gwyn's stomach rumbling at the prospect, for the outsize Cornishman needed to be refuelled every few hours and the last scratch meal on the *Saint Radegund* was poor fare by his standards. They followed the secretary through the door and down a narrow flight of steps to a dark vestibule with several doors.

'That one leads into the nave of the church, should you wish to leave your beds to pray,' said Ignatius. He pointed to one on his left but unlatched another door, which opened into the ambulatory walk around the cloister.

They walked along the flagstoned arcade, which opened between pillars to overlook the sparse lawn of the garth. At the other end of this side of the square, yet another door admitted them into a short corridor. It was noticeably warmer in here than the cellarer's building or the dormitory, and the cynical Gwyn suspected that the head of the house made himself far more comfortable than his minions. Their guide waved a hand at several rooms on the left.

'Those are various offices, including mine, but the prior's parlour is up here.' He turned into an alcove on the right, where a flight of wooden stairs led to the upper floor. The atmosphere got milder still as they ascended, and when they reached a square hall above it was positively warm, helped by the fact that a window in one wall actually had glass instead of a shutter, a rare luxury indeed. An open door in the opposite wall revealed a small chapel, which Thomas decided must be for the prior's private use.

The thin monk tapped on another door and entered, reappearing a moment later to beckon them inside. The coroner strode in, determined to assert his royal authority from the start, as he had long experience of some churchmen, with their superior and often supercilious attitudes, coupled with a reluctance to cooperate with his investigations. However, it transpired that in Bermondsey Priory he need have no fears on that score, for Prior Robert Northam was only too anxious for any help he could get. He rose from behind his table and bowed his head courteously to the coroner.

'I am glad to see that you have arrived safely, Sir John. Your reputation goes before you and I only hope that you can settle this distressing matter expeditiously.'

He had a mellow voice, but there was a strong undercurrent of anxiety in his tone. De Wolfe explained that his clerk and officer were indispensable to his work as coroner, and Robert Northam acknowledged them warmly. He was a stocky man of about fifty, with a bush of dark brown hair, which contrasted all the more with the baldness of his tonsure. His face was square and his features strong, deep lines being etched at each side of his mouth and across his forehead. Though the priory was a French foundation and many of its monks were from Normandy or further south, Northam was English. He had spent some years at the mother house on the Loire before being sent as prior to Bermondsey in 1189.

At a gesture from his superior, Brother Ignatius fetched a chair and placed it for the coroner on the opposite side of the table to the prior, who motioned for Gwyn and Thomas to sit on a bench near the fireplace, where a sea-coal fire threw out a comfortable glow across the chamber.

With his secretary standing dutifully beside him, Robert Northam sat down again and began explaining the situation to de Wolfe. 'I do not know how much you know of this tragedy, Sir John. I doubt that Hubert Walter was very informative, knowing his nature.'

John nodded his agreement. 'He told me virtually nothing, prior, other than that a ward of the king had been found dead and as the regular coroner of the verge was gravely ill I was to get here with all speed.'

Northam sighed and steepled his hands beneath his chin as he prepared to tell the story yet again.

'This house is blessed – or possibly cursed – with a reputation for being a refuge or perhaps a lodging for ladies of high rank. Sometimes I think we should have been a hostel rather than a priory!' He sounded more resigned than sarcastic, but John sensed a certain bitterness in his tone.

'We are too conveniently placed for London, virtually within sight of the great city across the river. When the king, God bless him, or one of his high officers of state has a lady in need of protection or safe accommodation, they tend to get landed on us here. We seem to specialize in royal wards, of which there seems an endless supply!' He folded his arms and leaned on his table, bending forward so that his dark eyes were fixed on de Wolfe.

'A month ago we had a message from the Archbishop that yet another ward of King Richard was to be housed here, though thankfully Hubert Walter said it was only to be for a short period – in fact, until she was married in the great church of St Paul on the other bank.'

John felt it was time he broke into the monologue. 'Was that an unusual request, prior?'

Northam turned up his hands. 'It has happened before – we are within easy riding distance of both the abbey of Westminster and the city's cathedral. This particular lady was from the midland shires and thus a more local domicile was needed for her to be prepared for the nuptials.'

John waited with more than his usual patience for the prior to continue.

'The lady – or really girl, for she was not yet sixteen – arrived in mid-January, with her tirewomen and some of her guardians. She was Christina de Glanville, distantly related to Ranulf de Glanville, the renowned former justiciar of England, who died six years ago at the siege of Acre in the Holy Land.'

De Wolfe grunted. 'I was there myself, as was my officer Gwyn. We well remember de Glanville and his tragic death.'

The prior rapped his table with his fingertips. 'Then tragic death seems to run in the Glanville family, for two days before the wedding his great-niece was found dead in one of our cellars!'

'Why was she a royal ward, prior?' asked de Wolfe.

'When she was a child, her mother died giving birth

to a son, who would have been the heir except that the infant died as well. Christina was the only child of Sir William de Glanville – and to complete the tragic circle, he also died alongside his uncle while fighting the Mohammedans at Acre.'

'Is the Glanville family not from Suffolk, sir?' ventured Thomas from across the room.

Robert Northam nodded. 'They are indeed – and the girl's father left a very substantial estate there, as well as other property elsewhere. As there was no heir of the age of majority, it all escheated to the Crown on his death and his only surviving child was made a ward of King Richard.'

'But presumably she was placed in the care of a guardian, unless she was sequestrated in some other religious house?' suggested the coroner.

'Indeed she was, Sir John. At first she was placed in the Gilbertine convent of Sempringham in Lincoln-shire, being only ten years of age at the time of her father's death. Then her uncle, her late mother's brother, arranged for her to live with his family as a more congenial home for a young girl.'

'Wasn't that a long way from her own estates in Suffolk?' asked John.

'Her father had had several manors and mines in the shire of Derby as well,' replied the prior.

Brother Ignatius diffidently murmured further details from alongside his superior's chair. 'The lands of Sir Roger Beaumont lay adjacent to the Glanville manors in Derbyshire, so it was convenient for him also to be appointed administrator of the escheated estate. The king agreed and Chancery drew up the deeds.'

De Wolfe, cynical fellow that he was, felt the first twitchings of suspicion when he heard this. 'No doubt there was some financial advantage for him in this arrangement?'

The prior took up the tale again. 'Roger Beaumont took half the income from the Glanville properties, the remainder going to the Exchequer on behalf of the king. It was reasoned that this was his due for sheltering Christina and the labour of running the very extensive estates, which were scattered over three counties.'

John suspected that the labour involved would have been deputed to a bevy of bailiffs and reeves and that Roger would need to do little other than to sit back and rake in the profits from the farming of sheep and cattle. If Derbyshire was included, quite probably there would be lead-mining and quarrying as well.

Thomas was wriggling a little on his bench, as his quick mind was looking further ahead. 'Prior, what would have occurred when this young lady reached maturity?'

Northam looked across at the little priest with interest. He had already formed the opinion that here was a sharp fellow and this last question confirmed his view.

'This is where motive rears its ugly head, I suppose. Whether Christina married or not, she would have recovered the ownership of her estates on reaching sixteen.'

Robert poured some wine for them before continuing.

'Her father's last will and testament plainly stated that when she came of age, she was to inherit the whole estate. The Curia Regis would no doubt have found a reliable steward to run the lands for her, though legally she would have been entitled to do what she wished with them. Of course, the king could have disregarded this and kept them for himself, but as both Glanville and his illustrious uncle had died fighting alongside the Lionheart at Acre, it would have been an unpopular act.'

De Wolfe thought that the prior was going to say 'churlish act', but he avoided this potentially seditious remark in time. Instead, John's bushy black eyebrows rose a little as he questioned the priest again.

'Sixteen? But she was about to be wed, so when would she have reached that age?'

Robert Northam sighed again, his worried features telling of the stressful time he had recently endured. 'She was to be married at St Paul's on her sixteenth birthday, coroner. And that would have been the day after she was found dead!'

There was a silence as the three visitors digested the significance of this news

'Might we ask to whom she was betrothed?' asked Thomas tentatively.

'A young man called Jordan de Neville, again from a well-known family. He was about five years older than the girl, the third son of the Nevilles, a rising family from the north country – Durham, I believe. The match was sponsored by several members of the Curia Regis and Hubert Walter was himself keen on the union, at the direct behest of the king, so I understand. King Richard, in a rare burst of interest in English affairs, decided that Jordan de Neville would make Christina an ideal husband and incidentally bring his manors as a useful addition to the Glanville lands. There must have been some covert petitioning going on in Rouen that I was not aware of.'

'And who inherits, now that she is dead?' asked John bluntly.

The prior shrugged, holding his hands palm upwards, after the fashion he acquired in France. 'It is not settled – but unless the king steps in to take the lot, Roger Beaumont has the best claim. He was Christina's guardian and nearest relative, and has been administering the estate successfully for six years.'

21

Again the coroner's index of cynicism rose another notch. A political marriage, drafted by the machinations of the court. He wondered what the prospective bride and groom thought of being pushed together by external pressures – the fact that it had happened to him sixteen years ago made his doubts all the stronger. Still, that aspect was none of his business and he returned to the duty that had brought him to Bermondsey.

'I need to know something of the background of the people who were with the girl before she died. What possible motives can there be for her murder, for she was not yet sixteen?'

'Many a child younger than she has been killed for less than is at stake in her case,' answered Robert sadly. John downed the last of his wine and looked quizzically across at the prior.

'So who could gain what from killing the poor girl?' he demanded.

Robert Northam shrugged. 'The obvious choice is Roger Beaumont. He had been sitting on a very handsome income for six years and had dug himself well into the administration of the Glanville lands. Now it would all be whipped away from him on the day of her marriage.'

'Would her death make that much difference?' asked de Wolfe. 'The estates were not his, whatever happened.'

The prior gave a cynical chuckle. 'Possession is a very potent persuader in the eyes of the law – and of King Richard. Much as we both admire and loyally serve him, we must admit that he has a great attraction for money. He said not long ago that he would sell London itself if he could find a rich enough buyer! With no heir apparent after the girl died, Roger Beaumont no doubt could expect to be offered her escheated estates at a bargain price, after looking after them for half a dozen years.'

De Wolfe nodded his understanding and got down to more immediate issues.

'So how did the poor girl die, prior? What is it that requires the attentions of a coroner?'

Robert Northam took a deep breath and used his arms to brace himself against his table. John had the feeling that his preamble so far had been partly to delay having to recount the more distressing events.

'On Tuesday morning of last week, one of the obidentiaries who assists the cellarer had occasion to visit the vault beneath the cellarer's building in order to make an inventory of some goods or other. This was a frequent task, often undertaken daily. When this brother descended the stairs, he was shocked to find the body of a woman lying at their foot. He raised the alarm by seeking out the cellarer, Brother Daniel, who with several other monks and lay brothers rushed down to the crypt. The infirmarian was called, as he was most skilled in physic, but he found that she had been dead for some time.'

'But why should there be any suspicion?' persisted de Wolfe.

Robert shook his head sadly. 'There were several factors, Sir John. Firstly, she was an honoured guest, a lady of high rank, and was to be wedded the next day, so what on earth was she doing in the cellarer's store-room?'

He wiped a kerchief over his worried face, as if he was sweating.

'Furthermore, none of us could understand why she was lying face down, with her head almost touching the bottom step. If she had fallen down the stairs, how could she have ended up in that posture?'

He stopped and looked at John almost appealingly.

'And it has to be said, coroner, that there had been some discord among the party that accompanied Christina. That cannot be overlooked!'

De Wolfe sensed that the prior was in the grip of some strong emotion, and a sixth sense told him that it was time to create some diversion.

'Perhaps it would be best if we were to view the scene of this unfortunate happening,' he said gruffly. In addition to the prior's acute discomfiture, John could hear Gwyn's stomach rumbling and felt it would be a good time to break off for some sustenance. Robert Northam took the hint and sent them away with his chaplain to meet the monk who was in charge of the guest accommodation. He was waiting outside the prior's parlour, a younger man with a smooth olive face and jet-black hair which suggested his origins in the south of France or even further afield.

'I am Brother Ferdinand and I will attend to your wants while you are staying with us,' he announced in a low sibilant voice. 'No doubt you wish to eat without further delay.'

He glided off in front of them and they retraced their steps through the cloister walk to the cellarer's building and the refectory where guests and visitors were fed. It was a large, square room with a long table flanked by benches, capable of seating at least a dozen people. It was empty, and to Gwyn's relief the lectern from which the Gospels were read aloud during regular mealtimes was unoccupied. Ferdinand invited them to be seated and went off to the nearby kitchen to organize their victuals.

'Odd sort of place, this priory!' rumbled Gwyn. 'What the devil do they do here all day? It must take a mint of money to keep going.'

Thomas glared at him. 'What do they do? They praise

God, what d'you think they do? And between times they meditate on life and heaven and earth.'

'Bloody waste of time, I reckon,' growled Gwyn. 'At least in places like Buckfast Abbey back home, they breed thousands of sheep and cattle and till the soil and keep bees for honey and mead.'

The perennial argument between them over religion was cut short by the arrival of two lay brothers with aprons over their habits, one of them bearing pitchers of ale and cider. The second servant, an arthritic skeleton, stumbled in with a large tray, which he set on the table. Thick trenchers of stale bread carried slabs of fatty bacon surrounded by fried onions. A wooden platter of roasted chicken legs was accompanied by a dish of boiled beans, dried from last autumn's crop. Another bowl contained hot frumenty, wheat boiled in milk and flavoured with cinnamon and sugar. The potman came back with a large wheaten loaf, a pat of butter and a slab of hard cheese on a wooden board. Pottery mugs appeared for the drink, then the two minions vanished back into the kitchen.

Conscious of their surroundings, Thomas stood and chanted a short Latin grace before sitting down to eat for the first time since he set foot on the ship in Dawlish.

'When you have eaten, Brother Ignatius will return for you, Sir John,' hissed Ferdinand before leaving them in peace to eat their fill.

'Maybe this is not such a bad place after all!' conceded Gwyn, eyeing the pile of food with relish.

His friend the clerk was not so enthusiastic. 'Much as I enjoy being in another of God's houses, there is something about this place that troubles me,' he said, his peaky face looking about him uneasily.

'You mean this eating chamber?' said Gwyn through a mouthful of bacon.

'No, the whole establishment. There is a feeling of

anguish about it, somehow, which I can't explain. It is not a happy place.'

'The prior looked more than a little drawn,' agreed de Wolfe. 'But I suppose it is wearying to have the Chief Justiciar breathing down your neck after some favourite of the king is found dead!'

He tucked into his food enthusiastically as, like Gwyn, he had the old soldiers' philosophy of always eating, sleeping and making love whenever the opportunity presented, in case it might be their last chance. By the time they had finished, it was mid-afternoon, calculated by the paling of the light seen through the solitary window opening, with its half-open shutter. The patch of sky was grey, and a cold breeze came into the unheated chamber.

'Must be freezing outside,' observed the coroner's officer, wiping the last of the ale from his moustaches. 'I wonder where they've left this cadaver for the past week or so?'

He was soon to find out, as the prior's secretary returned at that moment and ushered them out into the corridor of the cellarium.

'I would like to see the place where this unfortunate lady was discovered,' said John, deciding that it was time for him to show his authority a little more strongly.

'Then you have not far to go, Crowner,' replied Ignatius smoothly.

He led them outside into the inner court, which they had entered an hour or two earlier, and walked along the wall of the building for a few yards. As Gwyn had prophesied, it was bitterly cold now, with a north wind whipping down towards them, a few flakes of snow twisting in its grip. Shivering, Thomas limped along in the rear, wishing he had not left his cloak in the dormitory. However, they were soon inside again, as Brother Ignatius opened another door and led them into a dark alcove. A tallow dip burned on a ledge and, feeling alongside it, the monk produced two candles, which he lit from the weak flame of the floating wick. Handing one to the coroner, he kept the other at shoulder height and cautiously advanced into the dark to pull the bolt back on another heavy door.

'Be careful here, Sir John, or you'll suffer the same fate as that young girl.'

When his eyes had grown accustomed to the poor light, de Wolfe saw a flight of stone steps going down into the Stygian blackness below. The chaplain preceded them and cautiously they trooped down the precipitous stairway, the stone walls of which were barely wide enough for Gwyn's massive shoulders. Thomas, as inquisitive as ever, counted twenty treads from top to bottom, each two hands' length deep, the angle being very steep. On the packed earth floor below, Ignatius had stopped and turned to face the bottom of the stairway, his candle held high.

'This is where she was found, Crowner. Spread-eagled on the floor, face down and arms outstretched. Her head was about there!' He placed the toe of his sandalled foot a few inches from the bottom step.

'You saw her yourself?' asked John. When the monk agreed that he had been one of the first to respond to the lay brother's agitated call for help, the coroner dropped to a crouch at the spot. At first, Thomas thought a sudden urge to pray for Christina's soul had overcome his master, but then he saw that de Wolfe was holding his candle close to the ground and was searching the damp floor where the body had lain. After a few moments he clambered to his feet.

'Nothing to be seen there. I gather you saw no blood at the time?' Ignatius shook his tonsured head. 'None at all, sir. She looked as if she were asleep, what could be seen of her face. Her clothing and nether garments were not disarranged.'

He said this with a prim indifference that made John wonder if he had a deeper interest in a woman's apparel than he wished to admit.

'So where is the unfortunate lady now?' he asked. 'In the church, perhaps?'

The chaplain looked slightly offended this time. 'Indeed not, Crowner! She has been dead these past twelve days. We could not have the corrupt remains where we must hold our many offices each day. She is here!'

He waved a hand into the deeper darkness behind him. Bemused, the trio followed cautiously into the gloom, the two wavering candles showing piles of kegs, crates and bales stacked on either side. Above them a vaulted stone roof was festooned with cobwebs, and an ominous rustling of rats could be heard from the corners. They passed through a wide arch into a similar store filled with old furniture, mattresses and discarded material, then another, similar arch led them into another large bay. This was an empty space with a blank wall opposite. Even de Wolfe, as insensitive a soul as could be found anywhere in England, felt a chill as he entered, a frisson that was not related to the temperature, which was the same in here as in the rest of the subterranean vault.

There was something about this third chamber that he did not care for – but a moment later he decided that he had found the reason. Around the corner of the arch, the flickering lights fell on a makeshift coffin, resting on a pair of trestles. It was a crude box made from rough planks, larger than the usual coffin. In the sudden silence that the sight engendered, there was an eerie sound, a steady drip, drip as water fell from the seams into a widening pool beneath the trestles.

Thomas jerkily made the sign of the cross and then repeated it several times for good measure. There was something about this empty vault that deeply disturbed him, apart from the ominous sight of a coffin as its only furnishings.

The prior's secretary seemed oblivious to any oppressive miasma and walked to the wooden box and peered in.

'Not yet completely melted,' he observed. 'She is due for replenishment before evening.'

De Wolfe and Gwyn walked across to stand beside the monk and stared down into the coffin. A linen sheet covering a still figure was soaked with water oozing from shards of melting ice spread over the corpse beneath.

'Twice a day, two of the servants fetch a barrowful from the frozen pools on the nearby marshes,' explained Ignatius. 'It is fortunate that this tragedy occurred in the depths of winter, or your task would have been much more unpleasant.' He seemed to revel in the prospect and John began to dislike him.

'We need more light than this,' he said gruffly.

'There are candles on a shelf near the foot of the stairs,' said the chaplain. Immediately, Thomas volunteered to fetch them. He felt an overwhelming desire to get out of this chamber – and though he was still not fully hardened to the sight of violent death that was the coroner's business, his present unease seemed unrelated to the presence of a cadaver. He borrowed his master's candle and went off, taking his time in finding the spares, before reluctantly coming back with three more lit in his hands.

In the improved illumination, John de Wolfe and Gwyn went to work. Though they had developed a routine for examining the dead, this was the first time they had had to operate under these strange circumstances, in the semi-darkness and with numb fingers. Gwyn peeled off the sheet that shrouded the body, to an accompaniment of splashes of icy water and the tinkling of innumerable fragments of thin ice. A young woman was revealed, dressed in a plain nightgown of cream linen, all soaked with freezing water. Her long hair was black, but stuck in wet strands to her face and neck.

'We'll have to get her out, Crowner. We can't look at her properly like this,' grunted the Cornishman. 'Shall I lift her on to the floor?'

They spread the linen sheet on the ground and Gwyn lifted the girl with surprising gentleness and laid her on it, her arms by her sides.

The four men stood and looked down on the mortal remains of the young woman. In the dim light she looked as if she was asleep. The effect of the ice had been to blanch her features, so that her cheeks, forehead and chin looked parchment-white, especially by contrast with her dark hair. The eyes were closed, and for some reason she did not look pathetic in spite of the tragedy of a young life snuffed out a day before her wedding. There was even the hint of a smile on her pallid lips, as if she was amused at the havoc she was causing to the monastic community at Bermondsey.

Brother Ignatius was holding his candle in front of his chest, and when John happened to glance at him the light threw his face into sharp relief. The coroner was momentarily startled to see what looked almost like the mask of a devil, with an expression of loathing amounting to hatred as the monk stared down at the girl on the floor. De Wolfe blinked in surprise and a moment later the image had passed, leaving him to wonder if he had imagined it.

'Are we going to take a look at her, Crowner?'

Gwyn's down-to-earth voice brought John back to

reality as he heard the doubt in his officer's tone. This was a high-born young lady, and it was unseemly to make any extensive examination, especially with no woman available to act as a chaperone. At home in Exeter, if any intimate examination was required, especially in suspected rape or miscarriage, he usually called on the services of Dame Madge, a formidable nun from Polsloe Priory, who specialized in the ailments of women.

'We'll confine it to her head and hands for now. If necessary, we can find a woman to help us later.' De Wolfe squatted on one side of the corpse, with Gwyn on the other, a routine they had carried out innumerable times in the past eighteen months since he had been appointed coroner. He gently lifted her eyelids and looked at the whites of the flaccid globes, now collapsed so long after death. 'No blood spots there, no marks on her neck, so she's not been throttled. The windows of her eyes are clouded over after ten days, ice or no ice.'

His long, bony fingers then explored her hair, feeling the scalp underneath.

'Lift her a little, Gwyn,' he commanded, and his hands slid under the back of her head. 'Ha, what have we here?' he exclaimed. 'Pull the lady right up, will you?'

His officer lifted Christina by the shoulders until she was in a sitting position, her head lolling loosely to one side. The coroner steadied it and let her chin sink to her chest as he felt around the top of her head and then down to the nape of her neck, all covered in the wet, dark hair.

'A boggy swelling, almost on top of her skull,' he announced in a low voice. 'I can feel the bone cracked beneath it.'

Gwyn repeated the palpation, to confirm what his

master had said. 'And her neck must have gone, too, Crowner. Her head wobbles like a bladder on a stick!' He was likening it to the child's toy, an inflated pig's bladder tied to the end of a twig.

John felt it for himself, flopping the head back and forth in his hands, then motioned to Gwyn to set the cadaver back on the ground. He looked at her hands and arms, visible up to the elbows when he pushed up the wide sleeves of her gown. There was nothing to be seen, and he risked a look at her legs, lifting the skirts as far as her knees, again confirming that there were no visible injuries.

As Gwyn carefully rearranged her clothing, de Wolfe stood up and contemplated the dead girl lying on the floor in the flickering candlelight. It was Brother Ignatius who first broke the strained silence.

'From what you said, sir, I understand that she has suffered an injury to her head. This is what our infirmarian suspected.' His tone suggested that he thought it a long and unnecessary journey from distant Devon to confirm what they already knew.

'She has indeed, brother. And her neck is broken.'

'But this is surely what would be expected in a fall down those treacherous stairs?' persisted the monk.

'We shall see,' replied de Wolfe enigmatically. 'Meanwhile, we must place her back in the ice. I will suggest to your prior that arrangements for burial be begun without delay. In spite of the cold, my nose tells me that we cannot arrest the normal course of events much longer.'

Gwyn lifted the body as if it were a feather and placed it back in the icy slush, which was dripping ever faster through the poor seams of the box. He gently covered her with the linen sheet and stepped back, as Thomas murmured a funereal litany in Latin.

'Where will she be buried?' asked Gwyn. 'Will they

put her here in that graveyard we saw when we arrived or take her home to this Derby place?'

There was a low mumble from the chaplain, which John could not catch, but Thomas's sharp ears picked it up, much to his surprise.

'What did you say?' asked John sharply.

Ignatius shook his head. 'I do not know where, Crowner. I expect the prior will have to consult her guardian before a decision can be made.'

'Well, you had better hurry up about it,' advised de Wolfe. 'And keep using that ice for as long as she's here.'

They left the crypt-like basement with a feeling of relief, Thomas looking almost fearfully over his shoulder as they made their way back through the barrels and boxes stacked in the rest of the cellar. It seemed warmer – or, rather, less cold – in that area than in the further chamber, where the oppressive atmosphere seemed to bite at the skin and lungs.

On the way out, John stopped to look again at the area around the foot of the stairs. He tapped the earth with his foot, then scraped at the moist soil with the toe of his riding boot. Looking up, the steep staircase was dimly lit by the tallow dip at the top, revealing the narrow passage between the walls of grey stone and the regular blocks of the same granite that formed the treads.

He made no comment and led the way up to the door that opened into the courtyard. The snow was now coming down more thickly, though none had yet settled on the ground, and again Thomas shivered, this time from the undoubted cold that permeated his thin body to his very bones.

As the chaplain closed the door, he noticed the clerk shudder and took pity on him. 'There is a warming room at the side of the dorter, where a fire is kept going between November and Good Friday. You are welcome to sit there at any time in this inclement weather.'

Thankfully, they took up the invitation and found the room sandwiched between the frater and the dorter, which joined at right-angles. Other than the prior's quarters and the kitchens, it was the only place in the priory that was ever heated. There was a chimneyed hearth with a large log fire and a charcoal brazier sitting on a stone slab at the other side of the chamber. There were a number of benches around the walls and several hooded settles, whose wooden sides kept off some of the draught. Two older monks were fast asleep in a couple of these and several more were reading or dozing on the benches.

'If you wait here for a while until the chill leaves you, I will send down when the prior is able to receive you again, Sir John,' promised Ignatius before he glided silently away.

'I can't take to that fellow, somehow,' rumbled Gwyn, as they found themselves a bench to one side of the hearth, out of earshot of the nearest Cluniacs. 'Not that I'm all that partial to anyone in holy orders!' he added with a meaningful dig in Thomas's ribs.

For once, the clerk failed to rise to the bait, as he leaned nearer to de Wolfe to whisper in a conspiratorial undertone. 'Crowner, did you catch what he said in the crypt, when you asked where the girl was to be buried?'

'I know he muttered something, but I couldn't make it out,' said John.

'He said, "It should be at a crossroads, with a stake through her heart"!'

'I said he was a nasty bastard!' growled Gwyn, as de Wolfe digested this peculiar piece of information.

'I saw his face at that moment too,' he said slowly.

'There is something very wrong in this place, so keep your eyes and ears open and your mouths shut!'

'I trust you are refreshed after your long journey, Sir John,' said Robert Northam courteously, rising from behind his table to greet the coroner. 'I also understand that you have visited the scene of this tragedy and . . .' He hesitated, at a loss how to phrase his question.

De Wolfe helped him out without any finesse. 'Yes, prior, I have also examined the corpse.'

The priest sank on to his chair. 'I see you have not brought your two assistants with you?'

'No, I must speak to you alone.' He looked meaningfully at Ignatius, who was standing in his usual protective position alongside Northam.

'You may speak freely in front of my secretary, Crowner. He is also my chaplain and my confessor.'

John shook his head firmly. 'Some things must be held in total confidence,' he said. 'I have strict instructions from the chief justiciar to that effect.'

This was untrue, but he was quite prepared to lie when he considered it justified. The prior looked surprised but waved at Ignatius, who reluctantly left the chamber and closed the door. John wondered if he was outside, pressing his ear to the panels.

'You have something to tell me?' asked Northam anxiously as de Wolfe sat in the chair he had occupied previously.

'Christina de Glanville was murdered,' he said bluntly. 'Your own instincts were correct. She did not fall down those stairs, alive or dead!'

Robert's fingers played agitatedly with the bronze crucifix hanging from a chain around his neck. 'I suspected as much. But how can you be so certain?'

'As you told me, the fact that her head was near the

bottom step and that she was face down makes it a near impossibility for a fall downstairs. If she had pitched forwards, the likelihood would be for her feet to be nearest the step. It would be just possible for her to land on her head and somersault over, but then she would almost certainly land face up.'

The prior frowned. 'Is "almost certainly" enough?' he asked.

'There is more,' growled de Wolfe. 'She had a severe injury to the top of the back of her head, which had fractured her skull. Again, it is just possible, though unlikely, that she could land on the back of her head from a fall, but she would have had to twist in mid-air to achieve that. The stairway was so narrow that was almost impossible, and she would have struck the floor with her face first.'

The prior was following this with quick nods of his head.

'Furthermore, her neck was broken,' went on de Wolfe. 'But it was snapped in a backward direction, which is impossible from a heavy fall on the back of the head, which would have forced the chin downwards. The break occurred in the opposite direction, by the head being pulled backwards.'

There was a pregnant silence. 'You are absolutely sure of this?' asked Northam, almost in a whisper.

'She had not a single bruise nor scrape on her legs and arms,' persisted John. 'For someone to fall down twenty unyielding granite steps with sufficient force to crack the skull and break the neck, without striking their limbs on the edges, is beyond belief!'

The prior gave a deep sigh of resignation. 'So what do you surmise happened, Crowner?'

'Someone struck her a heavy blow on the back of the head with some object. It must have been flat not to rip the skin, but heavy enough to shatter the bone.

She would have lost her wits instantly, then the assailant gave her the *coup de grâce* by breaking her neck.'

'How is that possible?' wailed Robert Northam.

John shrugged. 'Quite easily. I have seen it done in the mêlée of combat. One hand cupped under the chin, the other on the nape of the neck – then a quick jerk backwards.'

The prior shuddered. 'We must be looking for a brute with great strength, surely?'

The coroner shook his head, his jet-black hair bouncing over the collar of his grey tunic. 'Not at all. Any determined man could do it – or woman, for that matter!'

The prior crossed himself in horror, reminding John of his clerk's habit. 'God preserve us from that! There were several ladies about the poor girl, but none of them could possibly be involved.'

'Who exactly were those ladies?' demanded the coroner.

'There was Margaret de Courtenay, who was to be the maid of honour at the wedding. She was a friend of Lady Christina, from the time they were in Sempringham together, so I understand.'

John could feel that Robert Northam was trying to distance himself as much as possible from any close acquaintance with the dramatis personae in this tragic drama.

'Then there was Lady Avisa, who was virtually the mother of Christina, being the wife of her guardian, Roger Beaumont, together with their daughter, Eleanor. And, of course, there were various hand-maidens and tirewomen who attended the three ladies,' he added dismissively.

'Were they all staying here at the priory?'

'They were indeed, as we have ample accommodation since we became so popular with the king and his ministers as a place to safely house their guests in London.' The prior sounded a little cynical at this demotion of his monastic retreat to an aristocratic lodging-house.

'Where would they stay exactly?' asked de Wolfe.

'Sir Roger Beaumont and his wife had a parlour and bedroom next to the inner gate, while Christina de Glanville and her bridesmaid Margaret de Courtenay were lodged in a pair of guest-rooms near where you are placed, Crowner. It is at the top of the stairs, but opposite the dormitory, through a locked door.'

'What about their personal servants?'

'They slept on pallets either in a corner of the same room or in an antechamber, in the case of the Beaumonts.'

John turned this over in his mind for a moment. 'The bridegroom-to-be, this Jordan de Neville – was he here at any stage?'

'Certainly. He visited almost every day for the week that the party was here. He spent several nights in the guest dormitory, where you yourself are lodged, but did not stay for the few nights before the wedding, as I gather it is unseemly for a groom to be with his bride immediately before the ceremony.'

He hesitated, as if doubtful whether to continue, then plunged on. 'However, he was here the night that Christina was last seen. Then he rode back with his squire to Southwark late at night, where he was lodged at an inn.'

John rose to his feet and thanked the prior for his time and patience. 'I will have to see everyone concerned before I can hold an inquest. In the circumstances of the long delay that was inevitable for me to get here from Devon, I will not demand the usual requirement that the corpse be viewed during the inquest. In fact, I do not know if the Coroner of the Verge is obliged to adhere to all the usual rules of procedure for common cases.'

Robert Northam stood to see de Wolfe to the door, and as John reached it he turned before Northam could lift the latch. 'One matter occurs to me, prior. Is there anything I should know about your chaplain?'

The priest stared at him, not understanding his meaning. 'Brother Ignatius? In what regard?'

'Does he have any strong opinions about certain matters? Any obsessions, for instance?' John felt awkward about asking such questions, but he felt it had to be done.

Robert Northam cleared his throat self-consciously. 'He tends to take a very literal view of the Scriptures. One might say that he holds a rather extreme view of certain religious precepts.' The prior's tone indicated that he was not going to be more forthcoming than this about his secretary.

'Do you know what his relations with the dead girl might have been?'

The prior looked somewhat offended. 'Relations? There were no relations. She was a guest in the priory, as there have been very many others.'

De Wolfe recognized that Northam was being deliberately evasive, but he felt that this was not the time to pursue the issue. After speaking to other witnesses he might return to it, but for now he was content to take his leave. Outside, Ignatius was ostentatiously standing in the entrance to the small chapel, well away from the door. As he escorted the coroner back to the warming room, John took the opportunity to probe his attitude to the dead girl.

'What did you think of Christina de Glanville?' he asked.

'I had very little to do with her, sir. The guests are housed in the outer part of the priory and my duties are with the prior and in the church.'

'But you must have met the young lady a number of times! She presumably attended services at least once a day?'

The chaplain shook his head. 'No females attend the Holy Offices in our church. It would be against all the tenets of our order.'

'But surely she must have gone to Mass with her friends and guardians?

Brother Ignatius grudgingly admitted that the prior had offered his private chapel for that purpose. 'I administered the Sacrament to her several times, as part of my duties to the group that she was with. But I knew nothing about her personally and have no opinion about her character.'

John's long experience of interrogating witnesses told him that the secretary was holding something back, but the stubborn set of his mouth told him that, like the prior, he would get no further today.

That evening they ate well in the guest refectory, being joined by half a score of pilgrims from the Welsh marches. A large proportion of Bermondsey's casual lodgers were pilgrims, either going to or returning from the new shrine to St Thomas at Canterbury, though some were going further afield, a few even to Rome or Santiago de Compostella. They were a cheerful lot and in spite of the cold turned an otherwise sombre meal into a pleasant evening, as they had some wineskins of their own to supplement the ale and cider supplied by the priory.

When the drinks had been consumed, everyone clambered up to the dormitory and wrapped themselves in every garment they possessed, as well as in the one blanket provided to each of them by Brother

Ferdinand, then curled up on their palliasses and tried to ignore the east wind that moaned through the shutters, carrying in an occasional flake of snow.

The next day de Wolfe found the confinement of the priory oppressive. Though Thomas insisted on attending most of the frequent offices in the church, John borrowed a pair of horses from the stables and took Gwyn for a ride into the surrounding countryside, such as it was, being so close to London. They rode towards the city and reached Southwark to look again at London Bridge, which they had crossed less than a couple of months ago, when they came from Exeter to visit Hubert Walter. This time they stayed on the south bank and visited a nearby tavern for some food and ale, before turning back into the flat heathland, dotted with a few manors with their strip-fields, barren at this time of year.

Today there was a dank mist rather than a dense fog, and when they reached Bermondsey the priory loomed eerily though the haze, like a grey fortress perched on the edge of the bog that stretched down to the river. As the porter let them in, even the unimaginative de Wolfe gave a shiver that was not altogether due to the biting cold. At noon they ate again in the guests' refectory, now empty of the boisterous pilgrims who had gone on their way to Canterbury. In the warming room afterwards, Thomas timidly asked his master how they were going to proceed with the investigation.

'The prior says that today all these people who were with Christina will be here to attend the funeral tomorrow,' replied John.

That morning he had asked Robert Northam about the disposal of the body and had been told that the Beaumonts had already requested that Christina be interred in the priory cemetery, as ten days after death it was already impracticable to take the remains back to Derbyshire.

'I will question them all in turn and try to get some sense of their feelings for the victim and where they were the night on which she was killed,' he grimly told his clerk. 'And today I'm going to twist a few arms in this place, see if I can squeeze some information from the Cluniacs.'

Knowing of Gwyn's fondness for kitchens, he told the big Cornishman to haunt the servants' domain and see if any useful gossip could be gleaned. The more menial tasks in a religious house like Bermondsey were carried out both by lay brothers, who, though they had taken no vows, wore the habit and the tonsure, as well as by ordinary servants, who either lived in the priory or came in daily from nearby cottages. Gwyn, an amiable but cunning fellow, was adept at befriending these lower ranks of society and could be trusted to ferret out any local scandals.

Thomas de Peyne had a similar gift, but one that worked best on clerks and priests like himself. Though now restored to grace as a priest, he had spent three years in the purgatory of being unfrocked, after a false accusation of indecent behaviour with a girl pupil in the cathedral school at Winchester. Before being re-instated, he had on a number of occasions helped the coroner by masquerading as a priest to worm his way into the confidence of various ecclesiastics. John now sent him on a similar expedition around the priory, a task in which Thomas revelled, as it allowed him to steep himself in the atmosphere and rituals of a religious house. He made first for the church, to attend vespers, then paraded around the cloister, talking to some of the monks as they perambulated around the garth.

Meanwhile, de Wolfe went to the dormitory and sought out Brother Ferdinand and made several requests, the first of which was a room in which to interview witnesses, and the second a view of the chambers in which Christina de Glanville had been lodged. The olive-complexioned monk took him along from the cubicle where John slept, to the head of the stairs and, with a key selected from a large ring hanging on his girdle, opened a door on the other side of the upper landing.

'This is where she resided, together with her friend Margaret and their two maids,' he said in Norman-French that carried a tinge of an accent that John guessed was the Langue d'Oc of southern France. He stood aside to let the coroner into a short corridor with two doors. Each opened into a vestibule that had a mattress, which opened into a larger room with better furnishings, the palliasses being raised on low plinths, with several tables and some leather-backed folding chairs, as well as tall cupboards for clothing.

'This first one was where Lady Christina stayed and in the next was her friend, Mistress Courtenay. Their tirewomen slept in the outer part,' added Ferdinand somewhat needlessly. 'All the more important guests ate in a separate dining room near the inner gate, where further accommodation is situated.'

De Wolfe looked around the rooms and saw no signs of occupation. 'What happened to her possessions, her clothing and personal effects?'

'Her guardians, the Beaumonts, took everything last week. They are lodged near Bishopsgate, I understand, but I had a message from the prior's secretary this morning to say that they are returning here tonight, ready for the funeral tomorrow.'

Ferdinand ushered de Wolfe out and locked up, then took him down to the ground floor of the cellarer's building, where one of the small offices next to the guests' refectory was given to him for an interview room. A bare cell with a shuttered window-opening, it had a table, a bench and two hard chairs.

'I will see that a charcoal brazier is brought in when you need to use this, Sir John,' offered the monk and made as if to leave the coroner to his own devices.

'Wait a moment,' commanded de Wolfe. 'I need to speak to everyone who was in contact with the dead girl, and that includes you.'

Ferdinand stopped and slowly returned to the centre of the room. 'There is little I can tell you, sir,' he said quietly, the dark eyes in his almond-shaped face searching the forbidding features of the coroner.

'Did she seem happy and excited at the prospect of her wedding? To most young women, this would be the most important day of her life.'

The monk remained impassive. 'I really cannot say, coroner. She did not appear to be effusive over it, but I had little chance to observe her.'

'When did you last see her?'

'At the evening meal on that day. I usually look in on the small dining room set aside for special guests to check that all is well. The whole party was there, eating and drinking, including Lady Christina.'

'Was Jordan de Neville there?'

'He was. He ate his supper and later went back to Southwark with his squire.'

De Wolfe was hard put to think of any more questions for this silent man, but he tried a new tack. 'Tell me, does Brother Ignatius have any peculiarities, so to speak? An unwelcome comment fell from his lips in the basement when we were examining the corpse.'

John expected another stonewall denial, but surprisingly Ferdinand's impassive face creased into a smile.

'Ah, you mean his strange obsession?' he asked. 'My fellow monk is something of a mystic. He regularly sees devils, angels and witches, though he is harmless enough and is an excellent support for our good prior.'

The coroner scowled at this rather dismissive opinion about a weird streak in the chaplain. 'What does that have to do with the dead lady?' he demanded.

Ferdinand spread out his hands, palms upwards. 'He was convinced that she was a witch, sir! He claimed that she was left-handed, had a fondness for the store-room cats and had long lobes to her ears or some such nonsense. He often made strange claims about visitors – and even our own inmates. He was convinced that our lay brother who used to tend the pigs was a re-incarnation of Pontius Pilate!'

'What happened to him?' growled de Wolfe.

'He drowned in the marshes outside last year,' replied Ferdinand blandly.

Further questions produced nothing of use and the monk departed, leaving John sitting in irritable frustration at his table. A servant brought in an iron brazier in which charcoal glowed dully, sending a moderate heat into the room, together with some acrid fumes. In spite of the warmth, John felt chilled and, though of an unimaginative nature, he realized that where he sat was just above where the corpse of Christina de Glanville lay in her box of ice. Eventually he rose and, with an illogical feeling of relief, left the room and went across the cloister to the prior's house, where he found Ignatius in his little office, busy writing on a scroll of parchment. He stood over the secretary and spoke without any preamble.

'I understand that you had certain convictions about Lady Christina. Is that true?'

The lean monk stared up at him, a sullen expression on his face. 'I don't know what you mean, Sir John,' he answered gruffly.

'You thought she was a witch,' snapped the coroner. 'Did you do her any harm?'

Ignatius jumped up, his sallow cheeks suddenly flushed. 'She was an acolyte of He with the Cloven Hooves!' he brayed. 'But I did nothing to her; it was not my place. God will settle all such matters on the Day of Judgement!'

'Are you sure that you didn't give Him a helping hand?' suggested John, thrusting his menacing face closer to the monk's. 'Where were you late on the night when she went missing?'

Ignatius looked around him wildly, as if hoping the prior would appear to save him from this avenging angel, though de Wolfe looked more like a cloven-hoofed acolyte at the moment.

'My opinions about certain persons go no further than speculation and prayer, Crowner! I had no hand in her death. Why should I?'

De Wolfe recalled a situation in Exeter some months earlier and a phrase from the Scriptures came to his mind. 'Does not the Vulgate say "thou shall not suffer a witch to live"?' he snarled.

Ignatius paled and stuttered a reply: 'The Book of Exodus does, yes – but I had no authority to intervene. I have detected a number of imps and devils and witches over the years, but it is not my place to banish them.'

A door opened across the passage and the prior's voice called out for his secretary. John did not wish to expose Ignatius to any trouble, in case his protestations of innocence were true, and went out to speak to Robert Northam.

'When your former guests return tonight, I need to speak to all of them as a matter of some urgency. I have been provided with a room in the cellarer's building and would be grateful if you could ask them to attend upon me there.'

The prior nodded and motioned for John to enter his chamber, where the coroner had more questions. 'I have heard rumours that not everyone was overjoyed at the prospect of this marriage. Have you any knowledge of this, prior?'

Northam sighed and tapped his fingers restlessly on his table. 'You will no doubt find out when you talk to them, though it may take some prising from their lips,' he said. 'Firstly, Roger Beaumont has a daughter, Eleanor, by his first wife, now dead. She had set her cap at Jordan de Neville, and the king's insistence on him marrying Christina was by no means welcome to her – nor I suspect to her father and stepmother.'

'Because of the loss of their exploitation of the Glanville estates when Christina delivered them to her new husband?' queried John.

'That and the fact that, instead, Eleanor might have married into the Neville family, who are rising stars in the nobility, with extensive lands in the north.'

The prior seemed to have no more gossip about his guests, and John wondered where a senior man of the cloth had unearthed this titbit about Eleanor Beaumont. He suspected that his chaplain-secretary was the channel for such hearsay.

Leaving Robert Northam's quarters, he went back to the warming room, as he wished to spend as little time as possible in the dank, inimical chamber above Christina's corpse. He sat there for some time and eventually dozed off, joining two old monks who were snoring their way through the afternoon. The return of Gwyn and Thomas woke him up, and they thankfully warmed their icy feet and hands as they told him the meagre results of their spying mission.

Thomas had been consorting with a few monks and senior clerks in the church, cloister and infirmary, which he had visited with the excuse that he wished to compare the priory's facilities with those at similar religious houses in Devon.

'There is a general consensus that Brother Ignatius is slightly mad, as he sees goblins and imps possessing many of the people who enter the priory. But it seems a harmless obsession and gives rise more to pitying jibes than to any real concern,' reported the clerk.

De Wolfe nodded agreement. 'I have heard the same sort of comments about him. Doesn't necessarily mean that he *is* harmless, though. Anything else?'

The little clerk rubbed his hands together to warm them. 'I raised the subject of the wedding and the death. There were many sidelong glances and shrugs. I got the impression that this marriage was well known to be a sombre affair rather than the usual happy event.'

'What did they say about it, then?' demanded the coroner.

'I gathered, more from their attitudes than outright words, that the people gathered here as guests made little secret of the fact that this was a union forced on them by King Richard. I could get no more detail than that, though a clerk in the scriptorium claimed that he had seen this Jordan fellow ogling the bridesmaid Margaret.'

Gwyn grunted confirmation of this. 'The kitchen servants, where I went seeking some fresh bread and cheese, said much the same thing when I brought the conversation around to it. They have long noses and sharp eyes – they suggested that though Jordan fancied this Courtenay woman, it was Roger's daughter who wanted him.'

De Wolfe pondered their words for a moment. 'This is something I must pursue with these grand folk who are coming here tonight. Though why the bride should be killed to avoid a wedding is beyond me at the moment.'

Thomas rather hesitantly raised another matter. 'Crowner, several of the brothers to whom I spoke muttered words about history repeating itself. I tried to worm more out of them, but they were very reluctant to answer. All I could gather was that there is some vague legend about the early years of this priory, when another king's ward vanished.

'I asked one of the oldest monks, Brother Martin, who is in charge of the scriptorium, but he said it was idle tittle-tattle. He claimed there was nothing in the priory archives to show that anyone had disappeared and blamed Ignatius for encouraging the belief that the place was haunted by the spirits of devils and incubi!'

'God's guts, what's that got to do with a girl getting killed last week?' objected Gwyn.

Thomas looked crestfallen, but John patted his shoulder. 'Every bit of information may help, even if it only shows the mood of this place. I admit, it's a cheerless house, even for a monastery!'

Just before nightfall, a small cavalcade arrived at the priory. There were two curtained litters slung between pairs of horses, accompanied by several well-dressed men on caparisoned steeds and half a dozen mounted servants, leading several packhorses. In addition, there were three women sitting side-saddle on palfreys. With much jingling of harness, they trooped through the outer gates and dismounted near the entrance to the inner courtyard. One older lady was helped down from the first litter and two younger ones climbed from the other.

The prior, his chaplain, Brother Ferdinand and several of the obidentiaries were there to receive them outside the door that led into the superior guest-rooms adjacent to the inner gatehouse, joining that to the cellarer's building.

For the better part of an hour, there was much coming and going as the guests were installed in their various chambers, together with their personal body-servants and luggage. Eventually the main players assembled in the refectory for wine and refreshments, where Prior Robert told them of the coroner's presence and his requirement that they attend upon him in turn in his makeshift office along the corridor in the cellarium. There was some indignant grumbling about being ordered around by some knight from some outlandish place called Devon, but Robert Northam firmly impressed on them that it was on the direct order of the Chief Justiciar, and hence the king himself.

After a flurry of messages conveyed by a couple of kitchen boys, some form of timetable was agreed and as darkness fell in the late-February afternoon John sat in his small room awaiting his first witness. He kept Thomas with him at a small table in the corner, supplied with pen, ink and parchment, ready to record anything of importance. Two three-branched candle-sticks gave a fair light as Brother Ignatius shepherded in a large florid man in middle age.

'Sir Roger Beaumont,' announced the monk. 'A noble baron of Wirksworth Castle in Derbyshire.' He declaimed this as if he was herald at a coronation, as de Wolfe rose and courteously motioned the new arrival to the chair opposite his table. Roger grunted a reluctant greeting and sat down, revealing himself as a square-faced man with a high colour, his bushy grey eyebrows matching his bristly grey hair, which was shaved up to a line level with his ears in the old Norman fashion. He was dressed in fine though sober-hued clothes, a long brown tunic under a green surcoat, all covered with a fur-lined pelisse of heavy black wool.

'This is a bad business, coroner,' he boomed, his voice suiting his burly appearance, heavy-boned and short-necked. John guessed his age as middle forties, a few years older than himself.

After a few formal exchanges, de Wolfe went straight into the meat of the matter and went through the history of Roger's guardianship of Christina, confirming what he knew from others.

'You were on good terms with the lady?' he asked

'She was like another daughter to us, for we have Eleanor, who is a few years older.' Roger had a forthright, almost aggressive manner, sticking out his jaw pugnaciously even when the subject matter was not controversial.

John avoided mentioning the prior's suggestion that this girl was a competitor for Jordan's hand in marriage and went on to ask about the night she died.

'I saw nothing of her after supper,' said Roger abruptly. 'My wife and I were accommodated where we are now. The two girls, Christina and Margaret Courtenay, were lodged upstairs. The first I knew of the tragedy was in the morning, when all hell was let loose on finding the poor maid's body.'

'Was she looking forward to her nuptials – excited and happy?'

Beaumont rubbed his square jaw. 'Not all that keenly, to be honest, but the king's command and perhaps her feelings of duty to her late father to preserve his estates overcame her personal desires.'

'And the bridegroom? What of him?' asked de Wolfe.

Roger scowled at the question. 'You had better ask him that, but I suspect he would rather have plighted his troth elsewhere.' He refused to be drawn as to where 'elsewhere' might have been, saying bluntly that it was Jordan's business, not his.

'With Christina dead, what will happen to her fortune?'

The baron shifted uneasily and his face became even more ruddy. 'Effectively, the king has acquired her estates. I am merely the caretaker. But perhaps in view of my faithful stewardship, he might allow me to purchase the manors myself, as I know their management so well.'

And at a knock-down price, thought John cynically. After some more questions that got him no further, he decided to take the bull by the horns, perhaps an apt expression for the bovine-looking man sitting opposite.

'I have to say this, Sir Roger, but you had a good motive for seeing the girl dead. Had this marriage gone ahead, you would have lost your half-share of the revenue and all chance of acquiring her large estates.'

The reaction was violent.

Roger Beaumont sprang to his feet, his chair going over with a crash as he confronted the coroner. 'Damn your impertinence, sir! Are you accusing me of killing my own ward, whom I have nurtured like another daughter for so long?'

Thomas, cowering in his corner, saw that the baron's face had turned purple and was afraid that he was going to have a seizure.

De Wolfe held up a placatory hand. 'I am accusing you of nothing, but it is my royal duty to explore every possibility. I must ask you, as I will ask everyone else, where were you on the night Christina went missing?'

Roger stared at him as if he had gone mad, but his rage seemed to have passed and he sat down heavily on the chair, which Thomas had hurried to put back in place. His voice was dull and thick when he answered.

'I spent the whole night asleep in my chamber with my wife. She will vouch for that, though I doubt you would consider that of much value.'

John inclined his head in acknowledgement. 'I consider everything most carefully, I assure you. Perhaps it would be convenient if I did speak to your good wife next.'

Roger left with an air of obvious annoyance, muttering under his breath, and a few moments later a buxom maidservant ushered in his spouse.

Lady Avisa Beaumont was a tall, handsome woman at least ten years younger than her husband. Her fair hair was plaited into two coils above each ear, contained in gold-mesh crespines, over which was a samite veil trailing down her back and over her shapely bosom. The cold was kept at bay by a heavy brocade mantle lined with ermine, covering her ankle-length kirtle of blue velvet. A slim, high-cheekboned face bore a pair of large brown eyes, and John, an experienced connoisseur of elegant women, could easily see how Roger had wanted her for his second wife.

There was virtually nothing Avisa could add to what he already knew, in relation to the night of the girl's death. She had spent it all in a bed an arm's length from her husband's in the guest-chambers near the inner gate and knew nothing of the tragedy until the hubbub in the morning. She produced a fine-linen kerchief, which she used to dab at her eyes when she related this part of her story, and de Wolfe had no reason to think that her grief was anything but genuine.

'Your husband tells me that Christina was not over-joyed at the prospect of marriage?'

Again the wife confirmed what Roger had said, but with an addition. 'Until a few months ago, we had hoped that my stepdaughter, Eleanor, would have joined the Neville family. She has long admired Jordan, whom she has known since childhood. In fact, it was on his visits to us at Wirksworth that he became acquainted with Christina.'

John scratched his stubble and out of the corner of his eye watched Thomas's pen scribbling away on his parchment.

'Was Christina or Eleanor the attraction that brought him to Wirksworth?' he asked.

Avisa Beaumont dropped her long-lashed eyes. 'Neither, really. He came to accompany his mother, who is my cousin. But we hoped that some attraction might develop between him and our daughter – as, indeed, it still might!' she added hopefully.

'So Christina's death has left the field open for a match with a young man who was heir to considerable property?' ventured John.

Just as a critical remark had fired up her husband, Avisa's face darkened and she glared at the coroner. 'That is not an issue, Sir John, and it is improper of you to suggest it! Anyway, she is not the only contestant on the field,' she added obscurely, but refused to enlarge on the remark.

De Wolfe's questions went on for a few more minutes but, as with Roger Beaumont, nothing useful was obtained. The lady seemed very reluctant to accept that the girl's death was deliberate and firmly declared it to be a terrible accident – though she could not hazard any guess as to why Christina should be found in the crypt of the cellarium.

When she left, with a rather haughty promise to send Roger's daughter down next, John turned to his clerk shivering on his stool, as he was furthest away from the brazier.

'Anything strike you so far, Thomas? You have the sharpest mind among us,' he said. The rare compliment warmed the little priest more than any fire and he hastened to offer his opinion.

'As you said, Crowner, both those persons had a motive to see Lady Christina out of the way, though whether they would – or could – stoop to murder is another matter. Sir Roger is easily capable of striking the girl unconscious and breaking her neck ... I'm not sure about the lady, but she looks tall and strong.'

They were interrupted by the arrival of a younger handmaiden who was acting as chaperone to her mistress, Eleanor Beaumont, whom she ushered into the room. She was eighteen and, though comely enough, had none of the beauty of her stepmother, following her father more in her solid physique. Thomas thought that she might have done better as a boy, as she looked capable of wielding a sword or drawing a bow.

Again, she repeated the claim that Christina had been like a younger sister to her for the past six years and, though she was not moved to tears, de Wolfe thought that unless she was a very good actress she was genuinely sorry that her friend was dead.

'I understand that you were lodged in the guest-chamber next to your father and mother?'

Eleanor nodded and turned her head to indicate the young woman who stood behind her. 'Sarah slept on a mattress near my door, but in the same room.' This was a hint that she could not have left the room that night without the maid being aware of it.

'I understand from Lady Avisa that you had hopes of marrying Jordan de Neville yourself?' John asked as delicately as his nature would allow.

The girl bristled visibly. 'She should not have said that! True, I had great affection for Jordan, but I doubt he noticed me in that respect.'

'But she is gone, so who will he marry now?' persisted John.

Eleanor flushed, looking more like her father than ever. 'You had better ask him yourself, sir!'

The coroner did just that a short time later, when the man who had been deprived of his nuptials arrived. Jordan de Neville was twenty-three and had spent some time at the Lionheart's court in Rouen, thanks to the noble connections of the various ramifications of the Neville family, who were a rising faction in the corridors of power.

He was a tall, thin man with a shock of black hair that sat like a thick cap on top of his head. He was dressed in the most modern style, the toes of his shoes being elongated into long points stuffed with wool and curled back almost to his ankles. A rather supercilious manner did nothing to improve his looks, which were average, to put it kindly. John felt that here was a fellow unlikely to set a girl's pulse racing, unless she had an eye on his undoubted family wealth and influence.

After he had seated himself before the coroner, John made sympathetic noises about the tragic loss of his bride-to-be. Jordan looked appropriately mournful and expressed his devastation at such a tragic loss. The words were perfectly phrased, but de Wolfe felt that their delivery lacked conviction. He came straight to the point with almost brutal directness.

'I am aware that this marriage was not your own choice, but arranged by your family at the behest of our sovereign lord, King Richard?'

The tactic was successful, for the young man broke into a flood of words, as if he had been yearning for someone on whom to unload his feelings. John saw that he was a weak character, easily persuaded by those in authority. He confessed that though he liked Christina, he had not wanted to marry her, being greatly attracted to her friend Margaret Courtenay, whom he now hoped to wed. He dismissed John's suggestion that Eleanor Beaumont might make an alternative bride, though he was aware that she had done all she could to ensnare him.

'My parents and uncle were the architects of this pact with the king to fuse the Neville and Glanville lands – it was a political arrangement. I had no say in the matter,' he concluded sadly.

De Wolfe moved on to more immediate issues. 'You were here at Bermondsey the night that Christina vanished?' he asked abruptly. Jordan looked affronted at the implications.

'I was indeed! Until about an hour before midnight, when all the monks trooped off to their church for Matins. Then I left with my squire and rode in the moonlight back to our lodgings.'

'Where did you spend the evening?'

'The whole party was in the guests' refectory. We ate supper and sat talking until about the ninth hour, when Christina went to her chamber with her lady-in-waiting, as did Sir Roger and Lady Avisa. I stayed talking to Margaret and the prior for another hour or so. Eleanor insisted on sitting with us, rather to my annoyance, but eventually she left for her bed as well.'

'So you were with your favourite lady until quite late?'

Again Jordan looked offended, a frequent mood of his, thought John.

'Not alone – it would not be seemly. Her handmaiden was there as a chaperone, as well as Prior Robert – and the two monks, Ferdinand and Ignatius, came and went on various errands.'

As with the others, more questioning failed to extract anything useful from the dandified young fellow, and the coroner waited impatiently for the last of the guests to present herself.

Margaret Courtenay dispensed with a chaperone, telling her maid to wait outside and firmly shutting the door on her as de Wolfe rose to greet her. A very self-possessed young woman, she was quite different from Eleanor Beaumont. A few years older, probably of twenty-one summers, she was a pretty blonde who fell just short of being beautiful. Strong character showed in her face, and her garments, just visible under a heavy cloak, were plain but elegant. She had a veil of heavy white silk over her head, but her fair curls peeped out of the front.

Once again, John went through the familiar routine of questioning. She was the third daughter of a baron from the West Country and had been sent to Sempringham as a novice some years earlier to test her suitability for becoming a nun. This was where she met Christina, but when the latter left for Wirksworth Margaret abandoned any intention of taking the veil and returned home to her parents. She stayed at Wirksworth on a number of occasions, and it was here that she met Jordan de Neville. She made no secret of her aspirations to become his wife, but their plans had been ruined by the forced marriage insisted on by the higher powers.

De Wolfe had left questioning her until the end, as she might well have been the last to see Christina alive. 'You returned to your chamber later than her, I understand?' he asked.

'I took the chance to be with Jordan a little longer,' she said rather wistfully. 'I thought it might well be the last time we could meet as single people. Christina was in bed when I entered the chamber next door to say goodnight. At least, her maid, who was sleeping in the outer part, whispered that she thought her mistress was already asleep.'

'And you went to your couch yourself then? Did anything wake you that night?'

Margaret shook her head. 'Nothing, and neither did my maid hear anything from her outer room – though she sleeps like a log, so nothing would disturb her,' she added disdainfully.

De Wolfe grunted, to cover his frustration at being unable to get anything useful from all these folk. 'You knew Christina for some years. Have you any reason to think that someone would wish her dead?'

She dropped the lids over her blue eyes. 'Only the obvious ones, Sir John,' she said very quietly.

'I crave your pardon, Mistress Courtenay, but it is not that obvious to me,' he rumbled.

Margaret looked up again, almost defiantly. 'Sir Roger and his wife have always been very good to me, having me to stay at Wirksworth. I would not wish to defame them, but surely everyone knows that he would lose a great deal – including his further expectations – concerning the lands that would have come to Christina on her sixteenth birthday, if this marriage had gone ahead.'

De Wolfe thanked her for her frankness and suggested that she remain while he asked her maid a few questions. However, there was nothing that this young woman could add, as she merely repeated Margaret Courtenay's account of that last evening. Outside in the corridor, the lady who had attended upon Christina de Glanville was waiting, and John took advantage of the presence of the other two women to bring her in for questioning. She started off the proceedings by bursting into tears, distressed by the reminder of the death of her mistress, whom she had served for over two years. When she had composed herself, all she could offer was a similar lack of help to his investigation.

'My lady left the refectory some time after supper ended and we both went up to our chamber. I helped her to dress for bed and then settled her for the night. She asked me to blow out the candle, so I knew she wished to sleep at once.'

Her snivels began again. 'That was the last time I ever saw her alive!'

De Wolfe made his throat-clearing noises – he never could abide weeping women; they made him feel helpless.

'There was no disturbance in the night?' he asked, for something to say. 'She never called for you or left her room?'

'No, not that I knew of. I slept soundly until dawn. She had said she wished to go to the prior's chapel to take the Sacrament, so I went to awaken her, but she was not there!'

Her sobbing began anew and John looked helplessly at the other two women.

'If you have finished, sir, we will take her back to Sir Roger and his wife,' offered Margaret Courtenay. 'We should all seek our beds, for tomorrow will be a sad and stressful day.'

'We are little the wiser for all that talking,' growled de Wolfe later. He, Gwyn and Thomas were sitting in the warming room, the only habitable place unless one wore three layers of extra clothing. There were half a dozen monks in the chamber, some dozing, others in murmured conversations, giving the coroner's party covert and often suspicious glances. However, the place was large enough for them to talk in low voices without the others hearing. John had given Gwyn the gist of the interviews, and his officer agreed that it took them no further forward in discovering the culprit.

'This Roger Beaumont is the obvious suspect,' he grunted. 'But he's hardly likely to admit it, even if he's the guilty one.'

'I wonder if he already has something to hide?' mused de Wolfe. 'What if he was embezzling some of the portion of the estate profits that were supposed to be going to the Exchequer? If he suddenly lost control after Christina's marriage, might not Jordan's new stewards and bailiffs discover the fraud and report it to the king? Beaumont could literally lose his head over that!'

Gwyn looked dubious, not because he could not believe that a lord was capable of such greed, but because they had no means of proving it.

Thomas ticked off the candidates on his spindly fingers.

'His wife has no obvious motive, other than what she gains by her husband becoming richer. The daughter Eleanor no doubt felt that she might have a chance with Jordan de Neville if Christina was out of the way, but would she kill for it?'

Gwyn reached across and grabbed Thomas's third finger. 'This one's for Jordan, for he wanted to marry the Courtenay woman, not Christina.'

'So that leaves only Margaret Courtenay, who also wanted an unmarried Jordan for herself,' finished John. 'But the dead girl was a good friend, for God's sake!'

They sat around the fire in silence, digesting the unpromising situation.

'Does it have to be one of the family guests?' ruminated the coroner. 'What about the people in this place? They're a queer bunch, right enough.'

'There's that chaplain, Ignatius, who thought Christina was a witch,' agreed Thomas.

'I suppose the prior himself had no motive,' said Gwyn in a hoarse whisper. 'Maybe he was tired of the court using his priory as a lodging-house!'

Thomas sneered at his big colleague, his reverence for priests making the very idea sacrilegious, but the idea set John's mind working. It seemed unlikely that Robert Northam could be implicated, but he was an important man and knew many of the barons and bishops who wielded power in England. God knows what plots and schemes were going on in the higher echelons of government – could he be involved in any of them?

However, there seemed no way forward to accuse anyone of the killing, let alone the prior himself, and their discussion faded into silence until an old monk approached them and sat down uninvited. He was a wizened man, with no hair left to demarcate his tonsure, his head being covered in wrinkled pink skin. His lined face was relieved by a pair of sharp brown eyes that suggested an active mind inside that shrivelled exterior.

Thomas smiled a welcome at him and shifted along his bench to let the old man get nearest to the fire. 'This is Brother Martin, whom I spoke to earlier,' he explained. 'He supervises the scriptorium next to the chapter house and keeps the archives of the priory.'

In a quavering voice that spoke of his advanced years, the monk enquired after their health and their lodgings and bemoaned the cold weather, which 'plagued his old bones', as he put it. The conversation, prompted by the eager Thomas, got around to the history of the priory, by which time Gwyn was nodding off with boredom.

'It was much smaller than this in the early days, some ninety years ago,' explained the archivist. 'But it grew fast with patronage. I hardly recognize it from what it was when I was a novice here, about fifty years ago. Old buildings knocked down and new ones springing up.'

'The priory received many gifts, then?' asked John politely, though he was not much interested.

'A lot of money and land from wealthy donors, sir. At one time it became fashionable to give to Bermondsey ... lands, rents, advowsons, even whole manors sometimes. Rich folk would pay a lot for Masses to be said for their souls to spend as little time as possible in purgatory!'

His face took on a faraway look as he peered back in time. 'Only a few months ago I was required to check on an old covenant dating back to the early years of the century, as there was some dispute about our right to the manor of Kingweston in Somerset. It was strange, for there had been parts of the entry scratched out, which made my task difficult.'

'This is the matter you told me of when we spoke in the cloister?' said Thomas. 'There was some reference to another chronicle, you said?'

'Long ago, I found another old parchment from those days, which listed the witnesses to Count Eustace's grant of the manor and advowson of Kingweston, one of which was a Brother Francis of this priory. His name had been erased from the deed itself and there is no other record of him ever existing. I told the prior of the irregularity and tampering, but he became quite annoyed and told me to forget all about it, as it was of no consequence. He took the old document from me and I've not seen it since.'

John wondered what this had to do with anything and soon the old monk had warmed himself sufficiently and wandered off.

'What was all that about?' he demanded of his clerk, prodding Gwyn to silence his loud snores.

Thomas smiled slyly; he was always keen to probe into old stories and gossip. 'From talking to several older monks, it seems that there was some scandal here many years ago. It was hushed up but refuses to be extinguished. The odd thing is that it also involved a royal ward – of the first Henry. She vanished along with a monk, and it is thought they eloped, though some claim she was murdered and is the cause of all these rumours of ghosts and evil spirits. Much of Brother Ignatius's obsession with devils and imps seems to be fostered by this legend.'

De Wolfe grunted. 'Then maybe poor Christina's ghost will join the spirit band that haunts this place. But it doesn't help us discover who killed her.'

An hour later Roger Beaumont and Jordan de Neville came to the warming room and sought out the coroner for a private word. The lord of Wirksworth was still offended by de Wolfe's insinuations about his having most to gain by Christina's death, but he concealed it under a stiff manner as he made his request.

'I realize it is late, Sir John, but some of the family – as we consider ourselves to be – wish to see the spot where our poor Christina came to her death.'

De Wolfe looked surprised at this unexpected supplication. 'Why ask me? The prior is the ultimate authority in this house.'

Beaumont scowled at the coroner, his face as red as a raw side of beef.

'He has already consented, but as you are the law officer investigating the matter I thought I should have your agreement.'

John was mollified by this deference offered by the pugnacious baron and asked when they wished to visit the basement chamber.

'Now, this very minute! The prior is to accompany us.'

Somewhat grudgingly, John followed Beaumont to the door, motioning for Gwyn and Thomas to accompany him. As they walked through the cloister, lit by hazy moonlight and a few guttering torches, he expressed surprise that the girl's guardian had not seen the cellar at the time of her death.

'The poor girl had been removed by the monks before we were informed,' snapped Roger. 'She was taken to the infirmary, where we saw her body. It was returned to the crypt when the justiciar insisted on you being called – for the sake of preservation, no doubt.'

Jordan de Neville, who had not yet said a word, added a few now. 'We will all be leaving straight after the funeral, so this evening is the last opportunity. We do not wish to view her again,' he added hastily. 'Merely the fateful spot where she was found.'

In the corridor of the cellarer's building, at the end furthest from the guests' refectory, was a door which led into the alcove at the top of the steep stairway down into the vault below. At right-angles was the external door into the courtyard, through which John had entered the previous day. Gathered in the corridor were the prior, his chaplain and Brother Ferdinand, escorting Lady Avisa, her tirewoman, and Margaret Courtenay and her maid. Another portly monk, the cellarer Brother Daniel, was also hovering behind.

'My daughter Eleanor is of too nervous a disposition to wish to accompany us,' announced Avisa.

Robert Northam moved to John's side and murmured conspiratorially in his ear. 'I regret any inconvenience, coroner, but they were quite insistent. I thank God that this will all be over tomorrow.'

De Wolfe shrugged his indifference as they waited for Brother Daniel to open the door and waddle into the alcove, where he lit a bundle of candles from the tallow dip and handed them to each of the guests.

'Be very careful on these stairs,' warned the prior in a loud voice. The last thing he needed now was for one of the notables to fall down the treacherous steps.

With the cellarer in the lead, holding his candle high, the procession trooped cautiously down the steps, John and his two assistants bringing up the rear with Brother Ignatius. At the bottom they all stood in a wide arc around the lower opening of the staircase. The flickering candlelight on the faces made the scene like some demonic ritual ceremony, until Prior Robert made a wide sign of the cross in the air and uttered a solemn prayer in Latin and led the others in a recitation of the Lord's Prayer and the creed. The loudest response came from Thomas de Peyne, who was almost overcome by this religious drama. The four guests seemed less moved by the solemn moment, but all followed the monks in crossing themselves and genuflecting.

'This was the spot where the poor lady was found,' said Daniel the cellarer, pointing to the floor near the bottom step. One of the maids began to sob but was sharply reprimanded by Lady Avisa, who seemed immune to the baleful atmosphere of the forbidding vault. Margaret Courtenay's face was tense and drawn, but she made no sound as her hand stole out to grasp that of Jordan de Neville, who stood close to her. He and Roger Beaumont stared stonily at the patch of bare earth but said nothing.

There was a long silence, which soon became embarrassing and then unbearable, until Robert Northam felt forced to break it.

'Have you seen enough, friends? Dear Christina still lies a few paces away, if you wish to see her before she is coffined in the morning.'

John frowned and began to protest that she was hardly in a fit state to be viewed by sensitive ladies, but the prior forestalled him.

'Of course, I directed that offer to the two lords here, not the ladies.'

Though Jordan had not long ago declared otherwise, he reluctantly followed Roger Beaumont when the older man began to stalk after the prior deeper into the darkness of the vault. John and his men tagged on, and the coroner was surprised to find Margaret Courtenay at his side.

'Mistress, this is not really a venture for a lady. You will appreciate the reason.'

The young woman shook her head and spoke in a determined voice. 'She was my friend and I owe it to her to say goodbye, Crowner.'

He gave one of his habitual shrugs and walked on in silence. Brother Ferdinand was on his other side, but he noticed that Ignatius had declined to come with them, having followed the other women back up the stairs.

In the end bay, with the uneven far wall brooding over them in the wavering light, they all lined up around the ominously dripping box. This time it was Gwyn who had the task of uncovering the corpse and lifting the top of the wet linen sheet once again to reveal the features. Both he and John were mildly surprised to see that the signs of corruption had hardly advanced since their previous visit, thanks to the frequent replenishment of the ice.

Roger and Jordan looked on her face briefly, with stony expressions set firmly in place, possibly as a manly shield against showing any emotion. Margaret Courtenay swayed slightly and gave a choked sob, then again made the sign of the cross and whispered some private farewell to her young friend, before stepping back and stumbling with her candle towards the staircase. Thomas hurried after her, solicitous as ever to anyone in need of comfort.

'Have you seen enough?' asked the prior rather abruptly. He led the others away, leaving John and Gwyn with the makeshift coffin.

'I suppose they've got a better box than this some-where?' grunted the Cornishman.

'They are taking her into the church for the Requiem Mass, then to the cemetery on the other side,' said de Wolfe. 'We had better give them a hand here in the morning to move the body.'

Gwyn looked with disfavour around the empty bay at the end of the long crypt. 'Something about this place gives me the shudders,' he said. 'Must be my Celtic blood, though you have plenty of that too, Crowner, from your mother.'

John shivered and agreed. 'No wonder some of these monks get these crazy notions, spending years stuck in this place on the marshes.'

He pulled his black cloak more tightly around him and made for the stairs, thankful to leave this forbidding place with its lonely corpse.

In spite of all the activity that day, it was still quite a few hours until the first of the religious offices at midnight, which inevitably Thomas de Peyne wished to attend. After another doze in the warming room, the coroner's trio went back to the refectory, where Gwyn cadged bread, cheese and ale from the kitchen before they retired to their fleece-stuffed mattresses upstairs. De Wolfe disappeared into his cubicle, and the other two wrapped themselves in their cloaks and a blanket in the main chamber. Gwyn was snoring almost immediately, but Thomas catnapped, long used to waking himself in the middle of the night to attend Matins. When the bell of St Saviour's tolled, he got up and padded down to the far door, where the night stairs led him down to join a stream of obidentiaries making for the church.

After the service, he returned to the dormitory to sleep until Lauds, the next office around dawn. Gwyn was humped on the next palliasse like a beached whale, making blowing and whistling noises. There were no pilgrims here tonight to close a loose shutter at the further end of the dormitory, which was tapping in the icy breeze. The clerk walked up to secure it and on returning glanced into the open cell where his master slept. His candle revealed a rumpled but empty mattress, there being no sign of the coroner.

Puzzled, Thomas went back to his own bed but lay awake waiting for de Wolfe to return. After a quarter of an hour, there was still silence and he reached out and prodded Gwyn on his large backside. It took several jabs to awaken him, and when he did surface he was irritated by the clerk's concern.

'He's probably gone for a piss or a sit-down in the reredorter!' growled the officer. 'Shut up and go to sleep.'

However, after another half-hour went by, Thomas could stand it no longer and got up to shake the Cornishman again. Grumbling, Gwyn stumbled out of bed, still fully dressed, and after a sleepy discussion they decided to go back to the warming room to see if de Wolfe was there. It was deserted, and now the two men were becoming concerned.

'Let's try the cloister and the cellarer's building,' urged Thomas, leading the way in the gloom, which was relieved only by moonlight and a few guttering torches fixed in brackets. The cloister walk was empty, and only when they went the length of the corridor in the cellarium and went out into the inner courtyard did they see anyone. In the lodge at the inner gate, a night-watchman sat dozing under a tallow dip. He was a lay brother, not the usual monk who kept the gate in daytime, but he denied seeing the coroner or indeed anyone else for the past two hours.

Gwyn and the clerk stood indecisively outside the porter's lodge, unsure of where to look next.

'Maybe he's with the prior?' suggested Thomas, but Gwyn scoffed at the idea of him visiting anyone at this time of the morning. In the hope that he had returned to his bed, they began retracing their steps and went back into the cellarium corridor.

'What the hell's that?' suddenly demanded Gwyn, as they were passing the inner door to the basement. Thomas cocked his head and heard a muffled thudding. With images of the icy corpse down below still fresh in his mind, he blanched and made to hurry on to the shelter of the dormitory, but Gwyn was made of sterner stuff.

'Let's get this damned door open,' he growled and slid back the bolt, which squealed in rusty protest. Inside the alcove, the thudding was louder and obviously coming from behind the stout oaken door to the vault.

'Give me a light, Thomas. This is no bloody ghost!' snapped Gwyn.

The clerk fumbled for some half-used candles in the niche and lit them from the feeble tallow lamp. By their light, the coroner's officer wrenched back the heavy bolt on the inner door, and as it swung open a tall figure stumbled into his arms. De Wolfe was dishevelled and blood was running from his nose and several grazes on his face. He staggered against the wall and slid to the floor, shivering and blaspheming roundly.

'I thought I was going to be there until they came for the dead girl in the morning,' he groaned. 'They might have had to move two corpses by then!'

His two assistants helped him to his feet, and in the next few minutes they examined his injuries while he told his tale. Thankfully, he had no more than multiple bruises and a few cuts and grazes, though on the upper part of his forehead he had a lump under his hair the size of a pigeon's egg.

'Some bastard pushed me down the stairs and locked the door on me!' he snarled when he had finished cursing. 'I must have lost my wits, for I was lying on the floor at the bottom when I got my senses back. Jesus, these bruises are tender!' He winced as he touched the front of his shins.

'Who did it, Crowner?' demanded Gwyn angrily. 'I'll go this minute and punch his lights out!'

John raised his hand painfully. 'Cool down, Gwyn. I heard and saw nothing. I've no idea who did it; he was behind me – or possibly she! Now help me to my bed. I'll be recovered by dawn.'

As they helped him hobble down the corridor and supported him up the stairs, Thomas ventured to ask him why he was going to the vault at that time of night, fearing that there was some supernatural reason for him to visit a decaying cadaver. John pointed to the large circular ring of silver that secured one corner of his cloak to the opposite shoulder, bearing a stout pin passing through holes in the material.

'When I was going to my bed, I found this was missing. The only place I could have lost it was when we all went to that damned cellar.'

'Couldn't you have left it until morning?' grunted Gwyn as they entered the dormitory.

'It's valuable – and a certain lady gave it to me many years ago,' growled John. 'With God knows who coming to fetch the body tomorrow, I wanted to make sure of it. With my candle out when I came to, I had to crawl and grope on my hands and knees to find it in that bloody cellar.'

Thomas shuddered to think of being in the dark with a dripping corpse-box for company and decided that John de Wolfe must have stronger nerves than anyone he knew. After their master gingerly lowered himself on to his mattress, Thomas went off to the far side of the priory and roused the old infirmarian, who hobbled across with bandages and salve to clean up the coroner's scrapes and bruises. They told him that de Wolfe had fallen downstairs, but omitted to mention which ones.

'Shall I rouse the prior as well?' enquired Gwyn, who was still simmering with anger at this outrage on his master, but John wearily forbade him.

'No point in hauling him from his bed. I just want to rest now. I'll see him in the morning.'

'Perhaps he was the sod who pushed you down the steps,' muttered Gwyn under his breath.

The day of the funeral dawned with a pale clear sky and an iron-hard frost in place of the snow flurries of previous days. Every drop of water was frozen, even in the jugs in the guest dormitory. Stiff and aching, but otherwise none the worse for his fall, John de Wolfe rose shivering from his pallet and joined Gwyn and Thomas in the refectory downstairs, where hot gruel and warm bread, combined with ale mulled in the kitchen with a red-hot poker, helped them to thaw out.

'What are we going to do about it, Crowner?' demanded Gwyn. 'I reckon it was that bastard Beaumont, trying to put you out of action!'

Thomas nodded excitedly. 'Perhaps he had been fiddling his share of the estate profits and was scared you would find out. Maybe that was why he killed his ward, to keep his embezzlement secret by hanging on to the lands?'

John paused in his attack on a slab of boiled salt ham and three eggs fried in beef dripping, for his injuries had not blunted his appetite.

'Don't get carried away. We've not a shred of proof to accuse anyone. I'm off to see the prior after this, Gwyn, but you had better get down to see what's happening to that corpse.'

Thomas was thankful that this order seemed to exclude him, and he hurried away to yet another service in the church, where he could gossip and question the monks again. When de Wolfe accosted Robert Northam as he returned from Prime, the prior was aghast at being told of the attack during the night.

'That vault is accursed!' he said with a vehemence that seemed too extreme for the occasion. 'I should have it bricked up, but the cellarer is adamant that he needs the space for storage. That place has been nothing but trouble for this house since we were founded.' He did not enlarge on this, and John was more concerned with discovering who had tried to kill him.

'I was lucky to receive nothing more than cuts and bruises, though I was knocked senseless for a time.' He grinned wryly. 'It proves beyond any doubt that Christina never fell down those stairs, when her lack of injuries are compared with my poor face and legs!'

'Who could have done such a thing?' expostulated Robert. 'Surely not one of my flock!'

'Then that leaves only your guests, prior,' observed de Wolfe.

Brother Ignatius, who lurked like a shadow behind his master, muttered something about the power of the Horned One surviving after death, but he was ignored as the prior and coroner discussed possible motives and culprits. They came to no conclusions and soon Ignatius was tugging at Robert's cloak to remind him that they should prepare for the coffining of Christina.

De Wolfe had other business and limped rather than strode over to the favoured guest-rooms near the inner gate. Here he rapped on the door and confronted Roger Beaumont, who appeared with Jordan de Neville close behind.

'Were you abroad in the building in the early hours of this morning?' he rasped without any pretence at diplomacy. 'And if you were, did you attempt to kill me by pushing me down the cellar steps?'

After the first shock, Roger became almost apoplectic with enraged indignation. He raved at the coroner and, if Jordan had not restrained him, would have thrown himself at de Wolfe in his temper.

John sometimes used this ploy of making others so incensed that they dropped incautious words that betrayed them, but this time it failed, even when he voiced his suspicions that Beaumont might have been cheating the Exchequer of some of Christina's revenues.

Eventually the incandescent language of the baron persuaded de Wolfe that he was getting nowhere, and with ill grace and no apology to Roger he backed off and went down to seek Gwyn. In the lower corridor, he found him helping a couple of lay brothers, fussily overseen by a trio of monks, to manhandle a new coffin into the alcove and down the now notorious stairs. Made in the priory workshops, the sarcophagus was of fine elm, but the corners were already suffering because of the narrowness of the walls on each side of the granite steps.

With much grunting and not a little sacrilegious cursing, the men managed to navigate it into the vault below and then carry it into the forbidding end bay. John followed them, the place now being better lit by a dozen candles and several horn lanterns. The coffin was placed on the earthen floor, now soggy with meltwater from the cold box.

Daniel the cellarer, Brother Ferdinand and Maglo the gatekeeper were restlessly milling around the servants, all giving competing advice on how best to get the corpse from the ice into the coffin. Gwyn solved the problem by casually dipping his brawny arms into the slush and lifting Christina bodily out of the crate and laying her gently in her last resting place.

'Is she not to be dressed in finery or at least a new shroud?' asked Daniel.

'The ladies' attendants will see to her in the church,' replied Ferdinand, crossing himself as he gazed down sadly at the girl's remains.

At that moment a melancholy procession came into the vault. Brother Ignatius was in front, swinging a censer that wafted perfumed incense into the chamber. John was not sure whether this was for ceremonial purposes or to dispel any noxious vapours from the corpse. Whichever it was, the chaplain appeared deeply unhappy, as an angry scowl disfigured his face. Behind him, Prior Robert held up an ebony staff topped by a silver cross, a brocade stole around his neck. Martin, the old archivist, came next bearing a tray covered with a lacy white cloth, and inevitably he was followed by Thomas de Peyne carrying a silver cruet in his gloved hands. Lastly, Roger Beaumont and Jordan de Neville formed a reluctant audience as the group moved in to fill the space around the coffin and stood with bowed heads while the prior began chanting in Latin, the monks responding appropriately, especially the devout coroner's clerk.

Robert Northam took a small wafer from a pyx on the archivist's tray and, with slight hesitation, placed this consecrated Host on the tongue of the dead girl, her mouth now sagging open as the death stiffness had at last passed away. With more Latin prayers and crosses made in the air, he took the cruet from Thomas and dribbled a few drops of wine saved from the last Mass on to her swollen lips.

At this, there was a sudden crash, which made even the phlegmatic John jump with surprise. His first thought was that perhaps God had intervened at this most solemn moment, but it was Ignatius who had dropped the censer, which rolled along the floor shedding dull sparks.

'This is not right, prior!' he hissed. 'You should be exorcizing her, not blessing her!'

Northam glared fiercely at his secretary. 'Behave yourself, brother! If you cannot, then leave this place at once!' he thundered.

Cowed by years of obedience, the lean monk's short-lived rebellion subsided into silence and he retrieved the fallen censer from the floor. The prior completed his valedictory ceremony by sprinkling a little holy water over the already soaking cadaver, while the surrounding monks intoned the final responses. Now the cellarer and Brother Maglo lifted the heavy lid from where it had been leaned against the far wall and put it in place temporarily with four nails driven in halfway. As he straightened up, the Breton monk slipped on the muddy floor and fell heavily against the back wall. There was a rumble from above and a lump of granite the size of his head fell in a shower of old mortar and crashed on to the coffin. Everyone ducked, half-expecting the arched roof to cave in as a trickle of rubble followed the stone. There was a momentary silence, while a cloud of dust slowly drifted down from the top of the wall. It was broken by a shout of agonized triumph from Ignatius.

'A sign! A sign! Beelzebub is among us! See what the witch can still do, brothers, long after her black heart has stopped! I was right, I was right!'

At a sign from the prior, the chaplain was seized by

Daniel and Maglo and hustled off to the stairway, where he vanished, still yelling about this vindication of Christina's black arts. As the prior stood apologizing to Roger and Jordan for the behaviour of his unstable secretary, the lay brothers, who had waited unobtrusively in the main vault, came forward and began carrying the coffin down the crypt towards the exit.

Gwyn stood with de Wolfe, looking up at the roof, apprehensive that more was waiting up there to come down on their heads. Dimly visible, there was a ragged cavity where the roof joined the wall.

'I think the roof is sound, except the courses of stones that meet the top of the wall,' said Gwyn. 'It's that which is so badly built.'

John, still aching in every limb from his bruises, had little interest in the art of masonry. 'Let's get out of here. I can't stand this bloody tomb! We've been here for two days, and I've learned absolutely nothing about who killed her.'

An hour later the tirewomen, together with two laundresses, the only other females allowed in the priory precincts, had completed their dressing of Christina's body. The coffin lid was nailed down permanently before being taken into the church, where the funeral service was held at what John suspected was a much faster pace than usual. The prior had banned Brother Ignatius from attending, and Thomas wondered what massive penance he would be given for his unseemly behaviour.

When the prayers and chanting were completed in the church, the congregation, swollen now by the ladies and their maids, together with the lay brothers and monks of Bermondsey, followed the coffin out of the west door of St Saviour's. Pacing across the outer courtyard, to the accompaniment of more doleful chanting, they turned right into the lay cemetery, the monks having their own burial ground south of the church. Carried by Roger Beaumont, Jordan de Neville and two monks, the coffin was laid in a pit dug the previous day and the final prayers were spoken over it by the prior.

Given the age of the young victim, it was a moving ceremony and even the hard-bitten coroner, so used to sudden and violent death, felt touched. He was standing next to Margaret Courtenay as they all gathered closely around the grave to watch the earth being shovelled in by the sexton and his labourer.

'What a waste of a young life!' John murmured to Christina's friend. 'Done to death, a virgin not yet sixteen years of age!'

Margaret looked up at him, tears in her eyes. 'It is so very sad, Sir John. Though perhaps not a virgin: there was a handsome squire at Wirksworth who at least spared her that.'

The young woman said this with such affection that John smiled at her, not offended by her indiscretion, but there was a sudden howl from behind him. Turning, he found Brother Ferdinand close by, obviously eavesdropping. Before John could protest, the monk spoke, hissing almost like a snake.

'Not a virgin? No, it cannot be! Tell me it is false, woman!' He made to grab at Margaret, but John smacked his hands away. By now the others close by were staring at yet another confrontation with a crazed Cluniac.

'What's it to you, brother?' demanded John, grabbing Ferdinand by the front of his habit. 'Why should a celibate monk be concerned with such things? Are you perverted?'

The people around the grave now began to hurry towards them, the overwrought prior in the lead, but

Ferdinand twisted from de Wolfe's grasp and backed away.

'It was all for nothing! Oh God, how grievously have I sinned!' he howled like a starving dog. Staring at John with an expression of sheer terror, he dropped his voice to whisper so softly that the coroner could only just catch the words.

'I offered up my sacrifice to you, Oh Lord! But it was all in vain, you rejected me!'

Turning, he hauled up the skirts of his robe and ran rapidly towards the gate into the outer courtyard. Everyone watched him, bemused by the behaviour of yet another apparently demented monk. John caught Gwyn's eye, but the big Cornishman shrugged. 'They're all bloody mad in this place,' he growled.

As the prior was anxiously conferring with the cellarer, who was also sub-prior, Thomas sidled up to his master. 'Crowner, I think we ought to follow him. I have a bad feeling about Brother Ferdinand.'

John always respected his clerk's intuition, and with a jerk of his head to Gwyn they started for the main buildings, the coroner hurrying as fast as his aching legs would allow. Thomas pattered ahead and was in time to see the fleeing monk vanish through the inner gate. As he passed through, he saw the courtyard door to the underground vault still swinging. He hastened to it but hesitated to enter the utter darkness of the stairs. Gwyn was close behind and, while they waited a moment for de Wolfe to limp up to them, Thomas lit a few candle stumps ready for the descent. As they went down, they heard the rest of the burial party approaching but pressed on in their pursuit of Ferdinand.

Gwyn took the lead, and when they reached the bottom they heard a high-pitched keening echoing eerily from the far end. The distraught Cluniac was alternately wailing and sobbing, then gabbling incoherently either to himself or to some unseen presence – possibly Almighty God.

'The crazy fellow is in the pitch dark,' boomed the Cornishman. 'He must have felt his way down there without a light.'

'As I had to last night,' replied the coroner grimly. 'And I suspect it was because of this same fellow trying to kill me!'

When they reached the last arch, their candles revealed Ferdinand lying face down in the slimy mud, limbs stretched out in cruciform posture, as in total supplication before an altar. He was wailing like an injured animal, and the ever-compassionate Thomas went to kneel by him to offer comfort.

When he sensed the clerk's presence, the monk gave a piercing yell and jumped to his feet, spread-eagling himself against the back wall, his hands scrabbling at the damp stones.

'Keep away! Keep off me, all of you!' he screamed, his face contorted in the dim light. 'I tried my best, but now I am doomed to an eternity in hell!'

De Wolfe grabbed a candle from Gwyn and advanced to stand menacingly in front of Ferdinand, who cowered away against the wall.

'Was it you who tried to kill me last night?' he roared.

The monk cringed even more. 'You were going to ruin my exorcism! Why else would you come here at dead of night? I followed you and foiled your intent . . . but it was all in vain!'

The prior and the others had now arrived at the arch, delayed by the lack of candles to light their way.

'Sir John, what in God's name is going on?' snapped Robert. He glared at the monk still scrabbling at the stones. 'Ferdinand, explain yourself!' he demanded, but the monk had eyes only for the threatening apparition looming over him in the form of the coroner.

Ignoring the prior, de Wolfe grabbed the petrified monk by the front of his robe, pulled him away from the wall and shook him like a frightened rabbit.

'What exorcism? What have you done? Did you kill that poor young woman, damn you?' he snarled.

'It was a holy sacrifice!' screamed Ferdinand. 'This place is accursed. I have felt it for years. There is evil here, and the only way to cleanse it was to liberate the soul of a pure virgin into this awful space!' His eyes rolling wildly, he flung an arm around to encompass the gloomy vault.

'How did you get her to come with you, you disgusting knave?' yelled de Wolfe, giving him another shake.

'I went to her room, to tell her she had been chosen to perform a miracle . . . and it was the truth! Only her pure soul could drive away the evil in this place. She believed me and crept away willingly!'

'And for her reward, you took the poor girl's life, you bastard!' snarled the coroner.

'Her spirit would have conquered the depraved miasma that pervades this place – but it was all in vain, for she was not pure after all!'

He began wailing again, and John released him in disgust.

'You are not only mad, you are depraved and evil!' he yelled. 'No doubt belonging to this religious house will save you from being hanged, as you richly deserve – but I hope your own soul rots in hell!'

Prior Robert stepped forward with the cellarer to seize the demented monk, but Ferdinand, inflamed by the coroner's contempt, backed away and seized the large stone that had fallen on Christina's coffin. With a scream, he raised it high above his head, to launch it at the prior.

Fearing yet another death, Gwyn lurched forward

and grabbed the monk around the waist and hurled him and the heavy stone backwards.

He slipped on the slimy floor and the two men crashed into the wall. A second later there was an ominous rumble from above and a shower of grit and mortar fell from the roof.

'Gwyn, get back!' shrieked Thomas.

As the officer leaped clear, an avalanche of stones fell from the top of the wall and the edge of the ceiling vault. There was a blood-curdling scream from Ferdinand as he was showered with half a ton of masonry dropping twelve feet on to his head and shoulders.

When the rumbling ceased and the cloud of dust had settled, the coughing, dirt-spattered onlookers saw that the monk was half-buried under a pile of rocks. Aghast, the men fell silent, then there was a final sound as a last stone rolled down the heap. From beneath it, a trickle of blood seeped out and mingled with the meltwater from the ice that had cooled his victim.

'Well, we failed to cover ourselves with glory this time,' grumbled John de Wolfe as he hunched over the fire pit and tried to get some warmth into his hands from the mulled ale in his pot. 'The damned fellow condemned himself without any help from me!'

The three men had left Bermondsey that morning, the prior having given them horses from his stables for the long journey back to Devon.

The previous day, the coroner had held an inquest on Christina de Glanville but ignored the death of Ferdinand, deciding that he had no jurisdiction over a monk who died inside his own priory.

Now they were spending an uncomfortable night in a tavern a few miles from Guildford, with the prospect of sleeping on the floor of the taproom, wrapped in their cloaks.

Gwyn grunted and pulled the pointed hood of his leather jerkin over his head to keep out a draught from a broken window shutter. 'If that woman Margaret had not said that Christina was not as virginal as everyone assumed, the bastard would have got away with it.'

Thomas was not so willing to discount divine intervention. 'But also, Ferdinand had to be in the right place at the right time to overhear her – it must have been ordained by God that he should not escape disillusionment and retribution!'

Gwyn lowered his quart mug from his lips to guffaw rudely. 'Don't tell me that you believe that the Almighty caused that roof to fall on him! It was due to some lousy, incompetent mason, who years ago didn't know how to build a decent wall.'

De Wolfe cut in to stop them bickering. 'It doesn't matter how he died. It's why he killed her that bothers me. Can we really believe all this mystical stuff about exorcizing evil with virginal spirits? Or was he just trying to have his evil way with her, getting her alone in a dark cellar?'

Thomas was eager to offer his explanation. 'I spoke to the old archivist again after Prime this morning, before we left. He said it was all bound up with this legend about the vanished monk years ago. He said Brother Ferdinand was always pestering him for more information and spent long hours in the scriptorium searching the old archives.'

'Proves he was bloody mad!' was Gwyn's succinct comment, made to irritate the little clerk. 'Just like that Ignatius fellow who thought she was a witch.'

'Maybe, but he must truly have believed that the crypt was unhealthily possessed in some way,' retorted Thomas.

Even the usually unimaginative John could not disagree with that. 'There was certainly something very unpleasant about the far end of that cellar,' he admitted. 'I don't believe in ghosts and goblins, but the few hours I spent crawling about in there with a sore head, in pitch darkness, was something I don't want to repeat!'

'But what was the demented swine trying to achieve?' demanded Gwyn.

Again, Thomas was keen to share his erudition on matters spiritual and esoteric. 'It is part of ancient wisdom that things virginal are pure and holy,' he said earnestly. 'You only have to think of our young novitiate nuns who devote their lives to God – and above all our Holy Mother, the Virgin Mary.' He paused to cross himself vigorously.

'Ferdinand obviously believed that releasing the fresh soul of a virgin directly into that loathsome space would banish the evil and cleanse it with her innocent spirit!'

'But I don't see how he got the girl to go down there with him in the middle of the night,' mused de Wolfe.

Gwyn snorted. 'These bloody priests have an unhealthy power of persuasion, dinned into people since they were infants – especially over impressionable young women.'

He nudged Thomas suggestively, but for once the clerk refused to rise to the bait, and Gwyn continued to pontificate.

'However he did it, the bastard had no intention of becoming a martyr. He must have killed her in that last chamber, hitting her with something heavy from that storeroom, then breaking her neck to release her soul in the most effective place. But then he dragged her back to the foot of the stairs to make it look as if she had fallen down.'

'At least we got that right, though the prior already suspected it,' grunted the coroner. 'That ruined

Ferdinand's accident plot, but if he hadn't discovered she was no virgin he would have got away with it.'

There was a silence as they stared into the glowing fire pit, their only defence against the hard frost outside.

'What about this falling ceiling?' asked Thomas. 'Can you really doubt that it was divine intervention?'

Gwyn was scornful. 'Divine intervention be damned!' he said. 'Cornish intervention, more likely! When that maniac lifted that rock to hurl it at the prior, I charged at him and we went arse over head, crashing into the back wall! It was already shaky, and the shock of both of us hitting it dislodged some of the keystones at the top, where one had already fallen out of its own accord.'

John was inclined to agree with him, but a small voice in his head made him wonder why the roof fall had so efficiently killed the monk but left his officer unharmed.

'That place is unsafe,' declared Gwyn. 'The prior was right for once. They should brick up that staircase and forget the vault ever existed.'

'Perhaps they will,' said de Wolfe. 'Whatever happens, I'll not be going back to that dismal place. At least we can satisfy Hubert Walter and King Richard that this was no political assassination, just the mad escapade of a crazy monk.'

'Maybe they'll ask you to be Coroner of the Verge again?' suggested Thomas, proud of his master's reputation.

'God forbid!' said John fervently and for once he made the sign of the cross.

ACT TWO

30 September 1270

When they found him in the vicinity of the reredorter he was babbling.

'God is over the three, the three over the seven, the seven over the twelve, and all are joined together. There are thirty-two paths of secret wisdom. The number thirty-two is the sum of ten and twenty-two, being fingers and letters of the Hebrew alphabet. The decade and its elements are figures. One is the spirit of the living God, and two the spirit from this spirit. Three and four are water and fire. Do you understand?'

'Yes, Brother Peter.'

Prior John de Chartres assured him of his full comprehension, though he could clearly see that the monk was raving. Brother Peter looked gaunt, his sandy hair lank and unwashed. The prior suspected him of fasting himself into this agitated state and felt humiliated at not having noticed it sooner. The youth smiled broadly and pressed on, the words cascading from his lips.

'And five to ten are the six sides of a cube – that perfect form – each designating in its turn height and depth, and the four compass points of the world. Of course, this establishes nothing real but expounds the idea of possibility . . .'

'Yes, yes, brother. Nothing is real.'

The prior soothed the young man, squeezing his shoulder in an avuncular fashion. But his words were just balm. Prior John's heart felt as heavy as a stone. He had been sent from France to shore up the faltering establishment that was Bermondsey Priory. Sundry suits concerning the ownership of adjacent lands had drained the priory's purse. And there had even been unseemly scuffles between tenant farmers and some monks, resulting in complaints of rough treatment. After four years of hard work, Prior John had thought he had at last got on top of all these problems. Then suddenly, in late September of the fifth year of his office – 1270 – matters had deteriorated. There had been a disappearance, and now it seemed that evil had been visited on the priory. For the only possibility he could imagine was that Brother Peter Swynford had gone stark, staring mad.

William Falconer, Regent Master of the University of Oxford, had been on a wild-goose chase, and he cursed his friend, Roger Bacon, for it. The Franciscan friar had become obsessed with alchemy since discovering certain secret books, books the contents of which he refused even to share with his old friend William. As a result, Bacon had locked himself away for weeks in his little watchtower on Folly Bridge at Oxford. At night the glow of furnaces and the stink of bubbling alembics assailed both the eyes and noses of those in the vicinity. Even those merely passing were occasioned to hurry by, fearing they might be contaminated by the deeds of the devil. He had finally emerged only to beg William to make a small journey on his behalf. Bacon's monastic order forbade him free movement, preferring to keep their free-thinking brother under close observation. But it seemed that Friar Roger required further confirmation of his theories of 'species', or radiating forces that emanate from every substance, physical or spiritual, to affect other things. And for that he needed Master William Falconer, himself an inveterate fiddler in the field of the natural sciences, to go on a journey. Falconer was reluctant to comply at first. But Bacon knew an appeal to Falconer's curiosity would hit the mark. And it had.

At first, Falconer had urged his friend to remember his own admonitions about experimental science. Proof of theories could be obtained only by personal experience through the senses. The Regent Master prided himself on his adherence to logic. Indeed, he had often made use of Aristotle's rules in *Prior Analytics* to solve many a vexing murder case in Oxford.

'We must seek only truths. For two general truths, not open to doubt, often lead us to a third truth not previously known.'

'Exactly, William,' responded Friar Bacon sweetly, reining in the irritation caused by Falconer's schoolmasterly tones. 'And that is why I am doing what I am doing. I need to understand pulverization and distillation, mortification and the proposition of lime. For whoever knows these things will have the perfect medicine, which the philosophers call the Elixir, which immerses itself in the liquefaction as it is consumed by the fire and does not flee or evaporate.'

To Falconer, it all sounded like dark magic, and he feared for his old friend. Perhaps Bacon's long incarceration by his order had addled his brain. But he knew that in the end he would have to humour him. He sighed, stopped pacing and plonked his burly frame down next to Bacon on the bench outside his workshop. He ran his hands through his unruly, grizzled locks, aware not for the first time that they appeared to be thinning on the top of his head. He knew he could not refuse Bacon's plea. Besides, he had his own reason for wanting to consult an alchemist, and preferably one far from Oxford, where everyone knew everyone else's business. He gave in gracefully.

'Tell me what it is you want.'

He hadn't bargained on his acquiescence resulting in him travelling half across the country and back. To Canterbury, in fact. And with little to show for his efforts at the end of the day. Now, to make matters worse, on his return journey, the rounsey he had hired in London had gone lame in one hoof. Moreover, one of his headaches was beginning. He fumbled in the pouch at his waist for some of his medicament. Dusk was falling rapidly, and he was well short of the inn where he had obtained the nag several days before. With even London Bridge, built only twenty years earlier, beyond the capabilities of his mount, he knew he would have to seek somewhere to stay. But he was floundering in the marshy lands to the south of the River Thames. Exasperated, he was almost moved to call the lonely area godforsaken until he remembered. He had passed close by Bermondsey Priory on the outward leg of his trip to Canterbury's Jewry. It could not be far away now, and his spirits lifted. Through rising mists, he followed his nose and the stench of the tanneries located in the priory's vicinity and soon saw the heavy bulk of church buildings looming out of the darkness. The priory sat low to the earth, as though it were sinking under the weight of its own bulk into the surrounding marsh. But he was glad of its proximity. Falconer was now on foot, leading the poor, lame mare, and his own feet were pinched in the new boots he had treated himself to in Canterbury.

'The lame leading the lame,' muttered Falconer as he finally limped under the great stone arch of the priory gatehouse. A rumble of thunder from the heavy storm clouds that gathered over his head welcomed him in. Strangely, the gates were still ajar, but there was no one to meet him. The place was deserted. Before him the outer court was empty, with the church's ornate façade rising up steeply. Row on row of saints precariously perched each in his own niche looked grimly down on him. Large spots of rain began to spatter one by one on the cobbles of the yard. The only light he could discern was that cast by flickering torches inside the church. Long shadows and guttering flames played across the great rose window high above, creating a sense of something hellish going on inside the church. This impression was strengthened when a piercing scream surged out of the half-open great doors in the church's western façade. The scream was followed by another, and another, causing its own echo in the gasps that were rent from Falconer's breast. His headache was worse, and the screams pierced his brain like a knife.

'In God's name, what is going on here?'

He dropped the horse's reins and left the nag to fend for itself in the priory courtyard. Striding towards the source of the awful screams, he suddenly felt a deep sense of foreboding. All was not well in Bermondsey Priory.

He pushed through the heavy oaken doors and stepped into the cool and imposing interior. The church was lit by pitch-brands set in iron rings along the side aisles. But it was the central nave of the church that drew his gaze. His eyes were carried up the seven pairs of sturdy columns that marched down the nave and on to the high rib-vaulting of the ceiling. It spoke of open space and heavenly calm. But at the end of the soaring space, in the entrance to the choir and the holiest of sanctuaries beyond, a scene from hell was being enacted.

A dozen black-clad figures were in the process of beating what looked like a roped-together bundle of rags heaped on the floor at the foot of the steps up to the choir. Each in turn raised an arm and brought his birch rod down with fearful force on to the bundle. In solemn but remorseless motion, the beating rotated around the circle of men, their actions synchronized by one who stood at the top of the short flight of steps. This man's face was grim and set with firm resolve. At any sign of weakness on the part of those thrashing the bundle, he issued a stern admonition.

'Harder, Brother Paul. Brother Ralph, remember this is for his own good.'

At his next turn, the accused offender unflinchingly beat even harder. It was a while before Falconer realized that the bundle was not just a pile of rags but a person, bound by ropes. And the heart-rending cries were coming not from those wielding the rods but from their helpless victim – a monk, as his oppressors were. Falconer could not stifle his cry of horror.

'For pity's sake, stop this.'

The call echoed around the lofty nave, and one by one the rods ceased their awful downward plunge. Slowly, the monks turned to face the intruder, a mixture of shock and guilt etched on their faces. Only the older man who had guided their efforts was unmoved. His authoritative voice rang out down the central aisle.

'Where have you come from? Who are you?'

His face set in a mask of determination, the man strode down the steps towards Falconer. His flock parted like the Red Sea before him, stepping back into the gloom of the side transepts. A lesser man might have fled at his forceful approach, but Falconer was too old and wise to be worked on by outward show. And he stood his ground. So it was the prior who hesitated momentarily, breaking his stride. Suddenly a change came over his countenance. In a swift moment, he was the man of God, shepherd of souls, welcoming a stranger into his church. He spread his arms and stood before Falconer with an apologetic cast to his looks.

'Forgive me, good sir. You encounter us at an awkward time. I am John de Chartres, prior of Bermondsey. Please forgive me for your being witness to this unpleasant scene. It was not intended for others' eyes.'

'William Falconer, Regent Master of Oxford University. And I can imagine your not wanting others to see this. Do you often beat your monks into submission?'

The prior threw a glance back over his shoulder to where the other monks were stood frozen on the spot. Falconer's words had been loud and clearly spoken. The monks could not have failed to hear them and were wide-eyed in astonishment that the stranger could be so bold in the face of their stern and overbearing prior. They had experienced four years of his dominance and were well cowed by now. Previous governance of the priory had been lax, but they had been brought back to strict discipline after the arrival of the new head of their house. John de Chartres had remedied former faults, righting the bad reputation of the priory, and now the monks feared him. Prior John coughed out a warning, scattering his gawping flock, and took Falconer by the arm. He led him into the side aisle, where their conversation would not be overheard by those more innocent ears.

'You do not understand the situation, Master ... Falconer, was it? You see, Brother Peter is ill.'

Falconer snorted in derision, at least glad to perceive that the pains in his head were receding. 'And thrashing him to within an inch of his life will cure him?'

With difficulty, the prior retained his calm exterior.

'Indeed, I hope it will. You see—' he paused, clearly unwilling to divulge too much of the internal problems that beset him '—Brother Peter is vexed with demons.'

Falconer frowned, reluctant to brook such unscientific thought. Demons did not figure in Falconer's pantheon of ailments. He offered an alternative guess as to what troubled the unfortunate monk. He knew that all too often the illness that caused a man to fall down in a fit and froth at the mouth was seen as demonic possession. Whereas the more skilled in medicine called it epilepsy, Falconer chose to use its old name. 'He has the falling evil, then?'

Prior John de Chartres smiled sadly and shook his head. 'I almost wish it were that disease. At least we then would know what to do and could take care of our brother. No. Unfortunately, we found him *in frenesim* – in a frenzy – and I do believe he has gone stark mad. It is fortunate we have a hospital here, where we formerly confined those with leprosy. Now that curse is receding, we use the old lazar house for the mad, the lame and the dumb.'

Falconer had heard of such hospitals. The inmates were not there to be treated but merely to be confined. He did not doubt that the bound and beaten figure of Brother Peter, now lying groaning in the centre of the church, would be chained up in such a place. If, as was likely, his so-called treatment was deemed to have failed. Falconer's first impressions were vindicated. The priory did not seem to be a happy place to have stumbled on, and in other circumstances he would have moved on. But he had no other choices available to him. Outside the church, he could hear the rain beginning to fall heavily, and he needed a dry place in which to rest. With luck, it would be for only one night.

'Hmm. Much as I doubt you can beat out the

madness from his mind, I don't know of any other way he can be cured. Perhaps a little kindness would help, though.'

The prior smiled wanly in response to Falconer's admonition. He might have wished the man was not present to witness the problems he had suddenly had to deal with. But the requirement to provide hospitality to the traveller was paramount. He strove to change the subject to something less painful to his soul. 'I imagine you wish to break your journey with us, Master Falconer. Especially with the weather turning so evil.'

As if on cue, a flash of lightning illuminated the outer courtyard in an eerie bluish glow, and a crack of thunder followed close on its heels. The frightened whinny of Falconer's hired rounsey reminded him of the reason for his broken journey, and he hurried out into the driving rain to quieten the animal. Prior John de Chartres did not follow him out into the deluge. From the cover of the church's western archway, he called out above the noise of the rising storm.

'Take the horse around the rear of the church. A lay brother there will stable the beast for you. The guest quarters are in the hall beyond the infirmary. But beware, there is someone . . .'

There was a momentary hesitation in the man's instructions, as though he had suddenly thought of another impediment to his new guest's sojourn. However, Falconer, who was short of sight anyway, did not see the worried frown on the prior's visage at such a distance and through the sheet of falling rain. Merely that the prior cast a look over his shoulder before again waving his arms to the right to emphasize where Falconer should go.

'Well, you will see for yourself. Go that way before you drown. You will find the hall easily enough.'

He then disappeared inside the church again to deal with the problem of the mad monk.

Falconer shrugged his shoulders at the mysterious utterance of the prior and, bowing his head against the driving rain, led the rounsey around the north side of the church. Avoiding a brook that already ran in flood across the marshy ground beyond, he followed the prior's instructions. He turned to the right around the grey and looming structures south of the church. Most abbeys and priories were similarly laid out, and Falconer guessed that the first outbuilding he came to was the infirmary where Brother Peter would soon be confined. It looked a grim and depressing place, and by the evidence of his nose the main cesspit for the priory abutted it close by. The final building in the range should be the guest quarters. And indeed, hugging close to the walls to shelter from the worst of the rain, Falconer soon discerned a bedraggled figure lurking in an archway that led to another inner courtyard. This would be the lay brother who would stable his horse.

The man beckoned him over and took the reins of the lame rounsey with nothing more than a grunt to welcome the prior's unexpected guest. It was only as the man turned his back that Falconer's eye was taken by a light in one of the upper windows of the guesthouse. He thought he saw the pale features of a person in the light of a flickering candle. Delving in his pouch, he produced his eye-lenses and fixed them on. But by then the vision was gone, the window dark, and, besides, the rain was smearing his view through the lenses.

When first he had commissioned the device to rectify his poor eyesight, it had been nothing more than two pieces of glass fixed at either end of a V-shaped bar of metal. He had had to hold it to his face to see clearly.

Dissatisfied, he had eventually crafted folding side-arms that wedged above his ears. For the first time ever, he had been grateful for the jutting nature of those appendages. Still and all, the eye-lenses were heavy and cumbersome, and he didn't wear them regularly. He was thought eccentric enough already in the town of Oxford, and to wear eye-glasses all the time would invite ridicule. Taking the glasses off, and folding them, he called over to the lay brother.

'Who was that at the . . . ?' He paused, unsure what he was asking. The man glanced up to where Falconer was pointing. Seeing nothing, he frowned and shrugged his apparently already burdened shoulders. Falconer sighed and decided he had seen nothing more than a false image in the flicker of lightning in the sky. That or a ghost, and he didn't believe in ghosts.

'Brother, where do I go?'

The man, who might have belonged to a silent order for all the conversation he had at his disposal, pointed a stubby finger at the doorway at the other end of the range from where the ghostly image had appeared. Falconer trudged under the arch and out of the rain.

The prior sat at the long oak table in his private chamber twisting the seal ring that adorned the little finger of his left hand. Before him lay a precious piece of fresh parchment on which he was contemplating writing a letter. This sheet was no palimpsest, used and rubbed clean for reuse, but bore a pristine surface. It was to carry a significant message to the parent house of St Mary's, La Charité-sur-Loire. John de Chartres had thought long and hard about the contents of the letter, and even if it should be sent at all. But he was a cautious and meticulous man and did not want to be held to individual blame for the scandal he feared could soon be exposed. He cursed the day he had been given the commission of setting the priory back on its feet. Then, he had scorned the old tales of horror that went back to soon after the founding of the priory.

Shortly after his own landing on the shores of England, he had been told by a seafarer, who happened to reside near Rotherhithe, that the place he was going to bore a poor reputation. He had brushed off the remarks as the malicious rumours of tenants who resented paying the priory its dues. But almost as soon as he arrived at Bermondsey, one of the older brothers, Ranulf, had taken him aside.

'Prior, I have to warn you that all is not well here.'

John smiled to himself wryly. He knew that. After all, had he not been sent to sort out the financial mess the priory had slipped into?

'I am aware of irregularities with the accounts, Brother Ranulf.'

He was quite shocked at the look of scorn the old monk had then given him. He was not used to such disrespect and began to remonstrate. But Ranulf gave him no time to get into his stride, sneering at the new prior.

'No, no. That is nothing – a little laxity. No, I am talking about past deeds that still dog our heels.'

John stood in silence as the story flooded from Ranulf's hoary and bewhiskered lips. It was a tale of the priory's earliest time, almost two hundred years ago. Of chaplains who disappeared without trace, and ladies who were wards of the king, and who rewarded the ministrations of the monks by running off into the wide blue yonder. It had all apparently brought bad luck on the house. When the monk finished his diatribe, it was John de Chartres' turn to cast a scornful look on his informant. He was a prudent and worldly man despite his deep faith, and yarns about errant lords and ladies and bad luck did not impress him.

Besides, he had been vouchsafed a darker and more accurate account of the priory's early history by his superiors. An account with which he wasn't going to enlighten Ranulf.

He had smiled and patted the old monk on the shoulder in much the same way as he had done this very morning when Brother Peter had uttered his gibberish. He had at the time taken Ranulf's tale to be similarly outlandish. They had not bothered him then, those old stories. Now, he was beginning to wonder. He pulled the candlestick closer to his parchment, the better to write of the events he wished to detail by the yellowish flame. Beyond the window of his comfortable upper chamber, dusk had fallen. And the edge of the pallid moon was beginning to be eaten away.

Falconer crossed the cramped room that was the small upper solar of his guest quarters, the old floorboards creaking under his weight. He sank down on the rude bed, which also protested at his size. He was a large man, but even now, after years spent in study at the university, his frame carried little excess fat. He had been a fighting man in his youth and kept up an active regime to avoid the degeneration of the body that he saw in his fellow Masters. But now it was not his body but his mind that troubled him. After fifteen years as Regent Master at Oxford University, Falconer was afraid he was losing his mind. Not in the sudden way that the young monk called Peter was deemed to have lost his by the prior of Bermondsey, but in a slow and insidious manner.

It had all started when he was lecturing a bunch of new students on Aristotle's *Prior Analytics*. The subject was as familiar to him as his own palm, and he had intoned the tenets a thousand times. But suddenly he could not recall a simple set of premises.

'First then take a universal negative with the terms A and B. If no B is A, neither can any A be B. For if some A – we will call them C – were B, it would not be true that . . . not true that . . .'

Suddenly the sequence that he had rattled off to hundreds of students refused to emerge from his brain. And a sudden shaft of a headache arrowed through his left eye. He had covered the moment by brusquely harassing one of the more recalcitrant of his students. 'Finish the premise, Thomas Youlden.'

At least he had remembered the boy's name, if not the principle he had been instilling into unwilling brains for years. The boy had trembled but had fumbled his way through that which had completely escaped his dominie. Later, his old friend and constable of the town of Oxford, Peter Bullock, had guffawed when Falconer had privately confessed his embarrassing failure. Though he still didn't mention even to Bullock the accompanying megrims that troubled him periodically.

'Why, William, I do believe old age is creeping up on you too.'

The thought had mortified Falconer, who was only just into his forty-fifth year and several years younger than Bullock. That was the moment when he decided he needed to seek a herbalist. The Doctors of Medicine at Oxford were less than useless to him. Their so-called medical knowledge was based on philosophical thought, not empirical action. Be that as it might, the problem was that he didn't want anyone else in Oxford to know of his plight anyway. So that was why he had so easily complied with Roger Bacon's request for him to travel to Canterbury to enquire of a certain Jew there about alchemical matters. Falconer had seen straight away that he could combine the trip with a medical consultation.

Now, as he lay back on the bed, pondering on the results of his trip, an errant sliver of pain began to niggle at his left eye again. He dipped into his pouch and extracted another dried leaf. It would have been better to infuse it in hot water, but the persistent rain and the thought of seeking help from the intransigent lay brother put him off. He stuffed the leaf in his mouth and sucked on it, waiting for the light euphoria it would bring. Through the arched window of the solar, he could see that one edge of the speckled surface of the moon was being eaten away by darkness. He closed his eyes and tried to relax, but sleep did not come.

In the growing stillness, however, he was aware of a dim but persistent noise. He lay in the darkness trying to decipher the sound. The closest he could come to it was that it reminded him of the sound of a ship tossing on a worried sea. He rose and stepped across to the window, wondering if one of those cloud-ships he had heard tell of as a child had indeed sailed into view above the priory. He recalled his father swearing to the truth of coming out of Mass one morning to find a cloud-ship bobbing in the sky, its anchor caught on a tombstone in the churchyard. His father had looked up to see a strange-looking sailor cutting the rope to leave the anchor behind and so allowing the ship to sail away into the sky. However, his father had been unable to show the boy any evidence. No anchor lay in the churchyard. Falconer gazed up, but all he saw was a growing darkness as the moon was increasingly obscured. Then he heard the sound again and knew it for what it was. Someone was unceasingly pacing the floorboards of the adjoining room to his. The room at whose window he had thought he had seen a ghostly figure.

As the moon was slowly eaten away and the night darkened, John de Chartres picked up his quill and began his narration of the events of the past few days. He set down on the pristine parchment in lines of black ink the disconcerting disappearance of two brother monks and the madness of a third. It had all begun two nights ago at compline, when Brothers Martin and Eudo had failed to put in an appearance. A cursory search of the priory and grounds had established that they were nowhere to be found. Eudo La Zouche was a quiet, stable youth, whose absence surprised the prior, even though he had found him easily led.

Brother Martin was another matter altogether, and his past history made it all the more difficult for de Chartres to confess to his disappearance. But confess it he must, it seemed. Especially now that Brother Peter's precipitate descent into madness had occurred. He was afraid there were darker deeds to confess. All three young men had come to Bermondsey Priory by different routes and from different backgrounds – particularly Martin – but had somehow struck up a mutual friendship. The prior had been glad at the time that they had studied and prayed together, clearly finding mutual strength in their comradeship. He now wondered if he had been misled into thinking their alliance was one of innocence. And he began to examine his recollection of their friendship to see if there had been one who had exerted a stronger influence over the others. It was his greatest fear that Martin had led the others astray in some way.

'I now lay down my confession of sin . . .'

The prior stared at these opening words scratched on to the page for an eternity, before becoming bold enough to write down the final calamity.

'And now we have his mother to contend with.'

Knowing that the effects of the chewed leaf would not allow him to sleep, William Falconer decided to slake his curiosity. He crept across his room, barely making a noise, and descended the stairs. The two guest-rooms, while being next to each other, were not connected in any way. They were approached by two separate stair-cases from the inner courtyard. So if Falconer was going to discover who his restless companion was, he would have to descend his own stairs to access those of the other guest. It did not occur to him until he stood in the archway at the bottom of his own stairs staring at the continuing downpour that he had no reason to be intruding on the other man.

'Damn it all, William. You are an infernally nosy char-acter – you must be able to think of some cause to disturb his rest.'

He sidled along the wall of the guesthouse trying his best to keep out of the rain that still poured down. Despite his best efforts, several large drops of water fell from the roof overhang and subtly found their way down his neck and inside his robe. He shivered as the freezing water trickled down his back, soaking into his underclothes. Reaching the arch of the other staircase, he pushed against the door to escape the deluge. It resisted his thrust, and after rattling the latch several times he finally realized the door was locked.

'Who is it feels so damned insecure that he locks himself up inside the walls of a priory?'

Defying the rain that was already soaking him a second time, he stepped out into the yard. Putting his eye-glasses on, he stared up at the window where he had first seen signs of occupation. At that moment, like a providential stroke, a flash of lightning lit up the yard followed hard by a clap of thunder. Almost on the thunder's heels and in the returning darkness, a yellowish light once more appeared at the window. Falconer swiped his fingers across the lenses before his eyes to clear the blurred image and perceived the pale, anxious visage of a woman. She was staring up at the maelstrom that was the storm. And the moon that was half-disappeared from the sky.

'A woman. And locked away too.'

'She is a Jewess seeking her son. What else could I do, short of casting her out? And that I could not do.'

Falconer hadn't known he had spoken his own observations out loud, and turned to look over his shoulder at who had replied. There stood a black-clad figure who had appeared out of nowhere, his footsteps masked by the sounds of the thunderstorm. Though his hood was pulled over his features to protect him from the rain, Falconer could see it was John de Chartres. The prior was looking at him quizzically, and Falconer realized he still wore the heavy glasses that helped his vision. Embarrassed, he pulled them off, folding them up and returning them to his pouch.

'She . . . What is a Jewess doing looking for her son in a priory?'

De Chartres grimaced. 'That is simple. He is here . . . or he was. Until the day before yesterday, to be exact.' He took Falconer by his arm and guided him towards the archway of his guest-room. 'Let me explain somewhere more salubrious.'

Saphira Le Veske gazed down on the two men as they scurried back into the shelter of the doorway at the other end of the building where she had been incarcerated. Once they were out of her sight, she looked up at the sky again, to where the moon was experiencing a rare eclipse. As the curved shadow of the earth crossed the moon's sunlit surface, it appeared as though a greater and greater arc was being eroded from the orb. Superstitious folk might imagine that the moon was being eaten away. Saphira, an educated woman who had run her dead husband's businesses for more years than she cared to recall, knew better. But she still sighed at the phenomenon. It was so much more alluring to imagine the moon being consumed by a great invisible monster than to conceive of orbs in the vastness of the sky. She looked back down at the empty courtyard, now nearly pitch black as the moonlight was eroded. The big, raw-boned man with the strange eye-lenses had piqued her curiosity. Before he had put on his glasses, she had looked into his piercing-blue eyes and seen intensity and a wild intelligence. Maybe he was the man she needed to restart her stalled affairs at Bermondsey Priory.

She crossed her upper chamber and pressed her ear to the wall that separated her room from his. If she concentrated, she thought she could just hear the murmur of two voices.

'Though I have no obligation to do so, I wish to explain the circumstances to you.'

The prior was beginning his conversation with William Falconer rather too sternly, and he knew it. Still, he could not help himself, as he preferred to surround himself with an aura of infallibility. He was moreover a man who relied on his dignity to carry him through difficult situations and was unused to confiding in others. But somehow he felt the present circumstances would be served by sharing them with this erudite stranger. Especially as Master Falconer was someone whom the prior was unlikely to see ever again after the night was over. Falconer was seated on the edge of his pallet, legs spread wide, his hands planted firmly on each knee. He angled his head at the prior's comment, as if indicating his understanding of the monk's difficult position. The man seemed to have something to hide. But William knew the value of silence in eliciting further information from a reluctant witness and kept quiet. Prior John de Chartres paced the creaky floor, pulling on his lower lip with the thumb and forefinger of his left hand. He paused for a moment, looking out at the darkling sky outside the narrow window. Then he swung around to face Falconer again.

'The blight of Brother Peter's madness is not the only problem to strike this priory recently. In the last few days two of his fellow brothers, both his sort of age, have disappeared without trace.'

'I am used to the errant ways of young men, who give in to the lure of the fleshpots for a few days. But they nearly always come back repentant.' Falconer paused to look up at the prior, who clearly didn't take too kindly to his suggestion that the Cluniac order resembled in any way the rowdy hordes of Oxford clerks. He quickly softened his observation. 'On the other hand, there are those uncertain souls who often take flight back home to their families, having decided that learning is not for them.'

The prior shook his head. 'Neither case can appertain here, Master Falconer. Brother Eudo is an orphan, and Brother Martin . . .' His face crumpled, and he cast a glance sideways at the blank wall that separated Falconer's solar from the other guest-chamber. William wondered if he thought the mysterious woman was listening in to their conversation for some reason. 'Perhaps you will understand if I tell you that Brother Martin is called Le Convers.'

'He is a Jew.'

'Was a Jew, Master. Now a convert from La Réole near Bordeaux, and I am paid eight pence a week to instruct him in the Catholic faith. But now I am not so sure I should have taken such a viper into my nest of innocents.'

Falconer sensed there was some deeper matter here, and that it involved the woman locked away next door.

He could feel the prickle of a megrim beginning, but he thrust it aside. 'Tell me all the circumstances.'

The Jewess knew she could save her son if only she could escape the durance that had been imposed on her. It had been her misfortune to trust the prior of Bermondsey Abbey when she approached him openly the previous day and said she sought out the youth known as Martin the Convert. John de Chartres had obfuscated, from the outset appearing embarrassed by the Jewess's request.

'Why do you seek out this person?'

'Because he is my son, Menahem. And his conversion was an ill-considered and rash act hard on the death of his father. If he is here, as I believe he is, please let me speak to him. I have travelled long and far to find him, neglecting the businesses that my husband built up in his lifetime. And which Menahem – Martin – will in time inherit.'

'Not if he is a Christian, I dare say.'

'True. After all, it is the business of lending at an interest, which is forbidden those of the Christian faith. But it is equally only that which we—' she swept open her arms to encompass all of her own faith '—which is all we Jews are allowed to pursue.'

'Be that as it may, madam . . .' The prior pursed his lips in distaste at the tenor of the conversation. 'What makes you think Mena . . . your son is here?'

'Because I have followed his tracks across France and into this realm. I thought to have lost any trace of him then. But, having lodged in Jewry at Canterbury in the small parish of St Mary Bredman, I learned of a French convert lodged close by St Thomas Hospital there. I was too late to catch him there, though. He was said to have been moved here to Bermondsey Priory. Can you deny he is here?'

'I can in truth say that no one called Martin Le Convers is presently in this priory, woman. So your journey is in vain, and you must return empty-handed. However, as the hour is late, and the weather worsening, please accept my Christian hospitality for the night.'

Saphira Le Veske thought his words accurate only in their strictest sense. Perhaps her son was not presently in the priory, but she was sure he resided here normally. She sensed something uneasy in the manner of the prior, something she could not put down to his being confronted by a Christ-killer, and a mere woman. What had her son done that made the man so unwilling to admit to his existence? She was determined to find out, and after taking up her lodgings in the priory guest quarters she resolved to wait until darkness fell and then scour the priory in secret. It had come as some shock to her to find she had been locked in. She had been standing at the window puzzling over her predicament when the tall stranger with the peculiar eyeglasses had turned up.

Saphira Le Veske was a good-looking woman with a thick head of red hair and green eyes that were unusual in her race. And she had turned many a man's head with her looks, which even though she was now forty-one she flattered herself to imagine were still alluring. The stranger was somehow going to be her saviour, whether he was aware of it or not. But before she could properly attract his attention, the creepy old prior had materialized from the stubborn darkness cast by the eclipsed moon. Now she was back relying on her own resources and would have to think again how she could escape her chamber. She wished she had paid more attention to the esoteric faith that had so seduced her husband and son prior to the older man's death. The Kabbalah might have given her some mystical release from her prison, but in the absence of magic she would have to rely on something more mundane. She poked her head out of the solar window.

'Can I speak to Brother Peter?'

Falconer had a notion that, if only he could understand the boy, he would be able to decipher what had happened in this accursed priory over the last few days. John de Chartres had spun him a yarn about three young monks who had forged a bond in the months since the young former Jew's arrival at the priory, a bond that with hindsight the prior now deemed unholy and unhealthy. De Chartres now saw Martin Le Convers as the fount of all the evil that had occurred. Falconer was not so sure but would keep an open mind until he got to the truth. His experience of the Jews of Oxford told him that people of that race avoided conflict where they could. Naturally, there were just as many hotheads among the young Jewish men as there were in the Christian community. But they were by and large more circumspect, and more aware of their equivocal position in England. Still, this youth was a convert and might not be in the same mould. Falconer had only Peter to tell him what had really been going on.

The prior pointed out the problem of questioning Brother Peter. 'But he is mad. All he utters is gibberish.'

Falconer smiled. 'And many would say I utter gibberish every day of my teaching life. Especially my new students. But soon they learn there is a logic in my catechism. Sometimes it just takes a pedantic and logical mind to make sense of the apparent madness in the world. After all, once you have discarded the impossible, then even the improbable that remains must somehow be the truth.'

John de Chartres grunted, clearly not prepared to accept the veracity of Falconer's rather unusual statement. But he saw no other way out of his dilemma than to allow the Regent Master access to Brother Peter.

'Come, he is in the hospital close by.'

As the rain still beat down steadily, William took a cloak from his travel baggage and wrapped it around his still-damp robe. He followed the prior down the staircase and out into the yard. The men paused briefly at the archway, hesitant about diving back into the storm. Falconer instinctively looked right and left before stepping into the darkness. Out of the corner of his eye he caught sight of something pale halfway down the junction of the wall to the guest quarters and that of the monastic dormitory, something pale, topped by a flapping bundle of material. He smiled to himself and, taking the prior's arm, steered John de Chartres across the streaming courtyard – away from the shapely vision of a slim woman's bare leg topped by her rumpled, dark gown, which had apparently snagged on the leaden downpipe that she was attempting to shin down.

'This way to the infirmary, you said?'

Behind them, Saphira untangled her gown and slid down the pipe to the ground. She crouched in the shadows, the rain turning her fiery red hair a deep brown, until the two men turned the corner of the building opposite. Then she hurried to follow them, sure that the errand they were on would throw some light on the whereabouts of her son. The tall visitor to the priory – the one who had clearly seen her stuck halfway down the drainpipe – had mentioned an infirmary. Maybe her son was the one they were about to visit there. From one point of view, she hoped not – often such hospitals were used as lazar houses. She did not want to imagine her son as struck down with leprosy, though this might explain the prior's reluctance to acknowledge his existence. Barefoot, she crossed the courtyard and cautiously peered around the corner of the adjacent building to see the men duck under an archway to her right. Silently, she followed them.

Falconer cast a quick glance behind him as he and the prior approached the hospital. He was able to spot a shadowy figure sidling around the corner of the building. Despite his poor vision and the growing darkness as the moon was cast further into shadow, he was satisfied that the figure's slight stature was that of the mystery woman who had been locked away. His instincts told him she would help him unlock the puzzle surrounding the two missing monks and Brother Peter's madness. To have her on hand and free of the constraints of John de Chartres suited him perfectly. He ushered the prior ahead of him and deliberately left the hospital entrance door open behind him.

Saphira Le Veske padded barefoot behind the two men, oblivious to the freezing rain that steepled down from the heavens. She was getting closer to finding her son, and all her concentration was on the task ahead. After they had passed under the arched entrance to the building on the opposite side of the courtyard, she hovered for a while in the deep shadow of one of the buttresses to its outer wall. Then, certain that the men must by now have proceeded further into the building, she slipped across the cobbled yard and stood under the same arch. The door was slightly ajar, and she was able to slip through the gap without moving it any further on its hinges.

Inside, she could discern by the light of flickering candles a long, rib-vaulted room partially divided by wooden partitions. She could hear the sound of restless bodies tossing and turning on straw-filled pallets, a sound punctuated by occasional moans. It was the sound of suffering, both physical and mental. Still, she could not rid herself of the idea of this being a lazar house, and she shuddered. At the end of the room, a curtain had been pulled back from one of the partitioned spaces, and candles burned brightly in the space so revealed. Saphira could make out the prior and the stranger leaning over a bed, staring intently at the figure that lay on it. She tiptoed closer.

'Can you not take these chains off him? He looks so ill.'

Falconer was appalled at the way the poor, mad monk was being treated. He was gaunt, and his skin was papery and taut across his skull. Yet he had been manacled to his bed with chains sturdy enough to hold down a bull. Brother Peter was bearing the indignity with equanimity, sleeping placidly on the coarse blanket that formed his bedding. And his robes were clean and tidy. The prior looked at the sombre monk who had been sitting at Peter's bedside when they had arrived. The thin, grey-faced minder pursed his lips and shook his head briefly.

'I fear not, Master Falconer,' replied the prior. 'Brother Thomas here is our herbalist, and I trust his judgement in cases like this.' He suddenly realized what he had said and qualified it immediately. 'Not that he is familiar with cases of madness, you understand. It is quite beyond both our comprehensions.' The monk nodded solemnly in confirmation. 'As for his . . . wasted appearance, he and his friends were simply fasting and practising the ascetic life. A little excessive maybe, but I didn't see anything wrong in it. And, see, we have put him in clean robes and dressed his wounds. But as for the chains, Brother Thomas and I are in agreement. It is better for . . . Peter . . . that he remains under restraint.'

Better for the priory was Falconer's interpretation, but he kept his thoughts to himself. He leaned over the slumbering body to examine the boy's face. Suddenly, Peter's eyes started open, and he stared back straight into Falconer's own face. The Regent Master wondered if he had been feigning sleep and how much of the earlier conversation Peter had been following. The boy was the first to speak.

'Hello, Adam.' He raised his right hand as far as he was able, and with a clank of chains traced three marks around Falconer's head. 'One, two, three. The Crown, Wisdom and Intelligence. I see it.'

'I am flattered, Peter. But my name is William, not Adam.'

Brother Peter faltered a little, frowning at the correction.

'Not Adam, then? Well, never mind.' Quickly, another thought flashed in his eyes. He smiled. 'Have you found Eudo yet?'

'No, Peter. Do you know where he is?'

A sly look crossed his features, and he turned away from the prior. 'I might.'

'And Martin, where is he?'

Falconer's question seemed to bother the young monk, and he moaned, shaking his chains as though he wished to be free of them.

'Martin? He is the Sephirah of Darkness. No, no, don't talk of him. I have journeyed to Jezirah and seen the ten classes of angels. I know.'

Falconer frowned, not understanding any of this gibberish.

'What do you know, Brother Peter? Where are they both, your friends?'

'Oh! He is dead. He is dead.'

The young monk's pale face then screwed up in horror, and he clutched at the sleeve of Brother

Thomas's robe. Uneasy, the herbalist grasped his wrist and worked the cloth out of Peter's grasp. Behind them, Saphira Le Veske was shaken by the words emanating from the monk's quivering mouth. Did he mean Martin was dead, or was he referring to Eudo? Guiltily, she prayed for the latter to be the case. Besides, unlike the patient stranger, she knew what the boy's ramblings meant. Or thought she did.

'What have you done, Menahem?' she muttered, and slid back into the darkness of the gloomy infirmary.

Falconer, meanwhile, contemplated his next move. If one of the boys was dead, where was the body? The prior said they had scoured the whole priory when the young monks had gone missing. At that time they had not been found. But if what Peter said was true, one of them was dead and his body lay undiscovered somewhere, leaving the other alive and perhaps guilty of the murder. It had all happened so recently that Falconer could not believe that whoever it was who was still alive – Martin or Eudo – could have gone far. Indeed, it was more likely he was hiding until the awful weather passed and it was possible to travel abroad. Looking out of the window of the hospital, he saw that the rain was still steepling down, and once again the Stygian gloom caused by the disappearance of the moon in the sky was briefly illuminated by a flash of lightning. A thunderclap like the crack of doom followed hard on its heels, showing the storm was now almost directly overhead. The terrible sound roused Brother Peter, and he cowered at the end of the bed, dragging his chains taut. He began to gibber, using strange words.

'He is released, the Sephirah of Darkness – Samuel and all his Keliphoth . . .'

The prior and the herbalist stepped back in horror and crossed themselves. Falconer rose, too, and rubbed his forehead in the region where his megrim was advancing. Unseen, he slid another leaf into his mouth and chewed. He looked down at the prostrate form of the chained monk, seeing the fear in his eyes. He knew he would get nowhere in the presence of the prior and his minion.

'Prior John, if there is truly a body in the priory, I urge you to locate it as soon as possible. Before the other monks arise for prime. If the two of you go now and conduct a thorough search, I will stay with Peter.'

At first, Thomas balked at the idea, but the prior saw the sense of it.

'Come, Brother Thomas, what Master Falconer says is sensible. We must locate the body before anyone else rises and discovers it by accident. Besides, Brother Peter is chained and cannot escape even if he wished to.'

The herbalist picked up one of the candles burning beside Peter's bed and led the prior away on their search. Falconer turned to follow their departure, surreptitiously glancing around in the dark for the mystery woman. He had been aware of her presence as he questioned the monk, but now she was nowhere to be seen. He wondered where she might have gone. And what she was doing.

In fact, Saphira was doing nothing. She had no idea where to begin the search for her son, knowing only that he was not in the infirmary. She had quietly peeped in each cubicle as she had passed it on the way towards Brother Peter's bed. There were only old and sickly men inside the partitions that were occupied, men on their final journey to the heaven they prayed to every single day of their monastic life. None of the bodies on the beds was that of a young man. She had breathed a sigh of relief. But then when Peter had proclaimed that one of his companions was dead, Saphira had been stricken to her core. She could only hope he was referring to the other young monk, Eudo. Though she wished no one ill, his death was preferable to the demise of her only son. But what troubled her more were the words that Peter had used before his outcry. To the prior and the stranger – someone called William Falconer, apparently – they had clearly been nonsense, the ravings of a lunatic, but Saphira knew exactly what they signified. And it worried her deeply. She sank down on the thin mattress in the cubicle she had chosen to hide in, waiting until the prior and the other monk had walked past. Suddenly she felt cold and tired, and she was aware how her wet clothes clung to her. It caused her to shiver uncontrollably.

'Peter, Peter, they have gone. You can talk to me alone now.'

Falconer gently urged the somnolent monk to open his eyes and acknowledge his surroundings. After a moment, when Falconer thought his urging was going unheeded, the young monk's left eye abruptly opened, as he tested the truth of the Regent Master's words.

'Look, Peter, the prior has gone, and so has Brother Thomas. Tell me, who is dead? What has happened to your friends Martin and Eudo? What were you doing that has frightened you so?'

Peter opened his other eye and looked slyly into Falconer's face. 'Who says we were doing anything?'

He sounded like a little boy caught in the act of self-abuse, and it occurred to Falconer that all this might be nothing more than a tale of mutual self-indulgence. God knows, he was used to that at the university. Though it rarely ended in death, perhaps one of these monks had been mortified enough to have killed himself. But the fear in Peter's eyes suggested that the secret held between these three young men was deeper and more horrific. Once again Peter began to babble.

'Look for geometric perfection, where the entrance numbers six, between eight and nine is the flaw. There is the three, and the name of God is creation.'

He grabbed Falconer's wrist and pulled himself up to the limit of his chains. 'Repeat it to me.'

Falconer balked, but at Peter's insistence he recited the nonsense twice, fearful that his memory lapses might let him down. His memorizing of the puzzle seemed to calm Peter down, and he fell back on the bed, his eyes closed once again. Falconer waited until the boy's breath became even and deep, then he rose. He walked down the gloomy passage between the beds towards the door of the hospital. Suddenly he stopped, distracted by something unusual but not sure what it was. He sniffed the air and walked back a few paces. Peering into the darkness of one of the cubicles, he saw a person sitting on the coarse palliasse, knees drawn up to the chest and head down. Long chestnut hair tumbled over the person's knees. It was the scent of wet hair mixed with a delicate perfume that had told him it was no tonsured monk he had detected on walking past. He slipped into the cubicle and stood beside the bed.

'Madam,' he murmured.

The woman started from her reverie and stared up at Falconer. Her face was pale and her features drawn, but it was a face of great beauty, with a chiselled nose and high cheekbones. The eyes were green and almost almond in shape, suggesting some eastern origin. Falconer saw immediately it was indeed the pale figure he had seen at the window above the courtyard – the ghostly apparition occupying the room next to his. He spoke again, calmly and comfortingly.

'Madam. My name is William Falconer. I believe we have the same goals. You are searching for your son. I, too, would like to find Martin, and his friend Eudo.'

'Menahem. His name is Menahem, not Martin. Menahem Le Veske.' She spoke firmly, almost stubbornly. William could see it would be best not to cross such a determined woman, who apparently had travelled far to trace her son. Besides, he was now more certain than ever that she would prove an excellent ally in his search. Saphira, for her part, knew that this William Falconer could be the key to tracking down Menahem. If only they shared their knowledge.

'My name is Saphira Le Veske, and I think I can explain some of what that poor young boy was saying.'

Captivated, Falconer sat down on the edge of the bed, and in the encroaching darkness the Jewess began to illuminate him.

Brother Thomas, meanwhile, was given the unenviable task of searching the outer court of the priory. This involved the prior staying warm and dry under the cover of the porch leading to the cloister, while the herbalist trudged across the open marshy wastes towards the working buildings on the south of the site. He was soaked by the time he entered the yard that was enclosed on two sides by the granary and brewhouse. His feet were frozen and covered in filth, and he left muddy footprints as he poked around the brewhouse and its neighbouring bake-house. He knew that the task was hopeless. Everyone had looked here before, and there had been no signs of Brothers Martin and Eudo then. He reckoned they had run away, tiring of the discipline instilled by Prior John. After all, if the old stories were true, it wouldn't be the first time a monk and those in their care had fled. His search revealed that neither youth was here now, nor were they in the kiln-house or granary. But as the latter was warm and dry, Thomas lingered over his search until he thought the prior would begin to wonder where he was. Reluctantly, he forced himself out again into the heavy rain, getting soaked once again. It was therefore doubly annoying that the prior had not even had the courtesy to wait for Thomas to report the results of his search. John de Chartres was nowhere to be seen.

Falconer was deeply disturbed after listening to Saphira. It seemed the gibberish that had emanated from Brother Peter's mouth was more than it appeared.

'The Kabbalah? Though I know many Jews in Oxford, and call them my friends, I have not heard of this.'

'If they are traditional Jews, then you are unlikely to have done. Its roots are deep in our faith, but not everyone approves of it, nor its recent new flowering. But my late husband was seduced by it, and by the philosophy of Rabbi Azariel. He was obsessed with the idea that, given the knowledge of the right sequence of letters naming God, man could emulate His role as creator. To make a living man, which we call a golem. There are stories that someone succeeded. I suppose it only natural that my son, Menahem, also picked up some of the doctrines.'

'Unfortunately, it seems it is a case of a little knowledge being dangerous.'

Saphira Le Veske grimaced and nodded her head. Her unrestrained tresses were drying and recovering their startling copper colour. And their natural waviness. She swept the thick hair back through the fingers of her left hand. Then she returned to clasping her knees with both arms like some young girl hugging herself for security in a dark world. The pose was in contrast to her mature command of the situation, however, and her understanding of its dangers.

'Menahem, Martin – call him what you will – was

always a boy who sought others' approval. If he thought these other boys would cleave to him because of him imparting secrets to them, he would revel in the adulation. I think that is why, when his father died, he was drawn into the seductive promises of the local Christian priest. And I was too engrossed in my own grief to see it until it was too late.'

'Tell me. Peter talked of the Crown, Wisdom and Intelligence, and called me Adam. What does that signify?'

'They are the first three of the ten Sephiroth – the mediums between God and the real world. They are the head of Adam Kadmon, the archetypal man.' She sighed. 'Forgive me if I cannot explain this properly. I never subscribed to my husband's mystical beliefs, which some say grew out of a spiritual reaction against the rational world we are surrounded by. The world I am perhaps a little too attached to.'

A smile formed on Falconer's face. 'I myself am seduced by the logical. Too much so, some people say. And yet it seems we both have to let a little of the mystical into our hearts, if we are to solve this riddle and find your son.'

'But not the darkness. We should not let that in.' Saphira shuddered and looked out of the narrow slit of a window in the cubicle. As if in mockery of her words, it was pitch black outside. The moon had all but disappeared, and with it any light. 'Our faith warns of the dangers of esoteric doctrines, which no one ought to delve into, unless he is a scholar who has his own store of knowledge to protect him.'

Falconer leaned forward and touched her lightly on the bare arm. She did not recoil, and he felt a spark of common feeling pass between them.

'I can say that I am not exactly ignorant of the philosophies of life. Nor are you yourself, I think.'

As he drew his arm back, she grasped it firmly, preventing him from moving away. Her hand was warm and her look encouraging.

'I trust you, which is more than I can say for the prior. He gives me the creeps. But do take care. There is an old story that warns of the risks of meddling in dangerous knowledge.'

'Tell me. It may help us avoid disaster.'

Saphira took a deep breath and began. 'Four sages enter an orchard – which stands for dangerous knowledge – and have a mystical experience. The first gazed on it and died, the second gazed on it and was stricken mad, the third gazed on it and destroyed their creation, turning heretic.'

'Eudo and Peter are the first two. Martin perhaps the third. And the fourth?'

Saphira turned her startling green eyes on Falconer, a questioning look in them.

'You said there were four sages. What happened to the fourth?'

'He escaped with his mind intact, because he was wise and anchored to the here and now.'

'Then let me hope the last is I.' Falconer uttered the words confidently enough, but he felt a twinge of fear due to his errant memory. Was wisdom draining from his mind? If he pursued this quest, would he fail also, through not being wise enough? But it was only a momentary lapse, and a flush of euphoria abruptly filled his mind with confidence. He laughed.

'Is there something troubling you?' Saphira asked.

He looked at the Jewess sitting beside him on the bed. She had a look of concern in her beautiful eyes.

'Nothing. What makes you think there is?'

'You looked so . . . distant for a while. As though you were no longer present.'

A tendril of worry crept up Falconer's spine. Was he

lapsing into blank reverie as well as being forgetful? He laughed again, trying to make light of his fears, but this time it sounded forced. 'It's nothing, really. I have just been a little ... ah ... forgetful lately.'

Saphira looked hard at him but decided to make no more of the moment. They had more urgent matters to attend to now. Falconer pulled off his old greyish cloak and draped it over Saphira's shoulders. She began to protest – after all, he would get as wet as her in the teeming rain – but he insisted.

'It's more sensible this way. If I pull the hood up—' he did so as he spoke, enveloping her head of luxuriant red hair and obscuring her finely chiselled features '—then no one will tell who you are. Look. You could pass for a monk in that garb. A small, very shapely monk, but ...'

She giggled, despite the situation, and pulled the cloak close around her. It was true – dressed like this she and the Regent Master could search the priory for her son without arousing too much suspicion. He gently took her arm.

'But we will have to hurry or the priory will be rising for prime, and then it will be impossible to move freely around.'

Falconer picked up a stub of candle and cradled it in his hand. They would be in the dark outside where a strong wind was blowing, but maybe he would be able to relight it inside the priory buildings. As they left the hospital, he glanced back at the tableau of a recumbent Brother Peter, chained to his bed and lit by the glow of two candles on either side of him. He resembled some saintly icon glowing in the surrounding darkness. The woman pulled at his sleeve, and they went out into the stormy blackness of the priory grounds. The sky was invisible, the moon completely obscured. It gave Falconer the feeling of an oppressive weight bearing down on him, and he hurried along the eastern wall of the dorter and towards one of the doors.

'Wait! Look!'

Saphira Le Veske's call was shrill and peremptory, her clutching at Falconer's sleeve urgent and demanding. He turned around and saw the woman staring into the Stygian gloom.

'What is it?'

'There. By the stream that runs below the building. There's someone there.'

'The latrine block? Hold on . . .'

There were times when Falconer regretted his poor eyesight, and this was one of those moments. He fumbled in his pouch and withdrew his eye-glasses. Fitting them to his head, he peered in the direction Saphira was pointing in.

'There. Can you see him? It's Menahem, I'm sure it is.'

Falconer, cursing the rain, tried to make out what she was indicating. Then he saw a movement, but it was no more than a grey shape in a blacker world, until the figure turned to look towards them, alarmed perhaps by the woman's cry. Falconer discerned pale features beneath a monastic cowl, and he was about to ask how Saphira knew it was her son on such little evidence when she broke away from him. The cloak he had lent her flapped in the strong wind as she chased after the disappearing shape. Falconer pulled off his eye-glasses and sprinted after her. When they got to where the figure had been, there was nothing. There was no door he could have entered, no window he could even have clambered through. His escape was blocked to the south by the churning, muddy stream that ran in spate below the latrine block of the reredorter. And he could not have passed them to the north, as there were blank walls to either side. He had simply vanished.

'Are you sure it was your son?'

'A mother knows her son, Master Falconer. It was Menahem, or Martin as they call him here. But where could he have gone?'

She looked distraught at having been so close to the goal of her hunt and yet having missed him. Falconer wondered if her overriding desire to find her son had seduced her into superimposing his image on the fleeting apparition. He grasped her shoulder and turned her back the way they had come.

'Come. Let us stick to our task of scouring the priory. If it was him—' she looked hard at him, angry at his lack of confidence in her opinion on the ghostly figure. '—then we will find him. We at least now know he is here somewhere.'

The trouble was that their search was as fruitless as the earlier one. They combed all the buildings they could gain access to but found no crumb of evidence that either Martin or his companion Eudo were anywhere on the premises. Nor was there any sign of a body. Finally, bodily soaked, with their spirits drowned too, they took shelter under the porch that led into the cellarer's building. The long, low, rib-vaulted chamber was illuminated by a couple of sputtering candles and punctuated by gloomy corners where lurked dusty barrels and anonymous heaps. Used for storage, it was a convenient and dry means of reaching the covered way of the cloister. Neither Falconer nor Saphira wished to remain in the rain any longer. As they crossed the cellarium, Saphira grabbed Falconer's arm and hissed a warning.

'There's someone down at the far end.'

Falconer screwed up his eyes, making out a tall, angular figure that did not resemble the boy that Saphira had claimed to have seen earlier. He was rummaging around in a pile of crates, one of which toppled over on to his sandalled foot. A brief curse was followed by an expostulation to God for forgiveness. The monk turned towards them, and Falconer could tell it was Brother Thomas. Saphira slipped discreetly behind one of the columns as Falconer approached the monk.

'Have you found something, Thomas?'

The monk looked startled. 'What? Oh, it's you, Master Faulkner.'

Falconer silently excused the monk his mangling of his name and enquired if he had discovered something of significance.

'No, I doubt it. I was just wondering about the old cellar below here. It's somewhere in this corner behind all these boxes. No one's used it for years, but Brother Eustace was saying a few days ago that he had heard noises in the night coming from this region.'

'Noises?'

'It's probably nothing, really. Eustace is getting on in years, and his hearing isn't what it used to be, but . . .'

'But what?'

'Others claim to have heard strange noises too. But that was only after Brother Eustace mentioned it, and you know how hysterical people can get about ghosts and such. Personally, I don't believe a word of it.'

Falconer was now getting confused and asked the monk what he was talking about. The skinny fellow waved his arms in embarrassment.

'Oh, just old tales of the founding of the priory, and missing chaplains and disappearing ladies of noble birth. Old wives' tales, if you ask me.' He hesitated and gave Falconer a shifty look that suggested he was not as dismissive of the tales as he claimed. He leaned close to the Master and whispered in his ear. 'Some say there are ghosts down in the lower cellar there.'

Suddenly a peremptory voice rang out down the vaulted chamber.

'What are you doing there, Brother Thomas?'

The herbalist, looking abashed, scurried over to John de Chartres as he strode out of the darkness.

'Just searching, as you commanded, prior. When I came back to the porch, you were no longer there, and I suddenly thought of the old cellar room. Then I couldn't find the door, and—'

The prior cut off his minion's meandering story abruptly. 'It is not necessary to look in there. And I was not where you expected me because I had other business to attend to. Important business.'

Falconer stepped between the two monks. 'Not necessary to look in this room? Why?'

The prior seemed calm, though Falconer thought he detected a fleeting look of alarm crossing his features. He took the Regent Master's arm, as though trying to guide him away from the room in question.

'It is a . . . storeroom that is rarely used and mostly kept locked.'

'And in your search for the two missing monks, you didn't look there?'

John de Chartres now looked more than a little uncomfortable.

'As I said, it's normally kept locked by the cellarer. There is nothing much stored in it, as it's below ground level and it's rather. . .' He hesitated, trying to find the right words. 'It's rather cold and damp. Uninviting, shall we say?'

'Then let's find the key to it and see if there's a body down there.'

John de Chartres looked taken aback by Falconer's suggestion, as if unwilling to divulge the secrets that this chilling chamber might house. But then he shrugged his shoulders and turned away. 'Follow me, then. It is not convenient, however. We shall have to rouse the cellarer from his sleep.'

Falconer grimaced. 'Murder is a very inconvenient matter, prior. And it needs a full investigation.'

The cellarer, an impossibly obese monk whose robe strained at the task of covering his stomach, had not taken too kindly at being aroused from his bed in the dormitory, though Falconer imagined the other monks sharing the communal sleeping area might have been glad of his awakening. His snores had been audible from the bottom of the night stairs leading up to the first floor of the dorter. They had first been met by the elderly monk called Ranulf, who slept by the entrance. It appeared he was a light sleeper and had been stationed close to the door by the prior to ensure that none of his fellows roamed in the night. He had led them to the cellarer's bed. It had taken them much longer to waken Brother Michael than it had done Ranulf. Now, as the cellarer donned his heavy black robe, Falconer's gaze drifted over the long room. The darkness of the sleeping quarters was profound, deepened by the total eclipse of the moon outside the window arches. Then he saw the faint light of a taper moving between the beds, and he followed the grey shape of someone slipping out through the furthest doorway. Knowing the layout of such places and that the latrine block lay in the reredorter to the south, he guessed that someone who had been disturbed by them had taken the opportunity to rise and take a piss.

That was another symptom of advancing years that Falconer himself had become only too aware of. It also reminded him of his unsuccessful attempt to find a specific for his memory problem and nudged his niggling megrim to the level of sharp pain. He popped another leaf into his mouth and chewed, waiting for the euphoria it would soon bring. By the time the little procession was wending its way down the staircase towards the storerooms of the priory, he felt a lift in his spirits. He thought of the Jewess, Saphira, and hoped she was still undiscovered in the cellarium building.

Waddling ahead, the cellarer led them inside his storage area and thence to the corner where Brother Thomas still stood. He moved a few boxes and revealed a heavy studded door that showed all the signs of little use. Cobwebs were draped across the top of the stone arch, and the metal of the lock was badly rusted. The cellarer complained as he fumbled for the right key among the bunch he held in his chubby fingers.

'I don't know why you should want this place unlocked. I have not used it in my time as cellarer, which amounts to some dozen years. I was told by my predecessor that the cellar – which is below ground – is useless for storage purposes. It's cold and damp due to the level of the river and prone to flooding.'

The prior turned to Falconer and explained. 'In the early days of this priory, the monks diverted the River Neckinger to serve the water mill. But the stream will find its own way still. Given that, and the fact that occasionally the Thames itself sometimes breaks through its embankment if the locals do not maintain it properly, we are prone to flooding here. This room is kept locked, as you can see, and there is no possibility that anyone can enter it without Brother Michael here knowing. We are wasting our time.'

It was then that they all heard a strange, muffled keening sound coming from the other side of the door. Brother Thomas and the cellarer gasped, and the colour drained from their faces. John de Chartres merely looked grim, then, dropping his gaze away from Falconer's, he sighed.

'Open the door,' he ordered peremptorily.

The cellarer pushed the key into the lock, where it stuck until he forced it round. Together, he and Thomas pushed against the rusted hinges until the door opened. A wet, musty sort of darkness flowed out of the entrance. Falconer was the first to step forward.

'Let me go first.'

No one objected, and Falconer took the lantern that the cellarer had been carrying from his trembling hand. Thrusting it forward, William could see a steep flight of steps running down between narrow walls. The keening sound had ceased, and all he could hear was the sound of water dripping somewhere in the chamber. He eased his way down the steps, which were only slightly worn in the centre, suggesting they had indeed been rarely used even though the chamber was quite old. At the bottom of the steps he felt rather than saw a floor of packed earth that muffled his footsteps as he walked on to it. Raising the lantern, he looked around him.

The cellar was rectangular, but at some point a wall had been erected partway down, creating two rooms. The space he could observe by the light of his lantern seemed more like a crypt than a cellar. Hollows were cut into the walls, each roughly the size of a human body, though none of them was occupied by anything other than spiders and their webs. He sensed the sepulchral gloominess closing in on him and, feeling dizzy momentarily, leaned his free hand against the wall. Under his palm, the stones were cold and clammy. In fact, the very air he was breathing was chill, yet at the same time it tasted of wet, heavy mud. For a while he felt as though he was suffocating, as if being buried alive. He sucked in one more breath of the thick, fetid air and held it down, steadying his thumping heart.

Calmed, he returned to surveying his environment.

This first, oblong area had green mould growing in the dampness, though he could tell that the walls themselves were finely wrought. There were few remains of what had once been stored here. As he looked cautiously around at the shattered ribs of old barrels, Falconer became aware of a rustling sound beyond the archway leading to the second section. He cautiously paced across the earth floor, wary of rats.

Reaching the archway, he poked the lantern into the second chamber and saw two forms huddled in the furthest corner. As the flickering light played on them, one moaned and held up a hand over his eyes. The other person lay quite still under his companion. They were both dressed in the black habit of the Cluniac monks, though both robes were spattered with the reddish mud common to the surrounding marshy land. The monk who had responded to the light of Falconer's lantern turned a pasty face towards him and reached out a hand in supplication. It was a hand bathed in the blackish colour of congealed blood.

'Help me.'

It was just a whisper, but no less heart-wrenching to Falconer for that. The blood-covered monk was not much more than a boy, with a thin, drawn face. Falconer looked beyond him at his companion. This one was past any earthly help, his tonsured skull a mess of blood, shards of bone and grey matter. Falconer hesitated a moment, thinking of Saphira Le Veske and her search for her son. Then he framed the inevitable question.

'Martin . . . Menahem . . . is that you?'

The boy frowned and stared fearfully into Falconer's eyes. It was then that William noticed splashes of blood on the boy's face too.

'How do you know my name? My real name?'

William breathed a sigh of relief on behalf of Saphira. Her son was alive, and the body had to be that of the other missing monk, Eudo. The problem was that Martin had been found in a locked room, crouched over the body with no one else present. And Falconer saw, lying close by Martin's feet, the stave from an old barrel spattered with Eudo's blood and brains. Martin had to be the killer.

Falconer looked down once again at the body of Brother Eudo. The splashes of blood and brain that spread in nauseous pools on the earthen floor radiated from where his head lay. There could be no question of him having been killed elsewhere and brought here to be hidden. The deed had been committed here, and Martin had been found behind a locked door. How could he be innocent? How could another man have been the murderer, only to spirit himself away through the solid and subterranean walls?

'Menahem. We must be quick. Tell me, did you do this?'

A strangled moan escaped the boy's throat.

'No. Yes. It is all my fault. They wanted to know about the golem and the mystery of God's creation. I led them to this.'

The golem. That was the name Saphira had used when telling Falconer of her husband's dabbling in emulating God as creator. But he worried that Martin's reply had been confused. He tried again to pin him down to the truth.

'But did you kill Eudo?'

A sharp intake of breath from behind him made Falconer turn. Standing in the archway was the grim figure of John de Chartres. The prior was surveying the scene illuminated by the lantern and drawing the obvious conclusions from what he was observing. There was a strange look of satisfaction in his eyes, as if what he saw solved a problem for him. Falconer would have thought it made life even more difficult for the prior, but apparently not. While Falconer's brain still raced, de Chartres commanded Brothers Thomas and Michael, who hovered behind him, to remove Eudo's body. They shuffled reluctantly into the confined space and lifted the body at each end, flinching at the sight of the blood and brains. They might have expected Martin to try to flee, but he merely slumped to the earthen floor, stained with his friend's blood.

'This is what comes of introducing a viper into our midst.'

The prior's comment was bitter and yet also truculent, full of hatred for Jews and their supposed evil ways. Falconer pursed his lips, refraining for the moment from forming a sharp reply. If there was anything to be done for Martin, he would need the acquiescence of the prior. To make of him an enemy would not be productive at this juncture. Besides, if by some miracle the murderer was someone other than the young Jew, it would have to be someone in the priory. John de Chartres himself could not be ruled out.

The prior touched Falconer's arm, starting him from his reverie.

'I shall go ahead and arrange for the body of Eudo to be laid in the side chapel. Will you stay on guard outside after Brother Thomas has locked the door? The boy can stay in here until we decide what is to be done.'

Falconer nodded, not intending to stay the other side of the door for long. If he could have the key, he could question Martin more successfully. And it would give him more time to examine the cellar more carefully for some clue to the conundrum facing him. He wondered where Saphira was now, and whether she knew her son was accused as a murderer. He left Martin in the inner room and walked out to the outer room with the prior. Following the body, they both climbed the steps. Once outside the cellar, Falconer offered to lock the door.

'Let me take the key, Brother Michael. You appear to have your hands full.'

The cellarer grimaced at the thought of handing over any of his keys. But as he still had hold of Eudo's legs it was an easy matter for Falconer to hook the large ring holding the keys from his belt. The cellarer grunted, struggling to maintain his hold on the body.

'It's the—'

'Large rusty one. Yes, I noticed.'

While the two monks hefted the body on to one of a pile of hurdles stacked in the corner, Falconer locked the door and then detached the key from the ring. By the time Brother Michael had trotted back to retrieve his precious keys, one key was tucked safely in Falconer's pouch. Having followed the monks across the floor of the storage area, Falconer stood quietly under the south-western end of the covered cloister. He watched as the sombre procession of prior and pall-bearers, carrying their comrade's body on the make-shift bier, wended its slow way around the colonnaded cloister walk and into the priory church by way of the side door. When the candlelit procession had disappeared, he glanced up at the sky. A thin sliver of the moon was beginning to reappear in the cloudy sky. The heavy rain had stopped, but an intermittent drizzle still swept across the marshes, and in the distance shards of lightning continued to illuminate the land. Far away, thunder rumbled across the broad expanse of the seething River Thames.

'Saphira.' He called out the woman's name quietly, hoping she might simply be in the shadows. There was no response, and he tried again, a little louder this time. 'Saphira.'

Maybe she had thought the body on the bier was that of her son and had followed the procession towards the church. Whatever the case, Falconer had no more time to waste. He quickly made his way back to the cellar door. Using the purloined key, he let himself into the lower cellar, locking the door behind him. Descending the steps, he called out so as not to startle the boy.

'Martin.'

There was silence. He called out again as he got to the bottom of the steps.

'Menahem. I am a friend. I know your mother, Saphira.'

Even the mention of his mother's name failed to rouse the boy, and Falconer began to get worried. Had he been gone long enough for Martin to harm himself? He prayed not, and walked over to the inner room. It was empty. Bewildered, Falconer's initial thought was that Martin had secreted himself in the outer room, hoping to outflank the Regent Master. Maybe Martin thought he would leave the cellar door unlocked, and he could make his escape. William quickly turned back on himself and held the light up in the outer room. There were the same few rotten barrels he remembered from his first cursory examination, but nowhere for a person to hide. To make doubly sure, Falconer poked the lantern into each of the large niches recessed into the walls. Nothing. Martin had simply disappeared.

Falconer stood in the centre of the cellar, irrationally imagining that Martin was always just behind him, moving every time Falconer turned. It was all he could do to stop himself spinning around continually. He remembered his proud boast to the prior, that once you had eliminated the impossible, then the improbable stood as the truth. But if the impossible was that

Martin had somehow walked through solid walls, what was the improbable truth that remained?

He began to scan the cellar more carefully, lifting the lantern into all the corners. It was as he had originally observed – a space with a low, vaulted roof that had at some point been divided part way by a sturdy partition wall. This first chamber was rectangular, and the finely wrought walls were studded with niches that would do equally for bodies or provisions. The damp state of the cellar had probably called for such shelves, or whatever had been stored on the floor would have been rotten in a short time. As indeed had all the barrels that still remained, rotting and caved in, their contents long dispersed. Falconer could see that the only way out was up the flight of steps.

He paced back through the archway to the second chamber, noticing for the first time that there was a door hung in the opening. It had been pushed wide open, scribing an arc on the packed earth floor. The lantern was still in his hand, and he pulled the door closed behind him. He once again looked around, sensing that something was wrong. All he could see that was unusual was a scuffed-up mound of earth in the centre of the room. But even that was too shallow to be anything like a grave. He decided to ignore it as insignificant. He was aware of a swishing, gurgling sound, like running water, deep in the bowels of the priory. For a moment his head swam, and he felt a little sick. Maybe he had taken too many of the khat leaves that served to ease his megrim. He closed his eyes and shook his head to clear it. When he opened his eyes again, he was disappointed not to see anything different. Then he realized what it was that was niggling at his brain. The room was perfectly square. But the partition wall behind him had looked to have been constructed halfway down the original cellar space. He looked around again.

The side walls were exactly the same as those in the outer chamber – smooth and well finished, if a little stained with green mould. Even the partition wall had been carefully constructed. But the fourth wall, now facing him, was different. It had been hastily constructed of a different material and even bulged slightly. The mortar was old and crumbly, and some of the stones were loose. For the room to be square, this wall must have cut off a section of the old cellar, and he wondered what might be behind it. He began to scrape at the mortar with his fingernails.

Suddenly he heard a deep, unearthly, indrawn breath behind him. And a massive force slammed into his back, crushing him against the crumbling wall. The lantern clattered to his feet, and the room was plunged into darkness. He spun sideways but was pitched forward by the weight of his attacker, and he ended up face down on the floor. Whatever it was attacking him was cold and clammy and smelled of wet clay. It pushed him down into the earth of the cellar floor, half-suffocating him. It sat on his back, a heavy, dead weight that prevented him from turning over and defending himself. He recoiled from the fetid breath that exhaled over his shoulder, assailing his nostrils. He had a fleeting glimpse of clay-covered features, horribly distorted as if squeezed imperfectly out of mud from the surrounding marshes. His panicking mind formed the image of a monster. A golem.

He fought back, managing to grasp one of the creature's legs that straddled his back. But his grip was lost on the slippery mud, and he could no longer breathe as the golem's hands closed on his throat. Abruptly he heard a thundering noise from somewhere above him. He felt his face pushed hard into the ground, and then the impossible weight was lifted from his back. For a while he lay gasping for breath, and then he managed to sit up. Once again he was alone. The thunderous noise returned, and he recognized it as someone hammering on the door of the cellar. Of course, he had the key and whoever it was could not get in. But someone – or something – had done so, almost killing him. Ignoring the hammering on the door, he picked himself up and addressed the conundrum one more time. And it came to him like one of the flashes of lightning that had riven the sky that night. Feeling strangely light-headed, he laughed at his own stupidity, and the riddle that Peter had drummed into his skull came back to him.

'Now, what was it again?' A tendril of fear drifted across his mind as he worried about his errant memory failing him. But he need not have been concerned, as the riddle stood out as clear as day. '"Look for geometric perfection, where the entrance numbers six, between eight and nine is the flaw. There is the three, and the name of God is creation." Well, I know that geometric perfection can be exemplified by the cube. So . . .'

He stood in the centre of the room and slowly turned. A perfect cube – if you ignored the ribbing of the ceiling.

'Now, let me remember some of the number symbolism Saphira recited to me from what she remembered of the Kabbalah. Three is water, six is . . . six is . . .' It wouldn't come. 'Never mind for the moment. Eight is west, and nine is north. So the flaw is in the north-west corner.'

He held the lantern up to that corner of the room, but he could see no flaw other than the imperfect jointing of the crude wall that cut off the end of the room. Then he remembered.

'Six is below, or depth.'

He crouched down and shed some light on the dark corner at his feet.

'Aaaaah.'

There, close to the bottom of the side wall, was another niche. But this one was deeper than the others. Much deeper and stone-lined. Moreover, Falconer could hear the rush of water emanating from deep within it. Three is water. There was another way in and out of the cellar after all. He poked the lantern ahead of him and with a bit of effort squeezed his broad shoulders into the gap. He wished he was once again the slim young man who had sallied out as a mercenary soldier many years ago. But with a bit of wriggling he finally found himself head down in the entrance to a chilly tunnel that ran south. A thin strand of water lay along the bottom of the leat. It smelled stagnant and dank. Just beyond the edge of the light cast by his flickering lantern, he thought he detected movement. A sort of scuttling, and rustling accompanied it. Either rats or the golem, he was not sure which. Still, to prove what he was beginning to think about the comings and goings of the ill-fated trio of young novice monks, he knew what he had to do. He wormed his way back out of the tunnel entrance and sat on the floor of the room in which he was now sure the monks had met in secret. If he was to get down into the tunnel, it would have to be feet first, however. So he hoisted up the bottom of his dingy black robe and tucked it into the belt around his waist. Surveying his new boots, he contemplated the consequences of removing them and exposing his bare toes to the attentions of the rats in the tunnel. There was nothing for it but to take them off. He couldn't ruin them, as he would not be able to afford another pair for years. His pale legs and feet thus exposed, he took a deep breath and slid down into the void. The water at the bottom was cold and turbid. The mud squeezed up between his toes, giving him the sensation of being sucked down. Fearful of attack in this vulnerable position, he made a quick, anxious twist of his torso and was inside the tunnel.

He had to crouch almost double, but he could stand, and would not have to crawl along its length. That was a relief at least. Holding the lantern before him, he made his way down a slight slope, his shoulders brushing the roof of the tunnel. Whatever hid in the dark ahead receded before his progress. Soon his back was aching, and he yearned to stand upright. But at least he had not encountered the golem again. The thought of struggling in such a confined space did not bear thinking about. He pressed on, aware of the water level rising around his ankles. Finally he could detect a greyish shape ahead of him. Nothing too distinct; simply a segment of darkness that was not as Stygian as the rest. It was the end of the tunnel, and he was glad. The water was lapping close to his thighs and running a little swifter here. Finally he was able to poke his head out and stand upright. Even the persistent drizzle washing over his face did not destroy his elation. He looked around and saw that he was in the open leat that ran under the reredorter. The dark bulk of the building rose to his left, and the water flowed swiftly down the leat towards the kitchen block and water mill to his right.

He sat on the grassy bank to collect his thoughts, damp soaking him from beneath and above. He shivered and wished he was back in Oxford, in his own solar and surrounded by his books and experiments. Roger Bacon had sent him halfway across the country on what had turned out to be a wild-goose chase. He had not even found a cure for his own forgetfulness. True, a Jewish herbalist had provided him with an extract of a nut that was supposed to strengthen memory. He had drunk it. But the only change it had wrought on him was to turn his teeth black. He later discovered that the dark, resinous juice was from the marking nut, so called because scribes used it as an ink.

He rubbed his temples, determined not to consume any more khat leaves. They assuredly relieved his megrims, but they also altered his perceptions of the world. He could not be sure what it was that had attacked him in the cellar. Had it been a golem, a ghost, or something much more real? He pushed himself up off the bank and waded along the leat towards the rere-dorter building by the pale light of the nascent moon.

Falconer's emergence up through the long slot that formed the toilet seating in the reredorter had startled two bare-arsed monks who had risen early in anticipation of the prime bell. Their shouts of surprise had roused most of the dormitory, causing Brother Ranulf to scuttle off and find the prior before his charges ended up scattering like hens harried by a fox in their house. If Falconer's mission had not been so serious, he would have found all this amusing. And when John de Chartres arrived, Falconer was at the foot of the night stairs, at the top of which was a press of curious faces. The prior soon scattered them with a severe look, and Ranulf began to ring the bell announcing prime – an unnecessary act, as everyone was now awake, but one Ranulf thought would settle the monks back into a proper routine. The prior, meanwhile, was persuaded by Falconer to accompany him to the hospital.

'Why do you want to go there, Master? We should be deciding what to do with the boy Martin Le Convers down in the cellar. By the way, have you got the key to the door? Brother Michael thinks you might have ...' The prior struggled for the appropriate word that might not offend his guest, even though he had the deepest suspicions about the Regent Master.

'Purloined it?'

John de Chartres blushed.

'I did, actually. And made good use of it in your absence.'

'I hope you did not release the boy. He is a murderer, and I need not tell you the consequences for yourself of such an act.'

'Oh, I did not release Martin, but neither is he any longer in the cellar.'

The prior stopped in his tracks.

'Please do not speak in riddles, Master Falconer. Either he is in the cellar or you released him. There can be no other answer.'

'Believe me, Prior John, there is. And as I, too, was attacked down there, behind the same locked door, you will see there has to be another answer. But let us step into the hospital, and I will provide a solution for you.'

They had stopped in the entrance to the infirmary building, and the prior gave Falconer a cautious look but stepped inside. He clearly thought Falconer capable of some kind of evil magic. Making boys disappear, and claiming ghostly attacks on himself. He hoped the darker secret of the cellar that he had been vouchsafed did not enter into any of this current problem. He followed Falconer into the hospital. Inside, the space was much as it had been before. A few cubicles were occupied by elderly monks eking out the last of their days in a less harsh environment than was demanded in the priory as a whole. And at the end, Brother Thomas once again sat next to the prone figure of Brother Peter, whose chains still bound him to the bed.

The prior and Falconer walked down the central aisle with the solemn chanting of the first service of praise of the day washing over them from the priory church. They stopped at the foot of Peter's bed, and the boy's eyes opened. He looked blankly around him, as though in a daze. The prior and Brother Thomas turned their gaze on Falconer, both expressing curiosity at what was to come next. What Falconer saw in the cubicle finally convinced him of his already shaping view on the murder of Eudo La Zouche. He just needed one more person to be present and hoped that his guess as to his whereabouts was correct. For the time being he didn't need Martin to reveal himself, however.

'Prior, earlier tonight you feared that three of your monks had gone missing, only to find one of them – Brother Peter here – in a state of derangement. Your worry was that something evil had happened in the priory, and you were quick to blame Brother Martin.'

'And it is clear now that I was correct in my opinion that Martin Le Convers was at the centre of all this evil. This Jew . . .'

Falconer held up his hand, fancying he could hear a rustling from somewhere else in the infirmary. He needed to stop the prior's invective before things got out of hand.

'We will have no more about that, prior. Let us first ask Brother Peter what he and his two friends were doing in the cellar where Eudo La Zouche was found murdered.'

The prior sucked in his breath.

'The cellar? How could they be doing things in the cellar? It has been locked for years, and Brother Michael has the only key. You saw how difficult it was to open that door. No one has been down there for a long time. I have expressly forbidden its use.'

'And yet both Martin and Eudo were clearly in the cellar when we found them.'

The prior's face went pale when he thought of the implications. And Falconer wondered once again what it was that was down there that the prior wanted no one to know about. Something important enough to kill for? He filed that away in his mind and continued his present train of thought.

'Tell us, Peter, what you and Martin and Eudo were doing in the cellar.'

Falconer could see Peter's eyes clouding over as he strove to think of a judicious lie that he could tell. In the end he feigned incomprehension.

'I wasn't there. Never.'

Falconer smiled coldly.

'But there is someone else who can tell us the truth, isn't there, Peter? Martin was there. He knows what you were doing. Digging into ancient mystical philosophy and invoking the name of God to call up life from a heap of clay.'

The two other monks gasped and quickly crossed themselves as protection from such abomination. Peter just lay back, a blank look on his youthful features. His chains clanked as his arms dropped on either side of the bed. Falconer pressed on.

'Martin can tell us if you were there. Can't you, Martin?'

He called this out loud, startling those present. The prior was forming a question on his lips, when a woman's voice called out from the gloom.

'He is coming, William. And he is ashamed.'

From one of the nearby cubicles emerged Saphira Le Veske, still wrapped in Falconer's long grey cloak. She was pushing a reluctant Martin in front of her. His monk's garb was smeared with mud and soaked from the hem almost up to the boy's waist.

'Brother Thomas, take the boy and lock him away. Somewhere safe this time.'

The prior's command was peremptory, but Falconer held back the herbalist before he was able to comply.

'There is no need for all that, is there, Martin? You will not try to escape, will you?'

Martin Le Convers shook his head and looked shame-facedly down at the ground.

'How can you believe his promises?' The prior was inexorable in his denigration of the young monk. 'He has escaped once from his cell . . . And you still have not explained that, Master Falconer.'

'He used the same route all three of them used whenever they wished to meet for their secret gatherings. There is a tunnel that links the cellar with the leat below the reredorter. All they had to do during the night was to sneak to the toilet, drop into the leat and walk along the tunnel to the room. How they found it the first time, perhaps they can tell us.'

It was Martin who supplied the answer.

'Eudo found it. He saw the tunnel entrance one day when he was sent to clean out the leat as a punishment for laziness. He only meant to hide in it so no one would see he was not completing his task. But then he became curious and explored the whole length, coming out in the room. Later, when we sought somewhere to . . . practise our skills, he remembered it. It was perfect – in every way – a hidden room, and perfect in proportions.' His face crumpled. 'And then it all went wrong.'

'How?'

'I don't know exactly, but there was something about the room. One night, when we were . . . when we were . . . exploring the names of God, the candle that Eudo had brought went out, snuffed out just like that. And yet there were no draughts in the room. Eudo accused me of messing around, trying to scare him. But it wasn't me. We argued and left the room, crawling back down the tunnel in the dark. I felt there was something behind me. But Peter and Eudo had gone ahead, so what could it have been? It was a week before we were brave enough to go back again. That was two nights ago.'

Falconer gradually became aware of a droning noise that had begun as Martin spoke. Slowly it rose in volume, but it seemed to be made of indistinct sounds. It was coming from the mouth of Peter Swynford.

'Kether, Chochma, Bina, Chesed . . .'

The incantation rose in volume until it seemed to fill the room.

'Shut up. Shut up.'

Martin crammed his fists in his ears and pleaded with Peter to stop. The prior bent over the prostrate figure on the bed and slapped his face hard. The noise was abruptly cut off, to be replaced by a sobbing from the lips of Martin. Saphira drew the youth to her bosom and comforted him like a mother would a little child. But Falconer had to press on nevertheless. Dawn had come and gone, and he was short of time. Saphira was unlikely to be able to leave with her son, if he was truly the murderer.

'Martin, did you kill Eudo on that night? Or did Peter?'

Martin turned a tear-stained face on his accuser.

'You don't understand. It was neither of us. We both left, Peter and I, before it got light. Eudo said he was staying a little longer. We told him it would soon be light and that we would be discovered, but he was adamant. Peter went first, then me. When I dropped through the opening into the tunnel, I turned and looked back through the hole. Eudo was scraping up the earth of the floor . . .'

Falconer recalled the mound of earth he had thought unimportant.

'What was he doing, Martin?'

'He was making the shape of a man on the floor. A golem.'

Martin spoke the last word with awe and horror. And even Falconer's rational mind lurched to think of the creature that had attacked him. It was said that all you had to do was attach the name of God to base earth or clay, and you could create life just as God had. Was Martin suggesting that Eudo had died at the hands of a monster of his own creation?

'Enough of this blasphemous nonsense.' John de Chartres' abrupt tones sliced into the shocked silence. 'You are merely trying to shift the blame from yourself to some . . . some chimera. You have consorted with the devil and dragged two unfortunates with you. It is time we rid the priory of your evil influence.'

Falconer could see the fires beginning to burn in Saphira's eyes. Before she exploded and made matters worse, he stepped between the prior and Martin.

'It seems to me, prior, that there are more possible murderers here than merely Martin. Eudo may have been killed two days ago, in which case either Martin or Peter could have been guilty. Or it could have been another who found out what they were doing and hadn't wanted them poking around in the cellar room. Tell me, what is the secret *you* are so keen to preserve down there?'

The blood drained from the prior's face. 'Surely you are not accusing me of the murder? I didn't even know of the tunnel. Or why would I have been so ready to imprison Martin in there?'

'You knew where the key was, and, no doubt, if I asked Brother Michael if you ever borrowed his keys, he would not be able to deny it. You do keep a tight rein on the accounts and the supplies, do you not?'

The prior could not deny the truth of it, but he still stood firm. 'I have no reason to have murdered Brother Eudo. The whole idea is absurd. Whereas Martin has spoken already of quarrels and fallings-out. Dabble with magic and reap the rewards of your evil, I say.'

Falconer sighed, divulging another more problematic fact.

'I do have to say that the murder probably took place two nights ago. You see, when I saw the body last night I could tell that the blood was congealed and dry. Yet I believe the murderer was also the person who tried to kill me last night. And by then you were all engaged in caring for the body. It looks very bad for you, Martin.'

Even Saphira seemed to lose heart at this stage, and her shoulders slumped. Especially when Falconer waved a hand at the recumbent Brother Peter.

'For by that time, Peter was in chains. Isn't that so, Peter?'

Peter sat up as far as his chains would allow him and nodded. Falconer then went for the jugular.

'But then how did you know Eudo was dead, Peter? You did know that, didn't you? You told us yourself right here. And Eudo was murdered in the cellar without a doubt.'

Peter eyed him slyly, twisting his tongue in his mouth. He began to gibber as though the madness had returned. The prior pointed at the poor afflicted youth.

'You can see he is mad. It was the prophecy of insanity that simply happened to be true. You can see he is chained down. There is no way he could have been in the cellar in the night.'

Falconer pointed down at the youth.

'Then how did his robe get so muddy? Look, the hem is wet and stained and there are smears higher up. You put a fresh robe on him when you brought him here. His feet are muddy too. Yet he has never left this bed. Open your mouth, Peter.'

At Falconer's command, Peter's gibbering faltered, and he cocked his head to one side as if puzzled.

'Open your mouth.'

Slowly, Peter slid out his wet, pink tongue. It looked like a large, obscene slug. And lying on it was a key. The key to his chains that he had stolen from the herbalist earlier, when he had grasped the monk's sleeve. While the others recoiled in shock, he sprang from his bed, the chains slipping off his wrists, and he pushed past his tormentors with ease. Saphira Le Veske was the one to recover her wits first, and stuck out a pretty ankle. Peter sprawled on the floor, driving the air from his lungs. Falconer quickly straddled his back, surprised at the powerful resistance driven by the skinny boy's madness. A similar power had almost defeated him in the cellar. It had, of course, been human flesh – Peter's – covered in mud from the tunnel that Falconer had fought, not a golem raised up by Eudo La Zouche. Now Peter's raging voice echoed down the hospital with a sort of confession that carried no sense of repentance.

'How stupid you are, Martin. Eudo wasn't shaping the golem; he was trying to destroy it. The creation was all my doing, and Eudo would have ruined it. Just because he was scared. Just as you were too scared to go ahead, or even return to the dormitory that night. But I wasn't. I would have created him. I nearly did, too, after I had doubled back behind you in the tunnel. I tried to persuade Eudo to proceed, but he argued and argued. I had to stop him in the end. But it left me no more time before prime. I would have gone back to the cellar, but you caused the alarm to be raised by your absence. You made me so mad. I could have done it. I could have done it.'

Above their heads the church bell dolefully tolled the time for Mass.

At the junction of the road leading between Canterbury and London, William Falconer sat astride his rounsey, now rested and cured of its lameness. He surveyed the open marshland that surrounded Bermondsey Priory and reached as far as the glassy expanse of the Thames.

This morning, as the watery sun rose higher above the scrubby line of trees to the east, a yellowish shimmer filled his view. The river had freed itself from its confines and had stretched itself out luxuriantly across the low-lying fields. The priory now appeared to be floating in the middle of a glistening lake. Pewter clouds still loomed to the west, painting the vista a uniform grey. It was probably raining on Oxford town and its university.

Falconer eased himself in the saddle, the leather creaking beneath him.

'We go our separate ways, then.'

Saphira Le Veske, perched comfortably on a palfrey lent her by the prior, nodded her head. 'It would seem so. I have a business to run in La Réole that I have too long ignored. Oh, by the way, an infusion of sage is said to be good for the memory.'

'I'll remember that.'

Saphira laughed, and Falconer suddenly realized what he had said.

'. . . if I can remember it without taking some sage first.'

Still, he was reluctant to make their parting too soon.

'And now you have a capable partner to assist you.' He waved a hand at the boy who stood at his mother's stirrups. 'Martin . . . er, Menahem . . . will make a far better man of business than he did a Cluniac monk, I feel.'

The boy hung his head, but Falconer could detect a smile on his face. He had found his family and his path in life again.

'By the way, Menahem Le Veske, I never thanked you for guiding me towards thinking of a tunnel. Without your mother seeing you in the dark last night down by the reredorter, I would never have guessed it was there.'

Menahem's pinched face folded into a frown.

'The reredorter? I was never there last night. I was hiding under the water mill until it was dark enough to get back to the room. I could not leave Eudo on his own, you see. He was too frightened of the dark. And of something in the room itself.'

Falconer recalled the grey, ghostly shape he and Saphira had seen in the brief brightness of the lightning fork, a shape that had disappeared into stone walls like a phantom.

A cold shiver ran up his spine.

ACT THREE

Morrow of the Feast of St Andrew[1],
Eighteenth Year of the Reign of King Edward II,
Bermondsey, Surrey

The monk looked at the newlyweds standing smiling before him, each so obviously joyful in the company of the other, and knew only pleasure in their happiness at first. They were so *happy*, and yet he knew as well as they did what risks they ran. Suddenly his belly clenched, and for a moment he couldn't think why. Then he remembered the old story of Lady Alice and Brother Francis all those years before.

That was all long ago. A woman with no shame, a whoring bitch who tempted the poor chaplain from his vows and threatened his soul with her lusts. It was said that the two had disappeared soon after, snatched away by the devil himself.

'Brother Lawrence, we are so grateful to you.'

The two had walked to him, and Lawrence was uncomfortable with their gratitude. *Not so these two, please, God,* he prayed. She was so terribly young, he much more experienced. It was that reflection that brought on the sense of fear again. In Christ's name,

---

[1] Saturday 30 November 1324

he knew full well that it might matter not a whit that they adored each other. Their families might do all in their power to destroy them. Others had in the past.

'We have been wanting to marry since we first met here, on the afternoon of the feast of St Peter ad Vincula last year,' she said.

That day, he thought with a shock.

'The day that the *traitor* escaped,' her husband confirmed.

'We saw them, I think,' she continued. 'I saw the men coming over the river in the early darkness. It was my husband here who saved me. God knows what men such as they would have done to me. He pulled me aside until they'd all ridden away.'

John, the novice, was listening intently, Lawrence saw. The older monk motioned to him with a frown, and John walked off a short distance. Lawrence didn't want him listening to anything that might be difficult to keep to himself. A boy had enough to hold secret as it was. The fewer the temptations of gossip the better.

'What were you doing here at such a time?' he asked.

She flushed a little. 'I was a fool! I saw William that afternoon and came to speak to him. We remained longer than we should. It was only my husband here who saved me!'

Her expression was so joyous as she turned to him that the monk had to look away. He folded his hands, and as the two embraced he bowed his head and prayed for them. They would need God's help if they were to survive.

'When the men came, we saw the ghost. It terrified me, but my husband held me close and protected me. Of course, later we realized!' The monk's quick look made her nod sadly. 'Yes, I told my father.'

He motioned to her to be quiet and drew her away from the others, but when they were finished, and he had made the sign of the cross over her in forgiveness, he shook his head. It was a sad, sad confession to have to make. He only hoped no more harm would come of her actions.

The girl's maid, Avice, stood at the side of the novice, but the monk saw that in her eyes, too, there was little pleasure to see her mistress wedded. Only a certain reserved anxiety, as though she, too, was viewing their future and disliked what she saw. The only witness who genuinely approved of the match appeared to be John, his new novice, who stood with a fixed grin on his face.

Brother Lawrence sighed inwardly. He tapped John on the shoulder and nodded back towards the priory. John made a sign of acquiescence. Their order demanded silence as well as obedience.

The two turned away from the little clearing where the marriage had been sworn and witnessed, but as Lawrence walked away he realized that John had stopped and was now gazing back at the newlyweds again.

John gave a defensive shrug of his shoulders.

Lawrence could see what he meant. The two were so full of joy. But the older brother could not help but tell himself: 'For now, yes. She is the happiest woman alive. But when her family hears what she has done . . . my God! I only hope no evil comes of this!'

Vigil of the Feast of St George the Martyr[2],
Surrey Side of the Thames

Sir Baldwin de Furnshill was a reluctant visitor to this, the greatest city of the realm.

Content with his lot as a rural knight living in Devon, he would have been happy not to have returned. He

[2] Monday 22 April 1325

had been here many years before, when he had still been one of those fortunates, a respected and honoured member of the Poor Fellow Soldiers of Christ and the Temple of Solomon, a Knight Templar. But his order had been destroyed by that snake King Philip IV of France, and his dishonourable, mendacious lackey Pope Clement V. Those two had seen to the destruction of the Temple and the murder of many loyal brothers in their avaricious pursuit of the order's wealth.

Yes, the last time Sir Baldwin had seen London and Westminster had been more than ten years ago, when he had fled France after his order's dissolution. He had arrived here in the hope that he might find some few of his old companions and had made his way to the Temple. Once there, he stood and stared, dumbfounded. He should not have gone. It was depressing to see how his order's headquarters in Britain had been so pillaged. Where once the rich and powerful had congregated to petition the order, where kings had come to borrow money and others came to give up their secular lives, accepting a life of rigorous training, obedience, poverty and chastity, now beggars and peasants gathered. Drunks walked in cloisters meant for spiritual contemplation. He felt sickened to see how this deeply religious place had been so debased.

Still, the tall, bearded knight with the calm, square face could easily understand how a city like this must be thrilling to a man like his companion, Simon Puttock, from Devon. Just how impressed Simon was would have been perfectly plain to a less observant man than him.

'Christ's *ballocks*, Baldwin! Look at the size of it! I thought Exeter's bridge was huge, but *this*!'

Baldwin grinned to himself. His companion was more than a decade younger, and, although they had often worked together in the last eight years, he as keeper of the king's peace charged with capturing and prosecuting felons, Simon as bailiff to the Abbot of Tavistock with responsibility for law and order on the troublesome tin-mining lands of Dartmoor, Baldwin had never truly accustomed himself to Simon's parochial view of the world. 'Yes, I would say it is perhaps the most impressive bridge in all Christendom.'

Which was true. It might not have been as elegant as some, God knew. The bridges of Paris, of Rome and of Avignon were all marvellous to behold – but there was something about the immensity of this, with the gaudy red and white, blue and gilt paintwork on the huge buildings that stood over the roadway like an enormous series of tunnels, that was almost other-worldly. Nineteen arches, some hundred or more shops on it, the chapel, the drawbridge halfway along its length – it was an immense creation.

Men in other cities built from a desire to make their world beautiful; Baldwin believed that Londoners built to be rigorously efficient – and to overwhelm visitors.

They were here, to Baldwin's disgust, because he had been persuaded by the Bishop of Exeter. It was much against his better judgement, but he had a feeling that many in power were not to be trusted, and if the government were dishonourable, it ill behoved him to complain without attempting to do something about it himself. So here he was, recently elected to the English Parliament, ready to do his duty and uphold the honour and integrity of the nation's laws so far as he was personally able.

That thought made him curl his lip with self-deprecating amusement. It made him feel ridiculous. He was a rural knight. At home in Devon he understood life. Here he was aware at all times how alien the people seemed ... how *foreign* he felt. And that it was people here, like those in the Parliament, who had eagerly helped destroy his order.

The Bishop of Exeter had a house just by the Temple, he knew, west of the city walls, just by the Fleet river. Truth be told, Baldwin could have brought Simon by that route, but he hadn't. He needed to prepare himself before he took another look at the Temple grounds. Instead he had chosen to come here, south of the river, and to cross the Thames over the draw-bridge at London's great bridge. Once here, he could turn west more easily, he thought.

But when they had passed over the river and entered the city walls, Baldwin gazed that way with a heavy heart. If he must go there and see his old order's headquarters buildings, he would do so after resting. To go there now, tired and depressed, would serve no useful purpose to anyone.

'Follow me. I know a place to stay,' he said, and led the way into the great city, taking Simon eastwards, away from the bishop's London house – the enormous place just outside the Temple's grounds.

William de Monte Acuto stood pensively in his hall, a middle-height man clad in a rich scarlet tunic with fur trimming his collar. Few even in London had known wealth such as he had enjoyed – once, but no longer.

Only a short time ago he had been a strong, healthy, fair-haired man with chiselled features that were his own secret pride. His chin was powerful and square, his nose straight, his brow unmarked by scars even after a number of battles at sea, and he knew that women looked at him with lust in their eyes.

But no longer. Where once his calm blue eyes had exuded confidence, now there was a drawn introspection. Laughter lines were replaced by tormented tracks at either side of his mouth: the marks of anxiety and loss. Few had known such wealth, no – and fewer had seen it disappear so speedily.

'Continue,' he said.

This growing rage was hardly new to him. Since his fall from favour, the anger had never been far from him. Still, that someone could have betrayed him was unthinkable – it was almost a prerequisite in *business*, aye, but this was one of his *own*. Any man who had spent a little time on board ship to make money knew that many merchants were in truth little better than pirates. Nothing was ever intended as a personal insult, of course, but if a man could steal another's cargo at sea, far away from prying eyes, then he would be an arrant fool not to do so. It was natural.

But this . . . *this* was different. This was a man he had brought up, a man he would have trusted to the ends of the earth, just as any lord would trust his most devoted men-at-arms. This was *intolerable*!

'Master, I am truly sorry . . .'

'I said: "continue",' William stated softly. He didn't need to look at the messenger to know how his cold tone would have affected the man. Any man who had served him as long as old Perce would know that his voice was more often an indicator of his mood than were his eyes.

'As you ordered, I followed him. He went up towards the water, as you reckoned, near the Bishop of Winchester's house.'

Once William had owned properties in London itself. That was back in the past, when he had been rich. Not now, though. Now all he had was this small manor in Surrey, a short way south of Southwark.

'So he went to the whores?' William hoped so. Perhaps this was all: the lad was wandering up to the bishop's lands. The wenches were so common up there, they were known as 'Winchester geese'. The bishop waxed fat on their rents, and what could be more natural than that a lad of his age, almost twenty, should want to go and slake his natural desires?

'He didn't stop there. He carried on, master.'

William closed his eyes. 'And?'

'Master, I am sorry. I can tell you only what happened.'

'Then *do* so!'

'I saw him. He went up past St Thomas's and over to Bermondsey. There was a woman there. It was Juliet Capun.'

'So I was right. He is betraying me,' William said heavily. He turned and walked slowly to his table, sitting on his great chair, trying to hold back the tears. Looking up, he nodded. 'You've done well, Perce. Very well.'

He barely heard the man's sad apologies, and Perce's departure went unnoticed. At least Perce was still loyal to him. It was treachery that offended him more than anything.

Especially the treachery of his own son.

It was naughty to tease the novices, but it was also a time-honoured tradition, and when his novice asked about the ghost, Brother Lawrence was not the man to let an opportunity pass him by. There were brief periods during which he was permitted to instruct John, and he did have a duty to let the boy know about the appalling history of the priory.

Only later would he realize what had been happening as he slowly paced about the cloister, but at the time all he thought about was the expression of rapt horror on John's face as he told the story of the ghosts of the priory.

'Her name was Lady Alice,' he said with relish. The basics he knew, of course, but any story had to be embellished to make it believable, and twenty years here in the convent had lent his imagination wings. 'She was brought here for safekeeping, and her lover was a chaplain, a strong, bold fellow called . . . Francis. He was here to watch over her, but she had a lustful spirit that could not be tamed. She was tempted, and she succumbed and tormented poor Francis until he also yielded.

'Well, Francis saw that their love could lead only to disaster, so he tried to extricate himself from her clutches. Too late, poor man. Too late. Their passion would not permit them to keep apart, and I fear that they sought each other out. I know—' he held up a hand in pained agreement '—what they did was appalling. To sin in such manner here in the house of God . . . and not only once, so I heard . . . Well, God's fury was roused!'

Lawrence knew also how to maintain suspense, and while he tried to think of a suitable ending to this story he could sense the novice's increasing torment.

'And? Brother? What happened to them?'

Lawrence shook his head sadly. 'They died. Both of them. But it is said that no one ever found their bodies. You see, some say that they decided to flee the priory, where they were honour bound to live out their lives in the service of God as their oaths demanded, and while trying to cross the marshes in the night they sank into a bog and perished. Some say that they were so miserable with their sins that they went to the river and threw themselves in. But the truth is concealed in the prior's books. Did you know that there is a chronicle of the earliest times of our foundation? In there, I have heard tell—' and he dropped his voice and looked about him as the novice leaned closer, his eyes grown round with thrilled horror '—it says that a great devilish beast came and bore them away, John. So terrifying was it that all who saw it fell to the ground, and some were never right in their minds again after that.'

He withdrew, nodding with solemn sagacity, eyeing the novice. 'And ever since that day, men have said that they have seen their ghosts – especially in the undercroft just here. See that? There is where the two are supposed to have been captured in flagrante delicto. You understand that?'

The boy did. No one at the convent could deny that they had more thoughts about such indecent acts than about anything else.

'Well, let that be a lesson to you. A man who commits a mortal sin of that nature is accursed, but a *monk*! He is damned for ever, as is the whore with whom he consorts. Never forget that, John, or you, too, will see the ghosts, and they'll beckon you to join them. Great, tall ghosts, enormous, with grasping hands to pull you down to hell!'

A tolling bell caught his attention.

'Hurry, lad. It's time to wash your hands for vespers.'

'But . . .'

'What?'

'Would a crime like that be more evil than any other?'

'Perhaps not. The king ordering Prior Walter to be arrested and held in the Tower: that, too, is a great crime against God; He will punish the guilty.'

Lawrence watched as the lad nodded seriously. Dear heaven, but he must try to moderate his tone. He had let the boy see his own pain, and that was a dangerous thing, now that the prior had been arrested and marched away. Prior Walter was ever a strong defender of the rights and liberties of Bermondsey – for all the good it had done him. Accused of aiding the escape of King Edward's most detested traitor, Lord Mortimer, who had managed to get out of the Tower of London and make his way, so they said, to France, there was nothing he could say or do in his own defence. When a man was accused by the king, no defence was adequate.

That was the state of the kingdom now. No man was secure if once accused. The king's deplorable adviser, confidant and, so it was rumoured, lover, Sir Hugh Le Despenser, held sway. After the last civil war, the king and Despenser had emerged victorious, and both had sought all who had stood against them. Knights, bannerets and even lords were arrested and barbarically executed. Even priors had to tread warily.

Because the prior was thought 'unsound' by the king's special advisers, he was taken away and replaced with this . . . this affected, primping coxcomb. A vain, foolish courtier, John de Cusance, whose interest in the priory extended only so far as the quality of the food. He had neither interest in nor understanding of the holy mission of the priory, which existed solely to fight for the souls of the men of this world by the careful round of prayers and services. This new prior was no protection to them. Prior John had his position because his brother was close to the king's especial adviser, Sir Hugh Le Despenser.

Brother Lawrence watched the boy scuttle off in the direction of the laver to wash his hands. He could remember how enthusiastic he had been at John's age.

His face hardened. That was a long time ago. A long, long time ago.

Feast of St George the Martyr[3],
Bermondsey Marsh

Old Elena could scarcely see it sticking up from the mud and filth, her eyes were so tightly narrowed against the rain that slanted down that morning.

Foul weather, this, especially since it was so unexpected. In the past they had grown used to the swyving

---

[3] Tuesday 23 April 1325

rains that fell incessantly through the summer and into autumn, but for the last couple of years the weather had been better, and through the summer there had been food to eat and fewer deaths. This year, though, she wasn't sure that the houses wouldn't all be flooded again. She'd have to get her belongings up into the eaves again, just in case.

She had been to the market this morning, and when she left her home here by the Thames in Surrey the sun had been shining. There were no clouds, and if it was windy – well, when wasn't it up here?

It was on the way back that the weather had set in suddenly, a low, dark squall rushing up the river, and all she could do was lower her head and try to hurry homewards before she was drenched. Too late to worry now. A chilly trickle at the back of her neck told her that the bastard rain had already penetrated. Even if she hung up all her clothing in her hovel before her fire, it would still be clammy and dank in the morning. One day's rain spelled two days' misery.

Her home was east of the priory, and she averted her head as she passed it, trying not to shiver. Here, in the gloom of the late afternoon there was an unwholesome aspect to the place. Made her feel chilled to see it. When she was a mere bratchett she had been prone to wander, and her parents had told her tales of the ghost there to control her. It had been enough to stop her wandering about the countryside. The stories of a foul, grey figure calling to travellers and drowning them had been used by parents for generations to quiet noisy and froward children.

But she'd seen it. A pale, grey figure out on the mud-flats. Others told her that she'd just been taking too much of her ale and that she'd caught sight of one of the monks out on the marshlands, but she knew what she'd seen. A ghost.

That was her view, and no one would change it. Especially not some pissy priest. The fellow'd heard her talking about the figure on the marshes, and he'd gone to her to tell her not to be so 'foolish'.

She paused, squinting ahead with a surly cast to her mouth. 'Foolish,' he'd said, like she was some superstitious chit with chaff in her brains. He could go to the devil. Wasn't as though the priory was a bastion of honour and integrity. That idea had been discarded in the last year. It was only a short while ago that the prior himself had been taken away. Walter de Luiz, aye, because he'd helped rescue that traitor Mortimer from the Tower.

Elena made her way around the outer wall, casting a glance about her at the grey, stirred waters of the river as she went. There were always bits and pieces which a careful woman might collect and sell if she kept an eye on the shoreline.

There was little enough love in the world. That was Elena's view, and no one would persuade her otherwise. She was a God-fearing woman, none more so, and it made her anxious that God had forsaken them. He'd taken away the Holy Land, hadn't he, and that showed how He had turned His face from His flock.

She saw something in among the low, tussocky grasses and hesitated. With the rain slashing down, she really wanted to be indoors, not picking her way through the boggy wetlands to see whether this was a worthwhile item, but in the end poverty dictated her actions. She grunted to herself, threw a look of resentment at the heavens and began to make her way to it. It could be a spar of wood, from the look of it. Every item had some value to the poor, and few were poorer than she.

Once, when she was only a chit, she had heard a preacher foretell disaster. It was a little after the Holy

Land had been wrested from the Crusaders, and his words often came back to her. Famine, aye, and war and plague. Well, there was no plague of men, God be praised, but murrains attacked the sheep and cattle, and that was bad enough. Then the famine came. Christ Jesus! In the summer nine years ago, one in every ten folk about here had starved. There had been times a body couldn't walk along the road without seeing another poor soul tottering, only to fall and lie still at last in the mud. So many dead. So many starving and desperate.

For a moment she remembered her Thomas. His smile, his cheery hugs, his lovemaking . . .

Pointless. That was two years ago, nearly. She'd found him the morning of the feast of St Peter ad Vincula, the day after she'd first seen the ghost on the marshes. That was what the ghost did for her: it showed Elena that her man was about to die.

Last night she thought she'd seen the ghost again. A tall, grey figure out on the marshes, clad in hood and cloak.

'You can't take my man again,' she rasped to herself.

Since his death, life had been hard. Always more people about trying to scrape a living. The weak, the hungry, the halt and lame, all came through here to reach London, the great city that drew in all: the rich, the poor, the hopeful, the desperate. It took them in and spat out their bones when the life had been sucked from them.

In this weather the city was almost entirely concealed, she thought, glancing over the pocked river's surface. The bridge was a faint smudge from here, all of half a mile or more away in the murkiness caused by the rain. Opposite, on the far bank of the river, was the great Tower of the king where the traitor had been held until his escape. He'd have had to take a boat to here. Not that Elena had seen him, of course. He was over the river and on a horse early in the night. The night her man died.

The Tower was a glimmering white vision even in this dull light. When she had been young, not a worn old wench in her late forties, she had been used to staring over at that fortress in admiration, imagining all the rich lords and ladies who visited the place. Now she knew it was a place of terror, a prison for those who had fallen out of favour with the king, like Prior Walter de Luiz. He was in there even now.

It was in between her and the Tower, rising from behind a hillock on the very edge of the water. Grunting with the effort, she made her way to it, slipping and cursing on the fine, watery mud that made up so much of this landscape. Once she almost toppled headlong, but then she reached the hillock and recognized it.

No spar. Nothing but a long, slim, elegant arm sticking up from behind a hillock of muddy sand.

John the novice was studying in the cloister as she stumbled towards it, frowning as he tried to make sense of the words on the page.

A novice's life was harsh by some standards, but he had been happy here, and would have remained so if he'd be left to do God's work. There was a genuine delight in his work, a feeling that all was right while he was in here. Of course, he hadn't taken the final vows yet – he was too young still – but he would. So long as the new prior permitted him, of course.

Prior John de Cusance was an unknown figure. Walter de Luiz was the master of the priory when the novice first arrived, and all had loved him. Lawrence always said that Prior Walter was one of those rare men who would get on in the world even though he was invariably kind and generous. It made him unique. He was a man to emulate . . . as was Lawrence himself, of course. There were rumours that Lawrence had himself gone out to the muddy flats to help the notorious traitor and rebel Mortimer escape from the Tower. Not that Lawrence ever took any credit for such matters, of course. He was far too self-effacing.

No, John's friends had never understood his impatience about joining the monastery. They all wanted women, money, ale, or the chance to win renown and glory. There were plenty of them who'd be happy to throw their lives away in a tournament, or in some battle whose only purpose was to win a leader greater prestige, or his soldiers some profit at the point of a sword. What was the use of that?

John had always aimed higher. Yes, if he'd wished he could have joined the warrior monks, the Knights Hospitaller – but he couldn't in all conscience. No, if he were to do that, he'd be living in the secular world, and there was nothing in that for him. He had decided to renounce that life while a lad, and at the first opportunity he presented himself to the bishop and asked to be allowed to devote his life to God and His works.

Never had he been tempted to reconsider his choice. However, when he heard the shivering scream that burst from Elena up near the river, he was aware of a presentiment of terror that would grow to shake even his iron belief.

There was a fixed procedure here in Surrey when a body was discovered, and there were so often bodies washed up on the banks that all knew it. The First Finder had to go quickly to the four nearest neighbours. There were some folk who lived at the edge of the priory's lands, and Elena hurried there before sending for a coroner.

Brother Lawrence was quickly on the scene, splashing through the filthy puddles of this benighted land. When he saw her, he crossed himself hurriedly, his face twisted with sadness. 'This is indeed terrible!'

The vill's constable, a taciturn veteran from the old king's Welsh wars, glanced across at him. 'She was a pretty little thing.'

Lawrence nodded. 'Do you not know her?'

Constable Hob peered down at her and shook his head. 'I hadn't looked at her – why? Should I? There are often bodies down here. Folk are killed in London and the river brings their bodies down this way. She could have been from anywhere.'

'She was from London,' Lawrence said. 'I know her. She was called Juliet, daughter of Henry Capun.'

'Shite!' Hob reached down and turned the girl's head, staring at her features. 'Oh, God's ballocks!'

'Yes. Her father is a paid banneret in the household of Sir Hugh Le Despenser,' Lawrence said mournfully.

The constable gripped his heavy staff and leaned on it. 'That will make for a pretty fine.'

Lawrence could not help but agree. It was bad enough to discover a body in the vill, but to have a wealthy and important man's daughter found dead was doubly so. And any man who could call on the aid of my lord Despenser was a very important man indeed.

Constable Hob looked at the monk with a speculative air, and Lawrence submitted to the question. He beckoned the man to walk with him, and they meandered over the damp marshlands away from the body and eavesdroppers.

'You know something of this?' the constable asked.

'I do not know . . . How did she die?'

'She was stabbed.'

'And then thrown in the water?'

Hob shot a look over his shoulder to see that no one could hear. 'No. That's what we always say because sometimes the coroner will give us a lower penalty if it's clear that the body's nothing to do with anyone in the vill. This girl was stabbed right here, from the look of her. There's a dagger in her hand, so perhaps she killed herself?'

Lawrence looked back. 'She had everything to live for. I cannot believe that.'

'You knew her?'

Lawrence looked at him steadily. He knew Hob well. Quietly, he said, 'I saw her married. I was witness to it. It was a match of love. Which is why it was not declared: they did not wish for her father to grow angry and harm them.'

'It was a concealed marriage?'

'They gave their vows in front of me and two witnesses. It was a legal match.'

Hob puffed out his cheeks. 'This will be a . . .'

But before he could say more, there was a harsh bellow from a man nearer the river.

'There's another body here!'

Morrow of the Feast of St George the Martyr[4],
Bishop Stapledon's Hall, Temple

There was a roiling in Sir Baldwin's belly when he first saw the bishop's London home – not because of the house itself but because just south and east of it, like a giant peering over a smaller man's shoulder, he could see his order's chief preceptory in England. It made him want to bow and pray for his comrades who had

[4] Wednesday 24 April 1325

once inhabited the place. As it was, he was glad of the thin rain that fell so steadily. It persuaded him to keep his head down, so he caught only fleeting glimpses.

'That's a huge place,' Simon said, seeing where his eyes were gazing.

'A good size,' Baldwin agreed, but then realized his friend was looking at Bishop Stapledon's home.

Marching up to the gatehouse, Simon told the porter who they were and asked for the bishop. Seeing how Baldwin's eyes remained fixed on the building between them and the river, the man said: 'It's the old Templar estate.' He spat into the street. 'God damn the evil bastards.'

Simon knew Baldwin's background and hurriedly led him away. The knight's jaw was working, and he had a sour look on his face, like a man who had bitten into a sloe.

'He knows nothing,' Simon said.

'No.'

It was a flat statement, but it was clear that Sir Baldwin found no comfort in the knowledge. The sight of the preceptory was enough to bring back to his mind all the injustice of his friends' deaths. Baldwin was aware that many people here and abroad knew that the Templars were innocent of the obscene crimes of which they had been accused, but that scarcely helped in the face of such blind contempt. It made him aware of a quick loathing for the man. He could have swept out his sword and taken the fool's head off without a second thought.

'Come, Baldwin.'

'Yes. I am all right. He is just a cretin. He has no understanding of the truth.'

'No,' Simon agreed soothingly. He could never confess it to Baldwin, but he found it hard to believe Baldwin's often-repeated assertions of his order's innocence. There was no smoke without a spark, was his view.

The bishop's main hall was an imposing chamber. On all the walls were pictures of saints, while in one corner stood a small row of bookshelves. Richly decorated books stood there, while on the opposite wall were more shelves, this time displaying a series of the bishop's best plate. Pewter and silver shone in the light from the enormous window in the south wall, and tiny motes danced as the two entered, ushered in by an obsequious clerk.

Bishop Stapledon, Walter II of Exeter, was sitting on a leather-covered stool at the far end of the room where the light was best. He was reading a parchment, spectacles held near his nose as he peered down, and when he looked up there was a peevish look about him, as though he had been reading disagreeable news.

Even as he stood and smiled in welcome, Baldwin found himself trying to remember when the bishop had last seemed truly happy. It was a long time ago – perhaps before he had been given the post of Lord High Treasurer to the king. So much had happened since, with the depredations of the appalling Despensers.

No man was safe from the intolerable greed of Sir Hugh Le Despenser. Once, it was said, he had confessed that he cared for nothing so long as he became rich. That he had achieved. Since he had launched his acquisitive campaign, he had become the richest man in the kingdom, save only for the king himself. In this cruel environment even the widows of men killed in the king's service were deprived of lands and money. One woman, Madam Baret, had been tortured with such irrational ferocity that she had been driven mad, all in order that Despenser could steal her property. Stapledon had once been a moderating influence, but now he could *surely* see that he had achieved little.

'Sir Baldwin, I am glad to see you again. And you, bailiff. I hope your journey was not too arduous?'

'It was almost relaxing,' Baldwin said shortly. He did not want to be here. If he were to look over his shoulder through the great window, he knew he would see the preceptory again. It was a constant reminder of hideous injustice. He could almost hear again the burning pyres as the Templars were roasted to death.

'I wish my own had been,' the bishop said heavily.

'Your journey?' Simon enquired.

'The news at every stage,' Stapledon said. He shook his head, glancing down at the papers again, then set them on the table. 'We are still so near to war with France . . . the queen has gone to Paris to deal with her brother, but no one can say how successful she may be.'

'Which is why you asked me to come here to London as a member of the Parliament,' Baldwin stated.

'Yes.' The bishop grunted to himself, then looked up through the window. 'You know what has happened to that site?'

Simon quickly interrupted. 'That was the Templars', wasn't it? The porter told us just now.'

'Yes, it was. And it was to have been handed to the Hospitallers,' the bishop agreed. He dropped his gaze to his lap and fiddled with a loose strand of wool. 'But now the king has given it all over to Hugh Le Despenser. He will enjoy it, I am sure.'

Baldwin did not need to listen carefully to hear the bitterness in the bishop's voice. He would have liked to have believed that its cause was the blatant nature of the theft of a religious order's property and not merely jealousy that it had not come to him. 'Despenser is most fortunate,' he observed.

Stapledon shot him a look. 'Perhaps. But now he has asked me to help *him*. Yesterday the daughter of one of his servants was found dead. Out on the marshes between the Rosary and Bermondsey Priory.'

'The coroner has been informed?'

'A coroner will be there today, I believe.'

'Then surely there is little I can do to help.'

'You are here as a Member of Parliament, Sir Baldwin, but I would be grateful if you could help enquire into the matter. My Lord Despenser has requested an enquiry, and as an unbiased witness I would ask you to go and see what you may learn.'

Henry Capun hurled his drinking horn across the room. It struck the wall and shattered, throwing shards of green pottery in every direction. Two servants ducked, expecting his intolerable burden of rage to be expended on them, but as soon as it erupted it was gone, and all he knew was the return of that terrible emptiness.

She had been his little princess. He could still recall her birth. At the time he'd wanted a lad, of course. What man didn't? He was a knight banneret, a man of standing, and a boy child was worth more in his world. A boy could be trained to be a warrior; he could earn a father some rewards for being brought up in a good warrior's household. He might win new allies, hopefully gain a wealthy wife, and should always be a delight to his old father. A daughter? Nothing but a damned drain on a man's resources.

He had gone to see her soon after the midwives allowed him into his wife's chamber. God, he could remember that time. He had been slightly drunk. Well, fairly gone, truth be known. He'd not meant to do it, but when he got in there he'd looked at her, and when he heard he had a daughter he'd shouted with anger. His moods were always quick when he was that bit younger.

'My lord, be silent!' the midwife snapped, drawing his daughter away as though fearing that he might kill her.

'Don't command me, bitch! I wanted a boy, and she's given me *that*!'

'Your child was in God's hands.'

'In His hands, eh?'

'Yes, and He sent you this babe in His mercy, perhaps to show you the error of your ways and give you a happier life.'

'Leave your moralizing, gossip. I have no need of it,' he spat, and lurched from the room. But not before he'd seen his wife's face. She'd been very upset. Indeed, later that night, as he sat in his hall drinking morosely, he'd heard her weeping. That noise stabbed at him – in truth, he had always loved her, ever since he first clapped eyes on her in the company of his best friend.

To his chagrin, he had soon taken a liking to the child. She had a smile that struck at his heart. When she looked at him and gurgled, it made his mood lift. Later, when she was learning to talk, her attempts made him chuckle with delight. Her little mistakes were to him the very essence of joy.

Yet she was also a reminder to him of his callousness towards her mother. If he had not been so harsh on that first night, perhaps his wife would not have insisted on trying to conceive again so soon after Juliet's birth, and that might have meant that she wouldn't have . . . well, there was no point raking over dead soil. She had died in the next childbirth. Her womb wasn't strong enough so soon after Juliet, the midwife had said, the poisonous old . . . She'd seemed to have a reproving tone in her voice, as though accusing him. *Him!* The one man in the world who'd never have hurt his wife intentionally.

But Juliet grew too quickly. He blinked – and she had become a woman. A woman with the desires of all women. And she committed the one crime she could neither help nor regret – any more than he could forgive.

She had fallen in love.

'Oh, Christ Jesus!' he blurted, and covered his face with his hands.

Simon had been on many investigations with his friend. The two had proved themselves adept at seeking felons back in their own lands.

Here, though, he felt completely out of his place.

They left the bishop's hall and made their way along the paths that followed the line of the Fleet River, down to the Thames itself, and there Baldwin gazed up- and down-river before setting two fingers into his mouth and emitting an ear-piercing blast.

'In God's name!' Simon protested, clapping a hand over his ear.

'Ach, you have to get these men's attention somehow. Lazy devils, all of them,' Baldwin muttered almost to himself. But as he spoke he was waving, and soon Simon saw a man in a rowing boat leave a little group of boats a few tens of yards down the river and make his way against the current towards them.

'Over the river, masters?'

'We need to get to Bermondsey in Surrey,' Baldwin stated, grasping the prow.

'That far? You realize how long it'll take me to work my way back upstream from there?'

Baldwin gave him a beatific smile. 'No. Why don't you tell us as you row?'

The news of Juliet's death had struck the whole house dumb. Servants went about their business but with a quiet, nervous urgency, scarcely daring to speak to each other, the master's distress was so evident.

In the main chamber, where her mistress used to sit, her maid Avice sat staring at the needlework Juliet had been working on.

'Avice? God's blood, wench, stop that whining.'

She looked up to see Juliet's brother, Timothy, in the doorway. 'Master, don't you know?'

'That she's dead? Yes. You expect me to play the hypocrite? No. She was an embarrassment to us all. And a cause of shame. Better that she is dead than carries on to do any more damage to us.'

'Oh, master! But she was so . . .'

'They found her with that man. She betrayed us. *Us!* Her own flesh and blood. She is better gone. Now, dry your eyes. I won't have all the maids in the house looking like mourners at a wake. Fetch me wine. I'll be in the hall.'

Simon hated boats. He always had. The damned rocking motion made his belly rebel at the best of times, whether it was calm or rough sea weather, but at least here the movements were moderately gentle. As though in sympathy, the drizzle had also stopped. In fact, he could almost have described the journey as soothing were it not for the continual swearing of the oarsman, who kept up a running commentary all the way over the river.

He appeared to have it in his mind to explain every little detail of the view to these obvious foreigners.

'That there, right? That's St Benet Paul's wharf. Just here, that's St Paul's wharf. Serves the great cathedral there. See the spire? Fuckin' huge, eh? Then that river there, that's called the Walbrook Stream, that is. And that there's the great bridge. Never seen one like it, I dare say. Shit, look at the size of the fucker! Huge, eh? Like a . . . oh, right, and this here, just beyond that open land. That's the Tower.'

It was here that his voice grew quieter, as though the

mere mention of the name of the Tower was to bring misfortune.

Simon studied it with interest. There was a strong wall about the place, and the White Tower rose within it. 'It looks impregnable.'

Baldwin nodded. 'And as a prison, it is hard to equal it.'

The oarsman hawked long and hard and spat a gobbet of phlegm over the side of the boat. 'Hard, perhaps. Let's hope no bastard tries to. Enough poor bastards have died in that fucker.'

'And one escaped,' Baldwin commented.

'Him? Yeah. Must have been lucky,' the man said with a shifty glower.

'They say that Mortimer escaped over the water to the far bank?' Baldwin pressed him.

'So they say.'

Simon followed Baldwin's gaze. 'What is it, Baldwin?'

'That place – is it a new palace?'

The oarsman threw a cursory look over his shoulder. 'That? Haven't you heard? It's called the Rosary. King himself is having it built. Suppose he wants to wake up and see his pretty Tower each day.'

'And it may make it harder for a man to escape from the Tower and reach this shore,' Baldwin commented.

'Don't know about that. We're here.'

Baldwin took a coin from his purse and passed it to the man, then climbed out pensively.

'What is it?' Simon asked him as Baldwin stood watching the wherryman laboriously making his way back upstream.

'Nothing. I was just considering how everyone here must fear that place.'

Lawrence saw them as soon as they began to make their way over the marshes towards the bodies.

'Who are they?'

'Christ knows. I don't,' Hob muttered.

The first, Lawrence saw, was the younger of the two. He was clad in a green tunic and hard-wearing grey hosen, with a leather jerkin. He had brown hair and was clearly used to the hardships of travel, from his sunburned features and scuffed boots. The other was an altogether older man, with a red tunic that had seen many better days. He had a greying beard and hair, and his eyes appeared particularly penetrating even at this distance. The beard followed the line of his jaw, delineating the strong features, and he had a scar that wandered down one side of his face. Lawrence could see that his eyes were darting hither and thither as they approached. He was no foolish man-at-arms who put all his faith in his weapons; he clearly had a brain.

'Lordings,' Hob said.

Lawrence was amused to hear the deferential tone in his voice. There was clearly something in the new man's appearance that persuaded Hob to be cautious.

'I am Sir Baldwin de Furnshill, and this is my companion, Simon Puttock, bailiff. We have been sent by my Lord Bishop Stapledon to see if we may assist with this dead person.'

'Which one?' Hob asked.

It was clear that his question surprised the two men. 'How many corpses do you have here?' Simon said.

'One girl, one man.'

'The girl is the daughter of a man named Capun?'

'Yes. Juliet. The lad was a friend of hers. A lad we all knew as Pilgrim.'

'Why was he called that? He had made a pilgrimage?'

'He was quite religious,' Lawrence said earnestly. 'He once made the journey to Canterbury, and several others to our Lady of—'

'I apologize, brother, but my time is short. Did you know him quite well?'

Lawrence pursed his lips. It was rare for a man of the cloth to be cut short quite so bluntly. 'Well enough. I would like to think of myself as a friend of his.'

'But surely you are a monk. You are enclosed within your walls, are you not? I had thought that the monks of Cluny were dissuaded from conversation. Is it not true that a Cluniac monk should not speak?'

'It is preferable that we do not. We try to ensure our own passage to heaven by virtue of our prayers, and by our performance of all that is pleasing to God. We know that the perfection of the world demanded that there be peace and silence, so we try to do all we can to keep the world in harmony.'

'Yet you are here?' Simon asked.

Lawrence met his gaze with mild reproof. 'Friend, even a priory has need of men who can discuss the requirements of the brethren. I am the cellarer. If I may not be permitted to walk in the world and purchase all that is needful, our convent and our order must soon collapse!'

'You knew this "Pilgrim", then. What was his real name?' Baldwin asked.

'His name was William de Monte Acuto, the same as his father. That was why his alias was so commonly used.'

'How did you know him?' Simon asked. He was not sure he liked this man. The tone of superiority was common enough among priests and monks, but it still irked him.

'He and his father used to be wealthy. They were wont to supply us with grain.'

'How kind,' Baldwin said drily. 'Can you tell us where this man William lives?'

'Naturally,' Lawrence said, and described the way to

the man's home. It was an easy enough journey: apparently William had a small manor just south of Southwark.

'You plainly knew him well enough,' Simon said. 'Was there anyone who disliked the man enough to kill him?'

Lawrence looked away, and the fingers of his right hand danced over his left sleeve.

Baldwin nodded. 'There were many?'

'You understand our language?'

'Enough of it. So he was a man who could upset many others?'

Lawrence sighed to himself. 'No, not generally. But his family had a certain enmity with *her* family, I fear.'

'Fascinating.'

Hearing a new voice startled Baldwin and Simon, and both spun on their heels to see who had arrived behind them.

With two servants, one holding their horses, stood a knight. He was a full three inches taller than Baldwin, so maybe an inch over six feet. He had shrewd brown eyes that flitted over Baldwin's frame, noting the scars, the squared shoulders, the over-muscled right arm.

'Coroner,' Lawrence said and bent his head respectfully.

Studying him, Baldwin was less than enthusiastic. The coroner was one of those foppish knights who valued fashion more highly than honour. This was one of those modern men who sought position and money rather than accepting a life of service. He was a mercenary.

He wore tight, parti-coloured hosen in red and blue, with a red surcoat trimmed with fur. Fine golden threads were stitched on his breast to create a pattern that glistened in the occasional flares of sunshine. On his head was one of those hats that, to Baldwin's eye, looked plain ridiculous. It bore a liripipe so long it was wrapped about his head and then dangled behind him.

A typical example of a modern warrior, Baldwin thought. More keen on fashions at court than real work.

'I am Sir Jean de Fouvilles. I am coroner here.'

'I am glad to meet you,' Baldwin said untruthfully.

Originally, so he believed, coroners had been installed as a bulwark against the overweening powers of the sheriffs, but more recently the coroners themselves had become symbols of corruption, and Baldwin distrusted them – especially this one. He *smelled* of courtly intrigue.

'Where are these bodies, then?' the coroner demanded.

While Hob marched him away to the first, the cellarer close on their heels, Baldwin and Simon trailed after them.

'You were not impressed with that monk?' Simon guessed with a grin.

'Was it that obvious? Well, I fear not. In my day our order depended on frugal living to keep ourselves in a state of readiness for war. We ate little, drank little and exercised regularly. These Cluniacs eat a great deal.' He added cynically: 'That must be why he is always out here dealing with others for more food.'

'What was that you said about being able to understand his language?'

'Monks who follow the Cluniac rule are expected to hold their tongues even under great provocation. There was a story I once heard of a monk who watched a felon steal his prior's horse and would not sound the alarm. So over time they have built up their own language using fingers and signs.'

They had caught up with the other three, and the coroner was peering down at the body with a speculative eye. 'This is the Capun girl?'

Hob was already at his side. 'Yes, sir. Juliet Capun.'

'Really?' the coroner commented, gazing about him at the view. 'What was she doing here?'

Simon could see his point. From here, all about them were low, reedy hillocks interspersed with little pools and puddles of brackish water. This land bordered the river, and the marshes all around were proof of the multitude of little streams that passed through this land on the way to the sea.

'That is the Rosary?' Simon asked, pointing as he took his bearings.

To the north and west of them stood the new palace that Baldwin and Simon had seen from the river. Massive walls were rising amid a scaffolding of larch boughs lashed together. It made for an apparently disorderly jumble of wood and cordage, although Simon could make out the basic structure. When complete, it would be a manor house, moated and easily defensible, with a short river trip to the safety of the Tower of London. It was easy to see why the king might seek to build on this new location.

'Aye,' Hob said. 'And the master in charge of the works is Master Capun. That is why he was so common over here, and his daughter often came with him.'

'What of the dead man?' Baldwin asked.

'Pilgrim? His father was William de Monte Acuto. He's a merchant. Rich once – not now.'

'He lost his treasure? How?' Baldwin wondered.

'*I* don't know. I'm only a constable.'

The coroner looked at Baldwin for a moment with mammoth disdain, then turned back to the constable. 'She was stabbed?'

'There is a blade in her hand,' Baldwin observed.

'It was a fierce wound,' the coroner commented. 'Very likely a self-murder. So common with young women.'

Baldwin gave him a long, considering look. 'You

think so? Strange that she should still grip the weapon, then. In my experience, suicides usually drop their weapons as they die. The muscles relax . . .'

'Yes, I am sure you are an expert in such matters,' the coroner said patronizingly.

Simon looked away, but not before he had seen how her tunic had been stained with blood. She lay on her back, a shortish woman, pretty enough, with dark hair and a pleasant, oval face. Her left leg was curled back underneath her, as though she had just slipped on to her back. There was but one stab wound, but it had entered under and beside her left breast, almost at her flank. A long dagger would easily puncture lungs and heart if angled correctly. The dagger in her hand was eight inches or more long.

It was an odd weapon for a woman. Everyone would carry a knife of some sort, of course, but most women would use daggers that were considerably shorter. This was more a man's tool, to Simon's eye.

The coroner was continuing. 'So she was guilty of self-murder, or another man was here and kindly left his dagger behind when he fled the scene of his killing. Not very likely.'

Simon saw Baldwin experimentally punching his left torso with a fist, testing the theory of self-murder. Catching sight of Simon's enquiring look, the knight shrugged and shook his head. 'Who would commit self-murder with so complicated a blow?'

Hob was apparently keen to take the men over to view the next body. 'Come this way, towards the river, but beware the pools! They can swallow a man, some of them.'

As the coroner cautiously set off behind Hob, Baldwin slipped down to study the girl's body. He peered at her face, her clothing, looked carefully at her fingers, and then took the dagger from her hand.

'A good blade, this – a little nicked and marked, but good and useful. And it smells,' he said, his lip curling, 'as though it's been used often to gut fish!'

'Hardly a feminine tool.'

'No,' Baldwin agreed. He stood and set his jaw. 'Come, let us catch up with our little cellarer.'

It took little effort. Lawrence was not a swift walker.

'How far to this man?' Baldwin asked Lawrence as the monk made his way cautiously over the soggy ground.

'He lies only some tens of yards away.'

'The constable said he was known to this woman?'

'Yes,' Lawrence said. He was silent for a moment, wrestling with his conscience, but he held his tongue. Hob was one thing, but the idea that he should vouchsafe information to a strange knight, no matter how apparently honourable, was alien to him.

Baldwin could sense his reticence. 'Tell me, how long have you been here in the priory?'

'Many years. I came here as a novice four and twenty years ago,' Lawrence said, smiling.

'Much has changed in that time.'

'And not all for the better,' he agreed.

'The priory is itself at least secure.'

'Mostly . . . but last year our prior was removed. It was a terrible, shocking incident.'

'Taken?'

'Walter de Luiz, one of the kindest, gentlest men on God's earth, and he was snatched by the king's men. He languishes there,' he said, nodding towards the Tower of London over the river.

'And you have a new master?' Baldwin was careful not to ask whether he was viewed as a prior.

Lawrence noted and admired the distinction. 'Yes. John de Cusance. He is more to the king's liking, it is said. Poor Prior Walter was accused of taking part in the escape of the traitor Mortimer from the Tower, and for that he remains incarcerated.'

'Politics are a terrible thing,' Baldwin said with bitterness. In his mind he saw again the pyres on which the Grand Master of his order, along with the Treasurer, were burned to death.

Lawrence shot him a look but saw nothing in his eyes to indicate that the knight was a threat. In these days of butchery and random executions at the whim of a foul king who demanded absolute loyalty as a right and stole from all in order to enrich his atrocious lover, Hugh Le Despenser, a man was always best served to watch his tongue.

Lawrence eyed the knight as they reached the other body. There, the monk looked down on Pilgrim, lying dead in a natural hollow in the ground.

Simon reached the edge of the dip and peered over. It was sad to see someone so young with his life ended, and this fellow was clearly not yet twenty. Hair of a golden hue, worn long in the most fashionable style, was fanned about his head like the rays about the sun. He lay as though sleeping, with his arms on his breast, and Simon almost expected to see them rise and fall with his breath.

All about him the water pooled black and oily, and the dark moisture had soaked into his clothing. Simon saw Baldwin reach down and touch the clothing, sniffing at his fingers afterwards. Blood had run from two wounds in his breast, both high, both capable of stabbing his heart.

'This is clear enough, then,' the coroner decided after a moment's contemplation. 'Surely this man wanted the girl, she refused him, and he chose to press his suit. To defend herself, she stabbed him, and then began to run away. Appalled by her homicide, the poor child took her own life.'

Baldwin turned slowly to stare at him. 'You seriously believe that this man, who was perfectly fit, strong, and taller and more powerful in every way than that young woman, you suggest that she was able to draw steel more swiftly and stab him twice without his being able to protect himself? And then what: she was so plagued by remorse for protecting herself that she returned to his body to prepare it as though for burial!'

'I suppose some other person came by, found him and decided to settle him in this manner,' the coroner said superciliously. 'Perhaps a monk from the priory.'

'Your confidence in the matter speaks volumes!'

'Sir knight, I am not sure that you realize to whom you speak. I am the king's own coroner here. I have experience of matters such as this.'

'How many murders have you recorded?'

The coroner glanced down at the body again. 'Enough.'

'I am sure you have often been taken up with other matters, coroner, but I have been investigating murders these last ten years with my friend Simon here. I am sure you have much experience yourself, but I would caution you against deciding too soon on any theory about this unhappy couple.'

As he spoke, Baldwin was circling about the area, looking at the ground. There was little to be concluded. All about here there was a mass of prints. The soft, stubby grasses had recorded little that he could make sense of, and yet there was one indication that made him pause and crouch.

In a direct line away from the two bodies, thus heading towards the river itself, there were a pair of parallel, scraped indentations. Where the grass was thinner, gouges had been made in the soil. Baldwin followed the trail for some little distance, until he came to a flat area that was a little more dry. Here he saw that there were more marks. Two or three pairs of feet had been here, and then he saw something else: a series of deep indentations. They were an inch to an inch and a half across, curious pockmarks in the soil. He could not understand them, but noted them as he looked about him. One thing was noticeable: this was higher ground.

Making his way back to the others, he scanned the landscape.

'I think he was killed over there and dragged here by one or two people. A little earlier, or later, the woman was killed over there. It is clear enough that she did not commit suicide.'

'You are sure of this, I suppose?' the coroner said.

'Quite certain. There are signs of the man with others over there, and signs of his boots scraping up the earth from there to here.'

'Well, it is an amusing theory. I look forward to learning what the jury makes of it tomorrow.' The coroner smiled. 'But for now I should like to know why a man should be dragged over here, when they could have rolled him into the Thames over there?'

Baldwin cocked his head. 'That is all? I should like to know why someone who hated him so much as to wish to kill him would then spend time settling his body.'

Lawrence watched the coroner dismiss the question with a sneer and march off, discussing setting a guard about the bodies as he went. Then the cellarer took a deep breath. He couldn't speak directly. It was too foreign to his nature. However, he did have a feeling that these two strangers were more interested in reaching the truth than most others, certainly more than that damned coroner. He wanted to tell them about the wedding. At least these men might make use of the information.

He felt himself in a quandary. If he held his tongue, the fool of a coroner might well decide to take the easiest suspect and accuse him. There were so many down this way who would have no opportunity to defend themselves if he set his face against them. There was no justice for the poor.

'Brother Lawrence,' Baldwin said, 'tell me: you appeared to be about to speak more when that fool arrived. This Pilgrim – did he have many enemies apart from this woman's family?'

'Well, Pilgrim was a young man, and who can tell what mischief he may have attempted? There could be someone somewhere who had cause to nurse a griev-ance against him. Juliet surely would not. She was an amiable, kindly soul. I always thought that she would make a good mother, although not with—'

'Not with whom?' Baldwin demanded.

'I was forced to swear an oath of silence before I could do this thing,' Lawrence said unhappily.

'What "thing"? Marry her?' Baldwin asked keenly, and Lawrence could do nothing but look away.

But he was relieved. The secret was out.

Timothy Capun had never been tall. He possessed the frame of a man who had suffered from malnutrition as a child, a permanent reminder of the famine eight years before. His face held evidence of the virulent malady that had caused his face to be pocked and marked with scars, so his appearance was not the most prepossessing.

Entering the great hall and seeing his father seated on one of the benches near the middle of the room, close by the great fire that had been relighted against the damp cool of this unseasonal summer, his face grew morose, and he crossed the hall's tiled floor to stand by Henry Capun's side.

'What do *you* want?'

'Father, I wanted to offer you my sympathy. We both loved her.'

Henry looked up at his son. His face was twisted, but then his pain left his features and he could stare at his son with entirely blank eyes. 'Did you do it?'

'What, father?'

'You *know* what. Did you kill your sister? Because even if it means I live the rest of my days in a gaol and depart this earth straight to hell, I swear if I learn you killed my little Juliet I'll see your body swinging.'

'Father, you don't think I could hurt my sister? I loved her too.'

Henry spat, 'You have no understanding of the word "love"!'

It was some little while later that Baldwin and Simon reviewed the monk's words while sitting in a dingy, noisome tavern near the south side of the bridge.

'I did not like that coroner,' Baldwin admitted. 'He struck me as too confident. A man who is that confident is a danger to justice. He ought to listen and gauge the evidence, not go rushing to assume only one solution to a problem.'

'You were not keen on the monk, either.'

'True,' Baldwin admitted. He considered, at last grunting: 'Ach – he is a monk from an order that holds to certainties in the same way as that coroner does. Cluniacs are so convinced of their place in the world and the security of their posts in heaven that there are rarely any chinks in their armour to allow even a small iota of doubt to enter. I do not trust men who never doubt themselves. Doubt seems to me to be an essential ingredient in an investigation. You doubt what each witness says; you question them because you doubt your own understanding; you *have* to doubt everything if you are to get to the truth.'

'You mistrust him simply because he is a monk?'

Baldwin nodded. 'Aye. I fear so. Still, he was useful, was he not?'

'We know that she was married, yes. Although to whom . . . to the dead lad?'

Baldwin grunted. After letting slip that tantalizing detail, the monk had clammed up, claiming that the whole affair was secret and he had sworn to hold his tongue. He would not answer any more questions.

'We must wait until tomorrow, anyway, to hear what is said at the inquest.'

'I look forward to seeing the First Finder describe what she found,' Baldwin said. 'Those two bodies . . . they were strangely set out. The man, Pilgrim, had been dragged down to be concealed, and then laid out neatly.'

'As though a monk had killed him and tidied him up?' Simon said.

'Possibly. But what reason could the monk have had for killing him?'

'The girl was attractive. Could a monk have desired her, killed the boy from jealousy and then killed her?'

'Possibly. And yet Brother Lawrence was convinced that the girl's family had a hatred for Pilgrim. They would think that their little girl had married beneath herself. Perhaps they sought to punish both?'

'I would like to speak to them.'

Baldwin eyed him. 'These are the very ones who have asked for Bishop Walter to enquire into the death.'

'It would hardly be the first time that the guilty were those who demanded the greatest efforts. And in any case, if they are innocent they may still be able to help us with some aspects of the girl's life. Any information can be useful.'

'True!' Baldwin said. He finished his drink. 'And yet I dare say that of all possible suspects this family is the one that is least likely.'

'Why?'

'Because if one of the corpses was to be set out neatly, surely any father would lay out his own daughter, rather than the bastard who'd ravished her – married or not?'

They found the Capun house with ease. London was a huge city, but men as wealthy and powerful as Henry Capun were not common.

Simon had never heard of the man, and he was comfortably certain that neither had Baldwin, but it soon became obvious that Henry Capun was a renowned man in London, and when they caught sight of his house Simon for one was daunted by the size of the place. He was perfectly used to seeing large houses, and he had himself participated in the questioning of noblemen and others – but that had been different. It had been in his own county of Devon. Standing here in the street they called the Strand, just outside the city's walls, not too far from the bishop's own hall, Simon was overwhelmed by a sense of his own insignificance.

If he had been alone, he would have left there and then, but fortunately it appeared that Baldwin suffered fewer qualms about questioning the man. The knight rapped sharply on the timbers of the porter's door and curtly demanded to be shown to the banneret.

Henry Capun looked as though he had been drinking too much for too long. His features were flabby and choleric. He had a circular face, with a neck that was thick from excess, and his paunch was like a barrel slung low over his belt. Simon privately thought that this was one of those men who wore his soul on his sleeve for all to see. He was an insipid fellow, weak and ravaged by the least setback.

His initial impression was to be quickly destroyed.

'Who are you?'

While Baldwin introduced them, Henry studied them minutely, Simon saw. Then he jerked his chin at Simon. 'You're a bailiff from Dartmoor? You knew Abbot Champeaux?'

Simon nodded. 'I worked for him these last eight years or so.'

'I knew him. A good man, and a damned hard one to win a bargain from. Aye, I knew him. He'll be missed.' He turned back to Baldwin. 'Not as much as my daughter will in this house, though. Bishop Stapledon told you to find her murderer, I hope?'

'He did.'

'And?'

'We have just come here from the place where she died. The inquest will be tomorrow – someone has told you of this?'

'Yes. The coroner was good enough to send a man to tell me when I may go to hear about her . . . her death.'

His voice dropped for those last two words, and his head sank on his shoulders as though its weight was insupportable. But then he rallied and fixed Baldwin with a stern gaze. 'I want the murderer found. I don't care who it is, how rich he is – I want him found and hanged.'

'Then you can help us. We are new to this city. My friend and I arrived only yesterday. What can you tell us about your daughter?'

'Juliet was a good, dutiful child. Always was. I adored her. Perhaps I spoiled her, but after her mother . . . There was a feeling . . . I suppose I saw much in her that I had loved in her mother.'

'Her mother died?'

'She fell pregnant too soon after Juliet's birth and died in the birthing. Perhaps it was natural that Juliet should be my most favoured child.'

'She was your only child?' Simon asked.

'I have a son as well. Her younger brother, Timothy. He is some compensation to me.'

Simon wondered at that. It was a curious turn of phrase and sounded odd from this man's mouth – but much of his tone and appearance was entirely out of keeping with Simon's first summing-up. Clearly this man was more mentally rigorous than he would have thought.

'We have heard – Sir Henry, I am sorry if this rakes up sadness for you, but I have to ask – we have heard that she formed a close liaison with a fellow.'

'Who?'

'Do you know of a man called Pilgrim?'

'William de Monte Acuto? That little shite? Yes, she knew him.'

'More than that? Did she know him well?'

Henry Capun's face darkened, and a flush rose from his neck. 'What are you saying, that my daughter was unchaste – even a whore? Do you think to insult her memory here in my house, Sir Knight?'

'Sir Henry, I speak only what I have been told. Did you know that she was married?'

Henry Capun gaped. He took a stumbling step backwards, a hand reaching out wildly for a chair. Hurriedly Simon ran to his side, grasped a stool and thrust it behind the banneret. Capun half fell into it, his hand gripping Simon's forearm as though it was the only thing to maintain his sanity. 'She . . . no!'

'This man Pilgrim was also murdered. His body lay only a short distance from your daughter's. She was married at the end of November last year. I have spoken to the man of God who witnessed the ceremony. Her marriage was fully legal.'

'My God! The *bastard*! If he had left her alone, none of this would have happened!'

'Do you think she may have married this Pilgrim?'

'I don't know . . . my God!'

'Well, can you think of anyone who would have had cause to harm them both?'

'Only that murderous son of a whore William de Monte Acuto, the boy's father!'

'Why should he want to kill them?' Simon blurted.

'Because he and I are enemies. I'll have nothing to do with him, nor he with me. Christ's bones, if he's killed my little Juliet, I'll have his heart!'

'Explain, please.'

Henry scowled. He had recovered from his first shock, but he was still shaky as he reached out for a mazer of wine on the table. 'When we were younger, William and I were friends. We were of a similar age, had similar backgrounds, and we were keen to do all we could to advance ourselves. But then I did better than him and started to win honours and money, and we lost contact. I think he blamed me for his own lack of opportunities, and that led to bad feeling. It was nothing to do with me, though. I treated him in the same way as I ever had. The trouble is, William has a lousy temper. He always did have.'

'How did your lives change so greatly?' Baldwin murmured.

'William sought to advance himself early on, and he allied himself to men in the early days of the century. When the king was still a prince, William did all he could to curry favour. Meanwhile I concentrated on money and left politics alone. When I had money, I was noticed by powerful men, and they advanced my cause for me.'

Which meant that he was able to bribe the powerful to achieve what he wanted, Baldwin reckoned, while his erstwhile friend and companion languished. 'You were allied with those who are still in power, then?'

Henry's mouth twisted. 'I can count the young Hugh Le Despenser as a friend. William was allied with Piers Gaveston.'

Gaveston, the king's companion, was so detested by the barons that he was captured and hanged like a common felon in the fifth year of the king's reign.[5] Baldwin began to understand the depths of the jealousy William de Monte Acuto might feel for this man – especially since as Gaveston's star waned the Despensers' waxed full mightily.

Simon was frowning. 'You say that this man de Monte Acuto might have killed your daughter – but that hardly makes sense. Why should he kill her when the only effect of her liaison with his son was to annoy you? And why kill his own son?'

Henry looked at him for a moment. 'Because, bailiff, he would look on any alliance with me as being a betrayal of his own honour. He hates me for all I have done.' He looked away, closed his eyes and shook his head. 'You see, there is one last thing I didn't mention. The woman I married, my poor wife Cecily, I won from him. He was wooing her when I snatched her away. He has never forgiven me for her death.'

And neither have I, he added to himself.

Thursday Next after the Feast of St George the Martyr[6],
Bermondsey Marsh

The next morning was bright and clear, with only a few clouds sitting stationary over the city. Baldwin and Simon rose early, and after a light breakfast they crossed

[5] 18 June 1312
[6] Thursday 25 April 1325

the bridge and turned left to go up to Bermondsey again.

The space about the two bodies was filled with people. There was huddled a jury of men, for the most part grim-faced at the stern duty before them, although one or two of those who were only twelve or thirteen were anxious at the sight of the coroner. People here were used to seeing the rich and powerful, but few enjoyed the sight of those who could fleece them unmercifully for any infraction.

Baldwin reckoned that the inquest itself was notable only for the severity of the coroner. In his own experience, many coroners could be too demanding, and frequently they were thoroughly corrupt, soliciting bribes to prevent a man being taken to court or demanding more to ensure that some other fellow was arrested in his place. There were any number of tricks that could guarantee a man a well-filled purse.

This man started proceedings by fining the vill because not all the men of over twelve years had appeared. Then he imposed another fine because Hob did not answer him in the required manner, apparently. Before they had reached the point at which the bodies were displayed, the jury was already cowed. Baldwin could see that their damp shuffling in the mud was stilled, and they stared at the ground with sullen resentment.

Not that the coroner minded. He appeared to relish their grim bitterness.

Soon, though, when the witnesses began to come forward, Baldwin found his attention being diverted – especially when he caught his first sight of the man he had been keen to question: William de Monte Acuto, the father of the dead Pilgrim.

To his surprise, for he had expected someone who would show the same dissipation as Henry Capun, William was a tall man with the physique of a warrior.

He had the same muscled neck, powerful right arm and thick thighs as a knight. Clearly this was a man who had fought in his youth. He had a calm face, and even with sorrow marking his eyes he was still a handsome fellow, the kind of man whom women would like. There was a softness and soulfulness in his features that was attractive and spoke of an inner gentleness. It was a great shame that he had allied himself with Piers Gaveston, but, as Baldwin knew, men would connect themselves with the greatest fools and felons in order to protect themselves politically.

'I am William de Monte Acuto.'

The coroner was questioning the witnesses in a bullying manner, as though he enjoyed cowing those who came before him. With William, he seemed a little unsure how to continue. At last he jerked his head at the woman's body lying on the ground before them. 'You know her?'

'I do.' William did not look down at her, but kept his gaze fixed forward.

'She knew your son?'

'Yes.'

'Where was your son on the night of the vigil of the feast of St George? That is two nights ago, Master William, the night of Tuesday and Wednesday.'

'He was with me at our house.'

'And no doubt your servants will vouch for you?'

'Of course they will – but I am happy to swear on the Gospels if you do not trust my word.'

Baldwin smiled at the man's suave courtesy. It was in marked contrast to the coroner's hectoring manner.

'I am glad to hear it. Perhaps we should have both you and your servants swear in like manner?'

'If you command it, coroner.'

'Your son desired this girl, did he not? Were they lovers?'

William de Monte Acuto's face hardened, but with pain, not anger. 'My son was a man. This young woman was lively and pretty, so perhaps it is so.'

'You were not aware that he was wooing her?'

'I guessed so, yes.'

'He lies dead there, stabbed through the heart. She holds a dagger in her hand. Perhaps she killed him, then herself?'

William looked at the coroner for the first time now, his face blank of anything but his sorrow. 'My son is dead, and you wish me to *speculate* about who did it?'

Later, Baldwin managed to push through the crowd and reach William de Monte Acuto. 'May I speak to you a moment, friend?'

'What – do you wish to question me like that *cretin* of a coroner?'

'No, I merely seek the truth – I act for my lord Bishop Stapledon.'

'Then how can a poor man like me refuse?' William said sarcastically. 'The king has many advisers, but there are few who can command the respect of my lord bishop.'

Simon said, 'Friend, I have a son. You have my sympathy. To lose a son is terrible . . . to then be questioned by that coroner is obscene.'

William bent his head. 'I could have happily taken his head from his shoulders.'

'Your son,' Baldwin said. 'When did you know he was missing?'

'The day he was found. I have a hall with a solar at each end. The servants sleep in the eaves between them. William used to sleep at the other end of the house, and recently . . . well, we were not on good terms in the last days.'

'Why?'

'Because of Juliet, of course!' His anger subsided as quickly as it had flared, and he hesitated. 'I had no wish for my son to be associated with her.'

'Her father and you were once friends?'

'Yes, we were. But then Cecily died because of him, and he started his rise to prominence and wouldn't talk to simple folks like me and my son. We weren't significant enough to measure in his estimation. No, he'd prefer to be spending his time with all those magnificent fellows in their great houses.'

'Whereas you . . . ?'

'I stayed where I had been born. I never lost my roots. I am a simple man, when all is said and done. I was born a serf, and I make my own way in the world. My business keeps me well enough. Henry Capun is a knight now, and he can claim Hugh Le Despenser as a friend. What use am I to him now?'

'Who could have wished to harm your son?'

'Only one man,' William said darkly. 'Henry Capun hates me and would seek to ruin me in any way he might. Killing poor William is just one way to attack me. Poor William!'

'You think he would kill his daughter in order to get at you?' Baldwin asked sharply.

William looked at him. 'My only love, Cecily, was taken from me by him. She died because she was desperate to give him a son. She wasn't ready for another child after little Juliet's birth, but he was ever a demanding devil, and she fell pregnant again. It killed her.'

'This son of his, Timothy – he is from another woman?'

'Yes. Henry married Edith after Cecily died, and Edith gave him Timothy, but then she, too, died in the famine seven years ago or more.'

'Still,' Simon suggested, 'he would have loved his daughter, surely?'

William wiped a hand over his face. 'God forgive me for saying it, but I doubt it. He looked on her as a chattel. Nothing more. If she was no further use, he'd have discarded her as easily as a man throwing away a broken staff.'

When the carter arrived at the gates, John was sent to find Lawrence. The cellarer was the main contact for any tradesmen with food.

John could see him with the group about the body with the coroner and hurried to him just as he saw Simon and Baldwin approaching him. The two men were a little alarming, with their strange accents. Especially the knight, with his black, intense eyes. John only hoped that Lawrence was not in trouble.

The arrest of Prior Walter the previous year had alarmed all the monks. That their leader could be removed and replaced at the whim of the king was unsettling. For John it was worse, though, because he knew secrets none of the others had heard. Every day he feared that the men would come to arrest his master, Lawrence. The cellarer had been involved in the escape of Mortimer. He knew that. He'd seen Lawrence return that night.

Simon and Baldwin caught sight of the cellarer, and, while the coroner demanded refreshment and adjourned the inquest, Simon led the way to the monk, struck with a thought.

'Brother Lawrence – when you mentioned the marriage of Juliet, you said you heard the vows. Were there any witnesses apart from you?'

'I cannot tell you of that wedding. I swore.'

Simon was staring at him with a shrewd narrowing of his eyes. 'If a maiden weds, it is rare indeed that she will do so without her maid at least at her side. Was her maid there?'

'You must ask *her* that. Why?'

'I was wondering . . .'

Another voice interrupted them. 'Yes? What were you wondering, master?'

Simon could almost smell the man before he heard him. There was an unpleasant odour of sourness, and when Simon caught sight of his ravaged face he could see why. It was only natural that a man so terribly scarred by the pox or some similar malady should be noisome to others. 'Who are you?'

'I was going to ask you the same, master. You have so much interest in my household, I thought you might like to explain what you were questioning this man about?'

'Your household? You are son to Sir Henry?'

His knowledge of Timothy's father should have been no surprise, for as Simon had already noticed most people in London seemed to know of Sir Henry, and yet it seemed to make the son still more suspicious. The man laid one hand on Simon's arm, the other on his sword. 'I'd like to know more of you and your fascination with my family.'

'Good. When you have let go my arm, I shall be happy to talk,' Simon said.

In response, Timothy half drew his sword. 'You'll talk now, or answer to—'

As he spoke, Baldwin's bright blue sword blade rang, and rested gently on his throat. 'Master Capun, I would have you release my companion. And do please take your hand from your sword. We would not want more blood shed, would we?'

Simon took Timothy's hand and pulled his arm free. The younger man's eyes were filled with loathing, but he didn't try to prevent him. As soon as Timothy's hand had fallen away from the hilt, Baldwin whipped his sword away and sheathed it in one fluid movement.

'We wanted to speak to you,' Simon said, glancing about him to find Lawrence. The monk had disappeared as soon as Baldwin's sword flashed from its scabbard.

'Why?'

'Your sister is dead, and you ask why we want to talk to you? We are seeking to learn what happened that night.'

'Ask that bastard over there. That son of a diseased pig was there. William killed them.'

'Your father hinted as much,' Baldwin said. 'Except it really makes little sense. Why should a man like him kill his own son, just to have some form of revenge on your family? He could kill your sister, granted – but why harm Pilgrim?'

'Pilgrim loved my sister. Perhaps he tried to protect her from his mad father? I don't pretend to understand him.'

'You suggest that William the elder could have tried to kill your sister? Have you ever seen him threaten her?'

'I have not seen him attack her directly, but the man is insanely jealous of my father. He would do anything to hurt him.'

Baldwin eyed him. The fellow was arrogant and bitter, but he had lost his half-sister and such feelings were not unnatural. 'That is no reason to want to harm his own son.'

'Who else could have done that to Pilgrim? You saw the body there, laid out with love. Who else but a father could have done that to him?'

'Not you, eh?' Simon said.

'I would have spat on his face and cut his ballocks off for what he did to my sister! She may have been—'

'What?'

'My father's first-born. He loved her greatly,' Timothy

grunted. 'Look at me: is it any surprise? Would you prefer a son looking like this, or a daughter as pretty as she?'

Baldwin was not to be moved from his questioning. There were, after all, many others who suffered from scars. 'You say he raped her? That is why you would castrate him?'

'In a way,' Timothy said evasively.

'She knew him? They indulged in the natural pleasures of a man and woman?'

'Yes! I know, for I saw them together. And it was *disgusting*! He had his . . . anyway, I rushed in, and it was only because she grabbed me and stopped me that I couldn't actually run him through, the cunning bastard!'

'Where was this?'

'In my house, in the stables behind the hall. He had inveigled his way into the place, and she went to see him. It was only because she begged me that I didn't tell our father. It would have broken his heart to know what they were up to. Carnal behaviour like that, to a man of honour and integrity, would be insufferable. But I swore to her that if I ever saw Pilgrim with her again, I would have his head off.'

Baldwin nodded thoughtfully. 'His head yet remains on his shoulders, but that does not mean you are innocent.'

'Me? If I could have, I would have killed him, and done it gladly. He was a ravisher of women.'

He was about to push away from them, but Baldwin placed his hand on the fellow's breast and prevented him. 'A few more questions before you go. Did you know that they were married?'

'Don't be ridiculous!'

'I have spoken to the man of God who listened to their vows. They were married.'

Timothy's mouth opened, but no words came. Instead he looked from one to the other, and then down at the ground with a frown. 'But . . . she couldn't have . . . She knew what that would do to Father . . . Why didn't she tell me?'

'You can answer that for yourself,' Baldwin said unkindly. 'Are you sure she didn't tell you that she was wedded?'

'Never! My Christ, if I'd known that . . .' He looked up at Baldwin again, and now there was a fierce, cold rage in his eyes. 'If she'd done that and not asked Father first, she deserved what happened to her!'

Later, when the two sat to discuss the matter, Simon was unsure of Timothy's innocence.

'I'd not be surprised if the poxy fool mused and let the resentment build until he seethed against her. He might have reasoned that the affront to the family's honour justified a severe punishment.'

'Perhaps. I am certain of only one thing: that the coroner's tale is entirely wrong!'

Simon agreed with Baldwin. The coroner's summing-up had been devastating for the vill.

'So we come to the essential facts. The two bodies. One, the woman, held the knife. I do not doubt that the knife was the weapon that ended both these two young lives.'

'Clearly he doesn't doubt – he didn't even bother to measure the blade and test the depths of the wounds, the width of the injuries, nor any other comparative measurements,' Baldwin whispered with contempt.

The coroner had continued. 'The dagger will be sold as deodand. It is clear enough that the woman killed her lover, and, feeling remorse, she first settled his body into that comfortable posture, and then she walked away to commit self-murder, dropping to lie dead where she was discovered. For these crimes . . .'

It was at this point, as he was outlining the full total of fines that would be imposed on the poor peasants of the area for allowing this infringement of the king's peace, that Baldwin nudged Simon and began to make his way from the place, muttering angrily: 'I suppose that little child was strong enough to pick up her dead lover and dragged him across the mud?'

He paused and stared into the middle distance. 'We never answered why someone should have killed him up there and then dragged him away. Plainly the idea was to conceal his body. Yet why? Surely the likely reason was to hide him from Juliet when she arrived? So someone planned the murder as a double killing. The man was slaughtered first, his body hidden, but treated respectfully, and then the girl arrived and was killed in her turn. But she did not merit such respect. Instead she was left discarded. Why? Was she being punished for a crime of which the boy was innocent?'

Shaking his head, he continued onwards, glowering at the ground as he went.

Rather than make their way nearer to the river, which was invariably damp, especially nearer the king's new moated palace, the Rosary, the two walked down to the priory, intending to make their way past it and down to the road that led to the great bridge.

At the gate they saw Brother Lawrence with a carter. Lawrence saw them approach and suddenly grew curt with the carter, sending him into the priory, before standing and waiting for the two to reach him.

'You left us swiftly, brother,' Baldwin said.

'I had no desire to be involved with that whelp,' Lawrence admitted. 'Is it as I feared, then? More fines for the poor folk who can scarce support themselves as it is?'

'You will not find a more stern and forbidding coroner in the country,' Baldwin said.

'He is a measure of the government. Was any culprit selected?'

Baldwin showed his teeth in a smile. 'Who would you have picked?'

'Me?' Lawrence looked up at him, then considered. 'Clearly it is plain that Pilgrim was innocent. Someone killed him, and yet treated his corpse with reverence, so his killer at least recognized that he was a decent enough fellow. He didn't want to leave his corpse lying there . . .'

'Which says little for the man who murdered Juliet,' Baldwin said. 'He left her crumpled in a mess.'

Simon nodded. 'Perhaps someone else came along and the murderer was forced to flee?'

'It is possible,' Baldwin agreed. 'What do you think, brother?'

Lawrence sighed and peered up into the sky. 'Did you know that this priory has a reputation? Many hundreds of years ago there was an illicit affair between a woman and a chaplain. It is said that the devil came and took them and that the man's ghost is seen here on the flats occasionally.'

'Here?' Simon asked. He only stopped himself from gazing about him with superstitious concern by reminding himself how Baldwin would make him regret such a display.

Baldwin smiled airily and turned to peer at Simon. Saying nothing to the bailiff, he asked Lawrence: 'How would a woman come to be living here in a monastery?'

'I believe that she was here for safekeeping . . . some form of wardship, no doubt.'

'Hard to believe that someone could send a young impressionable ward to a place like this,' Baldwin commented.

'What happens to those who see the ghost?' Simon asked.

'They die, so the rumour says.'

'Well, neither of these two were taken away, and I do not believe that the devil would be overly concerned about the sudden arrival of a witness. Nor do I think he'd have set out young Pilgrim in so considerate a manner,' Baldwin said caustically. 'Personally I would be easier in my mind believing that there has been an entirely human agent at work here.'

'We all have our own beliefs, Sir Baldwin. Perhaps yours are more secular than mine.'

'Perhaps,' Baldwin conceded. 'Tell me, brother, where should we seek the woman who found the first body?'

'That was Elena. She will be out there on the shore. She seeks what she can from the Thames at low tide. There is often something discarded in the waters which she can make use of or sell.'

Elena cursed as she missed it, dragging the thin rope back through the waters and coiling it in a rough bundle beside her.

The plank looked hardly rotted at all. From the way it floated it was probably nicely dried, hardly green, and would have been worth having. Still, on it went with the river. Her rope with the weight had been too weak to haul it in to the beach. The cord had snapped, the weight falling into the water while the beam floated on serenely. She looked down at the remaining rope with disgust, half-tempted to fling that into the water as well.

'Mistress?'

'Who are you?' she demanded querulously. The sun was hidden behind clouds, but it was still bright enough for her to want to shield her eyes with a hand as she studied the two men walking towards her. 'You were in the crowds at the inquest, weren't you?'

'We were, madam,' Baldwin said. 'We wanted to talk to you for a moment about what you saw that day when you found them.'

'I saw their bodies, that was all.'

'Was there anyone else out here on that day?'

'It was wet. There was no one out who had any sense.'

'You were.'

'I had to get to the market.'

'Were the bodies wet through? If it had been raining, did you notice whether they had been there for long or not?'

'I am no constable. I walk about here to try to earn what I can from what I find. There were two bodies there, but I didn't know about looking for how wet they were. No, I just found young Juliet, and seeing her there, that was sad.'

'You knew her?'

'A little. A pretty little thing she was, and so happy when she was out here.'

'What was she doing out here?' Simon asked, gazing about him with frank distaste. At least on Dartmoor there were some areas of dry pasture. Here all seemed waterlogged.

'Waiting to see her man. I had often seen her. Sometimes she was alone, with only her maid, but often she was with her man. Mostly it's been just the younger William in the last weeks,' Elena said helpfully.

'Perhaps she wanted company because of the stories of a ghost, eh, Simon?'

Elena scowled. 'Don't jest about the ghost. Us who live here know to fear that figure.'

'You know someone who's seen it?' Simon asked.

'I have seen it myself. It's a sign of bad omen.'

'What happened to you after you saw the figure?' Baldwin asked lightly. 'A corn on your foot? Or you found that you were growing wet while walking across this marsh?'

She looked at him with a chilly certainty. 'The first time I saw the figure, my husband Thomas died. Last time, next morning I found poor Juliet's body.'

Brother Lawrence watched them go to seek Elena with a sense of growing unease and anxiety.

It had seemed such a sensible idea at the time. When he and the prior had concocted their scheme, the idea of driving others away from the river had been essential. They didn't want Roger Mortimer escaping from the Tower only to be arrested as soon as he set foot on the Surrey side.

Lawrence had first mooted the idea of the ghost. All knew of the ghost. Those in the priory mentioned it in undertones and used the story to scare the novices when they could, but the locals had heard of it, too, and people like Elena believed in it. What better way could there be to keep unwanted eyes from the shore than by having a fearsome ghost wandering the place?

It had gone so well, too. Terrible, of course, that Elena's old man had seen them. Lawrence saw him, saw his gaping, stupid face, and raised his arms to loom over the fellow, and he had turned to flee, bolting over the flats like a rabbit from a hound. Next morning the fool was dead. A great shame, but Lawrence did not feel over-guilty. There were other considerations, and rescuing Mortimer was crucial. The country had to have him safe so that the muttered plans to remove this intolerable king could be put into action.

He saw John and began to make his way to the lad.

All would have been well, too, had not that woman seen him. Juliet. He hadn't realized at the time, but she had witnessed him and the men from the boat. Clearly, seeing the men pile from the boat while the 'ghost' held it steady for them made her understand that his costume was only a ruse. And equally, seeing where the boat landed, so close to the priory's kiddles, the salmon traps set out along the line of the river banks, made her understand that a man from the priory was probably responsible. So the officers came and took the representative of all power in the priory – the prior himself.

Lawrence could blame himself, of course, but that wouldn't have Prior Walter released. He was incarcerated in the same Tower from which they had rescued Mortimer. This new fool John de Cusance, Prior John, was installed, and there was little Lawrence could do about it.

Vengeance against those who had reported his and the prior's actions? That was not a pretty act. But he knew many would consider it justified. Reasonable, even.

So now an escape was needed. He had to find a way out – perhaps a boat?

Her conviction was enough to wipe the cynical amusement from Baldwin's voice. He apologized, eyeing her more closely than before, wondering whether she had reliable evidence. All too often he had found that those who claimed to have seen ghosts were in fact drunk at the time.

'Madam, I had not seen that such a figure could have so unfortunate a result. Tell me, that I should know this figure of evil, what does it look like? Is it clad in, say, the robes of a Cluniac monk?'

'You think I'm stupid enough to mistake the devil for one of the priory's men?' she scoffed. 'This man was tall, maybe a foot or more over your height, Sir Knight, and he wore a long cloak with a separate cowl and hood. I don't know the colour, because it was night-time, but I could see the cloak because it moved so strongly in the wind.'

'You saw no face?'

'I did not want to!' she stated firmly.

'It could not have been this unfortunate fellow, Pilgrim de Monte Acuto?' he hazarded, although he knew the answer before she spoke. The body had worn neither cloak nor cowl and hood.

'Pilgrim? I've seen him and his father up here often enough, I think I'd recognize them!'

'They are often up here on the marshes, you mean?' Simon said.

'Very often. The girl was a strong lure.'

Baldwin was struck by her comment. 'For Pilgrim, you mean?'

Elena was suddenly dumb.

'My God! You mean that the father wanted her too?' he cried, and turned away, slapping at his brow. 'Christ Jesus! Simon, the one aspect I could not accept was that William would murder his son for no reason. Yet here we have a reason: the father was a *competitor* with his son for this girl's affections. The two men discussed her, argued, and the father slew his son in a fit of rage.'

'Why did he drag the body away from the ground where he was killed?'

'Remorse? Or, as I suggested before: he wanted the body to be concealed, so he pulled Pilgrim's corpse from high ground where it would have been too obvious, instead setting it down in that malodorous little hollow, so that when he spoke to the woman he loved she wouldn't glance over his shoulder and see his son lying slaughtered.'

'Do you think he killed his son because he heard that his son had married her, and jealousy forced him to act as he did?' Simon wondered.

'Possibly,' Baldwin said. Now that he was following a definite path, he was feeling more confident by the moment. 'He told his son to leave the marsh and leave his lady love to him, and when he did I wonder if Pilgrim laughed at him and taunted him? So many people have said what a generous-hearted, kindly soul Pilgrim was, but even the kindest lad can be cruel to a parent. If his father did not know ... A father who doted on his son's wife would be cause for great humour, I would imagine. The poor man!'

It was mid-afternoon by the time they reached the city gate again, and there Baldwin stopped thoughtfully.

'I suppose we should go and tell the good coroner about our discovery,' Simon said, seeing his eyes flitting westwards.

'That was in my mind. Yet it was my lord bishop who asked us to investigate this crime. Let us inform him first, and then we may arrest William ourselves. I have no desire to inflate the coroner's reputation.'

So deciding, the two friends set off. Following the line of the Thames, they were forced to take a detour when they reached the Walbrook Stream, but then soon they were out through the west gate and crossing the Fleet river.

Bishop Walter was waiting for them in his hall, but this time he was shouting orders at servants, eyeing parchments full of lists and dictating to a clerk.

'Ah, Sir Baldwin, I am glad indeed to see you. And you, Simon, of course. Is it possible that you have had some luck in the mission I gave you? I heard that the inquest had been held, but I have to say that I did not feel that the coroner's conclusion was sound. The idea of the young woman committing murder and then killing herself seems most curious to me.'

'I think that I have a more credible answer which fits the facts more firmly than the coroner's.'

Bishop Walter listened intently, waving a clerk away irritably as he heard about the possible jealousy of the older William. 'But this is astonishing! As you say, were he suddenly to hear from his son that he was unable to marry the woman he adored, that might well tip him over the edge. After all, once she was married to his son, it would be impossible for him to marry her – even if she was a widow. No father may marry a daughter, and the wife of his son has become his daughter, naturally, in God's eyes.'

'It may be worse than that,' Baldwin considered. 'William had lost his love before, to Sir Henry. The thought of losing his only link with her, her daughter, may have added to his mental turmoil. The poor man!'

'So the shock drove him to kill his son, and then his daughter-in-law presumably rejected his advances, too, so he slew her. A terrible story, Sir Baldwin. Terrible. The poor man.'

'It is a shocking tale,' Baldwin agreed. 'And I feel that I should go and confront him with his crime. I have the king's authority to keep his peace. I am sure that with your approval it would be easy enough to go and have him arrested.'

'I shall raise a small force from my household,' the bishop promised. Then he hesitated. 'But one thing. As a courtesy to my friends, would you object to going and telling Sir Henry? He has a right to know how his daughter died, after all.'

'I should prefer to go straight to William.' Baldwin's tone was blank, but he felt angry to have the bishop ask this. It was clearly a political gesture, designed to satisfy the Despensers that Stapledon had done all in his powers to help them. Justice demanded that Baldwin confront the felon, not play the messenger to a politician's ally.

'William lives the other side of the river, while Sir Henry is but a short walk away. Would it really make a great difference? It is, as I suggest, merely a matter of courtesy.'

Baldwin considered, glancing at Simon. The bailiff shrugged, then nodded.

No, it was not against any principle of law, so far as Baldwin could see, but the idea of informing a victim's family of a deliberation before even arresting the man accused seemed wrong: putting the cart before the horse. But if the bishop insisted, Baldwin did not feel strongly enough about it to argue. 'Very well, my lord. Do you prepare a small force and I shall return here as soon as I may.'

The hall was still, and Baldwin was reminded of a calm before a thunderstorm. There was the noise of servants out behind the hall, but they seemed to be muffled. Baldwin had never before known an English house to be so quiet, and the idea that any master could persuade a rowdy, boisterous group of servants to be so respectful spoke volumes of the love all had for the daughter of the house – or perhaps the fear that all felt for their master.

'You have something to tell me?'

Henry had appeared in the doorway, and now he strode across the floor to stand near the two visitors.

Baldwin looked at Simon, then said: 'Sir Henry, we have had some fortune. As I told you yesterday, we have learned that your daughter had married Pilgrim. Their marriage was legal and binding. However, just as you did not know, I think it is likely that Pilgrim's father was also kept in the dark.'

'So I am not the only fool, you mean? Should I be grateful for the fact that his son held his father in a similar disregard as my daughter did me?'

'This is difficult for me to assess, Sir Henry. I never knew your daughter. However, I am convinced that she would not have intended to hurt you or your family. Yet it is all too easy for a young woman to fall in love with a man who . . . who may not be viewed as quite suitable.'

'So what are you telling me, then?'

A maid entered the room with a tray on which was one jug and one mazer. She set it on the cupboard, poured a generous helping and took it to her master.

As Baldwin continued, Simon noticed that the girl stopped at the screens entrance and waited, a hand on the doorpost, peering into the room with a pale face as she eavesdropped.

'We think that the father of Pilgrim learned that his son was going out there to meet your daughter. I read the facts as these: he remonstrated with his son. His son then taunted him with the fact that they were married. The news threw William into a rage and he killed his son and then, when he saw your daughter, he killed her too. Perhaps he was driven mad by the thought of his son's disobedience.'

Simon was impressed with Baldwin's cautious description of the events. There was no need to add to the burden of misery already felt by this poor man. He had lost his daughter already: best not to tell him that it might have been solely because this already acknowledged enemy of his had an infatuation for her.

'So . . . he killed her. Sweet Christ!'

Simon nodded – and then felt the stirrings of doubt.

Surely if this woman had been the daughter of William's first love, and he had slain her in a passion, he would have treated her with the same reverence he showed towards his son? Either the man would have left both bodies slumped messily, or both set out gently and kindly? Both had earned his jealous resentment; both deserved equal respect. And surely a man with love in his bones for either must later commit self-murder in disgust and despair? Yet at the inquest William had been so composed.

Baldwin continued: 'He will pay for his crime. We are going to arrest him even now, and I will see to it that he is held for the next court.'

Sir Henry drained his mazer, and as he held it out the servant ran into the room again, collected the jug and brought it to him, pouring another generous measure. It irked Simon that he should be so rude as to drink and not offer anything to Baldwin and himself.

Baldwin nodded and bowed, and the two men left the hall, walking along the passage to the front door. As they crossed the threshold to leave, Simon heard a pattering of feet, and he turned over-swiftly (he was not used to the presence of so many people at all times, and the evident violence of this great city was always in his mind) and would have drawn his sword, but he saw that it was only the young maidservant from the hall.

'Masters, I can't let you ... The story you just told my master ... It's not true!'

Baldwin eyed her doubtfully. 'What makes you say that? We have good evidence for it.'

'But the marriage! It wasn't Pilgrim who married my mistress! It was his *father* was wedded to her.'

Her story was all too swift to tell. She had been a witness with John and Lawrence when William and Juliet plighted their troths, in a quieter area of the marsh near the priory. The two had been seeing each other for some months, and after a while Juliet had agreed to make him a happy, married man again. However, she had stipulated that, although William could enjoy her, they could not tell anyone else until she had broached the subject with her father.

'She hoped that some day her father would be able to understand, masters. She hoped that he would forgive her. But he couldn't. He is a strong-willed man, firm of resolve, and once he has made a decision he will not alter it.'

'But what you have told us doesn't necessarily change anything,' Simon said. 'If William saw his son out there meeting his wife – again rage could well have overwhelmed him and he might have slain his own son in a fit of fury.'

'You think my mistress would be unfaithful to her husband?'

'You think she wasn't?'

'No! She was the most loyal, devoted wife!'

'Then why else would she have been visiting Pilgrim so often? We have heard that they were often together on the marshes.'

'That I don't know,' she said. Her eyes were already back on the doorway.

'Have you heard of this ghost of the riverside? Some say that those who see it soon after find that someone they know has died.'

She blanched. 'I have seen it! But no one died.'

'When?'

'Last year, when my mistress first met her husband. She and I were walking about the place in the middle of the evening, when we saw a large figure. Full tall, he was, and clad all in grey, with a hood and cloak.'

'What made you think he was a ghost?' Baldwin wondered.

'His height, and his gait. He went . . .'

In mute demonstration, she held her arms out wide and walked straddle-legged, her head low on her shoulders. It was hard for Baldwin not to smile. She looked like a man-at-arms who had been spending too long in the saddle. And yet . . . an idea flashed into his mind.

'You did not have a friend die?' Simon asked.

'No. But the next day I heard that Elena's husband was dead. Surely that was it.'

Baldwin was frowning, but there came a spark to his face as she spoke. 'This was the feast day of St Peter ad Vincula, wasn't it? The night that Mortimer fled the Tower?'

'Yes, master,' she said, but now her face was anxious, and her eyes moved back towards the house.

'Maid, did you tell anyone about that?'

'No.'

'Did your mistress see the ghost too?'

'Yes, but she was angry. She didn't seem fearful. She saw it at the water, she told me. I heard her talking about it with that monk, Lawrence.'

There was the sound of the main door opening. She said nothing more, but fled for the house as though fearing that the ghost of the marsh might be at her heels at any moment.

'There's something there, isn't there?' Simon said.

'I think someone was playing the fool pretending to be a ghost up there that night. It was the night of Mortimer's escape, and what better way to keep stray eyes at bay than to have a ghost who could kill your nearest and dearest. Probably Elena's husband met the good Lord Roger and was killed for his pains. Thank God we don't have to investigate that murder too!'

'Do you think William could have killed the two?' Simon asked, and explained his new doubts.

Baldwin considered. 'I think this ghost is a fiction, and Juliet saw through it somehow. And she told of her doubts. Perhaps she was killed because of that – in case she had seen something else? She was killed to silence her.'

'While Pilgrim knew nothing?'

'So he was left tidily, while she was left in a mess because she was guilty of speaking out? Ach, I do not know. Let's go to William and see whether he can help any further.'

* * *

They found William in his hall sitting in his chair. 'Excuse my remaining in my seat, gentles. I am still tired after that appalling inquest.' He spoke calmly, but when the small guard party appeared in his doorway behind Baldwin and Simon his eyes widened a little.

They had gathered the bishop's men quickly and taken the bishop's own little boat to cross the river, making their way down past the Rosary and grounding the boat in the shallows at the far side.

William's small manor was a scant mile the other side of Southwark. Bishop Walter had given precise directions to one of his men, and he led the way along the quiet Surrey lanes until they reached William's house.

For all that it was a small property, it was not maintained well. All about were proofs of the family's poverty. The limewash was streaked, and timbers were failing. When Baldwin looked about, it was clear that this was a sadly dilapidated property compared with others nearby.

The interior continued with the same impression. Where tapestries and rich hangings covered the walls of the manor houses in the Strand, here the walls were bare of all decoration. Not even a simple picture broke the grey, sombre colours. The only decoration in the whole hall was William's chair.

'You like this? It was given to my father. Alas, it is about all that remains of my inheritance.'

'We are not here for social purposes, I fear,' Baldwin said.

'I didn't think you were – I'm not a fool yet!' William said with a flare of asperity.

'We know you were there,' Simon said. 'It makes sense that you killed your son when you learned he was trying to ensnare your wife, but why kill her too?'

William leaned back in his chair, staring from Simon to Baldwin. '*What?*'

217

'Tell us the truth,' Baldwin said.

'I was out there, yes, to see my wife. I had no idea my son was there too. I assume he was dead before I went, but I wanted to see Juliet.'

'Why there?' Baldwin frowned. 'It is a miserable place!'

'She had an ally who was a boatman. She could always cross the river without fearing being followed, and the man would drop her off near the Rosary.'

'Damn the Rosary! It seems to appear in all conversations,' Simon muttered.

'You want to learn more about it? I can tell you much.'

'Finish your tale first. What did you want with her that night?' Baldwin said.

'She was my wife,' William said, and his voice was choked. He appeared to recover swiftly, but now his voice was thick, and he swallowed a great deal as though his throat was blocked. 'I wanted to see her every waking moment.'

He shouted for a servant, and shortly afterwards a wiry, sallow-faced man appeared. 'Perce, fetch ale. I apologize,' he continued. 'Money has been thin in my purse recently, and where I used to offer wine now I must resort to ale.'

When Perce returned and Baldwin and Simon were holding large mugs of ale, he continued.

'I wished to see her to try to persuade her again that she should announce her marriage to me. I didn't want her going back to her father, or that snake of a brother of hers. Have you seen him? Timothy, he is called, but a man less like a disciple of Christ I cannot imagine. He is marked like a leper almost.

'As was her wont, she refused me. The time was not yet right, she said. I spent too much time trying to persuade her, but she would have none of it. When I asked her about my son, she laughed at the thought that she might have had an affair with him. But there was something in her speech that worried me, I confess.'

'Why?'

'Because it didn't sound natural. I am an older man, Sir Baldwin. You are too. You know as I do that you can hear a lie in the tone of a lover's voice. I heard it then. Oh, don't look at me like that! I killed no one that night. I heard that note and knew then that she had been seeing my son. I was upset, I confess. But not upset enough to slaughter the only two people in the world whom I loved. That would be insane!'

'So what did you do?'

'I left her, with an immensely heavy heart and tears ready to spring. I couldn't force her to lie to me any further, and I sought solace in returning here and considering to myself that I would be cruel indeed to force her to join me here when she really wanted a younger man. I was prepared to perjure myself and declare that we had never married.'

'How did you? Your wooing must have been difficult in the extreme.'

'I think she came to love me as a father. Perhaps she never enjoyed the company of her own? It happened that we met one day near the Rosary while I was watching the building works. She saw me and came to apologize.'

'Apologize for what?'

'Didn't you hear? The Rosary was my manor. When it was taken from me, I lost all my lands.'

Baldwin was surprised. 'The lands about the Rosary? Marshes like them must be worth little!'

'My flocks were able to meander and pasture there, but more important was the fishing. I had traps all over the river bank, kiddles to catch salmon. My lands were worth a great deal.'

'How did you lose them?'

'I thought you must know all this. Ten years ago I was a companion to Piers Gaveston. I was loyal to him, even when the barons took against him and exiled him. I remained loyal, and when he returned to this country I fought for him. My reward was a series of manors from here all the way to Kent. But now Piers is dead I have no patron. And in the last few years Despenser has whittled away my possessions. The last act was to take my lands for the Rosary, along with all the rest of my lands. All I have left is this hall.'

'Under what pretext did he take them?'

'Oh, the easiest possible. He alleged that I was associated with the Lord Mortimer. He suggested that I had aided Mortimer in his escape from the Tower. But I swear I had nothing to do with it.'

'Many about here appear to have been accused of aiding Mortimer to escape,' Baldwin noted. 'The prior too. A new man has been installed.'

'That man Cusance. He is a companion to Despenser. They wanted a nice berth for him because he and his brother have served Despenser well. So Despenser had Walter de Luiz arrested and gave the living to his friend. It is a disgrace! To think that a politician could remove an honourable, godly man and replace him with a sham. All in the priory hate him. None trusts him.'

'Was there anyone else who could have wanted to have you impoverished?' Simon wanted to know. 'Surely Despenser wouldn't have simply picked on you for no reason. Someone must have suggested you had some part in that.'

'I have no idea who could have suggested such a thing,' William said. 'An enemy like that must have been obvious. I could hardly miss the fact that someone hated me so much as to want to take away my life. Look at me! Only two years ago I was a powerful man with a good livelihood. Now I have lost all – even my wife and son.'

'If you used to visit the marshes so regularly,' Simon wanted to know, 'did you ever see the figure? The ghost?'

William shivered and appeared to withdraw into his chair. 'I saw it once, with my wife. It petrified me. But then . . .'

Baldwin nodded. 'The next day you heard of the escape?'

'Yes. It made me think that the ghost was perhaps a clever ploy to scare away watchers. A clever ruse. And I believed it. So would you, out near the river with a fine mist coming down.'

'What did your wife think?'

'At the time she, too, was terrified.'

'Did you discuss it with her?'

'Yes. In fact she was proud afterwards to have reported what she saw to her father, and through him to the city authorities. It's probably because of her that the prior was removed.'

'Who would have known that?'

'I know Juliet mentioned it on our wedding day – but I don't think she talked about it apart from then. At the time she was so filled with what that marshland meant to her, you see. She was full of excitement. Joyful, just like me.'

A tear ran slowly, unregarded, down William's cheek. 'First I lost Cecily, now her daughter and my son. There is nothing left for me.'

'Master William, tell me,' Baldwin said. 'Sir Henry – would you doubt his personal loyalty to Despenser?'

'No, I think that he is entirely loyal. There are many things I say to his detriment, but I wouldn't disparage his faithfulness.'

Baldwin stood. 'I ask that you remain here in your hall until this matter is reconsidered. Others may seek to punish you if you leave here.'

'Any man could break into this place. There's only me and Perce now that my son is dead.'

'I shall leave these men with you. You will be safe.'

Baldwin turned to leave. 'One thing: how do people reach these salmon traps – kiddles you called them?'

'Mine were further into the water, and a boat was needed. Others, like the monks, have theirs nearer the shore. They sometimes use stilts to cross the mud.'

Baldwin commanded one of the bishop's men to hurry to the bishop and inform him that he was not convinced that William was guilty as they had considered. He asked that a man be sent to Sir Henry, too, to ensure that Juliet's father was aware that William was not arrested and was likely innocent.

Before they reached the water, Baldwin suddenly stopped. Simon saw him staring over the flats. 'Are you all right, Baldwin?'

'No, I don't think I am. My mind has been fogged. Juliet was killed and left; Pilgrim was killed but treated with respect. If Pilgrim was not murdered by his father, then who else could have left him in such a kindly manner?'

'As I said before – a monk?'

'Precisely. The only trouble is: Juliet. Who could have killed Pilgrim and Juliet and treated them in so different a manner?'

'A monk may be disinclined to touch a woman's body, I suppose.'

Baldwin gave a swift grin. 'Or more inclined, so I've heard. But this matter grows only more opaque. Why treat the two so differently?'

'Two killers?'

'Too coincidental. I cannot believe that.'

'Someone else came along and prevented the killer from treating the woman in the same manner?'

Baldwin nodded. 'I am still fascinated by Elena telling us about the figure. She must have realized we'd learn about men on stilts.'

'Yes, which makes me infer that she knew what she was saying and she was trying to give us a hint. Now I think I understand it, too.'

Friday Next after the Feast of St George the Martyr[7],
Bermondsey Marsh

Baldwin had woken Simon as soon as dawn broke, and long before most of the city had risen the two were already on the southern shore of the Thames.

'This affair is surely not so complex as it appears,' Baldwin said. 'Let us return to the place where the bodies were found and see if there is anything about the land which may lead us to an answer.'

The two men were walking away from the marvellous new development of the Rosary, their feet sinking into the thick tussocks of reed amid the meagre grass, before seeing some distance away a figure stalking about.

'I think that there we can see a part of the answer,' Baldwin murmured.

Simon followed his gaze. All he could see was a man standing at the water's edge, sometimes moving slowly about with great deliberation, like a toddler learning his first steps. 'There?' he asked.

But Baldwin was already striding towards the priory, and Simon had to hurry to catch up with him.

'What do you mean?' he demanded as he reached his friend.

'Look up there,' Baldwin replied.

[7] Friday 26 April 1325

At the gatehouse Simon saw a cart emerge. There was a man leading the pony, and alongside it a monk paced slowly. Even from this distance, it was easy to recognise the figure.

'Lawrence?'

Baldwin said no more as they approached the cellarer.

'Sir Baldwin! You are up and about early this morning.'

'As are you,' Baldwin said, eyeing the cart. 'You are off to the city?'

'There is always a need to keep friends content. We have rights to some fisheries, and every so often we send a gift to friends in the city.'

'Do you gather them yourself?'

'Me? Sir Baldwin, can you imagine an old fellow like me on stilts walking about the river's banks? Better to have a youngster do things like that.'

'Oh? I'd heard you might have been about during the evening when Juliet and her man were killed.'

'I don't know who'd have said that. I wouldn't leave the priory at night. Not with the ghost about. I've told you about that, haven't I?'

'Of course.' Baldwin smiled. 'And yet we've heard that Juliet told of the ghost out here on the night Mortimer escaped. A man could be upset to think that she had reported him – especially if it was her report that caused the good prior to be arrested.'

'Who would think in such a way?'

'I wonder,' Baldwin said coolly, and now he was staring intently at the monk. 'If a man loved his master and saw him punished by arrest, perhaps he would be so disgruntled and resentful that he might take matters into his own hands. A strong man, though. Clearly an older man would find it difficult to carry a body like Pilgrim's.' He glanced at the small cart. 'Who would these fish be for?'

Lawrence kept his face neutral. 'Sir Henry. I have been asked by the good prior to have this wagon-load delivered personally.'

'Ah. The same man who reported that your prior might have been involved in Mortimer's escape.' Baldwin smiled coldly. 'It is not a task to your taste?'

'Our prior has been installed to replace our poor brother Walter, who has been ripped from our fold. Naturally I seek to obey my prior.'

'*Naturally*,' Baldwin said drily. 'I would think many of your comrades would be as unhappy as you about the turn events have taken.'

'None of us is content. But we have the gratification of knowing that at least we are serving God in our own way, no matter what the powerful in the land may think or want. And God willing, our prior may one day return to us.'

'God willing,' Baldwin murmured in agreement.

'Was that any help to us?' Simon enquired.

Baldwin splashed into a puddle and gazed down at his boot in disdain. 'These were once good leather,' he muttered inconsequentially. 'Hmm? Yes, I think so. Do you consider that man to be a murderer?'

'Lawrence? No!'

'Nor do I,' Baldwin said. 'And I think that itself makes our task more easy.'

Simon glanced at him. 'What now?'

'Now we see if another fellow can help us,' Baldwin said with a smile, and turned to the gatehouse. 'A man utterly devoted to Lawrence or his old prior. Someone who is stronger, who could drag Pilgrim's body down into that hollow, but who's also young enough to be able to use stilts. Ah! Porter! We should like to see the novice, Brother John. Is he about today?'

'No. He's off to look at the kiddles.'

'Let me guess, he would use a small boat to reach them?'

'Trust a lad like him with a boat? He can make use of stilts like his master the cellarer!'

'Of course! Tell me, where would I see him?'

'Best to wait here. He'll be returning before long. Can I fetch you a quart of ale?'

William looked about him.

There had been a time, when he was a lad, when he had looked about himself in this room and seen only magnificence. There had been tapestries and fine pewter, silver catching the light from the fire in the middle of the floor, cushions on the benches, and great hounds pacing in and out. It had been a place of enormous comfort and elegance.

As he grew older, he came to this little manor less and less. He had the larger properties, and as his mercantile ventures bore fruit he would travel abroad more often, often dreaming idly of times when he would be able to settle down and find a wife. And then he had met Cecily.

She had been the beauty he had looked for all his life. A tall woman, with flashing blue eyes and dark, Celtic hair, she entranced him. So much so that he had mentioned her to his old companion, Henry. And then, the next time he saw Henry, Henry already had her heart. It all but broke William's.

Over time, he had healed. He had found dear Isabelle, who had been a congenial spouse who had borne him young William and two more children, and William had found his star rising with the influence of his master, Piers Gaveston. The king himself recognized William.

But then Gaveston was caught by his enemies and murdered. It was a terrible shock. Suddenly William learned what it was to lose his patron. Only three years later, the famine struck, and Isabelle and the children died. Christ's bones, but that had been a black time! Only eight years, but it was as though he had been living a different life.

It was after the famine that Henry grew in influence. And only eighteen months ago, William first clapped eyes on Henry's daughter, and in her face he saw the woman he had wanted to marry all those years before. Juliet ensnared him with her calm, elegant beauty, her ready wit and cheerfulness. He couldn't resist her.

There was a thundering on his door, and he tutted to himself. 'Perce, see who it is.'

When they had been young, he and Henry had been inseparable. The two of them had revelled in the same alehouses, whored after the same wenches in the stews, even fought together in the same actions when they came against pirates. Yet once Henry took his woman, all his love for his friend had dissipated like smoke before a wind. There was nothing left.

There was a shriek from the yard outside, and William spun on his heel in time to see Perce stumble inside. His hand was at his temple, and he walked with a dazed, unseeing expression. He entered, tottered, and then slowly fell to the floor, like a tree subsiding after the axes had hewn away one side, spinning a little to crash down on his back.

The men sent to protect and guard him were at the door, but they were reluctant to stand in the path of the force that entered now.

'So, William,' Sir Henry said. He thrust the war-hammer into his belt, casting a look about him. 'I think you'd best come with me.'

Lawrence walked up the lane towards the bridge, but all the while his mind was fixed on the knight waiting at the priory's gate. At last, with a sigh, he gave instructions to the carter about where to go with the fish, and with a heavy heart he turned back, walking along the river bank to the kiddles. There was one figure still there, a tall lad with his robes bound up to keep them dry, the stilts he wore hidden under the murky waters.

'John? Come here a moment.'

William felt the rope pulling at his throat again, but there was little he could do to protect himself as the horses trotted onwards. It was only fortunate that he had not lost all his strength.

Ironic. That he should have been innocent of crimes, that his greatest enemy should seek to destroy him, when his only offence had been to love the same woman and then love her daughter. He married her, and the result? She died, his son died, and now he was to die as well. For William had no doubt in his mind that this must be Henry's intention. The man was determined to remove him.

He was here between two horses, a rope about his neck gripped in Henry's fist, while other men-at-arms rode about him. His hands were bound behind him, his wrists already chafing, but the pain was bearable compared with the anguish of the losses he had already suffered.

They had left his manor as soon as William had submitted to being tied, the men supposedly left to guard him surprisingly quiet in the face of Henry's force. There was no point in their being killed to protect a felon. That much was obvious enough. And William had hardly covered a hundred paces from his gate when the little force passed him, one of them on his own horse. The man stared down at William, spat into the road and sped off towards the bridge and the city.

'He's coming back,' Simon said.

Brother Lawrence carried a large wicker basket, a

pair of stilts lying over the top. 'Good day again.'

He set the wicker basket on the ground, where it leaked brown mud and water. The stilts rolled from it.

'They look a handy tool,' Baldwin commented.

'On the flats they can be useful, and in the shallows.'

'And if a man wished to scare all the locals away from a place, such a device would make him appear greatly taller.'

'It would take more than—'

'Yes. Perhaps a good grey cloak and hood would be needed also.'

Lawrence nodded and sighed. 'You have learned much.'

'The night that the rogue Mortimer escaped from the Tower, he came this way. We know that. Someone was out here pretending to be a ghost to scare all the people away. You.'

'Yes. I confess. I walked about the marsh for some nights before the feast to remind people of the ghost and scare them away.'

'Elena's husband was killed. By you?' Baldwin demanded harshly.

'Me? No. But others were there, and if they met a man in a chance encounter, blood could have been shed.'

'You say one of Mortimer's men did it?'

'I say one of his men *could* have killed Elena's man. I do not know. That I swear on the Gospells.'

Baldwin eyed him narrowly. He spoke with conviction and apparent honesty, and Baldwin did not think him a murderer – and yet Brother Lawrence felt his guilt. His subterfuge at reintroducing people to the idea of this ghost had indirectly led to deaths. Elena's husband, the girl, and Pilgrim. All dead for nothing.

'Where is John?'

'Now? I am not sure. Some distance away.'

'You advised him to flee?'

'All he did he did for good motives.'

'I didn't think you would murder a girl, even if you thought she had betrayed your prior. That was the act of a younger, angrier man.'

'You may think so,' Lawrence said calmly. 'It is between him and God.'

'Juliet told her father about the priory helping Mortimer to escape, and then he told the king's men. That led to Prior Walter being arrested.'

'I think so.'

'And your novice knew of this. He heard Juliet tell you.'

'She was proud of telling her father about the escaping men, but she told me in order to apologize, I think. She never expected the prior to be taken. She was very young.'

'And innocent. But a lad like John, who was raised to the concepts of honour and obedience, he took a different view, didn't he? He thought her act was disgraceful treachery, rewarding the priory's kindness in marrying her by destroying the prior.'

Lawrence looked away. 'I can say nothing. My lips cannot be opened except to God. But whether it is true or not, John has the benefit of clergy. You may not touch him.'

Sir Henry was aware of the eyes on him all the way along to the bridge. There, he fully expected to be accosted, but the porter at the gate meekly accepted his words about his capturing a known felon, and he rode on with his little force to his home.

'You should have stayed away, William. I didn't want to have to hurt you, but you couldn't keep away, could you? What, did you want to upset me by stealing my daughter? Eh? Perhaps you did. Maybe you didn't even give me a thought. Well, you should have done, old friend. You should have. Because now I've got you here, and you're going to pay for the death of my little girl. And because you took her without my permission, first I'll have you castrated!'

And he clambered from his horse and tugged on the rope, pulling William onwards.

William had been in a daze while he spoke, and only now, as Henry drew him towards the stables, did he realize what was happening.

'Christ Jesus! No!'

The men grabbed him and pulled him bodily to the heavy wooden table set out by the brazier, the farrier's tools set out nearby. And Henry smiled to hear the screams of his old friend.

'You'll rot in hell for what you did to my daughter, William.'

'Sir Baldwin! Thank God I have found you! Sir Henry, he has come and taken William. You must help us. My lord bishop is in Westminster, and I can't get him . . .'

'Tell me all,' Baldwin said urgently.

The man explained quickly how the men had arrived at William's house, beaten down Perce and dragged William from the place.

'Where are they now?'

Baldwin took his horse, and then stopped a man with a small piebald rounsey. 'I am keeper of the king's peace, acting for my Lord Bishop Stapledon. I must have your horse.'

'You can't take it, I—'

In answer, Baldwin drew his sword. Its wicked blue blade flashed in the sun. 'Retrieve your horse from Bishop Stapledon's house later this day. For now, it is needed. Simon? Mount. Lawrence – send a messenger as swiftly as you can to my lord Bishop Stapledon's

231

house and tell him of this. He must send men to Sir
Henry's house if we are to save William.'

The man left with alacrity at the sight of the sword,
a fact that pleased Simon no end. Too many men would
have argued and drawn their own steel at being ordered
to give up their horse.

Soon they were cantering illegally and dangerously
along the thronging streets. Simon was almost brained
by a low-hanging merchant's sign, and then, peering
over his shoulder at that near catastrophe, almost rode
into a tavern's sign. After that he gazed ahead resolutely.

As they turned into the house's yard, the screaming
assailed their ears.

Baldwin had sheathed his sword after taking the horse
for Simon. Now he drew it again and clapped spurs to
the beast. It leaped forward, narrowly missing a groom
and making him dart away with a shocked curse.

'Free him *immediately* in the name of the king!'
Baldwin roared.

Simon was already on the ground. His sword was out,
and it came to rest at the throat of the man holding
shears near William's groin. 'Put that down,' he hissed.

There were seven men about the yard. There was a
man at William's arms, holding them by the rope that
bound them, while a man gripped each leg, holding
them apart. The man between them was very still, his
eyes fixed on the steel at his throat.

Baldwin saw Sir Henry and his son standing a short
distance away.

'Tell your men to release him, Sir Henry. If any harm
comes to him, I will have you pay for it. Release him,
I say!'

'You could fall from your horse here in my yard, and
no one need know what happened to you,' Sir Henry
scoffed. 'I could have you dropped by arrow, and all
would declare you had an accident. Go and leave us.'

'This man is innocent! He did not kill your daughter!'

Timothy stepped forward. 'So? He may not have stabbed her, but he raped her.'

'A man cannot rape his wife,' Baldwin grated.

'He didn't have permission to marry her. He took my sister and persuaded her to lie with him so he could insult my family, but there was no marriage – I deny that she was married!'

Baldwin looked about him at the men standing still and quiet. 'Sir Henry, you are safe. You are a friend of my Lord Despenser, and anything you do here today will be forgiven. But any man here,' he lifted his voice, 'any *other* man here who attempts to hinder me or harm this man will be arrested and held by my authority as keeper of the king's peace. And if William is harmed, I will have you all taken and I will see you hanged.'

'Where is your authority for that?' Timothy sneered. 'There are only two of you!'

Baldwin felt an unbounded relief as he heard the rushing of feet outside, and as men poured into the yard wearing the livery of Walter Stapledon he smiled nastily and glanced down at Timothy.

'Stand back.'

The bishop leaned back in his chair. 'You are quite sure of this?'

Baldwin had explained all. 'There is little doubt. John was utterly devoted to the cellarer, and through him his prior. The young lad was appalled by what the girl did, telling others about the ruse of using a ghost, and it was as a result of her informing that the prior was arrested. William's son was innocent, of course. That was why he was set out so neatly. John was sorry to harm him, I suppose, but he wanted revenge on the girl, and he wouldn't let a little thing like Pilgrim being there get in his way.'

Bishop Walter looked down at his hands. 'It seems far-fetched.'

'I was happy enough to believe that her brother was responsible. Timothy was very keen to preserve his family's honour. Not his father – he still loved Juliet, but not Timothy. She was only ever a half-sister after all. But then it seemed clear that it must have been Pilgrim's father. William was clearly hurt by his wife's change in affection. She once loved him, but then the attraction of a man nearer her own age overwhelmed her. Yet when I considered the strange disparity in the way the two bodies were treated and learned how her words may have affected the priory, it seemed more and more likely that there was an element of revenge involved. Perhaps in a way it was the same motive as Timothy's. A means of retaliating against an insult to the honour of a group. Not a family, but a monastery.'

'I shall discuss the matter with the bishop here and suggest that the boy be punished.'

'Please do so. And now I would like to re-enter the city and find my bed,' Baldwin said.

'You have done well, Sir Baldwin. I am grateful.'

Baldwin nodded, but as he followed Simon from the hall, along the screens corridor and out into the bishop's yard beyond, all he could see in his mind's eye was the faces of those whom he had suspected: Sir Henry's, twisted with pain and hurt; William's, torn with longing and despair; and, last, Brother Lawrence's. A man who had seen all that his faith stood for destroyed by a novice.

Of all, Baldwin felt that the monk's loss was somehow the worst of them all. The others at least had the strength of their hatred of each other to sustain them. Lawrence had nothing.

ACT FOUR

July 1373

Geoffrey Chaucer fiddled with his pen. He peered at the other pens that were lined up to his right. He counted them, although he already knew how many there were. Did any of them need sharpening? With his left index finger, he touched the end of the one he was holding. The goose-quill did not need sharpening, not really. He put down the pen. He reached out and brought the ink pot an inch or two closer to his writing hand. Then he straightened the few sheets of paper on the table. This particular task didn't need doing either.

He sighed. He was familiar with these little devices whose purpose was to delay the moment, the inevitable moment, when he'd actually have to put pen to paper and start writing. Anything to put that moment off.

He was sitting by an open window. Sounds of activity came from down below, from the area around the entrance to the gatehouse. On his arrival the previous evening, Geoffrey Chaucer had observed an excavated space in a corner between wall and buttress, a space large enough to hold a seated man. There was a neat pile of stone near the cavity, which was kept stable by stout wooden props. Water damage, Geoffrey supposed, looking up at the gargoyle that leered above his head. Rain pouring down over the centuries. Or perhaps water seeping up from an underground spring and slowly dissolving the mortar, for this was a marshy area.

Now there came the scrape of trowel on stone, or a shared joke or an inaudible curse as one of the workmen lifted an especially heavy block. Geoffrey considered shutting the window to keep out the sounds. After all, he'd come to Bermondsey Priory to get some peace and quiet. London bustled on the other side of the Thames, but you'd expect a silent order of monks to provide a bit of peace and quiet. The only noises should be the bells summoning the brothers to prayer. And, as if on cue, a bell rang at that instant. Closing the window would mean depriving himself of the soft airs and smells of a summer morning and breathing the stuffy air of the room. Chaucer glanced around at the room. It was barely furnished – a bed in one corner, a substantial chest in another, and the stool and table beneath the window where he was sitting. But, compared with the cells or dormitories that were reserved for the monks, it was like a chamber in a palace.

Geoffrey Chaucer knew something of palace chambers. His wife Philippa and their three young children had only lately left their private lodgings in John of Gaunt's little place on the banks of the Thames. John of Gaunt's little place was the Palace of Savoy. Geoffrey was sometimes employed by Gaunt – third son to King Edward – in private business or secret matters relating to the court, although that wasn't the principal reason for his family's residency at the Savoy. Geoffrey stayed in the palace from time to time when he wasn't on his travels. But he had never felt at home in the Savoy. Unlike his wife Philippa, who was the daughter of a knight and who in her earlier life had been under the protection of the late queen of England. Philippa felt at home in palaces.

Whenever he could, Chaucer retreated to the gate-house in the city wall at Aldgate, which he'd bought around the time of his marriage. That was home to him, that was where he kept his books and papers and his writing implements. And now, for various reasons, the Aldgate house had once more become the residence of Chaucer's entire family, his wife, his children and servants. The city gatehouse, which had looked so spacious when he'd first seen it, was transformed into a cramped dwelling filled with domestic demands. So Geoffrey was spending a few days on the south bank of the river at Bermondsey Priory to get away from them. Neither husband nor wife had expressed it in those terms, but both of them knew that he was, temporarily, escaping his family on the pretence of work.

By chance, Geoffrey Chaucer was staying in a room in another gatehouse on this summer's morning. It was a guest-chamber on the first floor of the inner entrance to the priory. It was where the more important lay visitors were accommodated or those to whom the abbot, Richard Dunton, wanted to show favour. Geoffrey had met Richard Dunton for the first time on the previous evening when he'd arrived at the priory. Geoffrey recalled with pleasure the prior's words at their meeting. He was a handsome man, with a commanding presence which he combined with an easy air. He seemed genuinely glad to see Chaucer. He'd said . . .

But Geoffrey's recollections of the prior's words were interrupted by a shout from outside. Then an answering shout. Then another and another. Not good-natured banter this time but real insults flowing between the workmen who were repairing the crumbling stone at the base of the gatehouse wall. Whereas before the sporadic chatter hadn't been audible, it was now all too plain. You'd think, wouldn't you, that workers in a priory would have more respect for their holy surroundings? But no, it was all 'hog's turd' this and 'bull's pizzle' that. None of Chaucer's business, but that was all the more reason to take a look.

Glad enough to be disturbed in his work – and at the same instant thinking, Work? What work? – Geoffrey rose from his stool and pushed the table slightly to one side so that he could get a clearer view out of the window. The downward angle was awkward, and he could at first see only a couple of workmen, hats pulled low over their brows to shield them from the sun, which was hot and high even this early in the morning. Chaucer could tell nothing more about them except that one seemed young, scarcely more than a lad.

The workmen were watching something out of Chaucer's line of sight. They stood, tense and expectant. Geoffrey recognized the stance of people on the edge of an imminent fight, wondering whether to weigh in, wondering whether to get involved or to separate the participants. Then two more men, out of view until now, shifted further away from the base of the wall. They were facing each other, a couple of yards apart and at a half-crouch. From his position by the window, Geoffrey couldn't see the expression on their faces, but their closeness to a fight was evident from their stance and the way in which each was clutching an ordinary tool – a chisel, a trowel – so as to turn it into a weapon if necessary. The man holding the chisel had the use of only one hand. The other one, his left, was withered and turned in on itself like the claw of a bird. Perhaps in compensation, all his strength and force seemed to be concentrated in the good hand and arm.

Geoffrey looked beyond the group of four. The area

south of the gatehouse, the inner court, was empty apart from a black cat slinking through a patch of sun between the shadows. But there were no black-habited monks walking – or slinking – anywhere. Not surprising, since the bell that had just rung was for terce, already the fourth of the day's devotional calls even though it was still early in the morning. Chaucer squinted into the sun-dazzled yard, willing someone to appear and intervene. Now the one-handed man raised his implement, the chisel. He was shorter than the other but looked the more dangerous. He shifted his weight on to his right foot, ready to attack.

Geoffrey leaned further out of the window. Without thinking, he shouted out. Not 'Stop it!' or 'What do you think you're doing?' Simply: 'Hey!'

It was enough. The man wielding the chisel looked up. The sun was in his eyes. He squinted, but Chaucer must have been no more than a shadow in the window. The man's mouth opened as if he was going to say or shout something in reply – it was a black hole of a mouth, with fewer teeth than he had good fingers. But whatever this individual had been about to say he thought better of. He lowered the chisel and shook his head, perhaps as a way of denying that he'd ever meant any harm. The second man, too, looked up before letting the hand holding his implement, the trowel, fall to his side. The two onlookers were also gazing in Chaucer's direction.

He felt that something more was required of him but couldn't think what to say. After all, an argument among the lay workers in Bermondsey Priory was none of his business. He was a guest in this place, with no authority over any of its occupants. It was enough if he had reminded these people that he was a witness to their goings-on and so managed to avert violence for the time being.

'Good day to you,' he said, withdrawing from his place at the window.

But Geoffrey stayed close to the window. He heard the beating of his heart. His breath was coming short, as if he had been on the verge of a fight himself. He strained to listen. Nobody was speaking as far as he could tell. It was the silence that follows a quarrel. After a few moments the sounds of work resumed, the scrape of the trowel, the thunk of a hammer.

He sat down at the table once again and picked up his pen. To work! Geoffrey Chaucer was supposed to be penning a report on some recent negotiations in the city of Genoa to do with the establishment of a trading centre for the Genoese on the south coast of England. The success of such diplomatic missions was measured by the amounts of paper they generated. But, in truth, the writing of the report was a pretext. What Geoffrey really wanted to do was to get back to writing his verses.

But the scene outside had unsettled him, and whereas before he hadn't wanted to concentrate, now he wasn't able to for thinking of the foursome by the gatehouse entrance. He hoped that the monks would soon finish their devotions in the great church and that one or two of them would appear, black-hooded strollers in the court. Their very presence would surely be a deterrent to any further trouble. If they noticed what was going on, that is. The Cluniac monks at Bermondsey Priory had a reputation for scholarship. They weren't like some orders, taking pleasure in hard sweat and calloused hands. Rather, they left that to the lay workers, like the quarrelsome individuals outside the window. They were the only ones privileged to get their hands dirty.

And a thought occurred to Geoffrey. Wasn't it rather odd that a man with a crooked hand should be employed as a mason, repairing a cavity in the fabric of the gatehouse? Although he might be able to use a trowel and perhaps shift blocks of stone, he could not wield a hammer and chisel (other than as weapons). Perhaps his continued employment was an act of charity on the part of the monks. Except that the last thing the crooked-hand man looked as though he'd require was charity.

Shrugging his shoulders, Geoffrey picked up his pen yet again and lifted a sheet of paper from the pile in front of him. Get going. You write verses, he told himself; you're a maker. Well, make something. That was evidently the reputation he'd brought with him to this priory. It was with these words that the prior, Richard Dunton, had greeted him the previous evening. 'Ah, Master Chaucer, the court poet.'

The court poet? Chaucer had never thought of himself like that before, or more precisely he had never heard himself referred to in that way. True, he'd written a piece in memory of John of Gaunt's first wife, and from time to time he recited his work to some of the nobility at the Savoy or at Windsor. The ladies and gentlemen seemed to appreciate his words. At least they applauded politely when he'd finished. And his invitation to spend a few days at Bermondsey had come about because of Dunton's links to the various royal households. But to be termed 'the court poet' now, as if it was an official title! Despite himself, he felt a little kick of pride.

Richard Dunton had personally escorted Geoffrey on a tour of the priory. This was an old foundation, he'd explained, dating from shortly after the Conquest. The conventual church loomed above the cloister, the upper reaches of it like a great cliff catching the declining rays of the sun. It had taken years, decades to build, and had been completed and dedicated within living memory, yet it might have stood on this spot for centuries. Dunton's deep voice echoed as they made a circuit of the cloister. The area in the centre was in shadow, and martins threaded the air between their nesting places among the eaves and buttresses. Geoffrey soon realized that the prior had his own kind of quiet satisfaction. He was the first Englishman to be appointed to the position of superior. He was new, he was relatively young, and there was vigour in his words and movements.

Geoffrey was surprised to find how knowledgeable Richard Dunton was about outside affairs. The prior knew the latest news about King Edward's health (declining) and that of the Prince of Wales (also declining). He was better informed than Chaucer on some of the most recent comings and goings at court. When Geoffrey commented, tactfully, on this, Dunton said: 'You must not think, Master Chaucer, that because we spend our time thinking of a higher world we are somehow not of this one too. It is very necessary for the prior of a great place like this to be aware of what the king is thinking and feeling – and of the state of his health. It's not so many years since we were taken under his protection on account of debt and other misfortunes.'

At one point, as they were rounding a corner in the cloister, a hooded figure almost collided with Geoffrey. The figure was carrying some books, which he dropped in his confusion. Another brother was following in his wake. This second monk busied himself retrieving the dropped books. After apologies had been exchanged, Richard Dunton said: 'This is well met.'

He introduced the brothers. The first, who'd been carrying the books, was Brother Peter, who combined the posts of sacrist and librarian. The second, who'd picked the books up, was a moon-faced young man called Ralph. He was described as the revestiarius and the sacrist's assistant. Chaucer was a little hazy on the responsibilities of the various posts in the order, but he had an idea that the revestiarius was in charge of the linen and vestments.

Richard Dunton explained the reason for Geoffrey's presence in Bermondsey and once again made reference to the 'court poet'. If Brother Peter had never heard of Geoffrey Chaucer, he made a good job of disguising the fact by nodding and saying: 'Of course, of course, Master Chaucer.' The librarian was old but with a stringy strength to him. He pushed his hood back and thrust his lined, spectacled face towards the newcomer as if to read Geoffrey like a book. The cloister was gloomy enough, but the gesture seemed like a lifelong habit, acquired from years of poring over texts. What little light there was reflected off Brother Peter's spectacles, making it hard to interpret his expression, in fact giving an odd impression of blindness. Meanwhile, Brother Ralph stood smiling pleasantly in the background.

'You remember that I wish to speak to you, Brother Richard?' said the librarian to the prior. When the other did not respond, he said: 'The matter cannot wait.' His voice was, like his body, creaky but firm.

'Come after compline,' said the prior.

Peter seemed about to say something more but, tucking his books under his arm, he nodded to his assistant and the two men rounded the corner of the cloister. Chaucer and Dunton resumed their walk.

'There is a man who does not live in the higher world or the lower one but only among his books,' said the prior.

'I can think of worse worlds,' said Geoffrey.

'No doubt his ceiling is leaking or a bookish mouse has chewed some manuscript.'

Geoffrey wondered that the prior needed to account for the librarian's wish to see him. He thought there'd been a greater urgency in Brother Peter's voice than would be justified by a leaking roof or a trespassing mouse. By now they had wandered out of the cloister and were walking near the chapterhouse. Beyond lay the monks' cemetery, with its modest white stone markers, all identical in the dying light, sheltered by willows and oaks. Richard Dunton gestured at some more scattered buildings. Like all great establishments, Bermondsey Priory was, if not a world unto itself, at least a township. It contained a bakery and an infirmary and, at some distance, even a farm. Around them stretched the flatlands of Surrey rising to gentle hills in the distance. This was marsh country, at risk from high tides and protected by ditches and dykes.

But now the prior took Geoffrey Chaucer by the elbow and, saying that there was something very precious that he wished to show him, led him back in the direction of the great church. Perhaps because of the nearness of water – in the river to the north, in the very ground under their feet – Geoffrey suddenly thought of the church as a stone ship. An upturned ark. Passing down the slype, or covered passage, they entered the building through a door off the cloister.

The interior was deserted save for a couple of figures who were kneeling in prayer. It was between the hours for vespers and compline, the final prayers for the day. Inside, it struck chill after the warmth of the evening. The mighty stone columns seemed to pass into dusk as they climbed towards the vaulted roof. The stained glass in the great rose window at the end of the nave burned with the last of the day. The prior once again guided Chaucer by the elbow until they reached a side chapel. A small cross, made of brass or latten by the look of it and studded with little gems, stood in a niche behind a grille flanked by burning tapers. Richard Dunton unlatched the grille so that they could see the cross more clearly. It was delicately fashioned and stood scarcely more than the height of a man's hand.

'I have heard of this,' said Geoffrey. 'The Bermondsey cross. There is a story that goes with it.'

'It was found during the time of the first King Henry by members of our order. You know the story, you say?'

'Not the details of it,' said Geoffrey, sensing Dunton's eagerness to tell the tale. As the two men gazed at the crucifix, the prior recounted how three of the Cluniac monks had been walking and debating by the banks of the River Thames one morning all those centuries before. It was a cloudy, workaday morning. Of course, the brothers should not have been outside the bounds of the priory, nor should they have been engaged in a theological discussion – given their vow of silence they should not have been talking at all, in fact. But perhaps things were not so strict in those days. Legend had it that they were discussing miracles and whether any such wonders were possible in these late times. One of the three monks, Brother James, was especially vociferous in his belief that the age of miracles had passed. At that instant they heard a flap of wings and looked up to see a great bird passing overhead, flying towards the river.

Fear struck deep into their hearts, for it was a larger bird than they had ever seen in their lives, larger even than the largest eagle. They clutched each other in their fear and watched as the bird reached the river. Some object appeared to fall from its beak before it began to climb higher and higher until it was no more than a speck against the clouds. Where before the brothers had been disputing noisily, they were now struck dumb. They were about to return, silent and chastened, to the priory when a narrow ray of sun shot through a hole in the cloud – at the very spot where the bird had disappeared – and seemed to fasten on a muddy stretch of the foreshore. 'Like a finger,' said Richard Dunton. 'That is how it is described in the account left by Brother James. Like a celestial finger directing him and his brothers to this particular point.'

Curiosity got the better of their alarm. They saw something glinting on the foreshore. They picked their way across the mud and muck of the shore until they reached the place. There, planted perpendicular in the mud, was the cross that now stood in front of Geoffrey Chaucer. The gems crusting its arms were untarnished, said Richard Dunton. There was no trace of mud or water on the cross. This, surely, was the very item dropped by the great bird. It was the strongest reproof to Brother James's words about miracles. When the brothers had recovered a little from their astonishment, they left him to guard the cross and ran back to the priory to get the prior who, like the present librarian, went by the name of Peter.

'Peter was an old man by then,' said Richard Dunton, 'but witnesses say that he ran to the spot. No one had ever seen him run before. And not just him, but the other brothers and the lay workers, too, since word spread fast that something remarkable had happened. Well, to shorten my tale, everyone agreed that this was a miraculous event beyond question. Brother James and the others were forgiven for their wilful wandering outside the priory, and they were even forgiven for breaking their vows of silence, since the results had been so happy ... so extraordinary. The cross was retrieved from the mud. Even that part of it which had been sunk into the river mud emerged fresh and shining. It was as if the metal had been freshly beaten and polished and the gems newly cut. It was ceremoniously carried to this place, and here it has stood for more than two hundred and fifty years.'

As if to mark the close of his story, the prior reached out and latched the grille in front of the cross. While he'd been speaking, Geoffrey had been examining the crucifix more closely. If he hadn't just heard this strange account, he probably wouldn't have spared the cross a second glance. It was a handsome enough item but not much different from what you might find in any religious house or church.

'You do not keep it locked away?' he said. 'Many people must wish to see this and even a priory may receive a thief unawares.'

'We welcome many guests here and there may be thieves among them. But who would dare to take it?' said Dunton, with a rare flash of unworldliness. 'Besides, this place is always occupied. And the cross will guard itself.'

Geoffrey wasn't so sure about that, but he said nothing. The two men turned away from the niche in the wall. The darkness in the nave had grown deeper, relieved only by the pinprick of scattered candles elsewhere and the embers of light in the western window. Geoffrey wasn't sure either how far the prior believed in the story he'd just told. There had been no trace of doubt or irony in his tones. When it came to miracles, Geoffrey put himself in the sceptics' camp. He didn't think they happened nowadays, or at least not with such convenient timing.

It was easy enough to see how the legend of the miraculous Bermondsey cross might have developed. The object was small enough to be carried in the beak of a large bird, which had probably been attracted by its bright sheen. But a bird wouldn't see much purpose in carrying it far and would soon drop it. By pure chance the cross had landed not in the water but on the Thames foreshore. Probably the monks had witnessed this straightforward event and, wittingly or otherwise, had transformed it into something wondrous. It couldn't be denied that the cross, like any relic and quite apart from its religious significance, must be useful to the priory. With such a history, it would draw pilgrims and the devout to this marshy spot south of the river.

After the tour, Geoffrey shared the monks' supper in the fraterhouse or refectory in the south cloister. The meal, simple but adequate, was eaten in silence while one of the brothers read from the Scriptures. Accustomed to the constant noise of his own house in Aldgate, Geoffrey relished the peace of it all. Even so, he suspected that after a few days such ordered calm would become tedious. He'd never been tempted by the religious life; he belonged too much to this world.

But, he reflected now, sitting in his guest-chamber on a bright summer's morning, such a life would do very well for a while. And he wasn't so much out of the world after all. The dispute among the artisans working at the foot of the gatehouse showed that. He dipped his quill in the ink pot and prepared himself to blot the white sheet in front of him. He'd had an idea!

All at once there was a violent shout from below, followed by grunts and the sounds of a scuffle. Geoffrey cursed under his breath, rose from his stool and went to the window once more. He was readying himself to call out when he saw that the situation had gone beyond that.

Again two of the masons were standing at a distance from the scene, but this time their faces registered not tension but horror. The man with the claw-like hand was crouching over the fellow he'd been exchanging words with earlier. This man was lying on the ground, and for an instant Geoffrey thought that the other was trying to help him to his feet, since his good hand seemed to be cradled about the other's neck. Irrelevantly he noted that the man lying down had lost his cap. He had prominent black eyebrows.

The crouching man leaped back. In his fist was clenched the chisel he had been wielding before. Chaucer's gaze flicked from the blood clearly visible on the chisel blade to the blood that was pooling on the ground beneath the fallen man's head. He was shaking violently, his heels thudding against the dry earth. He had no implement in his clenched hands, not even the trowel. If he'd been equipped for a fight, then he had either dropped or been disarmed of his makeshift weapon. Geoffrey had seen enough of death in battle to recognize that this unfortunate person had only a very short time to live.

For some seconds nobody moved. The two onlookers stood transfixed by the shock of what they were seeing, and by fear of the individual with the chisel who remained at a half-crouch a couple of yards from the body whose tremors were even now subsiding. The man held the bloody chisel out as if to ward off an attack, but neither of the others was going to approach him. Though Geoffrey hadn't moved or spoken, the killer must have sensed that he was being watched from the upper window. His covered head shifted upwards and he squinted as before. His black hole of a mouth widened in a type of grin, and Geoffrey felt the hairs on the back of his neck prickling. At the same time an inner voice told him that he must act, he must get down to the inner court and do something . . . Still he did not budge.

Out of the corner of his eye he saw flickers of black. The crooked-hand man must have noticed Chaucer's gaze shift, for he turned his head. Half a dozen monks, fresh from their devotions, were rounding the corner of the kitchen, which lay on the eastern side of the court next to the refectory. As one, like soldiers given a command, they stopped when they saw the scene before them: a man on his back on the ground, another crouched with his arm extended and two more standing by stiff as statues.

Then, as if to make up for the absence of movement, everyone started to act at once. The monks began to pace rapidly towards the group, their habits flapping. Either they were brave or they hadn't fully grasped what was happening. Simultaneously, one of the fellows of the dead man – he must be dead by now; he had stopped shaking, though the blood continued to flow from the wound in his neck – made to close in on the killer, but with great caution.

The claw-handed man was quicker. He darted through the tightening circle, lashing out to left and right with the chisel. Geoffrey turned from the window and left the room at a half-run. When he was halfway down the spiral staircase, which led to the ground floor, he realized he was still clutching the quill pen. For an absurd instant he debated returning to replace the pen on the table. Then he clattered down the stone steps, through the lobby and emerged blinking into the sun of the courtyard.

He skirted the pile of stones and wheelbarrows and leathern buckets and other equipment which was being used to repair the cavity in the wall. No one noticed him. Either they were staring at the corner of the yard by the kitchen or they were themselves moving in that direction. The murderer had evidently slipped around the corner moments before while Geoffrey was descending. A couple of the monks remained behind, together with one of the masons. No one had yet gone near the body.

As Chaucer came out from the shadow of the gate-house, the mason glanced around, fear and shock on his face. He was little more than a lad, with a round, freckled face. An apprentice, no doubt. His eyes flicked down to Chaucer's hand. He opened his mouth but no words would come. Geoffrey held up the quill as if to say, 'Look, it's harmless,' but he wasn't sure whether the lad really took it in. He placed the quill on a nearby block of stone. By now the two monks were bending over the body on the ground. Their black garb reminded Chaucer of crows in a field.

The other mason, the older man, returned. He was panting heavily from the chase, sweat running down his face. His shirt was torn at the shoulder and blood was seeping through. He took off his woollen hat and held it to the wound. He glanced briefly towards the freckle-faced lad but did not look at the body.

'Scraped me, he did,' he said to Geoffrey when he'd recovered his breath. 'I left it to them to catch the bastard. They know the holes and corners of this place – God knows there're enough of them.' Chaucer wasn't sure whether he was referring to the brothers who'd taken off after the one-armed fugitive or to the priory's holes and corners.

One of the remaining monks made the sign of the cross over the body while the other kneeled down beside it. Chaucer heard the murmur of prayer.

'What happened? Who did this?' said Geoffrey.

'Calls himself Adam,' said the man. 'Anyone can call themselves Adam, though, can't they? Argumentative bastard, looking for trouble from the moment we started this job.'

Both men spoke almost in whispers. The freckle-faced apprentice kept silent but gazed in fascination, it seemed, at the monks, both of whom were now on their knees.

'You didn't know him, then? He's a newcomer?' said Geoffrey, indicating the direction taken by the fleeing man.

'We were short-handed. Michael the cellarer wished Adam on us.'

The cellarer or bursar of the priory was responsible not only for provisioning the priory but also kept the office which oversaw the upkeep of the buildings.

'Adam has only the use of one hand,' said Geoffrey, reluctant to add that this might seem to disqualify the man from building work.

'Cellarer said we should show charity. Adam came to him with a sob story of how his hand'd been crushed by some falling scaffolding when he was working over Lewes way. There's another whatsisname over Lewes way.'

'St Pancras of Lewes. It's a Cluniac house,' said Geoffrey.

'That's the one. St Pancras. You're not a religious?' said the man, looking at Chaucer's clothes and apparently surprised at his knowledge of the Cluniac order. He continued to hold his cap over the wound in his upper arm.

'I am a visitor to the priory. Geoffrey Chaucer is my name. You are . . . ?'

'I am Andrew. This here is Will and that there on the ground is John.'

He meant the freckled boy and the dead man.

'Cellarer Michael says we should look after our own,' continued Andrew, 'so he takes this Adam on even though he only had the one good hand. Did enough damage to old John Morton, didn't he, with that one good hand? Though you might say it was a bad hand.'

The two monks who'd been attending to the dead man were joined by other brothers and some lay workers. One of them had brought a makeshift carrier made of coarse cloth fastened to two poles. He placed it on the ground and unfurled it. Several of them half lifted, half rolled the dead man on to the stretcher.

The irrelevant thought occurred to Chaucer that at least their black habits would not easily show the blood which must be staining them.

As they lifted up the stretcher holding the body, the apprentice gasped. It was the first sound Will had made.

'John on the ground is Will's uncle,' said Andrew. 'His father's sick, which is the reason we were short-handed. Will's a bit . . . you know . . .'

He rolled his eyes in his head. A bit simple, he meant. Geoffrey looked at the boy again. Will was watching as the group made its way towards the corner of the yard, presumably on its way to the infirmary.

'You know why he's simple?' said Andrew.

Geoffrey shook his head. He didn't know why the man was talking so much. Shock, he guessed.

'It's because his mother was sired by a priest. The boy's state is God's punishment for her father's sin, though you wouldn't know it from the way she carries on. Giving herself airs and all.'

Chaucer said nothing. The comments seemed out of place. He was familiar with the idea that the sins of the fathers might be visited on succeeding generations. It was not an idea that he liked very much, although, looking around at the world, there seemed to be a grain of truth in it. Rather than saying anything in reply, he continued to gaze at the retreating procession carrying the body of the mason. Before they'd gone far, Richard Dunton intercepted them. The carriers paused. The prior stood by the stretcher and bowed his head. His lips moved in silent prayer, then he strode briskly to where Chaucer stood with the mason and the apprentice.

'This is a bad business, Geoffrey, very bad,' he said. 'Did you see it happen?'

'Not altogether. This man was a witness.'

'Andrew, isn't it?' said Dunton. 'You are hurt, Andrew.'

'Yes, sir,' said the mason, pleased to have been recognized despite everything. 'It's nothing much, sir. Just a scratch.'

'It is your fellow that is dead? John Morton?'

Geoffrey understood that Richard Dunton had the knack, very useful in someone with authority, of knowing the names even of those in lowly positions.

'The boy here is his nephew,' said Andrew. 'John is – he was – brother to the lad's father.'

The Prior said: 'I know.' He reached out and grasped Will by the shoulder. The boy started and blinked as if he had been woken from a dream.

'Has the villain been caught, sir?' asked Andrew.

'He will be,' said the prior. 'I understand that he arrived here only recently.'

Andrew nodded and Dunton said: 'We will scour the grounds and buildings. He will find no home or sanctuary here.'

'Must go home,' said Will, picking up on the prior's last words. The boy's voice was surprisingly steady. 'My father, he is sick at home.'

'In the Morton house? I did not hear of any sickness,' said the prior.

'No reason *you* should hear, sir,' said Andrew. He removed the woollen cap from his damaged arm. The blood was seeping more slowly now. As he'd said, it wasn't much more than a scratch.

'Go to the infirmary, man. Get that wound attended to.'

'Home,' Will repeated. He made as if to set off but did no more than walk in a half-circle, as if he'd forgotten his whereabouts.

'Wait,' said the prior. 'You shall not go by yourself.'

Dunton's glance shifted between Geoffrey Chaucer and Andrew, who hadn't moved, despite being ordered to the infirmary. The prior said: 'Geoffrey, would you mind accompanying Will? I must stay here. But the boy should not go alone. There is a bad man on the loose and, besides, it may be necessary to . . . to give an account . . .'

Chaucer understood. The prior did not wish the news of John Morton's death to come from the mouth of the boy, even assuming he was capable of delivering it. Young Will would probably recover soon enough, but at the moment he was still affected by witnessing the mortal violence done to his uncle.

'Of course,' he said.

'The family live outside the main gate, Master Chaucer,' said Andrew. 'There is a row of dwellings. Theirs is a house apart. It is Mistress Susanna's you are looking for.'

Geoffrey indicated to Will that he should go with him. They walked through the gatehouse and turned left into the outer court. There was a second arched gateway at the end. Chaucer had been greeted here the previous evening by Brother Philip. Now a lay figure was lounging in the shadow of the gate. He was a hulky man. He was picking at his teeth with a twig. His face lightened when he saw Will but not in a pleasant way.

'Morning, young Will,' he said. 'How are you this fine morning? How's your mother?'

He cupped his hands under imagined breasts. The boy did not respond. Then the man seemed to notice Chaucer for the first time.

'You keep this gate?' said Geoffrey.

'I help the brother who does. Who wants to know?'

'Never mind that. What I want to know is whether anyone has passed through here.'

The large man pretended to think. He scraped between his teeth with the twig and examined the result with more interest than he was giving to his questioner. 'Many people pass through this gate,' he said finally.

Then, seeing Geoffrey's expression, added: 'What's happened?'

'A workman is dead. Killed by one of his fellows. If the killer attempts to pass, you must stop him.'

The hulking man stopped lounging and stood up straight. Geoffrey took pleasure at the confusion and fear which settled on his face.

'How will I know him? How can I stop him if there is only one of me?'

'Then you are equally matched because there is only one of him. You should recognize him easily. He has a hand like this.' Geoffrey held up his left hand like a crooked claw. 'Oh, and he may be running away. Adam is his name.'

The gatekeeper started. He obviously recognized the description. Without waiting to see any further results of his words, Geoffrey ushered Will through the arch and into the street beyond. He didn't really think that the murderous Adam would try to leave the priory by the main gate, but he was satisfied enough to have alarmed the deputy gatekeeper. The chances were that the fugitive would make his escape to the south or east where the priory's grounds joined the flat countryside surrounding them. It wasn't surprising that the insolent keeper had heard nothing. The scuffle and the murder had taken place in the inner courtyard a hundred yards away, behind thick walls and buildings that blocked the noise. Anyway, the monks did not go in for the uproar and the hue and cry which would have followed a similar attack in the city streets.

Outside the gate he paused. 'Where is it you live, Will? Where is your home?'

The freckle-faced lad hesitated, then pointed to his right. The wall of the priory continued for a distance. They passed the entrance to another cemetery. The crosses and stone markers here were dotted more at random than their equivalents in the monks' grave-yard. Chaucer guessed this was where the lay workers would be buried. Quite a few of them, accumulated over the two hundred and fifty years of the priory's existence. Never any shortage of the dead.

To their left the land stretched away to the muddy fore-shore of the river, which glinted in the sun. The further bank was half-obscured by the haze of the morning, although the White Tower of the great castle on the northern bank was visible. The sails of a few boats stood prominent against the flatness. Gulls swooped and squawked above the water. It must be somewhere here that the miraculous little cross had landed, dropped from the beak of a bird that was larger than the largest eagle.

They came to a row of mean dwellings, more or less single rooms equipped with a door and walls and a roof with a hole to allow smoke out and a window-space at the front to let light in. Each house seemed to be leaning against the one next to it for support. If you took away the end one, they might all topple down. A couple of children were playing outside a doorway. One of them waved at Will and he waved back. Chaucer assumed that they were heading for the row, but Will wandered beyond it, in the direction of a house standing a little apart from the others.

At that instant a woman emerged from the door. She was carrying a leather bucket. She was about to throw its contents beyond the door but stopped when she saw Geoffrey and Will. Chaucer realized who she must be from her face. She was attractive, with an ample figure apparent even under a loose smock, but there was an echo of her looks in the boy. This was the woman, he remembered, who supposedly had a priest for a father. It was possible. Priests were human. They might not be allowed to marry, but they had female housekeepers and other servants.

'What's he done?' she said to Geoffrey.

'He's done nothing. Are you Mistress Morton? Susanna Morton?'

'Yes. What's wrong?'

'Is your husband here?'

'Inside, sir.'

The woman moved from the door. She stood uncertainly clasping the bucket of water. Chaucer peered into the room. After the brightness of the day, he couldn't see much. The remains of a fire sent up a spiral of smoke, some of which found its way through the hole in the roof. On the far side was a large bed, which took up perhaps a quarter of all the available space. A man was lying on it, a blanket pulled up to his chin. Next to him was a great bolster. Since the bed would contain the whole family, the bolster was probably used to demarcate areas of it. Even as Geoffrey watched, the sleeping man groaned and murmured some inaudible words. Meantime, Will ignored his mother and father. He brushed past Chaucer and went to a corner of the room. He crouched down and busied himself about some activity.

'Have you come to report on him, sir?' said Mistress Morton. 'He's sick. Celler knows he's sick and cannot work.'

Celler? She meant the cellarer of the priory.

'He tried to get up this morning but his legs would not stand him,' continued the woman. 'He was sweating and very feeble.'

'What is the matter with him?'

She shrugged. 'Fever. He has had it ever since he was down underground.'

'It's all right,' said Geoffrey, not sure what the woman was talking about. 'I haven't come to check on your husband. Anyone can see he is too ill to work. Can we speak somewhere private?'

Even as he said the words he realized that it was a foolish question. This was as private as they were going to get. Already the presence of an unfamiliar figure had caused the occupants of other dwellings to poke their heads out, perhaps alerted by the playing children. Geoffrey moved into the shadow of the Mortons' doorway.

'It is the wife of John Morton I wish to speak to.'

'John's wife? He has a wife over Chatham way. But they had a falling-out and so John has been living here with us for as long as there is work at the priory. He is brother to my Simon.'

She nodded towards the man in the bed. Then, realizing the drift of Chaucer's words and picking up on his half-whispered tones, she said: 'Something has happened, hasn't it? Something's happened to our John?'

'I'm afraid so.'

Swiftly Geoffrey explained the circumstances of her brother-in-law's death. He thought it best to give her an unvarnished account. A fight of some kind in the inner court of the priory – and even as he said this, he realized he didn't know whether there had been a fight or a simple, unprovoked attack by the claw-handed Adam – which had resulted in a shocking death. In truth, there wasn't very much more to say. Mistress Morton dropped the leather bucket, and dirty water splashed over their feet and leggings. She stood wringing her hands. She swayed against the doorpost. Will looked up at his mother from the corner where he was still crouched.

'I knew it,' she said.

'Knew what?'

'Ever since they were working down in that cursed place, in that cellar, and brought back—'

The woman stopped herself and put a hand to her mouth. Chaucer noticed that she was gap-toothed.

'I don't understand, Mistress Morton. What cursed place? Brought back what?'

'They were down in the cellar last week. It is ghost-ridden. There are bones down there. Bad fortune comes to all those who go there. I wish I hadn't picked out—'

Again the woman paused as if on the verge of saying the wrong thing. Then she went on: 'My husband Simon has been afflicted with a fever and now you say that John is dead and, look, I scalded my arm only the other day.' She rolled up the sleeve of her smock and displayed a stretch of raw, puckered skin. 'The boiling water leaped out and took hold of my arm,' she continued. 'It has never done that before. And John is dead, too, God rest his soul.'

Geoffrey thought that, in her grief, the woman must be confused between an ordinary household accident and a violent death. By this stage some of the other women from the row had come bustling out, together with their children. There was a mixture of curiosity and pity on the faces of the adults, more curiosity than pity perhaps. All the same Mistress Morton stepped out from the shadow of the doorway and as if by instinct went towards her neighbours, who immediately surrounded her. There was a moment's silence, which was broken by a babble of questions and exclamations.

Geoffrey was relieved. He reckoned he could leave it to the neighbours to comfort Mistress Morton, if comfort was what she 'required on hearing of her brother-in-law's death. Nor was it his responsibility to stay and tell John's brother, Simon. The sick man was surely incapable of understanding or, at the least, it would make the blow even worse to inflict the news on him in his current state. Simon Morton was well out of things.

Geoffrey began to walk back in the direction of the

priory. He hadn't gone far when he sensed someone behind him and felt a tug on his sleeve. It was Will, the dead man's nephew. Looking at the smile on his freckle-filled face, Geoffrey grasped that the boy really was a little light in the head. He was all cheerfulness. It was as if he'd forgotten about the fatal violence he'd witnessed in the courtyard. Probably he had. He held out his clenched hands, the backs uppermost. He nodded at Chaucer, as if to say 'you know what to do next'.

So Geoffrey tapped the boy's right hand. Delighted, Will flipped it over to reveal a palm which contained nothing but grime. The boy put his hands behind him and, after a bit of fumbling, brought them round to his front once more. Wondering how much longer he'd have to humour the lad but unwilling to turn his back on him, Geoffrey tapped the clenched left hand, which the boy promptly opened. Chaucer had been half-expecting the left hand to be empty, either because Will had switched whatever he was holding to the other one or even because he wasn't holding anything in the first place. So it was with a small thrill that he saw that Will had indeed been concealing an object.

Chaucer made no attempt to take it but bent forward to examine a ring, an old and dulled golden ring. It looked valuable.

'Very good, Will. You had me fooled for a bit,' he said. 'You should take that back to wherever you got it from. Run along now.'

In the back of his mind was the thought that if the boy was caught with the ring he might be accused of stealing it. But Will seemed to have no intention of running along. His cheerful expression was replaced by a look of disappointment. He thrust the palm holding the ring towards Chaucer.

'No, I do not want it. It's not mine. It's probably not

yours to give away either, Will. Put it back where you got it, I say again.'

But Will would not budge. He stood opposite Geoffrey, insistently proffering the ring. Over the boy's shoulder, Geoffrey could see the gaggle of neighbours still clustered about Will's mother. He wondered whether the ring had come from the Morton house. It didn't look like the kind of thing a mason's family would have. He remembered that the sick man's wife had said something about an item brought back to the house from ... from where? The cellar she'd also referred to?

As if in confirmation, Will said: 'Down among the bones.'

Once again he shoved his hand forward so that the ring was almost under Chaucer's nose and repeated 'down among the bones' in a strange singsong, as if the phrase was part of a children's rhyme. The simpler course would be to take the ring, Geoffrey decided. The odds were that it did not belong to the boy or to his mother or father. He could make enquiries inside the priory, without revealing how he'd come by the thing. He could pretend that he'd found it by chance (which was correct, in a way). He didn't want to get Will or his family into trouble. Unless one of them really was a thief, of course.

Chaucer plucked the ring from the boy's open hand, and the grin that split the other's face told him he'd made the right move in the game they were playing. He slipped the ring into a pocket. Will moved a pace or two back, then turned and ran off in the direction of home.

Baffled, Geoffrey resumed his walk to the priory. Passing the lay cemetery, he reflected that his hopes for peace and quiet in this place had been destroyed and then rebuked himself: a man had just died, after all. His own hopes didn't count for much against that. Passing through the outer gate he was unsurprised to see no sign of the hulking gatekeeper. With a murderer on the loose, the man had obviously decided to make himself scarce. The inner courtyard where the killing had occurred was empty too. There was still blood on the ground, already dried and fading in the sun. Chaucer noticed that his quill pen was where he'd left it on the block of stone. He didn't imagine he'd be resuming a quiet morning of writing. He thought for a moment of his house in Aldgate and wondered what his family was doing.

He walked on past the cloister. Everywhere was deserted. It was eerily silent. His thoughts turning to the claw-handed man on the loose, he was startled to see a figure rounding the corner of the monks' sleeping quarters.

But it was only Andrew coming towards him, the other mason. There was dried blood on his shirt from the cut he'd received as the killer escaped. Presumably he'd had the wound attended to in the infirmary.

'Have they caught him yet?' Chaucer asked.

'I do not think so,' said Andrew.

'I have taken the boy home,' said Geoffrey. 'His mother knows now. Perhaps you can tell her more.'

'Don't know much more than you, Master Chaucer.'

'What was the cause of the fight?'

'It was no honest fight but a coward's attack. Like I said, Adam was new to us. A surly bad-tempered fellow, out for trouble from the moment he started. Possibly he was bitter on account of his withered hand. He made fun of simple Will and then, when his uncle defended the lad, Adam turned on *him*. But if you ask me . . .' Andrew's voice tailed away.

'Yes?'

'. . . I can't explain it, but it was as though Adam was

looking for an excuse to go for John Morton. There'd been strong words before you stuck your head out of the window, Master Chaucer, and afterwards there was quiet for a bit while we got on with our work. Then Adam suddenly leaped on old John and did for him with a blow to the neck. With the chisel. I tell you one thing, though. No true mason would use his tools in that fashion. We masons are a peaceable bunch. He was no proper member of our guild.'

Geoffrey nodded. Andrew was right. You rarely saw a quarrel among the masons. Their work demanded skill and concentration and a kind of rhythm, a combination of head and hand. Perhaps the physical labour left them too tired for scraps and fights; perhaps the fact that they were frequently employed in building churches and other holy places sobered them. While Andrew was talking, a question had been running through Chaucer's head. He decided to trust the other man and ask it.

'Have you been working on a cellar recently?'

At once Andrew turned wary. 'A cellar, sir?'

'Mistress Morton told me that was where her husband caught his fever. She said it was a cursed spot.' Chaucer said nothing about the ring in his pocket which might have been retrieved from the cellar.

'Oh, that place,' said Andrew. He seemed to debate with himself whether to elaborate, then said: 'Yes, Master Chaucer, there are all sorts of tales told of it. I don't believe the prior himself would venture down there after dark – though it's always dark down there, of course. Yes, it's true. John and Simon were sent down to do some repairs by the cellarer, Brother Michael.'

'But not you or Will?'

'Will is a delicate creature. In truth, he is not fitted for much. Me and the boy were seeing to another job – a boundary wall. I prefer to work outside.'

'Not Adam either, the one-handed man? He wasn't working down in this cellar?'

'I tell you, Master Chaucer, Adam had been with us only a couple of days since Simon fell sick. I didn't know him from, well, didn't know him from Adam.'

Geoffrey sensed the mason's unease – or perhaps it was simple impatience with his string of questions. And, indeed, he could not have said exactly why he was asking them.

'Where is this, ah, cursed spot?'

'It lies under the cellarer's chamber on the other side of the cloister.'

Since the cellarer was the person in overall charge of provisioning, naturally there would be storage areas under his part of the priory. Geoffrey might have gone on to enquire exactly what 'tales' were told about the cellar, but at that moment there was a strange flurry of sound and Prior Dunton burst into view, accompanied by Brother Peter the librarian with other monks trailing behind. They were walking fast but turning to look behind them. At first Chaucer thought they were being pursued but, seeing him and Andrew, Richard Dunton changed direction.

'You've caught him? Or he's escaped, the murderer?' said Chaucer. He could think of no other reason for the strained expression on the prior's face.

'Oh, he has been caught – or escaped if you like,' said Richard Dunton. 'He's over there. In our cemetery. He's dead, too, now. Come and see.'

At this point, or shortly afterwards, Richard Dunton became concerned at the two deaths at Bermondsey Priory, not so much because of the events themselves but because of their effect on the priory's standing and reputation. Two violent deaths, with the second coming hard on the heels of the first. At least the claw-handed

Adam had had the foresight to die in a cemetery. Or rather he had been struck down there. Or had struck himself down. He'd climbed a tree in the graveyard, wrapped one end of a rope about his neck and the other around a branch. Then he'd toppled off the branch and hung there, slowly throttling.

Dunton and Chaucer had stood looking up at the body suspended from the branch of an oak. The face was livid, and the man's tongue poked like a stick out of his almost toothless mouth. His torso shivered and his feet swayed in the breeze. A few paces behind them stood Brother Peter, the librarian and sacrist. Chaucer had been surprised to learn that, in addition to his other duties, Brother Peter had charge of the burial ground. He was muttering and crossing himself at the sacrilege of a man committing suicide in the bounds of the cemetery. Keeping him company was the moon-faced monk who had the post of revestiarius.

'Well, he has met a quick retribution,' said Geoffrey.

'It had been better to have him arrested and brought to trial,' said the prior.

Geoffrey didn't remark that the result would have been the same: a noose tightening about Adam's neck until he expired. Nevertheless, Dunton was right. It would have been much better if the murderer of John Morton had been apprehended in the proper fashion. Now it rather looked as though the murderer had taken the law into his own hands. Geoffrey reached up and touched the trailing end of the black girdle wound about the dead man's neck. It was similar to the girdles that the monks used to secure their dark garments.

Richard Dunton was no fool. He nodded and said: 'I can see where your thoughts are directed, Geoffrey. But it would not be so difficult to come by one of those cords. It is obvious what has happened here.'

'It is?'

'This man Adam, overcome by remorse, flees to the cemetery, where he plans to die. He is already equipped with the cord that will snuff out his wretched life. While we are searching the place for him, he is quietly preparing himself for death. Remember Judas the Apostate, who hanged himself from a tree after betraying our Saviour. Remorse can call on the most unlikely men, and call quickly and unexpectedly too.'

'Judas had the use of his two hands, I believe,' said Geoffrey, indicating the withered hand of the man swaying from the oak.

'Men in despair can accomplish great and terrible things,' said the prior.

Yes, thought Chaucer, but not impossible things like clambering up an oak, crawling along a branch, fastening one end of a cord about his neck and the other around the branch, all the time employing only one hand. However, he could not have said for certain whether the dead man did not have some limited use of his left hand, and the prior was surely correct when he claimed that men in desperation can do things they'd be incapable of in normal circumstances.

'If only he had chosen some other place,' said Brother Peter, speaking aloud for the first time. 'Why did he have to choose this sanctified ground?'

'Hush now, Brother Peter. The circle is closed,' said Dunton. 'This man killed another man and now he has done away with himself, God rest both their souls. We must cut him down.'

He beckoned to a gaggle of lay workers who'd been standing at a distance, out of respect for the prior or the dead man or both.

'But why did he kill John the mason?' said Chaucer as they left the cemetery while the murderer's body was being cut down.

'I do not know. You were there. A quarrel, wasn't it?'

The prior suddenly broke off and said in a more anxious tone: 'You intend to report on this back at court, Geoffrey?'

And Chaucer, who'd been thinking of no such thing, said: 'You cannot keep it a secret.'

The reality was that, at court, no one would be remotely interested in a spat between a couple of artisans which had resulted in a murder and an apparent suicide. But it seemed to Geoffrey that Dunton had been too quick to declare the matter closed. If the prior hadn't been worried for the reputation of his house, he began to show some concern now.

'Very well, Master Chaucer, if you consider that there is anything . . . untoward . . . about this sad affair, then you are welcome to pry into it and ask questions. I know how much influence you have at court. Go where you like. Talk to whomever you wish. I shall even give the brothers dispensation if you need to speak to any of them. Ask away to your heart's content and satisfy yourself that this case is exactly what it seems, a vicious man who hanged himself after being overcome by remorse. Meanwhile, the life of this place must continue as though nothing has happened.'

Chaucer noticed the coolness and relative formality in Richard Dunton's tone. He thought that the prior was overestimating his influence at court but, of course, he didn't say so. It was a touchy subject. Any influence was largely because of the connections between his wife Philippa, her widowed sister Katherine Swyneford and John of Gaunt himself. Officially Katherine was resident in the Savoy Palace as *magistra* to Gaunt's children by his first wife, and unofficially she was there as Gaunt's mistress. The *magistra* pretence was necessary for Katherine because Gaunt's second wife – the noble Constanza, from the kingdom of Castile – lived under the same ample roof. It was because of her sister

Katherine's status that Philippa Chaucer and her family had been given choice lodgings on the south side of the palace overlooking the river, even though they'd recently moved back to Aldgate.

Chaucer wondered how far knowledge of the affair between John and Katherine had spread. Certainly it was whispered about at court. Had the rumours reached as far as Bermondsey Priory? Did people believe that Chaucer, because he was brother-in-law to the woman who was Gaunt's lover, had to be humoured? Or was Richard Dunton's belief in his 'influence' connected only to his reputation as a court poet? Whichever version was right, it was sufficient to open a few doors.

And opening doors was what Geoffrey Chaucer was about to do now. He slipped inside the entrance and peered at the precipitous flight of steps running down into darkness. This must be the place: the storage space under the cellarer's area of the priory, the place where John and Simon Morton had been sent to carry out some repairs before one fell sick and the other died prematurely.

He'd waited until the next call to prayer (the life of the priory continuing as normal) before searching out the spot first described to him by Andrew. He had a kind of licence to wander and investigate, yet he preferred to do it more or less unobserved. He had a particular reason for descending to this subterranean chamber. It was as a result of the hints dropped by Mistress Morton and Andrew the mason and a conversation with the cellarer, Brother Michael.

The monk who went by the name of Michael was a significant figure in the life of the priory, responsible not merely for overseeing provisions and fuel supplies but also for the upkeep of the house. The individual who held the position of cellarer or bursar had to be capable – and preferably devout – since his job entailed frequent absences and therefore exemption from other monkish duties. He was out and about in the world, dealing with suppliers and carriers. Chaucer had noticed the cellarer at supper the previous evening. Brother Michael conformed to the traditional, slightly hostile picture of the monk. He had a generous shape and a round, cheerful face. Chaucer was reminded of a tavern-keeper he knew in Southwark, a man called Harry Bailey, who was all teeth and smiles on the surface but shrewd and watchful underneath.

Later in the morning and after the discovery of Adam's body in the monks' cemetery, Brother Michael had sought Geoffrey out, no doubt under instructions from the prior. It was wonderful, thought Chaucer, what having a foothold in court – or being related to a royal mistress – could do. People became so willing to help.

'The prior says that you wish to know about Adam, Master Chaucer. I don't know much but I will tell you what I can if you come with me.'

They entered the cellarer's building on the western side of the cloister, and Brother Michael ushered Geoffrey upstairs to a well-appointed chamber. Chaucer was surprised to see there the lay person who'd been standing by the outer gatehouse and who had teased the simple Will. He was hovering in the region of a table piled with papers. He seemed about to speak to the cellarer when he observed Chaucer entering the room behind Brother Michael. The monk didn't trouble to keep the displeasure out of his voice when he said: 'What are you doing here, Osbert?'

'I thought I dropped something when I was here earlier, master, but I must have been mistaken.'

Osbert brushed past Brother Michael and left the

room, without looking either man in the eye. 'Insolent fellow,' said the monk. Then, without asking his guest whether he wanted a drink, he poured red wine into a goblet, which he passed to Chaucer, indicating that he should make himself at ease in one of the chairs. He filled his own goblet and sat down with a plump sigh opposite Geoffrey. Chaucer noticed a black cat extended on the windowsill, probably the one he'd seen earlier in the inner court. He waited. He was interested to see what approach Brother Michael would take.

'Of course, I took the man on only as an act of charity,' were the cellarer's first words. 'He said he had been working at one of our sister houses, St Pancras of Lewes. He said that his hand had been crushed by a falling block of stone.'

'You say "he said",' said Geoffrey. 'It sounds as though you didn't believe him.'

Brother Michael shrugged and spilled some wine on his habit. He didn't appear to notice. Like blood, the wine stain would hardly show. 'Master Chaucer, I am not a man of the world as you are. If someone tells me something, I tend to believe it. If a man comes to me desperate for employment and claims to have received an injury while working in the service of our order at another house, then it is almost my duty to see that such a person is accommodated. He had already applied to me once and I had turned him down because, to be truthful, I didn't much care for his looks. But when he asked again and since we were short-handed on account of sickness, I took him on.'

'Shouldn't it have been the responsibility of the Lewes house to show him charity in the first place, Brother Michael? And why did the dead man end up here in Bermondsey?'

'I don't know, Master Geoffrey, if I may call you that.

The man hinted to me that he had a falling-out with someone in St Pancras, and in view of the tragic events that have occurred here I think that that is more than likely. As for why he finished up in the priory, well, some men prefer to wander where their feet take them . . . and his feet brought him to Bermondsey. Another drink?'

Chaucer shook his head. The cellarer poured himself more wine. His large fingers were loaded with rings. Geoffrey was reminded of the ring still in his pocket, the one handed to him by simple William together with the comment about bones. Something about Brother Michael's story didn't altogether convince Geoffrey. Whether it was the cellarer's claim not to be a man of the world, a sure sign (in Chaucer's eyes) that the speaker was the opposite of unworldly, or whether it was his defensive readiness to explain why he'd taken on Adam, he couldn't say.

'We needed another man, you understand. One of the masons – what's his name? Simon – he was sick. Still is, I think.'

'I understand that Simon Morton fell sick with a fever after working with his brother in a cellar below here,' said Geoffrey. He was surprised, and gratified, at the change in Brother Michael's expression at these words. The broad, cheerful face closed up. Chaucer was again reminded of the Southwark tavern-keeper, the way Harry Bailey's expression would alter if there was a dispute over a reckoning. To conceal the change, Brother Michael carried the goblet to his full lips once more. When he brought it down again, he'd recovered.

'That's true. He caught a fever after working in the cellar. *Post hoc sed non propter hoc*, though. You understand me?'

'It was a coincidence that Simon Morton got sick, and nothing to do with what he was working on in the cellar. Yes, I understand. What were he and his brother doing, by the way?'

'Some stonework had given way down there. They were repairing it. They are masons, Master Chaucer. That is their job.'

'I hear there are tales told about the place.'

'This is an old foundation. It is built on dead men's bones. Of course, there are tales told about every corner of the priory. There is nothing remarkable about the cellar, nothing at all. Is there anything more you wish to know? I have a heap of business to attend to.'

Brother Michael gestured towards the table laden with papers and parchment. At some point during their conversation the black cat had removed itself from the windowsill and settled itself among Brother Michael's papers. Noticing this, the cellarer tut-tutted but made no move to shift the animal. Chaucer would have wagered heavily that the cellarer was not really concerned about the business he had to attend to. The cat would remain undisturbed as a paperweight. But he took the hint and got up to leave, thanking Michael for his time.

Yet when he was in the open air, he wondered what he'd achieved despite the undercurrents of the interview. The only help to an investigation was the ring which was still in his pocket and which might have been discovered in the underground room. So he armed himself with a lantern from his room and went in search of the entrance. It was easy enough to find on the western end of the cloister.

He descended the steep steps. At the bottom was a stout door. Half-hoping that it would be locked and so frustrate his search, he tested the iron handle. But the door wasn't locked, and it opened smoothly and silently to his touch. He jumped when he felt something brush against his leg. But it was only the cat, the large black cat he'd recently seen stretched at ease on Brother Michael's windowsill and among his papers. Now it was eager to get into the vault ahead of him. Be my guest, he thought. There's no accounting for taste, especially a cat's.

Holding up the lantern, Geoffrey emerged at one corner of what seemed by the uncertain light to be a long, rectangular chamber. Old sacking and fragments of wood were strewn along one side, while on the opposite side man-sized niches had been cut into the walls. Nothing at present seemed to be stored here, perhaps on account of the damp. It struck chill, and he could hear the drip of water. He should not stay down here long. The air was bad, bad enough to have put a man on his sick-bed. Geoffrey Chaucer felt uncomfortable. Was it because he felt like a trespasser even though the prior had given him permission to wander? Not just that, he decided. It was as if a weight was pressing on his shoulders. No wonder the masons didn't enjoy working here.

Nevertheless, now he'd got himself down here he ought to have a proper look for . . . for what? After a few moments of investigation with the lantern, Geoffrey thought he'd discovered the spot where the Morton brothers must have been doing their repair work. Most of the niches in the wall were veiled in cobwebs but a couple were clear. The mortar appeared fresher in these recesses, and there were crumbs of stone on the ground. He wondered why repairs were necessary, since nothing of value was stored in this place, then supposed that there was a risk of ground water breaking through the skin of stone and rendering the chamber quite unusable in future.

Geoffrey walked the length of the chamber, which was solidly vaulted. The cat accompanied him, then lost interest and went to investigate something in a dark corner. As Chaucer drew towards the further end, the sense of oppression grew stronger, and by the time he'd reached the wall he was almost gasping for breath for all that the chill in the air was increasing. He gave a cursory inspection to the wall that closed off the room. Curiously, it appeared to be of a later date than the other stonework. No, not later, he decided, looking more closely by the lantern-light. But finished more quickly and carelessly – the blocks were not so neatly aligned and the mortar was slightly crumbled. Lantern in his left hand, he put the palm of his right to the wall and at once removed it, as though the surface was either very hot or very cold (but it was neither). It was curious that the masons had not been instructed to carry out repairs here as well as on the niches in the longer wall. The only reason could be that there was no danger from water seeping through from the other side, and that therefore whatever lay beyond this wall was not earth but a hollow space or cavity. Geoffrey might have confirmed this by rapping on the wall, but something kept his free hand by his side. In any case this was not the area of the chamber which concerned him. There was no more to see at this end.

Thankfully, he turned back towards the entrance. His eyes were absorbed by the circle of light as he picked his way across the flagged floor, but he was abruptly aware of a dark flicker in the area at the bottom of the steps by the half-open door. All at once it occurred to him that he'd been foolish in descending to this chamber by himself, apart from the cat. But it was human company he had now, not company inside the chamber but beyond the door, which thudded to with a draught of air. Chaucer ran towards the door, but it was firmly shut by the time he reached it. He heard the scrape of a key being turned on the other side and then feet – very rapid feet – ascending the steps.

He rapped on the solid wood and called out. The black cat joined him and miaowed loudly. One of the brothers or lay workers must have been making a tour of inspection and observed the open door to the crypt. Without bothering to check whether anyone was inside he'd closed it and turned the key. Yet even as this inno-cent explanation ran through Chaucer's head, a more sinister one was keeping pace with it. This action was deliberate. Anybody coming to lock up would surely have glimpsed the light of the swaying lantern or heard the sound of steps within. But the decisive evidence was the running feet. No one honestly engaged on fastening doors would run away from the scene as if his life depended on it.

He tried the door again but it was well secured. Then he called out more loudly. Not a cry for help but 'Hey!' and 'Is anybody there?' He paused and waited for the sound of descending feet and rattling keys and the breathless apology that would follow.

No sounds came.

Geoffrey took a few deep breaths in an attempt to calm himself. He felt his skin crawling. Ever since child-hood he'd had a fear of being shut in. He did not relish being imprisoned in this place even for a few minutes. For it would only be a few minutes, surely, before someone heard his cries?

Then he recalled the thickness of the walls, built to last, built as if to muffle sounds. No one knew he was down here either, no one except the individual who'd locked the door on him. Geoffrey's absence would be noticed after a time, certainly. But would anyone come looking for him? And, if they did, would they trouble to explore a deserted, unused crypt? Wouldn't it be assumed that he'd simply decided to quit the priory, perhaps unsettled by the day's events? After all, he wasn't bound by the rules of the place. He was free to come and go. If he didn't appear at mealtimes, would Richard Dunton conclude that he had got fed up with his Bermondsey sojourn and returned to his wife and family across the river?

A sudden, grim vision flashed through Chaucer's over-active brain. The discovery of a starved, desiccated corpse after some weeks. It was an absurd image, yet not so absurd as to prevent him breaking out in a sweat. He renewed his pummelling on the door and his shouting. He listened. Nothing, apart from the drip of water some-where in the depths of the chamber and the bell for prayer resounding distantly – very distantly – outside. He might as well save his breath. There would be no one around to listen to him for the next half-hour or so.

He examined the candle in its socket inside the cylindrical lantern. It was reduced to a stub. It was the candle he'd been reading by in bed the previous night, trans-ferred by him from a candleholder to the lantern in preparation for this little expedition. It would have been prudent to have equipped himself with a fresh candle. Too late now. Unpleasant as it was being stuck down here, it would be many times worse being without any illumination at all.

Well, no doubt someone would appear in answer to his calls sooner or later, but in the meantime he must explore his temporary prison. The door was immovable but perhaps there was some other way in and out of the chamber. If he hadn't noticed it on his first inspection, then that would be because he hadn't been searching for it. And if he was going to find it, he needed the few remaining minutes of light from the candle stub. He made a more thorough tour of the vault, running the light over the walls and fetching up once more at the end wall. Again the sense of airless oppression grew stronger even as the candlelight began to give ominous flickers. Geoffrey was on the point of giving up and returning to the main door – the monks must surely have finished their prayers by now – when he felt a draught at knee height.

Geoffrey dipped down with the lantern and his heart leaped to see what he hadn't observed before, a small aperture at the base of the wall. He got down on hands and knees, observing that the black cat had rejoined him.

'Is this a way out?' he said to his companion.

Depositing the lantern beside him with care to keep it out of the draught, Geoffrey pushed his head into the opening. It was a little wider than his shoulders. A waft of dank, odorous air met his nose. The hole gave on to a kind of shaft, sloping down at an angle. He held the lantern over the hole to reveal ancient stonework. He could hear nothing but had the sense of water below. Probably the aperture gave access to the priory's drainage system. Somewhere, the descending shaft would connect to a system of channels which would eventually emerge into the open. The prospect of slithering down the shaft and then making his way like a rat through a besmeared and confusing network of underground passages, perhaps for hundreds of yards, did not appeal.

He had a choice. He could make his way back towards the main door and resume his attempt to get noticed, or he could launch himself down the stone shaft. At that moment the candle in the lantern gave a final flicker and went out, and a blanket of dark fell on the chamber. Geoffrey was still on hands and knees, debating. He felt the whisk of the cat's tail against his sweating face.

At the same instant, and to Chaucer's overwhelming relief, he heard a banging on the door and a voice calling: 'Is anyone there?' He shouted in reply and there was a jingle of keys and the sound of the door swinging inwards. A figure stood at the entrance. It was one of the brothers.

Geoffrey levered himself to his feet.

'Who's there?' said the monk.

'Geoffrey Chaucer, a visitor to your priory.'

'What are you doing down here?'

By now Chaucer had reached the door. He recognized the monk. It was the revestiarius, the young man who was assistant to old Peter and whose name was . . . what was it now? . . . ah yes, Ralph. The brother also recognized Chaucer as he drew closer to daylight, which reached the bottom of the steps.

'Why, sir! I did not know it was you.'

'A foolish error. I was exploring the place and stupidly got myself trapped in here somehow.'

The cat appeared and shot past the two men. Brother Ralph smiled and said fondly: 'Magnus, you foolish thing.'

Chaucer reflected on the appropriateness of the Latin name. It was a black barrel of an animal, well fed on kitchen scraps. He'd been on the point of describing how he'd been deliberately locked inside but something checked him. Better to treat it as an accident.

The young monk stood fingering the bunch of keys. He said: 'Someone reported shouting from down here. I dismissed his words, then thought I'd better make certain after all.'

'I'm glad you did.'

Brother Ralph glanced at the lantern which Chaucer was holding. 'You were searching for something?' he said.

'No, I was only curious to see this place. I have heard stories of it.'

'Stories?'

'Of spirits and hauntings and suchlike,' said Geoffrey.

He was truthful enough in claiming he had not been searching for anything in particular, but he grew a little uneasy to find himself blathering away about spirits. Brother Ralph said nothing but stood aside to allow Geoffrey to pass him and then secured the door to the underground chamber. They climbed the steps to the outside. It was early afternoon. The sun shone full into the inner court, giving Geoffrey a better glimpse of Brother Ralph. He was a short young man whose pale complexion was emphasized by his black habit. He had a bland, amiable look. Chaucer noticed the sacrist and librarian, Brother Peter, passing in the background. The sun caught Peter's spectacles, making them glint under his cowl. It was hard to tell but he seemed to be looking with curiosity at Geoffrey and Brother Ralph.

'Is that place down there your province?' asked Geoffrey, indicating the steps they'd just climbed. 'I thought the revestiarius dealt only in linen and hangings.'

'You are right, Master Chaucer,' said Brother Ralph. 'This whole area is the cellarer's and the sub-cellarer's, but I could not find them so I took the keys from their office. I must return them now.'

'My thanks, Brother Ralph. You saved me from an unpleasant stretch in the dark. I am well rebuked for my curiosity.'

What next?

For the second time that day Geoffrey passed through the outer court of the priory. The hulking gatekeeper was back in position. That is, he was leaning against the wall and picking at his teeth with a twig. Geoffrey wondered if it was the same fragment of wood as before. He halted opposite the man as though a thought had just occurred to him.

'Did you find it, Osbert?'

'Find what?'

'Whatever it was that you had mislaid in Brother Michael's chamber.'

As on the previous occasion, when he'd warned Osbert of the murderous fugitive, Chaucer was speaking more to discomfit the gatekeeper than anything else. Something about the man set his teeth on edge. But Osbert was ready to give as good as he got. Removing the twig from his mouth, he said: 'Where are you off to, sir?'

'To visit a grieving house.'

'Prior Dunton gave orders that no one was to leave this place.'

'That was when there was a murderer on the loose. Now he has done away with himself there is no more danger.'

'Done away with himself! Believe that and you'll believe anything.'

This chimed with Chaucer's own opinion. He approached Osbert. The deputy gatekeeper was almost a head taller. Yet Geoffrey was accustomed to dealing with people like this, people with a little authority who turned into jacks-in-office.

'What do you know, Osbert?'

'I know what I know.'

'I expect you do,' said Geoffrey, turning away. He hadn't gone more than a few feet before the other said: 'Don't you want to know what I know?'

'If you wish to tell me, man, then do so. Do not waste my time with riddling utterances.'

'You are going to visit a grieving house, you say. It is the Morton house you mean, isn't it? But the grief will not be that of a living brother for a dead one. Simon will not be so sorry at the death of John. The only sorrow there will be Mistress Susanna Morton's. Her you've seen?'

Again Osbert made the cupping gesture with his hands at chest height. Geoffrey nodded. The deputy gatekeeper licked his lips.

'I've seen 'em too, all unbuttoned and loose.'

'If I want dirty talk, Osbert, I can find better sources than you, more inventive ones.'

'Wait, sir. Listen. I've seen Mistress Morton down by the river. I came across her and him one morning lately, going at it hammer and tongs behind some bushes. That woman and her husband's brother, the one that's dead and gone. She saw I saw too. He didn't, he was too busy. But she saw me with her great goggle eyes over his heaving shoulder.'

'Did her husband know?'

The gatekeeper shrugged. 'He could smell it on her, I expect. She's loose in the hilts, that one. For all that she gives herself airs. That's on account of her parentage.'

Parentage? Chaucer recalled that Mistress Morton was supposed to be the daughter of a priest. But he wasn't going to indulge Osbert by joining in the slurs on the woman, especially over something for which she bore no responsibility. Instead he said: 'You've tried it on, too, haven't you, Osbert? You've chanced your arm with Mistress Morton.'

And not succeeded, he thought. Otherwise you would not be talking about the woman in quite these terms.

'So what if I have?' said the other.

'What has this to do with anything, though?' said Geoffrey. Then an idea occurred to him. 'Are you saying that Simon Morton wanted to harm his brother because of his wife's infidelity?'

'He wouldn't have the guts to do anything himself,' said Osbert. 'Little shrimp of a man who could only sire a half-wit. Could've been her, couldn't it?'

'Why would Mistress Morton want to get rid of her brother-in-law?'

'Perhaps she got tired of his great hands wandering all over her—'

At that moment a monk came out of the gatehouse door. It was Brother Philip, who had official charge of the outer gatehouse. He dipped his cowled head on seeing Chaucer. Osbert had the grace to look uncomfortable. He said to Geoffrey: 'And a good day to you, too, sir.'

Chaucer went through the shadow of the gate and turned right towards the artisans' dwellings. He pondered over what he'd heard from the gossipy, lascivious porter. He wondered whether Osbert was telling the truth about what he'd witnessed behind a bush on the river bank. Chaucer recalled something revealing that Mistress Morton had said when he had brought the news of John Morton's death. She'd referred to 'my John'. So was this whole business to be explained by domestic jealousy? Was that what Osbert was hinting at? Had Simon Morton discovered that his wife was carrying on with his brother ('He could smell it on her') and, lacking the nerve to take action himself, did he persuade . . . suborn . . . bribe someone else to do the job for him? Adam of the crooked hand? How would a poor mason have paid for such a desperate task? With a valuable ring, perhaps? Or was it Mistress Morton, trying to get rid of an importunate lover? She'd find it easier to pay Adam, and not with a gold ring either.

Geoffrey tried to get the sequence of events clear in his mind and almost straightaway dismissed the hypothesis. Because Adam had not been taken on at the priory until after Simon fell sick.

But wait: hadn't Michael the cellarer said that Adam had earlier approached him in the quest for work and been turned away? Was it possible that at some point before he fell ill Simon had gone to Adam and urged him to assail his brother, perhaps even to kill him? Andrew the mason had claimed that Adam seemed to be looking for an opportunity to go for John Morton. But if Simon – or even his wife – had hired Adam, then the murder had been carried out in a strangely public manner. Perhaps Adam had intended to provoke an attack, to pass the whole thing off as a brawl with unintended, if fatal, consequences.

This string of hypotheses seemed too vague. And anyway, they would never know the truth of it now that Adam was dead.

Geoffrey had mentioned to the insolent gatekeeper that he was planning to visit a grieving house. The idea hadn't entered his head until he'd spoken the words. But now he found himself re-passing the lay cemetery on the far side of the priory church. The somnolence of an afternoon in mid-summer extended itself across the scene. The far shore of the river was obscured in the heat haze. There were no boats visible nor was anyone there to observe his progress towards the door of the Morton dwelling. He knocked but did so gently, mindful of the sick man within. The door was unfastened and gave slightly under his hand.

Chaucer peered around the corner. The fire smouldered in the centre, a thread of smoke twining up towards the hole in the roof. The interior was hot and airless. It smelled of the sickroom, and of something else besides. The large bed contained the diminished figure of Simon Morton. Of Mistress Morton and Will there was no sign.

Geoffrey pushed the door further inwards. He called out, but in a muted way. There was no word or movement from the bed. But then Simon was a sick man, a feverous one. He must be asleep, still. Yet Geoffrey feared the worst. He advanced across the uneven floor of the chamber. As his eyes adjusted to the gloom, he could see Simon Morton lying on his back, outstretched beneath a thin, patched blanket. Whether he looked peaceful and at ease, as the dead are sometimes said to look, Geoffrey would have been unable to say. For the great bolster that he'd noticed earlier was now lying crosswise over Morton's face. That someone had deliberately placed it there and then held it down was shown by the deep indentations on either side. Chaucer wondered how long it would take a man to die under such circumstances. Not long, probably, given Morton's feeble state.

Geoffrey lifted the bolster off Simon Morton's face. It was heavy enough almost to stifle a man by its own weight. Morton's mouth gaped, but otherwise he did look as though he might have died in relative peace. Geoffrey was glad at that. He'd never seen Simon at close quarters, but he would have known him for John's brother by the prominent stripe of his eyebrows. The man had been murdered. There could be no question of suicide here.

Chaucer's first thought was that this deed might have been carried out by Susanna Morton. Easy enough to kill a weakened man, and with the nearest weapon to hand, the great bolster. Somehow this seemed too obvious an explanation, like the self-killing of Adam. Yet, if it had not been Mistress Morton (or her simple son), then it must have been an outsider. And if a stranger had come through the door, he surely ran the risk of being observed by someone from the other dwellings. There was no other way in.

But, Geoffrey suddenly noticed, there was another means of access to the Mortons'. In the back wall was a low entrance, covered by a piece of sacking that shivered slightly in the afternoon air. He had to stoop to make his way outside. At the back of the house lay a strip of land, planted with a few vegetables wilting in the heat. Each dwelling in the row had a similar patch of ground, no doubt tended by the women while their menfolk were off working.

On Geoffrey's right hovered the bulk of the priory church. As he was gazing at the central tower, the bell rang. He had lost track of the canonical hours. There was no one in sight on the patches of land, which were roughly delineated from their neighbours by rows of sticks or a few rags of washing.

A raised path ran along the back, parallel to the line of dwellings. It would not have been difficult for someone who knew which house they were searching for to gain access from this side, once they'd checked that the coast was clear. The Morton house was easiest to find since it stood alone.

Chaucer was reluctant to enter the dead man's house again. He did not need to gaze on Simon's gaping mouth for a second time. Nor did he want to emerge by the front door like a regular visitor. Instead he walked past the flattened stems of leeks and battered cabbages and turned eastwards on to the path, with the priory at his back. He was gripped by the desire to get away from this place. He regretted that he'd ever come here. For peace and quiet, ha! There had been two – no, three – suspicious deaths in the course of a few hours. An air of gloom and menace seemed to hang over all.

The area beyond the houses was flat and empty, save for a few clumps of trees and the odd, even more ramshackle hut or hovel. The tide was coming in, and the river seemed to be on the verge of spilling over on to the adjoining land. Geoffrey wondered who had taken the decision to site the Cluniac house here all those hundreds of years before. And why. Because of the remoteness of the spot? For its closeness to the river? Or was it for the great expanse of sky, which might inspire pious thoughts?

He saw two figures walking along the river foreshore. They were hand in hand. A young couple, he thought at first, but as they drew closer he recognized Mistress Morton and Will. The mother was leading the lad. They must have been out fishing, for the boy was carrying a kind of net attached to a pole, which he toted on his shoulder. In her other hand the mother was grasping a bucket, perhaps to hold whatever they'd caught or scavenged on the foreshore. Cockles or winkles perhaps. Tuneless sounds were borne through the air. The boy was singing.

They had not noticed Geoffrey Chaucer and he turned inland off the track, putting the rise of the ground between himself and the mother and son. He felt a pang at the thought of what they'd discover when they returned to the house. He debated for a moment warning them, but the fear of being the bearer of bad news for a second time that day – and the stronger fear that he might be implicated in Simon Morton's death (hadn't he been first on the scene following the murderer?) – held him back.

If he'd had the suspicion that the wife could have disposed of her husband by pressing the bolster over his face, then it was dispelled by what he'd just seen, mother and son returning innocently from a fishing expedition.

No woman could murder her husband and then go for a walk with her son, surely? He had thought Mistress Morton impatient with her Will, but here she was escorting him by the hand and he was singing.

Geoffrey felt guilty even for suspecting her. And with the guilt came anger. He determined he would get to the bottom of whatever it was that was happening at Bermondsey Priory. He owed that to the woman who'd lost both husband and brother-in-law within the space of a few hours. He hastened back in the direction of the priory. He would squeeze the truth out of the one man he'd talked to who seemed to know more than he'd let on.

'You have one last chance to tell me what you know, Osbert. After that, I shall go to the justice.'

Chaucer spoke more in regret than with menace. He'd already hinted at his position at court and implied that he had the power to have Osbert summarily dealt with. He even gestured vaguely towards the other side of the river and dropped a reference to the white-towered castle which stood there, as if he had the authority to whisk Osbert across the water. He hadn't, of course, but how useful those connections with the Savoy Palace could be!

The two men were in a kind of cubbyhole off the outer gatehouse. There was an unglazed slit of a window, which did nothing to dispel the stale, sour air. This was where Osbert lived, as was shown not only by the smell but by the palliasse in one corner and a small chest in the other, doubtless containing a spare shirt and leggings. For a deputy gatekeeper in a religious house must look presentable. Not that Osbert would be entrusted with the task of ushering in important visitors. That would be left to Brother Philip, who'd welcomed Chaucer the previous day. But Osbert would do to receive – or turn away – the flotsam who always wash up at the doors of a great institution like the priory.

Now Chaucer was attempting to put the fear of God or of the law and the royal court into Osbert. It seemed to be working. He'd said nothing about the latest death, that of Simon Morton.

'Come on, man. Your story about Simon Morton wishing to do away with his brother was balderdash, wasn't it? There was no such plot.'

'I said only what I thought.'

'You said what you'd like to think, maybe. But the truth is that you wanted Mistress Morton for yourself. You claimed you'd seen her and her husband's brother together—'

'Oh, I did, sir. See them, see them going at it hammer and tongs.'

'You told her what you'd witnessed, didn't you? You said she'd seen you. You probably said that if she didn't, ah, do what you wanted, then you'd expose her.'

Osbert's grudging silence showed Geoffrey that he was on the right lines. He pressed home his advantage. 'So what was her reply?'

'She laughed in my face. That woman has the dirtiest laugh this side of Gravesend, sir. Laughed and said that no one would believe me.'

'So to get revenge on Mistress Morton or just to cause mischief, you insinuated that her husband had cooked up some plot to hire a killer for his brother. And then for good measure you said she might have done it.'

'Insinuated, sir? I don't understand the word.'

'But you get my drift. You invented a plot where none existed.'

'There is a plot, all right. I admit I made up what I said about Simon Morton. Fellow wouldn't hurt a fly. But there are funny goings-on here in the priory.'

'There are funny goings-on everywhere. You're telling me nothing.'

'Ask Brother Michael.'

'The cellarer?'

'That's the one. He knows what's going on. All I know is that a few days ago I was in here and heard the Morton brothers as they were passing through the gateway. They were arguing. Not about Mistress Morton but about something they'd found during their work. They stopped right outside that window there. I was lying on my bed and I heard it all.'

'What had they found?'

'A parchment with writing on. And something else of value. I couldn't tell what from their words. It might have been a brooch or a ring.'

Despite the stuffy air inside Osbert's room Geoffrey felt a chill. A ring? Like the one that still nestled in his pocket?

'What would a parchment mean to the masons? They wouldn't be able to read it.'

'No, sir. But they knew it was important because it had a seal attached and it was old.'

'So why were they arguing?'

'Over what to do with the items they'd dug up.'

'Dug up? You're sure of that?'

'They had been working in a cellar somewhere. They were having words about whether to keep what they'd found or to hand them over to one of the monks. Perhaps there'd be a reward, one of them said. It was John's voice, I think.'

'How does Brother Michael come into this?'

'You'd better ask him.'

'That's what you were doing in his chamber today, wasn't it? You were going to see what you could get out of him.'

Osbert shrugged. 'He won't talk to me but he'll talk to a gentleman like you. All I know is that I saw Brother Michael talking to John and Simon Morton. Saw them talking in a quiet and private place one evening.'

'Quiet and private.'

'As the grave. They were in the graveyard.'

Osbert nodded his head in the direction of the cemetery that accommodated the lay folk, the one beyond the main gate.

'You were spying on them.'

'A man may be out and about for an evening stroll and see things. You can't blame his eyes for seeing.'

'What did his eyes see?'

'They saw money change hands between the monk and the masons. A purse was given by him to them. Why, I ask myself? If you want to know more, you must ask Brother Michael.'

In the event Brother Michael was willing enough to tell Geoffrey why he had been having surreptitious dealings with the Morton brothers. It seemed that the cellarer of the priory had decided that it was less dangerous to reveal things than to attempt further concealment, particularly after Geoffrey told him that Simon Morton had also died. He implied that it was from sickness and not murder. He hinted, too, that he'd heard of dealings between Michael and the dead masons. Hearing of the second death, Brother Michael crossed himself and sat in silence for a moment. But it was only when Chaucer produced the ring, given him by Will, that Michael sighed, leaned back in his chair and nodded. He reached for the ring, which Chaucer held out. It was perhaps not as splendid as any of the ornaments circling his own fingers, but the monk scrutinized it for a long time.

'Where did you get this?'

'I believe it came from the vault beneath this place.'

'Most likely it did. It is old, like the testament.'

Geoffrey waited. He reckoned that if Brother Michael was going to say more, then he would do so unprompted. The cellarer held the ring between thumb and forefinger and peered through it, as if it were a keyhole.

'Most likely, this, too, belonged to Brother James.'

'Brother James? I have not met him but his name is familiar.'

'No more have I met him, Master Chaucer, since Brother James has been dead two centuries and more. He was buried down there in the vault all those years ago. I had no idea he was there when I gave orders for the stonework to be made good. The masons discovered some bones when they went to repair the recesses in the wall. There were bones and a skull together with fragments of monkish garb, and evidently this ring, which I have not seen before. The Morton brothers must have kept it back. It doesn't matter now. The remains didn't matter either. They were what you might expect to uncover in any holy site which is old and which has lain undisturbed for centuries. I gave instructions that the bones and cloth fragments were to be resealed in the wall. What mattered was the testament which was found with the bones. From the seal and the signature we knew that it belonged to Brother James.'

'He died violently?'

'I do not believe so. There were no marks of violence on the skull or other remains. And, in fact, his testament shows that he was expecting to die a natural death very shortly after he wrote it. He was more than seventy years old.'

Geoffrey suddenly recalled where he had heard the name of Brother James before. He was one of the monks who'd been walking on the banks of the river and witnessed the miraculous appearance of the Bermondsey cross, dropped from the beak of a giant and mysterious bird. Hadn't the prior, Richard Dunton, mentioned an account or testament that Brother James had left? Was it this, or a copy of it, to which Michael was referring?

'The masons informed me of their discovery, as was their duty. But they held back two items. This ring, it seems. And the document. No doubt they were wondering how to profit by it.'

'The document was in Latin, surely?' said Geoffrey. 'How could they know its contents. They would not have been able to read.'

'You are right, more or less. One of them, Simon, could read a little but only words in English. Somehow, though, the two men had got hold of the idea that Brother James's testament contained matter that was both valuable and dangerous. A day or two after the discovery of the bones, they came to tell me what else they'd found, half in the spirit of discovery, half in the desire to see what they could gain by it. They did not produce the document but merely hinted at what it contained. I told them it was all nonsense, that they should at once hand over what they'd found. It was the property of the priory. I think that Simon Morton might have been persuaded. He already looked sick and feverish and he said the vault was a cursed place. But John Morton wasn't so easily swayed. He is an outsider from Chatham way. "What's in it for us?" he kept on saying. So in the end I agreed to give them something in exchange for the testament.'

'You gave them money?'

'Yes. I met them in the lay cemetery. They had visited this office once too often, and I preferred to see them outside the priory. Simon Morton looked sicker than ever. I don't think he came back to work after that. Much good the discovery did him or his brother, and now they will both finish in the place where we met.'

'You have the parchment still?' asked Geoffrey, glancing at the pile of papers on Michael's desk.

'It is destroyed. I burned it on instructions from the

prior. But I would have burned it anyway without his say-so.'

'Whatever it contained must have been ... "dangerous" was your word.'

'It was dangerous, in its way. I do not mind telling you, Geoffrey, as a man of the world. But I would be obliged if you did not spread the story abroad. If you did, then it would be denied by us.'

'Us?'

'The Cluniacs of Bermondsey, the few who know what was contained in Brother James's testament.'

'As long as it is nothing seditious or connected to wrongdoing, I'll keep quiet,' said Chaucer. 'And since the man who wrote it is long dead, I don't see how his words can be seditious or criminal.'

'They were not. Rather they were righting an old wrong – as Brother James saw it.'

'Where is the harm, then?'

'You've been to Winchester, Geoffrey? You have seen the great table which is in the castle there?'

Geoffrey shook his head, but he understood what the monk meant by the Winchester great table. It was reputed to be the very board at which King Arthur and his knights had sat in the ancient days of romance and chivalry, a table that was circular so that none of those sitting at it would be able to claim precedence over the others. However, he wondered what Brother Michael meant by raising the subject.

'The round table is supposed to be many hundreds of years old,' the monk continued. 'Supposed by the ignorant, that is. But I have heard that it was made much more recently and that our present king, Edward, is glad enough to bask in the reflection of its lustre. For chivalry is all his care, or it was during his days of health and vigour. You must know this, Geoffrey, you who spend so much of your time in the royal courts.'

'I do know this. What I don't understand is how it's connected to the testament of a dying monk.'

'I mention the round table to show how things are not always as they appear. Objects may be thought old or hallowed when they are nothing of the kind.'

'You are referring to the Bermondsey cross, are you not?' said Chaucer, sensing Michael's reluctance to get to the quick of the matter. 'Brother James was one of the monks who witnessed its miraculous appearance on the Thames shore. He left an account of it, according to the prior.'

'Brother James left two accounts of the discovery of the cross. One of them is in our library even now, the story of the great bird and the precious object dropping from its beak and the shaft of sunlight and so on. It was dictated and signed by the three monks who witnessed the miraculous, ah, descent of the cross. This is the story that is enshrined in the history of our priory.'

'Richard Dunton told it me only yesterday evening,' said Geoffrey. 'He spoke as if it was the undisputed truth.'

'I've no doubt the prior says only what he believes,' said the cellarer. 'Men are able to convince themselves of what they need to believe. Yet it was only days earlier that Brother Richard instructed me to burn Brother James's testament – his second testament, that is, the old parchment that was found in the vault. You can guess what it contained, Geoffrey?'

'I have a good idea by now.'

'The story of the Bermondsey cross was a fiction from beginning to end. There was no great bird, the cross never fell from the sky, there was no shaft of sunlight pointing like a celestial finger to the spot where they discovered it. If you've seen the cross, then you'll know that there is nothing very remarkable about it. Only the circumstances of its appearance give it meaning. One of the three brothers probably had it already in his possession. However they came by it, they planted it on the river shore then concocted the legend of the bird and all the rest.'

'In God's name, why?'

'Not for profit, not for fame either. Remember that these were the early days of the priory. We were an obscure foundation, hundreds of miles away from our origins over the sea in France. What better way to put the place on the map than to chance across a miracle that sanctified the place? And Bermondsey did become famous on account of its cross. Not for that only, of course. We have achieved much over the past two centuries and by God's grace survived and prospered. But the devout are still drawn here by the miraculous cross. It has served its purpose and it will do so in the future. And who can say that, by this time, the cross has not acquired some sacred tinct, whatever its history.'

'But Brother James told the truth in his dying testament? He described how the cross had actually been found – or planted.'

'Yes. Before he died he wanted to set the record straight. His conscience pricked him as he was preparing for his deathbed. I do not know whether he wished the testament to be sealed up with his bones or whether it was done on the orders of the prior at the time – or, indeed, whether it was no more than chance that everything was buried together. But the secret rested with him until it was uncovered by two masons carrying out some workaday repairs.'

'How many others know of the testament?'

'A handful. Brother Peter, who keeps the library. He has been agitated about it and keeps badgering the prior. Prior Dunton himself, of course. But this is not something to share with the brotherhood at large. We should not disturb belief without good reason. Those who know will say nothing. I am relying on you to say nothing, Geoffrey.'

'And the Morton brothers cannot speak for they are both dead.'

'Coincidence. One was killed in a brawl by a reprobate who has done away with himself, pricked by his conscience.'

Chaucer raised his eyebrows. Seeing his scepticism, Brother Michael said: 'Who can tell what a man *in extremis* will do, except that they will be great and terrible things? And the other brother has died of natural causes, you say. He was a sick man. I saw him white and shivering in the graveyard. For sure, he caught his death in that vault beforehand.'

He did catch his death on account of that place, thought Chaucer, but perhaps not quite in the sense that you mean. He remembered the man on the bed, the great bolster pressed down hard over his gaping mouth. It was ... convenient ... that all those lay persons who were aware of Brother James's testament were not around to blab of it. But to Brother Michael he said nothing of his suspicions.

'So the matter is closed now?' said the cellarer.

'It seems so.'

Brother Michael sighed again, this time with satisfaction. He clenched his fist around the ring, which, throughout the conversation, he had been rolling between the thumb and forefinger of his left hand. Then he held out his right. Geoffrey extended his. The monk might have been plump and somehow soft-looking, but he had a strong grip and held Geoffrey's hand for a fraction longer than necessary as if to reinforce his words. Then the cellarer said that they would no doubt meet at supper in the refectory, and Geoffrey took his leave.

* * *

When Geoffrey agreed with Brother Michael that the matter was closed, he did so because there seemed to be no prospect of discovering any more from the cellarer. Chaucer regarded himself as a fairly shrewd judge of people and considered that Michael had given him all that he knew, after an initial show of reluctance – the monk's reluctance understandable because the affair of the false cross – or, more precisely, the false legend of its appearance – did not reflect well on the priory. There was an irony, however, in the fact that even if the 'truth' became widely known it would probably make little difference to the value and attraction of the relic. Why, the prior himself already seemed to have reverted to the legend, judging by what he'd told Geoffrey the previous day. In the same way he'd jumped to the convenient conclusion that the death of the claw-handed Adam was a suicide.

As Brother Michael had said, people convince themselves of what they need to believe.

All of this, however, did not necessarily clear up the three deaths – of the Morton brothers and Adam. If Chaucer hadn't witnessed for himself the stifled corpse of Simon, he might have accepted that the business was finished. It was like a tapestry in which each of the threads was neatly woven to make up a picture, albeit a crude one. Adam had killed John because he was a violent, bad man, and then done away with himself in contrition. Meanwhile, Simon had died from natural causes – an impression that Chaucer had done nothing to counter. In reality, the tapestry wasn't finished. There were some loose threads.

One of the threads was to do with the circumstances of Adam's 'suicide'. Geoffrey didn't accept that the man could have hanged himself. He could not have assembled the noose and slipped it over his neck with a withered hand. Then there was the strange episode when Chaucer had been shut up in the vault beneath the cellarer's quarters. Someone had slammed the door and turned the key and run away. But why? To give him a fright? To keep him out of the way? Or even as a roundabout way of disposing of him?

Yet it was something else that tugged at Geoffrey's thoughts as he wandered about the priory grounds. It was late afternoon. In the distance, to the south and beyond the flat river lands, the Surrey hills could be glimpsed through the haze. Chaucer struggled to pin down what was bothering him.

It was to do with the testament that had been written (or dictated?) by Brother James as he neared his death while his conscience was pricking him. The testament told the true story of the Bermondsey cross. A testament now destroyed by Brother Michael. No one would ever read it again. Perhaps Brother James had never intended it to be read in the first place. Merely writing it down would have been sufficient to clear his conscience. The document would have been penned in Latin, of course. Latin was the language of monks and priests and other learned persons. Geoffrey himself had translated work from Latin. That ancient language was the natural choice of educated people, especially two centuries ago. It could not be understood by the common folk, which was one reason for using it.

Yet the masons, Simon and John Morton, had somehow grasped the contents of James's testament. How had they managed that? Only through one of the Bermondsey monks, surely. Yet none of the monks would have revealed the secrets of a dangerous document to a couple of artisans. Rather they would have gone to some lengths to keep it out of their hands, as was shown by Brother Michael's willingness to pay the Mortons for the recovery of the testament.

So, if not one of the monks, who might have deciphered the Latin document – or at least made some rough sense out of it? And he suddenly recalled what he'd been told of Mistress Susanna Morton. That she gave herself airs, that she was a cut or two above the other womenfolk dwelling near the river. That she was reputedly the illegitimate daughter of a priest. Priests could read and write Latin. Was it possible that a priest who'd fathered a child might – out of guilt or a sense of responsibility or even out of affection – have tried to foster some learning in that child of his? Have tried to pass on the rudiments of another language, of Latin? Could it have been Mistress Morton who had unpicked the secret of the testament and told her husband or the brother-in-law, who had in turn taken their knowledge to Brother Michael in the hope of gaining by it?

Chaucer struggled to recall Mistress Morton's words when he'd escorted Will home and given her the news of John's death. She evidently regretted something. She'd said, 'I wish I hadn't picked out . . .' before breaking off. He'd assumed she was referring to some object, perhaps the ring Will had presented to him. But supposing she'd meant to say 'I wish I hadn't picked out the words'? The words of Brother James's testament, the words that revealed the truth of the miracle of the cross.

Had she passed the secret on, or fragments of it, to her husband and her supposed lover?

If so, they hadn't gained much by it, as Michael had pointed out. They would shortly be buried in the graveyard. But Mistress Morton was still alive . . .

And at once Geoffrey Chaucer turned around and half-ran through the inner court and then the outer one. As he passed through the gateway, two thoughts flashed through his head: firstly, that he was not created for running and was already out of breath, and, secondly, that he must reach the Morton house before Mistress Morton, too, was murdered.

The man slipped along behind the raised path, which ran parallel to the workers' dwellings. He was not completely concealed from anyone working on the garden patches, but fortunately no one was about at the tail end of the afternoon. This was the second time in a single day that he had made a foray outside the priory and to the same house. On the first occasion he had waited until the woman and the lad had left the place. They were going fishing, the boy carrying a net. That meant they would be gone for some time.

The man waited until they were no more than tiny figures on the foreshore before he crept through the back entrance to the house. Inside, the air was fusty and sickly. Simon Morton was lying on the bed, scarcely breathing, it seemed. For an instant the man debated leaving nature to take its course. But, no, that was too risky. Giving himself no time for further thought, he heaved the bolster from where it lay by the sick man's side and pressed it down over Morton's face. The body under the blanket twitched and there was a sound somewhere between a groan and a gurgle, and then nothing more. But the man kept his hands firmly in place until there could be no chance of Morton ever waking up again. Then he retreated by the route he had come, forgetting in his haste to remove the bolster from the dead man's face. He strode back in the direction of the priory, heart beating hard and breath coming short, but curiously satisfied. Duty done, and for the second time.

He had already overseen the death of Adam, the man with the crooked hand whom he had hired to dispose of John Morton. He had met Adam in the monks' graveyard. It had been comparatively simple to catch

Adam off guard, to slip the girdle over his head and pull it tight and tighter yet. An unholy glee filled him during the act. His legs were shaking as Adam's slack body fell to the ground. Then he had hurriedly set the scene to make it appear as though Adam had killed himself.

The man would not have believed that he could have found the strength to kill another human being and then arrange his body just so. Yet in an hour of crisis strength comes from somewhere. Had the prior not said that men in despair can accomplish great and terrible things? It was a gift from above . . . or the other place. The man dismissed the thought. He had done his duty, that was all. When this was finished he would get absolution, he would cleanse himself.

With the deaths of John Morton, then Adam and now Simon, all those who knew the story of the cross were dead. All, that is, apart from the very few Cluniac brothers who were privy to the secret. And they would not talk.

When the man had heard the story, the supposed true story, of the origins of the cross, he had been outraged. It was as if a segment of the sky had fallen to earth. At all costs, the cross must be defended and the story of its origins suppressed. Those who had uncovered the secret must be silenced. The priory was in mortal danger and all measures were justified. Even God himself would wink at the act. Unwilling at first to do the necessary work himself, the man had approached Adam, recognizing his desperate and bitter character. He had envisaged a silent act, a killing conducted with decorum. But Adam had disposed of John Morton in the crudest and most public manner. Therefore it was necessary to deal with Adam. Once the man had surprised himself by finding the deed easy enough, the killing of Simon Morton followed naturally.

And with that the man thought it might be over. Absolution alone remained. Cleansing.

But then he turned to puzzling over how it was that two simple masons had understood the words of a Latin document uncovered in a vault. Too late, he recalled the gossip, familiar enough in the priory, that Mistress Morton was the bastard child of a priest. Too late, he considered that having such a man for a father – a wicked man who had defaulted on his duty – might mean that it was the woman who was at the root of all this trouble. Women were at the root of the world's ills, beginning with Eve. And now there was this one, the offspring of a priest. Susanna Morton, well named after the woman in the Book of Daniel whose beauty had tempted the elders into gazing on her naked, bathing body. Susanna might have unpicked the secrets of Brother James's testament. No sooner had the thought occurred to the man than it hardened into a certainty. It was Mistress Morton who was responsible. She had read what she shouldn't have read. She, too, would have to be dealt with. Even as he strode along, the man fingered his girdle, which he would use around the woman's white throat. Something in him relished the close quarters he would have to engage in to dispose of Susanna.

So now the man crossed over the path at the point behind the Morton house. It was fortunate, he told himself again, that the place was set a little apart from the other dwellings. But what was this? Far from the quiet of the afternoon, there was a throng of people around the Morton hut. Neighbours and even a couple of monks. Her foolish son was there too. Too late, the man recalled that Mistress Morton would have returned to find her husband dead. He almost giggled to think how fast he had forgotten that earlier murder. These people had come to condole with her. He could do nothing to her at present. He'd have to wait for a later opportunity.

He made to turn round and came face to face with Geoffrey Chaucer.

'Brother Ralph,' said Geoffrey.

Chaucer just about managed to pant the words out. He was red-faced and running with sweat.

The young man paused indecisively. Guilt and rage were written across his usually placid face like the mark of Cain.

'What are you doing?' said Geoffrey.

The monk seemed to consider the question before saying: 'I am doing my duty. What are you doing?'

'You were in on the secret, weren't you?' said Geoffrey after a time. 'The true secret of the Bermondsey cross.'

'I heard about it from Brother Peter. He was deeply troubled.'

'But not as deeply as you,' said Geoffrey, reflecting on how he'd recently thought of himself as a good judge of men. But there really was no way to winkle out a man's inner self from his appearance. Here was Brother Ralph, innocent and bland-seeming but with the fire and fury of a fanatic. He already knew the answer, but for form's sake he said: 'Why did you carry out the killings?'

'I have already told you. Duty. To defend the cross and the priory.'

'They do not need defence of the kind you have given.'

'I should have left you shut up in that vault. The chances were that you wouldn't have been found for several days. Nobody goes down there. It is a cursed place.'

'Why did you let me out?'

'Not you, Master Chaucer. It was Magnus the cat. I knew I must have left him shut inside. He should not be shut in to starve.'

Geoffrey did not know whether to laugh or weep in the face of this murderous man who had already done two others to death and was undoubtedly on his way to kill a woman but who could still care about the life of a cat. He was about to call out to the cluster of individuals around Mistress Morton's hut for assistance in apprehending Brother Ralph. But the monk anticipated him and took to his heels, running not in the direction of the low houses nor back towards the priory but eastwards towards the river. As he went he shouted out something about 'cleansing waters'.

Chaucer set off in pursuit, but Ralph was younger, fitter and faster. He reached the edge of the shore. The mud was thick here, and he waded across it with difficulty, sploshing through the incoming tide. Geoffrey stumbled and fell on his face. Above him he heard the beating of wings and a shadow passed across. He glanced up but the bird, which he couldn't identify, was already flying higher. He watched as Brother Ralph reached the end of his glutinous passage across the mud and stones and then, deliberately, waded into the fast-flowing water. His black garb billowed out, then only his head and a single arm were visible. The man's white hand was the last of him that Geoffrey saw, a white and delicate hand.

Returning at the end of this long and murderous day to his lodgings in the gatehouse, and after supper in the refectory, Geoffrey noticed that the quill pen remained where he'd placed it at the start of the morning on a block of stone. He wondered who'd complete the work on the wall cavity now. He had said nothing about the details of the death of Brother

Ralph, though it transpired in conversation with Prior Dunton that the young monk had the reputation of being 'odd'.

'His mind must have been turned by all the deaths we have witnessed here today,' said Dunton. 'In a frenzy he threw himself into the waters of the river. Pray heaven that Ralph's death will be the last.'

'I think it will be,' said Geoffrey.

'We will say a Mass for his soul,' said the prior, 'and for those others who have died in Bermondsey today, of course.'

Nor did Chaucer mention the great bird that had passed overhead as Brother Ralph reached the waterline. A gull, probably. What else could it have been on the Thames foreshore? In fact, he mentioned nothing at all at supper in the refectory (there are advantages sometimes to eating in silence). Instead he slipped inside the great church after supper and before the hour of compline. Once again the church was almost empty, the summer evening fading in bright colours beyond the great west window. He went to gaze on the cross behind its grille. The cross was small, barely significant. As Brother Michael had said, its value lay not in itself but in the tale of its discovery.

Geoffrey Chaucer reflected on the two stories, the legend of the miraculous bird which had dropped the object from its beak and the more prosaic account of a band of monks who'd wanted to bring some fame and credit to the priory. Did it matter which was true? Not to him perhaps, but it was important enough to have caused a string of deaths. And now he alone was in possession of the secret. That Brother Ralph had hired Adam to dispose of John Morton, then himself killed the claw-handed man before going on to stifle Simon Morton. And no doubt Ralph would have done the same for Susanna Morton if he hadn't been intercepted by Geoffrey. He remembered Ralph's parting words about 'cleansing waters'. God knows, if you cannot read a man's face, how can you interpret what goes on in his head? Well, the fast-flowing Thames received everything and everybody cast into it, the pure and the impure, the innocent and the sinful, without distinction.

Geoffrey wondered whether the widow Morton would be without a mate for long. He didn't think so. She had too many attractions. But he did not intend to stay in Bermondsey Priory to find out. He'd had enough. He'd make his excuses to the prior and leave Bermondsey tomorrow morning and get back to the domestic bustle of the Aldgate gatehouse. Get home for a bit of peace and quiet. Why, he might even be able to do a bit of writing without the distractions of murder.

And as he was retrieving his pen, Geoffrey Chaucer remembered that early that morning before the murders started he'd had an idea for a poem. The subject had slipped his mind now. What was it he intended to write?

ACT FIVE

I

April 1663

Bermondsey House was a jagged black mass against
the night sky when Captain John Browne arrived for
his clandestine meeting with the conspirators. It had
rained all day, though the deluge had petered out after
dusk, and the air was rich with the scent of damp earth
and wet blossom. The house, built on the site of a
once-powerful monastery, had fallen on hard times.
Its stocky Tudor chimneys listed at odd angles, its roof
sagged, and boards replaced the glass in many of its
windows. Its grounds were in an equally sorry state.
What had been a stately avenue of oaks was now a
dismal tunnel of dead wood and ivy; the fish ponds
had decayed into treacherous bogs, and the orna-
mental gardens were a chaotic sea of nettles, bram-
bles and weeds.

Browne shuddered as he rode along the driveway.
He was not an impressionable or a sensitive man – the
long-suffering crew on his ship *Rosebush* could attest to
that – but there was something eerie and forlorn about
the house. When the wind whispered through the trees,
Browne thought he could hear voices, and that they
were those of long-dead medieval monks, hissing accusations and recriminations. He took a deep breath,
pushing such fanciful notions from his mind, and
turned his thoughts to the night's business. What he

was about to do was wildly dangerous, but he trusted his friend and fellow sea captain Dick York – and if York said it was important for him to meet the powerful shipping magnate William Hay, then that was good enough for Browne.

He jumped in alarm when an owl hooted nearby, and wished a more respectable time had been chosen for the assignation. Then he grinned at his own foolishness. That was impossible, given the subject that was to be aired – the hours of darkness were the only time for such treacherous transactions. The location was perfect too – this desolate, lonely, half-forgotten place that looked as though it was already full of brooding secrets. Browne considered what he had managed to find out about Bermondsey House before agreeing to the meeting.

William Hay did not own it – that honour went to some wealthy nobleman, who lived elsewhere and who never bothered to visit. Instead, it was rented to the Castell family, members of whom had been tenants for decades. Old Will Castell had been a talented shipwright, and he had originally leased the mansion as a statement of his commercial success. After his death, his fortune passed to his grandson, who promptly lost everything to his penchant for gambling. Creditors now snapped at the younger Castell's heels, and Bermondsey House was falling into decay for want of basic maintenance. To make ends meet, Castell hired out his home to men like Hay, who paid handsomely for the privilege of conducting devious business away from prying eyes.

And if anyone did ask questions about what went on inside Bermondsey House, then there were always the ghosts to blame. Browne had been told tales involving ancient coroners, ex-Templar Knights, Oxford scholars and even the poet Chaucer, who had delved into dark matters involving murder, theft and deception. People were superstitious about the site and perfectly willing to attribute odd happenings to the shadowy world of spirits and demons.

Yet even so, Browne was uneasy. He had never met Hay or Castell and did not know if they could be trusted, so he had brought two sailors from *Rosebush* to protect him, should matters turn nasty. He did not trust them, either, if the truth be told. The navy had not been paid since the Restoration of the monarchy three years before, and the only men left in it were those incapable of getting decent work elsewhere. Browne glanced at the two men who jogged along beside his horse. He had chosen his cooper, Ned Walduck, and a big, stupid sailor called Tivill, both surly villains who knew how to fight. He was under no illusions regarding their loyalty to him, though – they had agreed to come only because he had promised them two shillings apiece. Browne had never bothered to make himself a popular captain – he believed that winning the affections of his men was a waste of time – and it was the money that would induce Walduck and Tivill to defend him, should the need arise that night.

He dismounted, tossing his reins to Tivill, and was about to knock on the front door when it was hauled open. The man who stood there was probably in his thirties, but a life of debauchery made him look older. He reeled drunkenly, a mass of courtly ruffles, collars and lace, as he slurred a welcome. Castell, thought Browne in distaste, the man who had squandered his inheritance on vices and pleasure. Behind Castell was an elderly, shabbily dressed crone who was smoking a pipe. At first he assumed she was a servant, but when she shoved her lantern into Castell's hands and barked an order, Browne realized she must be Margaret, wife of the old shipwright and grandmother of the dissipated creature who tottered and grinned on the doorstep like a halfwit. Browne's misgivings intensified. Could such folk be trusted? After all, treason *was* a capital offence. He looked around for evidence that York had arrived, but it was too dark to tell.

'Come in, come in,' hiccuped Castell. 'I would offer you wine, but I have just finished it.'

'Why does that not surprise me?' muttered Browne, making no move to enter. His horse, sensing his unease, began to prance. Tivill struggled hopelessly to control it, while Walduck sniggered at his shipmate's ineptitude. Then Browne heard footsteps hurrying towards them, coming from the direction of the darkened grounds.

'Walduck,' snapped Browne, furious when the cooper made no effort to defend his captain but continued to laugh at Tivill. 'Your two shillings is set to become nothing, unless you tend to your duties. Draw your sword, man, and be ready to fight.'

'There is no need for that,' said Castell soothingly, while Walduck glowered resentfully at the reprimand. 'We are all friends here – you do not need men to protect you.'

'I shall make up my own mind about that, thank you,' snarled Browne. He squinted into the darkness, hand on the hilt of his sword, as he tried to see what kind of person was approaching. The figure came closer, revealing itself to be short, plump and obsequious. It wore a tight-fitting long-coat that was absurdly out of date and a wide-brimmed hat with a feather stuck in it, as if the man imagined himself to be a youthful Cavalier. Browne felt his jaw drop in astonishment as he recognized the fellow. 'Jesus wept! Is that Thomas Strutt?'

Walduck was equally shocked, chagrin forgotten. 'It is! Our old purser, God rot his thieving soul!'

'Shall I run him through?' asked Tivill, abandoning the horse to draw his sword with one hand and a dagger with the other. His eyes gleamed at the prospect of violence. 'He supplied *Rosebush* with rancid meat and stale biscuits last year, and we had no choice but to eat them.'

Walduck shuddered at the memory. '*And* he cheated us over gunpowder. He said we had thirty barrels, but there were only ten – and the lie almost saw us killed when we met them Dutch pirates.'

They were right, and Browne's misgivings about the night's venture intensified. Hay probably *did* need all the men he could get to help him remove the king and his government from power, but surely he knew better than to recruit a dishonest, unreliable fellow like Strutt? *Rosebush*'s old purser would sell his own mother for a cup of wine, so would think nothing of betraying would-be conspirators. Abruptly, Browne decided he wanted no more to do with Bermondsey House and its secrets.

'There has been a misunderstanding,' he said to Castell. He turned towards his horse. 'I should not have come here tonight – I *would* not, had I known villains like Strutt were involved.'

Strutt started to object to the insult, but someone emerged from the shadows near the door, where he had been listening unseen. William Hay, owner of the Hay's Wharf Company, was a small, neat man, who wore a massive yellow wig – a headpiece almost large enough to verge on the ridiculous. His clothes were made of dark red satin, cut tight to the waist to show off his figure and then flaring out into a froth of lace and frills around his knees. His shoes were small, buckled and elegant, and as far from Browne's practical riding boots as it was possible to be.

'You should hear what I have to say before you leave,

captain,' he said softly. 'It will be worth your while, I promise. Come, the others are waiting.'

Against his better judgement, Browne followed Hay along a weed-infested path that skirted the house's east wing. The two sailors were at his heels, and Strutt trailed behind them; it was too dark to see whether Castell or his grandmother had joined the procession. Tivill was again trying to soothe the agitated horse, although with scant success, because he was attempting to do it without sheathing either of his weapons. Walduck was scowling, because the purser's unexpected appearance had put him in a black and dangerous mood.

At a point where the shadows were thickest, Hay opened a door to reveal a flight of steep, slime-coated stairs. Browne balked. He disliked enclosed spaces, and a cellar was not his idea of a suitable place for a meeting, seditious or otherwise. Anger began to replace nervousness. He was damned if *he* was going to be enticed underground in company with the likes of Thomas Strutt. He glanced behind him and saw other figures beginning to converge on the door, too, all cloaked and hooded. Evidently, other conspirators were beginning to assemble.

'I have had enough,' he snapped, his nerve – and temper – finally breaking as he backed away. 'Good night, Hay. Do not contact me again.'

Suddenly there was a sharp crack, and he felt himself stumble, although there was no pain. He was aware of falling to the ground and of blurred, indistinguishable voices echoing around his head. He tried to open his eyes, but all he could see was blackness. Then the voices faded, and he knew nothing at all.

II

Late June 1663

Thomas Chaloner, spy for the Lord Chancellor of England, was pleased when Captain Browne's widow provided him with an excuse to leave London for a few days. The weather was unseasonably hot, and the city's sewage-splattered streets baked and sizzled under an unrelenting sun. Streams and brooks ran dry, tar melted on the ships moored along the Thames, and Chaloner's attic rooms in Chancery Lane were like tiny furnaces. The Lord Chancellor was preoccupied with weighty affairs of state and barely looked up from his paper-strewn desk when Chaloner asked if he might spend a few days across the river on business of his own. He waved a chubby, lace-fringed hand, and said Chaloner could do what he liked, just as long as it did not involve another interruption.

So Chaloner packed a bag and left the sweltering metropolis for the cooler pastures to the south. Or so he thought. He soon learned that Bermondsey was every bit as torrid as the city, and because its inhabitants also used their streets as sewers and rubbish dumps there was no improvement on the stench, either. Furthermore, the reek of urine-soaked hides from Bermondsey's tanneries was pungent enough to make his eyes water and mingled unpleasantly with the more earthy aroma of heat-spoiled beer from the riverside breweries.

While he walked, Chaloner thought about Hannah Browne. They had met when Hannah had accompanied her husband on one of his voyages, and Chaloner had been a passenger, en route to one of his overseas assignments. Ships demanded a lot of time from their captains, so Hannah was bored and had often sought out Chaloner's company. To pass the time, he had taught her to play the flageolet, though she had never been very good at it. Browne had been delighted with her new skill, though, and had encouraged her to play for him almost every night. It had revealed a softer, more attractive side to that cruel and uncompromising man.

Hannah Browne's letter had asked Chaloner to meet her at Jamaica House, a large, rambling inn with its own bowling green. He pushed open the door, then waited for his eyes to adjust from bright sunlight to the dimness of the room within. Although the window shutters had been thrown open in the vain hope of catching a cooling breeze, the tavern remained dark and gloomy. It smelled of spilled ale, smoke from its patrons' pipes, and sweaty, unwashed bodies.

Chaloner spotted Hannah immediately. She was sitting near the empty hearth, fanning herself with one of the newsbooks that had been left on the tables for customers to read. It warned loyal citizens about the threat of a new Parliamentarian uprising, although no one in Jamaica House seemed overly concerned about the notion of rebellion. Chaloner could not help but notice that the government's official publications had been variously used as beer mats, wedges to combat wobbly tables, and even as a plate for the large pig that obligingly disposed of any leftover food.

Hannah was staring at the ashes in the grate, grief and worry etched into her face. She was an attractive lady in her forties, with brown hair and pale blue eyes. Her flowing skirts and bodice – black, to indicate mourning – were patched and darned, albeit neatly, which was unusual for the wife of a successful and prosperous sea captain. Chaloner wondered why she was willing to be seen in garments that would normally have been passed on to the servants. Did she think she had donned some sort of disguise? If so, then the ruse had failed, because she held herself in a way that would tell anyone that she hailed from a wealthy home. She did not notice Chaloner until he was next to her.

'Thomas!' she exclaimed, resting a hand over her heart to indicate he had made her jump. 'I thought working in England, instead of hostile foreign countries, might have cured you of your penchant for stealth.'

Although stealth *was* a talent Chaloner had honed during his decade employed as a spy, he had certainly not practised it on Hannah that day. He had approached her table openly, and it had been her own preoccupation that had led to her being startled. He was sorry she still mourned Browne so deeply, but not surprised. She had been devoted to her husband, despite his many shortcomings – the spy thought Browne gruff, impatient and opinionated, and he had not liked him at all.

'Your letter sounded urgent,' he said as he sat next to her. 'What can I do for you?'

'You were John's friend,' she replied quietly. 'He told me many tales that involved him ferrying you to enemy countries and landing you under cover of darkness for the purpose of spying.'

'Did he?' Chaloner was unimpressed. The close relationship between the captain and his lady should not have included him sharing information about government affairs – information that even now might be dangerous for Chaloner and the other intelligence officers who had used *Rosebush* for their work. And Chaloner would not have called Browne a friend, either, though their adventures together had made him a colleague of sorts. It was that fact which had prompted Chaloner to respond to Hannah's summons – espionage was dangerous, and there was an unspoken agreement among spies that they would look after each other's families in the event of a mishap.

'John saved your life once,' Hannah went on. 'You were charged to steal some valuable documents in Lisbon, and he lingered offshore longer than was safe, waiting for you to return. He was obliged to use his cannons to help you escape in the end.'

Chaloner refrained from pointing out that Browne had been paid handsomely for the risks he had taken. 'You do not need to remind me of his courage to make me help you,' he said reproachfully. 'I would have done it anyway – assuming it is within my power.'

Hannah looked sheepish. 'I apologize, but I am at my wits' end, and you are my last hope. You see, John was murdered by someone who hurled a stone at him. He lay insensible for two days, and then he died without ever waking.'

'I heard,' said Chaloner gently. 'It must have been hard for you.'

Hannah regarded him oddly. 'What did you hear exactly?'

Chaloner tried, unsuccessfully, to determine what she wanted to know. 'Just what you said – that a drunken seaman threw a rock and knocked him out of his senses.' He did not add that he had been sceptical of the story, because he knew from experience that it was difficult to lob such missiles with sufficient force and accuracy to kill.

'The man *alleged* to be responsible was *Rosebush*'s cooper, Walduck. The jury was told that he killed John when in his cups, so did not know what he was doing.

At the trial it emerged that John was not a popular captain and his crew disliked him.'

'He was a strict master,' acknowledged Chaloner carefully. This was an understatement – Browne had been a martinet who had terrorized his people, and the spy was not surprised that one had decided to exact revenge in a moment of ale-fuelled madness. Then he frowned, puzzled. 'I have met Walduck. He *is* a violent lout and might well strike a superior. However, I also recall that he – unusually for a seaman – never touches strong drink. Are you sure they have the right culprit?'

Hannah slapped her hands on the table, hard. 'At last! Someone who questions what is being passed off as the truth! No, I am *not* sure they have the right culprit. In fact, I am certain they have the *wrong* one. Walduck was hanged the same day that he was found guilty, and, as far as the authorities are concerned, that marked the end of the matter.'

'The same day?' echoed Chaloner, startled. It was very fast, even for London.

'With what *I* considered unseemly haste. And there is a second inconsistency in what the jury was told – namely that John was murdered *here*, at Jamaica House. However, I know for a fact that he was going to meet a man called William Hay at Bermondsey House that fateful night.'

Chaloner found this evidence less compelling. 'Perhaps Hay changed the venue at the last minute, and your husband never had the chance to tell you.'

'Not so. The taverner is *certain* John was not here that night. He is an observant man, and I trust his memory. However, when he offered to testify at Walduck's trial, he was told it was unnecessary.'

Chaloner was beginning to be unsettled. 'Do you think your husband's death had something to do with his involvement in intelligence work? Someone wanted his silence about a voyage he made, and murder was the best way to ensure it?'

But Hannah shook her head firmly. 'I think it relates to his assignation with Hay. Hay does not live in Bermondsey House – it is the home of a destitute gambler called Castell. I asked around and learned that Castell will do anything for money. He often lends out his mansion for shady purposes.'

'Your husband was meeting Hay for shady purposes?'

'In a manner of speaking. Like many Londoners, Hay objects to the way in which the government squanders money on itself while the country is neglected. Did you know the navy has not been paid in *three years*? Hay thinks England would be better served by a different government.'

Chaloner regarded her in alarm, appalled that she should be confiding such matters in a crowded tavern. 'Lower your voice! If your husband did meet Hay with the intention of joining some treasonous plot, you would be wise to pretend you knew nothing about it. The government is terrified of rebellion, and you may find yourself stripped of everything you own in retaliation—'

Hannah interrupted him with a brittle bark of laughter. 'If only there was something for them to seize! John invested our entire fortune in a cargo he was going to transport to Jamaica, and his untimely death means we have lost everything.'

Chaloner supposed that explained her shabby clothes. 'You think his murder is connected to this investment? Someone killed him to prevent him from profiting from it? Do you suspect Hay?'

'Hay had nothing to do with our cargo. And before you ask, John was no rebel, either. He swore an oath of allegiance to king and country when he joined the navy, and he was a loyal servant. He went to Hay's meeting to *expose* the traitors, not to join their ranks.'

Chaloner was not sure whether to believe her. 'I see.'

'It should have been easy – attend a gathering, learn the names of the malcontents and turn the whole lot over to the government. But John was killed before he could act.'

'He was murdered because someone suspected his motives? One of the plotters?'

'It seems likely: Hay is a rebel, so perhaps *he* killed John when he realized John was *not* of a like mind – and Walduck was made a scapegoat for the crime so no awkward questions would be asked.'

Chaloner considered her theory. It was only five years since Cromwell had died, and Hay would not be the only man yearning for a return of the Commonwealth. The government was its own worst enemy in that respect, because there was little in that debauched, quarrelsome, ambitious rabble that inspired confidence, and rumours of wild drinking, gambling and womanizing were rife. London objected to subsidizing its vices with taxes, and Hay might well have decided to take matters into his own hands. Dispatching suspected infiltrators would be an obvious precaution to take, because Hay and his co-conspirators would face certain execution if their plot was exposed.

'Will you look into the matter?' asked Hannah when Chaloner did not reply. 'Please?'

Chaloner thought about it. Any threat to the government was a threat to its Lord Chancellor, so he, as the Lord Chancellor's spy, was duty-bound to investigate. Unfortunately, he suspected that Browne's intentions had not been as honourable as his wife believed. He knew for a fact that Browne had harboured anti-government sympathies, because he had confided them once during a drunken dinner at sea. Hence Browne might have been murdered *because* he was a rebel, not because he was attempting to unmask traitors, and if Chaloner did investigate, he might expose that fact. He was sure Hannah would not appreciate having *that* aspect of her husband's character revealed and made public.

'You owe John a favour,' pressed Hannah when he still remained silent. 'A debt of honour. I am asking you to repay that debt and find out who really killed him. I appreciate it is likely to be dangerous, given that you will be probing into the affairs of would-be dissidents and they will do all they can to keep their necks from the noose, but you must try.'

'Why did you wait so long before writing to me?' asked Chaloner, keeping his concerns about Browne to himself. 'Your husband died in April, and it is now June. Trails will have gone cold, witnesses been bribed or silenced, and evidence destroyed. It would have been easier to explore the matter immediately.'

'Because I had suspicions but no proof,' explained Hannah. 'But all that changed yesterday. John's meeting with Hay was arranged by his friend Captain York – another man eager to expose treachery. York went to sea within days of John's death, but he is home now. *He* does not think Walduck is the killer, either, *and* he has questions about the speed of Walduck's trial and execution.'

'I will need to talk to him.'

Hannah smiled for the first time. 'You will help me, then? Thank you! York is waiting nearby, in the grounds of Bermondsey House.'

Hannah led the way through the crowded streets, travelling south. Behind them the noonday sun glinted on the river, which was sluggish and depleted by the drought upstream. Some of the houses they passed had gardens, but most were ramshackle affairs that arched across the narrow streets above their heads, so only a narrow ribbon of blue sky was visible between them. Prostitutes made lewd offers in loud, brash voices, and sailors roamed in drunken bands. Chaloner wondered whether any were from *Rosebush*, which was still waiting for a replacement captain to be appointed. Rumour had it that no one wanted the post – her crew was notoriously mutinous, and it was common knowledge that only hard, bullying men like Browne would be able to master them.

In a surprisingly short period of time, Hannah and Chaloner had left the houses behind and were walking along a hedge-fringed lane that boasted rolling fields to either side. The air was sweet and clean, and a soft breeze whispered through the ripening crops.

'Bermondsey House,' said Hannah, stopping outside a dilapidated metal gate. Her voice trembled slightly. 'The place where John was attacked.'

At the end of an unkempt drive was a Tudor mansion that Chaloner knew had once been visited by monarchs. It was an elegant array of stocky chimneys, patterned brickwork and tiny gables, but it screamed of neglect and decay. Saplings sprouted from its roof, ivy climbed its walls and the whole edifice exuded the impression that it might give up the ghost and collapse at any moment.

Hannah opened the gate and led the way along the path that led to the main door. Halfway up it, she glanced around carefully, then ducked into a thicket of holly bushes, pulling Chaloner behind her. She followed a winding track until she emerged in a wood-land glade. A man stepped out of the trees to greet her. He was portly, florid of face, and wore the kind of hard-wearing coat and breeches often favoured by sea captains. Chaloner had met him before, when York had been serving under Browne on *Rosebush*. The two sailors had been good friends, and the spy recalled thinking uncharitably that the fondness had probably arisen from the fact that no one else had wanted anything to do with a pair of such opinionated, arrogant tyrants. York nodded a curt greeting at him, then turned to Hannah.

'Well? Will he do it?' The captain's hand was on the hilt of his sword, and Chaloner was under the impression that he might try to use it if the answer Hannah gave was not to his liking.

'Thomas has agreed to help us,' replied Hannah. 'You can trust him. He is loyal to the government, and – like my poor John – eager to expose these vile traitors.'

York regarded her unhappily. 'I sincerely hope so, because what you have told him may see *me* cracked over the head with a rock too.'

Hannah's expression was not entirely friendly. 'It is a pity you did not have the same consideration for John when you embroiled *him* in this nasty affair.'

The expression on York's face was one of deep guilt. 'I have already explained that. I would *never* have involved him if I thought he might be harmed. I assumed it was a case of taking names and leaving the rest to the government – in essence, I thought we could both be heroes, but without risk to ourselves. My intention was for him to share my glory in unmasking this plot, and I am appalled that he is dead when I thought I was doing him a favour.'

Hannah turned abruptly and walked away. Tears glittered, and Chaloner saw that she was torn between wanting nothing to do with the man and needing his help. York watched her for a moment, then indicated that Chaloner was to sit next to him on a fallen tree trunk.

'She does not believe Walduck murdered her husband, and neither do I.'

'Based on the fact that Walduck was unlikely to have been drunk at the time?'

York nodded. 'He never took anything stronger than water. The lawyers at the trial kept harping on the fact that Browne was an unpopular captain and that most of his crew – including Walduck – would have relished the opportunity to dash out his brains. Hannah does not believe it, but it is true. You sailed with Browne, so you know I am right: he was a hard taskmaster.'

'Then perhaps Walduck killed Browne when he was sober but hoped that saying he was drunk would save him from the hangman's noose.'

'Walduck was not *that* stupid – he would have known drunkenness was no defence.'

'Why was he accused in the first place?'

'Because he had the misfortune to be there when the murder took place. Browne had hired him and another sailor called Tivill as bodyguards. However, both seamen were carrying swords and knives, so why would Walduck have used a stone to kill Browne when he had far more familiar weapons to hand? Besides, Walduck was a greedy man and would never have harmed Browne before he had been given the two shillings he had been promised. If Browne had been killed on *Rosebush* that night, I would have said Walduck was as good a suspect as any. But here, before he had been paid? Never!'

'How did the meeting with Hay come about in the first place?'

York sighed. 'Last winter, Hay chartered my ship to transport a consignment of lead pipes from Ireland. It struck me as an odd commission, so I looked inside some of the crates. They contained muskets. Obviously, no one brings guns to London for innocent purposes, so I decided I had better find out what was going on. I thought such initiative might see me given a decent command, instead of the lumbering barges the navy foists on me these days.'

'And?' asked Chaloner when York paused.

'And I asked Hay to dinner, then made one or two treasonous remarks under the pretext of being drunk. The next day I was invited here, to Bermondsey House, to meet others who dislike the current government. Unfortunately, I was unable to learn their identities. I was about to give up when Hay suggested I bring other like-minded seamen into his fold.'

'Why would he do that?'

'So I could prove my commitment to his cause, I suppose. And because captains with ships are a valuable commodity in the world of rebellion. Most naval vessels are fitted with cannon, after all.'

'So you confided in Browne?'

York nodded. 'He is – was – one of few men I trust. He was going to help me discover the names of the men involved, then we were going to pass the information to Spymaster Williamson – the man in the government responsible for dealing with sedition.'

'Are you sure Browne thought foiling Hay's antics was a good idea?'

York stared at him. 'Of course I am sure! Browne was no traitor! Do you think I would have asked him here if he were? He railed against the government's incompetence, of course, but who does not?'

Chaloner rubbed his chin. Was that all Browne's drunken confidences aboard *Rosebush* had been – an indignant objection to an inept ruling body? Was Browne loyal to the king after all?

'But he was killed before he could help you,' he said. 'Were *you* there when it happened?'

'My horse went lame, and I was late for the meeting. By the time I arrived, Browne was dying and most of the conspirators had left.' York looked deeply unhappy. 'This is too dirty a business for me. I have done my duty now – I have told a government intelligencer about the plot, and that is all that can be expected of me. I shall return to my ship and—'

'You will stay and work with Thomas,' countered Hannah sharply as she rejoined them. She had composed herself, although she was pale. 'You will introduce him to Hay as a man interested in joining his rebellion, and you will remain with him until he has enough evidence to hang them all. That is what John was going to do – at your instigation – and that is what *you* will do now.'

York mopped his brow with a dirty handkerchief. 'I thought Hay and his cronies were just a group of men with more money than sense – that it would be easy to infiltrate them and put an end to their plotting. I wish to God I had never embarked on the matter.'

'Well, you did, and now it is time to put it right,' said Hannah harshly. 'Tell Thomas what you have arranged.'

York's expression was haggard, and Chaloner was impressed that Hannah was able to bully the man – York was no weakling, to be intimidated by just anyone. 'I told Hay that I might bring a Captain Garsfield to meet him today – Garsfield is one of the names you used when you sailed with Browne. Hay wanted to know why you were willing to see the government overthrown, so I told him your sister had been despoiled by the Duke of Buckingham. It was the first thing that came into my head.'

Chaloner regarded him uneasily. As a spy, he was

used to assuming false identities, but he preferred to invent them himself. He did not know enough about ships to be able to answer detailed questions about the sea, and he would be caught out unless he was careful. However, using Buckingham as an excuse for resentment was clever – the lecherous duke was unable to walk past a pretty woman without attempting to seduce her, and complaints from outraged brothers and fathers were myriad.

'Hay is expecting us this afternoon,' said York when Chaloner nodded cautious agreement to the plan. 'And there is to be a gathering of traitors at midnight.'

Chaloner left the glade only when he was certain that Hannah and York had no more to tell him. Both had theories about the identity of Browne's killer, and it was not easy to distinguish between fact and supposition. Eventually he managed to deduce that there were six possible suspects for the murder. First, there was Hay, the rebel leader. He had two deputies named Strutt and Parr. Strutt had once been purser aboard *Rosebush*; apparently he had proved to be dishonest, and he and Browne had ended up hating each other. Meanwhile, Parr had also crossed swords with Browne in the past, although Hannah and York did not know how or why. Both had been at Bermondsey House the night Browne had died, although only Strutt had exchanged words with him. Then there was Castell, who lent his home to anyone willing to pay – and Chaloner knew from gossip at White Hall that he was an unscrupulous rogue. And lastly there were the two sailors, Walduck and Tivill, one of whom had already been hanged.

'This is sheer madness,' said York when Hannah had gone and he and Chaloner were heading for Bermondsey House's main door. 'Browne was *murdered*, so why should *I* put my head in the lion's mouth too? You are a skilled intelligencer. Can you not listen at a few doors for the answers Hannah wants? I will wait in the nearest alehouse, and we will report to her together tomorrow.'

'Listening may not be enough. We shall need to ask questions too.'

'*You* ask them, then,' said York firmly. 'I intend to distance myself from you, lest there is trouble. After all, one of us should be alive to tell Hannah that her demands were unreasonable.'

Chaloner was not surprised to learn that he could not count on help from York, but he was still disappointed in the man. However, York kept fiddling with the elegant lace on his bib-like collar, a gesture that revealed increasing agitation, and Chaloner suspected that he would not make for a reliable ally anyway. As usual, it was better to work alone.

While he walked along the overgrown path, he thought about what he had learned. Had Browne really been killed because Hay or one of his followers realized he was there under false pretences? Or had Browne embraced the cause rather too eagerly, which had been regarded as equally suspect by the conspirators? He glanced at the man at his side, wondering whether *he* should be regarded as a suspect too. Was York loyal to the government, as he claimed, or had *he* killed Browne when he realized his friend intended to run to the spymaster with his tale of treason?

They reached the door, and their knock was answered by an elderly woman who was smoking a pipe. York murmured to Chaloner that she was Margaret Castell, grandmother to the current tenant. She wore a threadbare wig, the heel of one boot was tied on with twine, and she looked as dilapidated and disreputable as the house in which she lived.

'Have you brought it?' she demanded without preamble. 'The gunpowder you promised me?'

'Gunpowder?' echoed York with a nervous gulp. 'I promised you no gunpowder.'

'You said you have a ship,' snapped Margaret impatiently. 'And ships have cannon. When I said I was in need of a few barrels of powder, I thought it was obvious that I was giving you a hint.'

'Well, I did not understand your hint, madam,' said York, alarmed. 'I am a plain-talking man and not one for sly innuendoes. But we have business with your grandson. Where is he?'

'Out gambling, I imagine,' said Margaret coolly. 'Or drinking with his sottish friends.'

Chaloner sincerely doubted it. It was common knowledge that Castell did not have two pennies to rub together and that anyone drinking with him would be obliged to settle the bill themselves. Further, no one would accept him at a gambling table, because he was incapable of paying the debts he already had, let alone any he might incur in the future.

'Why do you want gunpowder, ma'am?' asked Chaloner curiously. Surely, *she* could not be part of the rebellion? If so, then Hay's plot was more of a joke than a genuine threat.

'The stable is falling down, which means it is useless, so I thought I might as well use the bricks for repairing the kitchen. It is cheaper to blow up a building than to hire labourers to demolish it, and we need to be careful with the finances these days. Speaking of money, you owe me a shilling for your usual chamber, York. Payable in advance, of course.'

She held out her hand, and York dropped the coin into it. He hastily added another when sharp black eyes expressed their disapproval at his meanness.

'It is hot today,' he said, sidling past her into the

relative cool of the hall. 'So I shall go to my quarters to freshen up. I am sure you will not mind showing Captain Garsfield to his room.'

'Wine,' said Margaret, watching him stride away. 'He cannot last an hour without consulting his flask. I do not suppose you have any spare powder on *your* boat, do you, Garsfield? I cannot pay in coins, but there are other ways of compensating a man.'

Chaloner regarded her askance, not sure what she was offering. 'I shall make some enquiries,' he replied noncommittally.

'Good – it is damned useful stuff to have around. Are you one of Hay's crowd? He told me to expect a multitude – and at a shilling per head I am delighted to hear it, although it means I shall have to loiter until everyone arrives. I cannot have my grandson answering the door and getting the money.'

Chaloner followed her into a hall that was paved with cracked tiles. Its wooden panelling had warped from years of damp, and any polish had long since been leached off. Several paintings hung on the walls, but dust and dirt had obliterated all detail except the occasional pink, self-satisfied ancestral face. The place stank of mildew and burned cabbage.

'I understand this was once a monastery,' said Chaloner, intending to lead the conversation around to the death of Browne gradually. The crone might become suspicious if he launched into questions too abruptly, and he did not want her to warn Hay.

'Then you understand wrong,' she said, heading towards the stairs. The pipe was still in her mouth, making her difficult to understand. 'It stands on the *site* of a monastery. The cellar is monastery, though – we call it the monastery *crypt*, because it reminds me of a tomb. I used to tell my grandson it was where they buried monks who drank and gambled – the law-abiding ones went in the cemetery. Unfortunately, he never believed me.'

'Are there graves in this crypt, then?'

'Probably, although I do not go down there much, because it is haunted. You will see it for yourself later, because Hay likes to conduct his business there. I have offered him the hall, but he says there are too many broken windows and he is worried about eavesdroppers.'

Chaloner was not surprised, given the nature of the discussions. 'Do you attend these meetings?'

'Lord, no! I suspect they are plotting to overthrow the king, but that will never happen. People were always promising to dispatch Cromwell, too, but that never came to pass, either. Assassination is more difficult than you might think, and I have no time for such nonsense anyway. I prefer more genteel pursuits, such as cock-fighting, smoking and wrestling.'

'You are not worried that you may be held accountable for what takes place in your home?'

'Not as long as members of the government come here to plot the deaths of old Cromwellians too.' Margaret grinned, rather diabolically, and tapped him on the chest with the stem of her pipe. 'I am well known for being neutral in politics, and conspirators have to meet somewhere, do they not?'

Chaloner raised his eyebrows, startled by the blunt confession. 'Then I assume you are careful not to lend them your house on the same day? Two cabals of opposing fanatics will not make for easy bed-fellows.'

'I am *very* careful,' said Margaret, opening the door to a bedchamber that reeked of cats. 'After all, dead men cannot buy my hospitality, can they? The meeting is at midnight, and most plotters go hooded. They probably know each other anyway, but a disguise makes the fools feel safer. If you did not bring one with you, you will find a spare on the back of the door.'

Chaloner spent the next couple of hours exploring Bermondsey House. Most of it had been allowed to slide too far into neglect for rescue, and another two decades would see it either demolished or collapsing of its own accord. It was riddled with secret corridors, spyholes and rooms that were too small to serve any obvious purpose. In one cupboard he discovered several barrels, and an inspection told him they contained gunpowder. Did they belong to Margaret or the conspirators? There was no way to tell, and he left them with the uneasy sense that the rebels might be further along with their preparations than he had imagined.

He had not been back in his room for long when he heard voices in the hall outside. Margaret was showing more plotters to their quarters, and York was greeting them. The captain's face was more florid than ever, and he had attempted – unsuccessfully – to conceal the wine on his breath by chewing garlic. The three new arrivals were keeping their distance. One, a short, elegantly dressed fellow with an enormous yellow wig, held a scented handkerchief to his nose, while the other two – a tall, lean Puritan, and an overweight clerk – pulled faces that revealed their distaste. Margaret did not seem bothered, though; tobacco smoke billowed around her, and Chaloner wondered whether she was capable of smelling anything at all.

'Garsfield,' breathed York. He sounded relieved. 'Where have you been? We knocked twice on your door, but there was no reply. I was beginning to think you might have gone home.'

Chaloner gestured to a window, where sunlight was

blazing through the vestiges of some medieval stained glass. 'Sleeping – this heat is exhausting.'

'There you have it, Hay,' said York, turning to Yellow Wig. 'He was asleep, as I told you.'

Hay gave a tight smile that suggested the answer was not one he believed. He had small, bright eyes, and Chaloner immediately sensed sharp wits. 'You did not go exploring?'

'It is far too hot for that,' replied Chaloner, affecting nonchalance, though an uneasy feeling made him wonder whether he had been seen.

'So you were here the whole time?' pressed the shipping magnate.

Chaloner pointed at his door. 'It can only be locked from the inside, and it has been secured ever since I arrived, as anyone who tried it will certainly know.'

Fortunately, it did not occur to Hay or his companions that jamming a door – from outside or inside a room – was child's play to a professional spy, and proved nothing about his whereabouts. However, the hairs Chaloner had placed across the latch had been disturbed when he had returned, so he knew someone had given it a good shake in an attempt to enter.

'You must forgive our wariness,' said Hay with another smile that did not touch his eyes. 'Our beliefs mean we are suspicious of everyone – an attitude that has kept us alive during these uncertain times.' He gestured to the two men at his side. 'But where are my manners? These are my associates, my deputies, Mr Strutt and Mr Parr.'

Chaloner studied the pair with interest. Parr was a clergyman, whose thin, dour face and drab Puritan dress indicated a fanatic – and thus a man prepared to go to any lengths to do what he felt was right. Strutt wore clothes that were too small for him – an old-fashioned doublet and loose knee-length breeches that did nothing to flatter his portly frame. His plump face was surrounded by sweaty jowls, and his oily smile was impossible to read. Chaloner distrusted both men instinctively.

'Preacher Parr is Rector of Bermondsey,' elaborated York. 'His sermons are . . .' He flailed an expressive hand, trying to find the right word.

'Colourful,' supplied Margaret helpfully. She began to back away. 'Not that I attend church, you understand. Waste of time in my opinion. But I shall leave you gentlemen to gossip. Your friends will be arriving soon, and I do not want to lose their shillings by letting my grandson answer the door.'

York grinned nervously at Hay when she had gone. 'Garsfield is master of a brig that conveys gunpowder to Jamaica. Quite often the supplies clerks make mistakes on their inventories.'

'I often end up with unwanted powder,' added Chaloner, taking the cue. 'And I never know how to dispose of it. However, York says you might be able to give me some ideas.'

'Well, he should not have done,' said Hay, casting York an admonishing glare, while Parr and Strutt exchanged uncomfortable glances. 'Not until we know you better.'

'You can trust him,' said York. Unease was making him gabble. 'He hates the government, because the Duke of Buckingham despoiled his favourite sister.'

'Apparently you have vowed to run him through for the outrage,' said Preacher Parr to Chaloner. 'Is it true?'

'*I* dislike the government because I fought for Cromwell during the wars,' York went on before Chaloner could reply. 'And I am still a Parliamentarian, despite the fact that I serve in the new Royalist navy. But *Hay's* grievance is financial. He owns most of the wharves along the river in Bermondsey, and he objects to the high taxes that the government imposes on him.'

'A vast quantity of imported goods passes through my hands,' conceded Hay cagily. Then a note of pride crept into his voice. 'More, in fact, than any other merchant in the capital.'

'The location of his wharves – on the south bank – means he is obliged to pay an additional tariff for sending goods to the north,' York continued. '*Two* taxes – one to unload at Bermondsey, and a second to ferry these goods across the river to the city.'

'That seems unfair,' said Chaloner. 'The government is ever greedy for its subjects' money.'

Hay's stiff manner yielded slightly at this remark. 'That is certainly true.'

'York says you have two cannon on your ship, Garsfield,' said Preacher Parr rather eagerly. 'And the current trouble with Holland means you keep them loaded.'

'Not always,' said Chaloner, suspecting it would be illegal or impractical in certain situations. Was Parr trying to catch him out? 'It depends.'

'How much powder can you lay your hands on at any given time?' asked Strutt.

'Strutt was a navy purser until an argument with his captain drove him to other business,' said Hay to Chaloner, to explain the man's question. 'He works for me now. He and Parr both know a lot about ships and armaments.'

Thus warned, Chaloner was reluctant to embark on specifics lest he make a mistake that would arouse their suspicions. 'Is it safe to talk here?' he asked pointedly. 'Only Margaret said you normally use a cellar, because of the danger of eavesdroppers.'

'True,' said Strutt, glancing around quickly. The

gesture was fast and furtive, and made him look like a ferret. 'This is no place for a discussion of fire-power. We should wait until later, when our trusted colleagues will be with us.'

'There are about thirty of us – all like-minded men,' said Preacher Parr to Chaloner, lowering his voice conspiratorially. 'When we gather in the cellar, we wear hoods to maintain our anonymity. It is a simple system – you will not recognize anyone, but neither will anyone recognize you.'

'As you wish,' said Chaloner, wondering how he was going to learn the names – or even obtain descriptions – of the conspirators under such circumstances. 'But I have nothing to hide.'

'Everyone has something to hide,' said Strutt. 'No one is perfect.'

'*You* certainly are not,' said York unpleasantly. 'Browne could never prove you stole the provisions that were supposed to go on his ship, but it was obvious that you were guilty.'

Strutt's greasy obsequiousness turned into something harder and more nasty. 'The Navy Board would not agree – they reviewed my case and deemed me innocent, although I resigned from *Rosebush* anyway. Browne was a brute, little better than the louts who served under him, and I am glad I am no longer obliged to deal with him.'

'He was my friend,' said York coldly.

Strutt shot him an ambiguous look. 'I know.'

Hay and his deputies had arranged a light supper of bread and pies before the meeting, and they invited York and Chaloner to share it with them. Chaloner hesitated, suspecting he would be quizzed about his mythical ship and knowing it would be only a matter of time before he was tripped up in a maritime inconsistency. However, he had already used the excuse of fatigue, and felt he had no choice but to join them in the dilapidated chamber that passed as Bermondsey House's main hall. Margaret also graced them with her presence, reluctantly setting aside her pipe in order to eat. Halfway through the meal, a foppish man slouched into the room and flung himself on a bench.

'This weather!' he drawled, reaching for the wine jug. 'You could fry an egg on me, I am so hot!'

'My grandson,' said Margaret, eyeing him with disapproval. 'You can thank him for your being here today, because I would never have sunk this low if he had not gambled away our fortune.'

'You spent a fair bit of it yourself,' retorted Castell, draining his cup and filling it again. 'You had an eye for fine clothes, handsome beaux and gay balls, so do not blame it all on me.'

Margaret cackled. 'Well, it was good while it lasted. Who has some tobacco? I am out again.'

'Tobacco is an agent of the devil,' declared Rector Parr grimly. His black clothes hung loosely on his skeletal frame, adding to the overall impression of dour self-denial and austerity. Chaloner noted that even his friends seemed to find his unsmiling piety a bit of a trial, and concluded that Parr was not a man who would be invited to many parties. 'And those who partake of it risk their immortal souls.'

'The devil had my immortal soul years ago,' retorted Margaret. 'And good luck to him.'

'He will need it,' murmured York, passing her a pouch. Although he had shown restraint with the wine over his dinner, he was still far from sober, and Chaloner sincerely hoped he would not lose control of himself and say or do something to give them away.

'I saw Widow Browne today,' said Strutt. He shot York a spiteful glance, to ensure the captain knew he was about to be baited. 'Her husband must have left her badly off, because she would never have donned such tatty clothes when he was alive. You should have seen the state of her gorget!'

'I heard his death came at an unfortunate time,' said Hay, speaking before York could reply. 'Apparently he had invested everything in a special cargo he was to transport on *Rosebush* and his demise meant his family lost everything.'

'Shame,' said Strutt with a gleeful smile. 'However, Browne damaged me with his false accusations, so I cannot find it in my heart to feel sorry for him.'

'God does not approve of grudges,' announced Preacher Parr. 'Not unless they are just.'

'Who decides what is just?' asked Chaloner provocatively.

'God's faithful servants,' replied the clergyman loftily. 'Men like *me*. It was my misfortune to run foul of Browne when I tried to preach the good word to his crew – he had me thrown into the river. He was a violent brute, and God gave him a violent end.'

Chaloner recalled that Hannah and York had mentioned some past disagreement between Browne and the preacher, which had led them to put Parr on their list of suspects. The incident did not sound very serious, and Chaloner imagined Browne would barely have given it a second thought, but he could imagine how it might have gnawed at Parr's fanatical heart. He would see it as an insult to his crusade for God and might well have decided to avenge himself with a convenient rock.

'It was a pity one of his sailors decided to brain him,' said Hay, his expression unreadable. 'Personally, I thought him a decent fellow, though we only exchanged a few words before he died.'

'Were you present when he was murdered, then?'

asked Chaloner innocently. 'I thought he was killed in Jamaica House.'

'No, he was attacked *here*,' said Margaret, almost invisible in a cloud of smoke. 'But Hay arranged for the law courts to be *told* it was Jamaica House, which was nice of him. I do not want my lovely home associated with sordid doings like murder, after all.'

There was a short, awkward pause, during which everyone thought, but did not say, that most people would consider treason and sedition just as sordid as an unlawful killing. Meanwhile, Hay grimaced, annoyed that she should expose his meddling with justice quite so readily.

Chaloner smiled pleasantly at the shipping magnate. 'What did you and Browne exchange a "few words" about?' he asked.

Hay was wary. 'I cannot recall now. The incident was weeks ago, in April. Why do you ask?'

Chaloner shrugged. 'Because I dislike the notion of seamen lobbing rocks at us senior officers. What led Walduck to strike Browne dead?'

Hay was thoughtful. 'Well, Walduck did not draw his sword to protect Browne the moment he heard footsteps approaching, and Browne reprimanded him for it. That annoyed him – I could tell.'

'Enough to want to kill him?' asked Chaloner. It did not sound a very powerful motive.

'Criminals do not behave in the same way as normal men,' said Hay sagely. 'After the spat, I led Browne to the cellar where we hold our meetings, but he must have lagged behind, because when I reached the bottom of the steps I looked back to find him gone. I assumed he was with Strutt.'

'He was not,' said Strutt, a little too quickly. 'I disliked him and did not want to be in his company. I kept my distance. His men were with him – I was not.'

It was a very vehement denial, and Chaloner regarded the purser curiously. Just how angry had he been about Browne's accusations regarding his honesty? Strutt was bitter and spiteful, just the kind of man to throw a stone at an enemy rather than confront him with a sword.

'I was some way away when the commotion started,' added the preacher helpfully. 'But I saw Walduck throw the rock.'

'How?' asked Chaloner sceptically. 'If you were some distance off, then how could you have seen what happened? Further, I understand this meeting was late at night, so it would have been dark.'

The rector grimaced. 'Well, perhaps I did not actually *see* the missile in flight, but it was obvious what Walduck had done. He made no attempt to deny the charge when I accused him of it.'

'He just stood there,' agreed Strutt, 'and refused to answer questions. All he said – kept repeating – was that masonry from the house had dropped on Browne.'

'Wicked lies,' said Castell, reaching for more wine. Margaret nodded fervent agreement. 'Our masonry has never hit anyone before.'

Hay continued his tale. 'When I went to see what had happened, Browne was lying on the ground. His two sailors were leaning over him, and – as Parr just said – it was obvious that one had taken the opportunity to commit murder.'

'Did they run away when you came?' asked Chaloner.

'No. They said they had been walking along behind him when he had just collapsed. Walduck was astonished when we later arrested him. He told us we would never be able to prove it.'

'You should have seen his face at the trial,' crowed Strutt. 'He could not *believe* the jury's verdict and kept insisting that masonry was to blame. A lump *did* fall, as it happened, but it was too far away to have hit Browne.'

'Walduck was a drunken fool!' declared Hay irritably. 'And the attention that accrued from Browne's death was something we all could have done without.'

'So Hay had words with his friends in the law courts,' finished Margaret. 'To protect us all from scandal. He had the matter expedited too – Walduck tried and executed at top speed, so he could be buried and forgotten.'

Hay regarded her sharply, as if he detected recrimination in the comment. Margaret merely blew a smoke ring and beamed benignly at him.

'How did you know *Walduck* was the culprit?' Chaloner asked curiously, looking at each person in turn. 'It could have been the other sailor – Tivill.'

'Because Tivill had a sword in one hand, a dagger in the other, and he was struggling with Browne's frisky horse,' replied the preacher promptly. 'He had no spare hands to lob rocks with. Besides, why use a stone, when weapons of steel were available?'

'The same could be said about Walduck,' Chaloner pointed out.

Parr sighed. 'Yes, but *Walduck* was a killer – you could see it in his eyes.'

Chaloner was acutely aware that all their accounts were based on supposition and prejudice, and he was not sure he believed any of them. His questions were clarifying nothing about the night of the murder, or about the roles played by his various suspects.

'I heard a thump,' said Strutt. He smiled, as if the memory afforded him pleasure. 'It was almost certainly Walduck's stone cracking Browne's skull.'

'Had any of your associates arrived at Bermondsey House when all this happened?' Chaloner asked, looking around at them. 'Or were you and the two sailors the only ones there?'

The preacher shrugged his thin shoulders. 'Others

were gathering for the meeting, but it was dark, as you have pointed out, and impossible to see much. Some came to see what had happened, but they usually wear hoods, so I could not tell who indulged his curiosity and who left before there was a fuss.'

'Did anyone ask Tivill what *he* saw?' asked Chaloner. 'He must have been the closest—'

'He saw nothing, because he was trying to control the horse,' replied Strutt, rather quickly. 'It was prancing about, and as he was holding a weapon in either hand he was trying to control the beast by gripping the reins in his teeth. The fellow is an imbecile!'

Chaloner recalled Tivill from *Rosebush* and concurred that he was not the kind of man who would know how to cope with a situation that required three hands. He had been a liability on the ship, and only escaped hanging himself among the lines and cables because his shipmates watched out for him. His only virtue, as far as Chaloner could tell, was his willingness to fight. He was perfectly happy to lead charges against an enemy, even when they appeared to be suicidal, and Browne had used him accordingly.

'I find this discussion distasteful,' said Preacher Parr with a fastidious shudder. 'Let us talk about *our* business instead. How many guns on your ship, Garsfield?'

'Two,' replied Chaloner. During one voyage, he had made a study of *Rosebush*'s cannon, for want of anything better to do, and knew a little about them. He spouted a few vague technical details that had the rebels leaning forward with interest.

'Do they fire best on the up-roll or the down-roll?' asked Strutt.

Chaloner did not have the faintest idea, although he realized the angle of the muzzle would make a difference to its efficiency. He glanced at York for help, but the captain was pouring himself wine and seemed oblivious to Chaloner's predicament. Strutt's eyes narrowed, and Chaloner knew he was about to be exposed as someone who did not know what he was talking about.

'I prefer the up-roll myself,' said Margaret, reaching out to take the jug from York. She glared at him when she found it empty. 'It gives you greater range, and there is less chance of damage to your vessel. I manned my share of the things during the wars, you know.'

There were some startled glances, and Chaloner stood to take his leave before anyone could question him further. Hay followed suit, saying he had work to do before the meeting, while Castell announced that he had booked a prostitute at a nearby tavern. His grandmother did not seem surprised, and only commented that she was tired and that it was time to sleep. She began removing garments before she was out of the hall; loath to be subjected to anything too horrible, no one lingered. Strutt disappeared to his chamber, and Chaloner said he had a book he wanted to read.

'The Bible?' asked Parr, giving the impression that anything else would be anathema.

'Tide tables,' replied Chaloner. 'The mariner's Bible.'

York laughed rather wildly, then said he had letters he wanted to write. Chaloner watched him leave and hoped he would drink himself insensible before the meeting. It would be safer for everyone – especially Chaloner himself.

The meeting was not due to start for at least three hours, so Chaloner jammed the door to his room again and set off to reconnoitre the cellar in which the gathering was supposed to take place. First, though, he entered a secret passage he had discovered earlier, which had spyholes cut into its wooden walls. These allowed the occupants of various rooms to be studied without the watcher being detected.

As he groped his way through the darkness, Chaloner thought about what the conspirators had told him regarding Browne's death. The testimony of each was questionable, and he found himself unable to determine who – if anyone – had lied. However, he *had* learned that no one had actually witnessed the incident, so why had Walduck been hanged? Surely, any jury would have seen there was reasonable doubt about his guilt? It was true that Walduck and Tivill had disliked their captain, but would Walduck really have brained him, then loitered around, waiting to be arrested? It made no sense. Chaloner also did not like the notion that Hay had managed to secure an early trial and a hasty execution, or the fact that the law courts seemed to have accepted a number of falsehoods – such as where the murder had been committed – without demur.

When Chaloner reached Hay's chamber, he peered through the spyhole to find it empty. Whatever 'work' the yellow-wigged shipping magnate had been going to do did not involve sitting at a desk. Hay was top of Chaloner's list of suspects, mostly because he had so much to lose from being exposed. Not only would he face a traitor's death, but he was wealthy and respectable, so his family, friends and associates would share his disgrace.

The next room was occupied by Strutt, who sat at a table, writing furiously. Was he doing something for Hay or – and Chaloner was deeply suspicious of the speed at which the quill was flying across the paper – was he making a record of what had transpired at dinner? If the latter, then why? Was Strutt also uncomfortable with rebellion, and was he planning to make a report to the authorities when he had sufficient evidence? Or was he penning some innocent missive that had nothing to do with revolt? Chaloner watched him for a while, thinking that if Hay was top of the list of suspects for Browne's murder, then Strutt was a very close second. No one could hate as fiercely as Strutt without being tempted to lob sly stones when the opportunity presented itself.

Parr occupied the quarters next door. The preacher was on his knees, hands clasped before him. His face was dark and savage, and Chaloner was certain the prayers would not be ones any decent God would want to hear. Parr remained indignant that Browne had declined to allow him to spout religion at *Rosebush*'s crew, and Chaloner knew casual murder would be seen as divine justice by the likes of the fanatical Rector of Bermondsey.

The next room was York's; the captain had a cup in his hand and was pacing back and forth in agitation. Had he recruited Browne to help him expose the dissidents, only to discover that Browne actually thought revolt was a very good idea? The two men had been close, it was true, but how much value did York place on friendship – especially when his own life and safety were at stake?

The corridor ended, and Chaloner was treated to a view of Castell and his grandmother in a hallway; she was counting the money she had collected, and he was watching with jealous eyes. If Browne *had* exposed the treacherous happenings at Bermondsey House, then they would have been in serious trouble. Trials for treason were notoriously unjust, and the Castells would have been punished for providing Hay with a venue for his activities, regardless of what they thought about his plans. Either one was capable of lobbing a piece of the masonry that littered the ground outside their home, although Chaloner wondered whether Castell would ever be sober enough to hit what he aimed at.

The spy visited more hidden passages before he headed for the cellar. He saw more men in other rooms but knew none of them. They were all wealthy, judging by their clothes. Some were alone, while others were in pairs, and he estimated there were roughly thirty of them. It was not many for a rebellion, but if they all poured money into the cause they could buy a lot more support. Such a movement was certainly something the government would want to suppress.

York had said the cellar used by the rebels was accessed via a flight of steps located not far from the main door, so Chaloner walked around the outside of the house until he found the stairs, tucked away among some ancient ruinous walls and all but invisible to the casual observer. He regarded them thoughtfully, then went back inside the mansion and made his way to the rooms that were built directly above the vault. Bermondsey House was riddled with so many secret spaces that he was sure there would be more than one entrance to the undercroft. He soon found what he was looking for – a low, slime-coated tunnel that sloped sharply downwards. It was concealed behind a fireplace in a pantry, and he had detected it because the chamber's dimensions were not quite right – as a spy, he had a good sense for such things.

He lit a candle and descended slowly, swearing under his breath when he slipped and fell a few feet. The passageway went further down than he had anticipated, and he was beginning to think it might actually go *underneath* the crypt rather than into it, when he finally reached the bottom. He shivered. It was icy cold – eerily so – and he was dressed for the warmth outside. His way was barred by a small trap door, but it did not take him many moments to pick the feeble lock that held it in place, and he pushed it open to reveal a low-ceilinged chamber.

He emerged cautiously, becoming warier still when he saw a torch burning in a brazier on a wall at the far end – the end where the steps were located – placed in readiness for the midnight gathering. He listened intently but could hear nothing except the steady drip of water on stone. The cellar looked monastic, like a crypt, with sturdy vaulting, and there were holes cut into its walls. They were roughly man-sized, curtained by cobwebs, and he supposed they had once held the bones of monks. Some were oddly deep, stretching so far into the wall that he could not see the back of them. The floor had been flagged in places, but mostly it was beaten earth, which had become packed as hard as stone over the years.

He touched a wall, marvelling at the quality of the work that had gone into its making, because although the stones were stained with the filth of ages, their edges were sharp and clear. As soon as his fingers brushed against the stone, a chill enveloped him, deeper and colder than the temperature of the chamber, and he was unable to prevent a shudder. There was something dark and sinister about the cellar, as though it had witnessed more than its share of evil deeds.

He shook himself impatiently – he did not have time for ghosts – and began a systematic search. Old barrels indicated that the undercroft had been used as a wine store at some point, while several desiccated rats suggested that grain or food had probably been kept there too. Marks in the walls and along the ceiling showed where partitions had once stood, dividing the chamber into smaller segments. Now, though, the cellar was just one large vault, full of shadows and eerie pockets where the light of his candle did not penetrate. He began to think of ghosts again, and the tales Hannah had related about old bones and murder. He took a deep breath and pushed such notions from his mind a second time.

He ventured further into the vault. Benches had been placed in the middle of the chamber, where another torch was burning. He was about to leave by way of the main steps when echoing footsteps told him someone was coming – fast. There was just enough time for him to snuff out his candle and dive into the shadows before the man arrived. Chaloner held his breath, certain he was going to be caught and not sure what excuse he could give to explain his presence there.

But the newcomer did not so much as glance in Chaloner's direction. Wearing a hooded cloak, so nothing could be seen of his face, he hurried to the tunnel end of the chamber and began scratching at the top of the wall. It was not long before a piece of masonry came out in his hands. Chaloner watched him insert something in the resulting gap, replace the brick, and leave as quickly as he had arrived.

When he had gone, Chaloner padded forward to inspect the wall. It was different from the rest of the crypt – it bulged outwards, indicating that the work had been carried out hastily, without the care that had been lavished on the rest of the cellar. Its crumbling mortar said it was ancient, even so. Chaloner removed the stone and retrieved what had been placed there.

It was a letter addressed to Joseph Williamson. Chaloner gazed at it in surprise. Williamson was spymaster-general – the man in charge of the government's intelligence services. The message was in cipher, which Chaloner could certainly have broken given time, but not in a matter of moments. He considered keeping it, but was afraid its absence might warn someone that something was amiss. Reluctantly, he put it back.

He was about to leave when he heard voices. More people were coming, although they were approaching at a more leisurely pace than the hooded man. Chaloner doubted he would go unnoticed a second time and did not want to be caught snooping quite so early in the game. He assessed his options. He could not leave through the tunnel or by the steps, because he would almost certainly be seen, while the only furniture to hide behind were benches – useless for the purpose. He glanced at the coffin-shaped niches. It was distasteful, but it was better than being caught.

Careful not to disturb the cobwebs that would help to conceal him, he crawled into one of the holes. He was hard pressed to keep himself from exclaiming his shock when he discovered someone else already there – and that the person was dead.

There was not much Chaloner could do, except shove the corpse deeper into the niche and lie hard up against it. He held his breath when the odour of decay wafted around him, concluding that the fellow had been dead for some time.

Three men entered the crypt – yellow-wigged Hay, Preacher Parr and Strutt the purser. The shipping magnate went straight to the wall and removed the loose stone. He shoved the document in his pocket and deftly replaced the brick. He did not so much as glance at what he had retrieved, indicating he had expected to find something there. Chaloner was confused. Had Hay taken the message because *he* intended to pass it to Spymaster Williamson? Or was he claiming it before the author could expose him? Of course, that assumed the document pertained to the brewing rebellion, and it was possible that it did nothing of the kind.

'Are you *sure* we are doing the right thing?' asked Strutt, clearly unhappy. 'It feels dangerous, and you know what they do to traitors these days.'

'We are *not* traitors,' said Hay firmly. 'We are men who want justice and equity – especially in matters relating to commerce. What is wrong with that?'

'I doubt the law courts will see it in those terms,' said Strutt miserably. 'But I am in no position to argue. I was destitute after Browne forced me to resign from the navy and would have been hanged or be in debtors' prison if you two had not offered me work.'

'*God* provided for you,' said Parr righteously. 'Not men. And He will help us fight His holy war against corruption, greed and the devil. And by the devil I mean the government.'

'Do not include greed in your list of vices,' said Hay with a wry grin. 'I want to make a greater profit from my wharves, and some would call that greed, so watch what you condemn.'

'I am a soldier of God,' announced the preacher in a way that should have told Hay not to try jesting with him. 'I shall combat sin wherever I find it – and sinners too.'

'What is in the letter this time, Hay?' asked Strutt, hastily changing the subject. Only men with plenty of time on their hands embarked on religious debates with zealots like Parr. 'Can you read it?'

'It will be encoded. They always are – and they take me hours to decipher.'

'We should move that body before the others arrive,' said Strutt practically. 'It is beginning to smell – and York's friend asked too many questions earlier. I do not trust him, and we do not want a peculiar odour encouraging him to pry more deeply into our affairs.'

'I am sure he *did* wander off earlier,' said the preacher, reluctantly dragging his thoughts away from his personal crusade against evil. 'I cannot prove it – indeed, he *did* lock himself in from the inside, as he claimed – but I knocked very hard. No one sleeps that soundly.'

'He is a sea captain,' explained Hay. Parr regarded him uncomprehendingly, so he elaborated with an impatient sigh. 'Ships' cannon destroy a man's ears if he hears them too often, as happened to Walduck. York is stupid not to have guessed that was why Walduck failed to object to our accusations – he did not hear them until after he was arrested.'

'And by then it was too late,' said Strutt rather gleefully.

Chaloner was horrified. Not only had an innocent man been hanged, but one who had been injured in the service of his country. The injustice of it made him all the more determined to learn the truth.

'Garsfield did not seem hard of hearing to me,' said Parr doubtfully. Then he shrugged, and a fervent gleam lit his eyes. 'But I am not really worried about him, because *God* will ensure all is well. I petitioned Him earlier, and He is unlikely to refuse the demands of one of His most ardent servants. Shall we move the body now? We may not be alone for long, because our members are impatient for news of our achievements and may arrive early.'

Chaloner stiffened as their footsteps tapped towards him. Now what? He doubted he could invent a reason for being there that would be believed, and discovery would mean the end of his plan to unmask the traitors. It occurred to him that he could climb across the body and hide on its other side, but the hole would be too shallow, and he would be seen anyway. Or would he? Earlier, he had noticed that some of the niches were very deep, built to hold sizeable sarcophagi. Perhaps there was a chance that it might be large enough to conceal him.

Trying to make as little noise as possible, he clambered across the corpse, aiming for the darkness on the other side. Strutt was right about the smell. It was not a pleasant thing to be doing, and Chaloner started to sweat, despite the chill of the vault. He was half-tempted to give up and opt for concocting some story instead, because there was a limit to what a man should be expected to do for his country, and climbing around on corpses was well past it. But then he was across the body, and into the space on its far side. It took only a moment for him to realize he was in luck: the shelf was an especially deep one, and he supposed it had been built to hold more than one coffin.

He slithered to the very back of the recess not a moment too soon, because there was a flash of light and Hay approached with a lamp. Parr pushed aside the cobwebs, and he and Strutt tugged the corpse from its hiding place. Chaloner braced himself for discovery, but the three men were hurrying, eager to finish the distasteful business, and did not bother to inspect the back of the niche once the body was out. Hay produced a blanket, and Parr and Strutt wrapped the corpse in it. As they began to haul their burden out of the crypt, the sheet fell open and Hay's lantern illuminated the dead man's face. It was the sailor, Tivill.

His mind teeming with questions, Chaloner followed the three men, wanting to see what they would do with the body. He was grateful that he had not taken the letter from the wall, given that Hay had been expecting to find it – the conspirators were already suspicious of 'Captain Garsfield', and Chaloner did not want to give them further cause for alarm. Strutt and Parr carried

Tivill up the main stairs and towards the nearest trees, while Hay kept watch. Fortunately for Chaloner, Hay was more concerned about being seen from the windows of Bermondsey House than being followed from the vault, because he did not once glance in the spy's direction. Thus, even though the moon shone in a cloudless sky, it was absurdly easy for Chaloner to trail the bobbing lamp to the wood and then edge through the trees until he could see and hear what was happening.

But he could have spared himself the effort, because he learned nothing new. Strutt dug a hasty grave, Parr intoned some insincere prayers, and Hay kept watch. Then all three left without another word. When they had gone, Chaloner scraped the loose soil from Tivill's face. He was not good at determining time of death, but he was sure Tivill had not died in April, when Browne had been murdered and Walduck hanged. Tivill was dead days rather than weeks. So how and when had the sailor met his end? And, more important, why?

A quick inspection revealed a soggy dent at the back of Tivill's head, consistent with a blow from something heavy, perhaps a stone. So, Chaloner thought, Tivill had been killed in the same way as his captain. But what would Tivill have been doing at Bermondsey House in the first place? Had he come to wreak revenge on the men who had seen his shipmate wrongfully executed? Chaloner immediately discounted the notion of Tivill as an avenging angel – he had not been that sort of man and would not have cared what happened to Walduck. It was more likely that he had come to demand money for his silence – and had been killed when Hay and his associates had been disinclined to oblige.

Chaloner wondered what he should do next. His first

inclination was to go straight to White Hall and tell Spymaster Williamson what was happening. Williamson would muster troops and catch the rebels in the very act of fermenting their plot as they gathered in the crypt. Unfortunately, it was a long way from Bermondsey to White Hall, and London Bridge would be closed for the night. By the time he had bribed his way across, located Williamson, convinced the spymaster that Hay's cabal was worth the expense and effort of raising a militia, the meeting would be over and the plotters dispersed. So Chaloner decided to stay, attend the meeting and see what more he could learn.

He judged he still had about an hour until midnight, so he elected to spend the time constructively. He returned to the cupboard where the gunpowder was stored and helped himself to a barrel. He tugged it down the tunnel to the crypt and placed it in the niche that had held Tivill. Carefully, he broke the seal and scattered a few handfuls in front of the cask, then added a layer of kindling he had filched from the pantry. He hoped his precautions would not be necessary and that he would be able to eavesdrop on the gathering without the need for fireworks. But he had not survived so many years in an occupation fraught with danger by being careless. Satisfied that he had done all he could to even the odds, he made his way back to his room.

Once there, he donned the hooded cloak Margaret had left on the back of the door, ensured there were no telltale cobwebs on his clothes and went to collect York. Unfortunately, the captain had not imbibed nearly enough to be insensible, as Chaloner had hoped. Like many habitual drinkers, that took time – far more time than York had been allotted that night.

'They are suspicious of us,' the captain snarled, hauling Chaloner inside his chamber. 'They know you are not who you say, especially after that business with the up-roll. Thank God Margaret piped up with a brag! We should leave while we can, or Browne will not be the only one with a dented skull.'

'Did you know that cannon fire had rendered Walduck hard of hearing?' asked Chaloner, declining to tell him about Tivill's fate.

York gazed at him. 'Did it? He never said so. Perhaps that was why he never heard the stone strike Browne. Strutt says *he* did, and he was further away, so there must have been a very loud crack.'

'Is there anything else you might have overlooked?' asked Chaloner a little caustically. York was a navy man and should have known about the effects of persistent gunfire on a sailor's ears.

York nodded. 'I did not want to say anything when Hannah was listening, but Walduck hated Browne more than she knows. There was a question about the allocation of some prize money, and Walduck thought he had been cheated. He had not, of course. Browne was not a dishonest man.'

'No,' agreed Chaloner, recalling that scrupulousness with money had been one of Browne's few redeeming qualities. 'Do you think Walduck's hatred was enough to lead him to murder?'

York nodded again. 'But he would have plied his sword, not a stone. And do not forget the two shillings he was promised – that is a lot of money to a man who has not been paid for three years. Even if Walduck did have murder in mind, he would have waited until the coins were in his pocket.'

'What did Tivill do when Walduck was arrested?'

York stared at him, trying to understand the implications of the question. He failed, so gave up with a shrug. 'Nothing. Hay took Walduck to the Marshalsea prison, but Walduck later told me he thought they were going to make a report to the coroner and was shocked when he learned he was accused of murder.'

'So he went willingly to the gaol?'

'Yes – he made a fuss only when he realized what was really happening, at which point he killed a warden. Meanwhile, Tivill also went to the prison, but Hay said he made himself scarce when the soldiers laid hold of Walduck. I have not seen him since, and he did not give evidence at the trial, although an order was issued for him to appear as a witness. He is probably at sea.'

'Perhaps,' said Chaloner, supposing that a voyage would explain why Tivill, like York himself, had only recently returned to the place of Browne's death. He had secured a berth that took him safely away from London and accusations of helping Walduck commit his crime. Then later, when his fear had abated, he had slipped back to Bermondsey House in the hope of securing some blackmail money.

York regarded him uneasily. 'What are *you* going to do now? I refuse to be part of any rash plan, so do not expect any heroics from me.'

'We shall just listen and watch – and leave as soon as we have enough evidence to put an end to this mischief.'

York was deeply unhappy. 'Very well. But if anything goes wrong, you are on your own.'

Chaloner had never doubted it.

Chaloner and York were descending the stairs to the hall when Margaret intercepted them. She was wearing a scruffy mantua – a loose nightgown – of faded pink velvet, and the inevitable pipe was clamped between her yellow teeth. A grey wig and a pair of substantial military-style boots that looked as though they belonged to a large man completed the outfit.

'That was good tobacco you gave me earlier,' she said to York. 'Got any left?'

The captain fumbled for his pouch. 'I must have left it in my room. I will fetch it for you.'

Suspecting he intended to escape, the spy put out a hand to stop him. York's flight would warn the conspirators that something was amiss, and then Chaloner might never acquire the information he needed to convict them. York would just have to control his fear – after all, he was a sea captain, paid to defend king and country.

'No matter,' said Margaret, not looking as though she meant it. 'It keeps me awake, and I am reaching the age where a bit of beauty sleep does not go amiss.'

'It would not go amiss for me, either,' mumbled York, when she went to straighten a painting that hung at an odd angle. It fell from the wall when she touched it, causing her to leap back smartly. 'I would give everything I own to be at sea right now. I wish I had never brought Browne here *or* introduced him to the man who sold him that cargo . . .' He trailed off, aware that he had said too much.

'I see,' said Chaloner, unimpressed. 'You injured Browne on *two* counts. Your plan to include him in the glory of unmasking traitors saw him killed, and the commercial opportunity *you* arranged has resulted in his family losing everything. No wonder you feel guilty towards Hannah!'

'I will give her what I can,' cried York. He looked as though he might cry; Chaloner sincerely hoped he would not. 'I promise! In fact, if you find me a priest, I shall swear on the Bible to make amends for my . . . poor judgement. Mrs Castell! Do you know any priests?'

It was an odd question to yell at someone out of the blue, but Margaret took it in her stride. 'Parr is a priest,' she replied, abandoning the ancestral art and coming to talk. 'However, I would not trust him if he was the last man on Earth. He is a fanatic and will stop at nothing to get what he wants.'

'And what does he want?' asked Chaloner.

'His vision of a perfect England,' Margaret replied rather wearily. 'A country ruled by religious maniacs, where God will be used to justify the bigotry of small, mean minds. I am a bit tired of their breed, if you want the truth. Religion and politics make for uneasy bedfellows and should be kept apart. And men like Parr should be kept in dark cellars, where no one can hear their poison.'

York frowned at her. 'Are you saying *Preacher Parr* cracked Browne's skull with the rock, to further his dream of a Puritan government?'

Margaret was bemused in her turn. 'No, I am not! Fool! Indeed, he is the one man who *cannot* have murdered Browne, because I was watching him through a window. I would have seen if he had thrown anything – and he did not. I am talking about his unpalatable godliness, which—'

But Chaloner was more interested in what she had witnessed than in her views on religion. 'You did not mention this when we were talking about it at dinner.'

She shrugged. 'You did not ask me, did you? You were more interested in what Hay and his silly henchmen had to say, and not once did you solicit *my* opinion on the matter.'

'We offended you by not consulting you?' asked Chaloner, a little taken aback.

She regarded him coolly. 'Actually, you did. I live here and know far more about what happens than occasional visitors like Hay, Strutt and Parr. Yet you dismissed me as though I was nothing. Still, it is what I have come to expect from youngsters. You have no respect for the wisdom of age.'

'*Do* you know who killed Browne?' demanded York. 'He was my friend and – as Garsfield here said earlier – we navy men do not like the notion of villains lobbing rocks at us senior officers.'

Margaret's eyes narrowed. '"Villains"?' she echoed sharply. 'Not "sailors"? Can I assume from that description that you do not think Walduck was the culprit, then?'

'Yes, you may,' said York, before Chaloner could warn him to be wary of confiding too much. 'I said from the start that his guilt was far from obvious, but no one took any notice of me.'

'Will you tell us what you saw, ma'am?' asked Chaloner, keen to encourage her to talk. If York was allowed to babble, he might inadvertently reveal that unmasking the killer was the real reason for their presence there that night.

She sniffed huffily. 'If I must. Hay, Strutt and the other plotters were too far away or in the wrong place to have lobbed missiles hard enough to have killed Browne. There were only three people who could have done that: the two sailors and Preacher Parr.'

'But you just said Parr was innocent,' said York. 'I do not understand what you are telling us.'

Margaret tutted irritably. 'Yes, I did say Parr could not have thrown the fatal stone. So what does that tell you?' She clicked her tongue again when York did nothing but stare. 'Think, man! It means one of the sailors is the culprit. It is a matter of simple logic.'

'But Tivill was struggling with Browne's horse, and Walduck would have used his sword,' objected York. 'And neither was drunk.'

Margaret looked superior. 'Are you going to hear my opinion or regale me with your own theories? I thought you would have learned by now that I am worth listening to.'

'Go on, then,' said York with a long-suffering sigh. 'Tell us what you think, woman.'

Margaret inclined her head, though Chaloner would have told York to go to the devil had he been in her shoes. It was hardly a gracious request. 'I suspect Walduck *claimed* he was drunk, because he thought it might see him acquitted. Not responsible for his actions. I would have done.'

York sneered his disdain. 'He was not *that* dim. He would have known inebriation was no defence, although . . .' He paused, and some of the irritable arrogance faded.

'Although what?' demanded Chaloner.

'Although, as a non-drinker himself, he despised men who let ale control them,' continued York thoughtfully. He turned to Chaloner, speaking in a low voice and rudely trying to exclude the old lady. She promptly stepped forward, head cocked. 'But it was the one thing Browne was lax about at sea – he was usually forgiving of men who transgressed while intoxicated, perhaps because he liked a drink himself and was no hypocrite. Perhaps Walduck *did* assume that his crime would be overlooked if he put it down to beer.'

'Well, there you are, then,' said Margaret with satisfaction. Her hearing was better than York had supposed. 'I was right: his experience aboard *Rosebush* told him he might be exonerated if he blamed ale. The ruse failed, but I imagine he was desperate, and desperate men resort to desperate measures.'

Chaloner watched her walk away. 'Her testimony tells us the killer was either Walduck or Tivill,' he said to York. 'No one else was close enough. We know Tivill had his hands full with weapons and horse, because several people have said so. That leaves Walduck. *You* said he bore Browne a grudge over prize money, and we know he was violent. It takes a lot of force and a deadly aim to hurl a stone with enough power to kill – something that has struck me as odd from the first. Ergo, I suspect no one threw anything.'

'But Browne *was* hit by a rock,' objected York. 'I saw the fatal wound myself.'

'Yes, he was hit,' agreed Chaloner. 'But by someone bringing it down hard across his head, not by a lucky toss. That means he was killed by someone physically close to him. Walduck.'

'Walduck would have used his sword,' said York stubbornly. 'I know he would.'

But Chaloner understood why the cooper had not bloodied his blade. 'Strutt said a piece of masonry dropped from the roof not long before Browne was killed. It seems to me that Walduck saw it, too, and it gave him what he thought was a clever idea – blaming Browne's death on an accident.'

York gazed at him. 'Walduck was dull-witted, but he did possess an innate cunning; such a notion might well have jumped into his mind. That would explain why he did not run away – he thought no one would be able to prove anything. He virtually said as much when I questioned him later.'

Chaloner felt weary. 'So the case is solved. The right man was hanged after all.'

A crafty look came into York's eye. 'Then we should go and tell Hannah—'

Chaloner grabbed his arm as he started to head for the door. 'Browne's murder pales into insignificance when compared with what Hay and his cronies are doing. There is gunpowder in a cellar, and you told me yourself that muskets have been shipped to London. We cannot go anywhere until we have learned what they intend to do.'

'Then you can tell your friends at White Hall tomorrow. This is work for a militia, not us.'

'Hay will deny our accusations, and he is a wealthy merchant with powerful friends. We need proof of his treason, and we are not leaving until we have it. So far, all we have is what you claim to have heard at his gatherings.' Chaloner did not add that no spymaster was going to take the word of a captain with a penchant for wine over that of an influential merchant.

York looked as though he was going to argue further, but his mouth snapped shut when footsteps sounded from along the hall. Chaloner grimaced in exasperation when York immediately ducked into an alcove. Such antics were unnecessary, because they were supposed – expected – to be heading for the gathering. He was about to order York out, when Strutt approached. The purser seemed even more ill at ease and agitated than York, and Chaloner wondered yet again whether he was as comfortable with rebellion as he let Hay believe.

'There you are, Garsfield,' Strutt said in a voice that shook. 'I shall show you the way to our meeting place, as this is your first time. You go first. I will follow.'

Chaloner knew instantly that something was amiss. He pretended to acquiesce, then spun around without warning. Strutt leaped in alarm at the sudden movement, and the dagger that had been poised to strike clattered to the floor. Strutt began to back away, moving unknowingly towards the place where York hid. The purser took a breath to shout for help, but York reacted with startling speed. Strutt's yell turned into a peculiar gasping sound, and when he sank to his knees York's knife was protruding from his back.

'That was unnecessary,' hissed Chaloner angrily. 'Now what are we going to do? If anyone finds the body before the meeting, they will know exactly who killed him.'

York glared. 'He was going to stab you! Besides, I am not sorry for ridding the world of that vermin. He caused Browne and the crew of *Rosebush* all manner of hardship with his dishonesty, and then he accused Browne of being a liar when he objected to the thievery. Strutt was a snake!'

Chaloner opened the door to the nearest secret passage and hauled the purser's body inside, hoping the corridor was not one Hay and his accomplices would use – at least not until Chaloner had made his report to Spymaster Williamson. With York still voicing his reservations, Chaloner walked quickly down the stairs towards the hall. Then he saw a shadow near the pantry and stopped abruptly, motioning York to be silent.

'Garsfield will *not* be coming to the gathering tonight,' Hay was saying in a low voice to Parr. 'Strutt is taking care of him and will join us when the matter is resolved.'

The preacher was uneasy. 'You should have asked me to do it. Strutt is weak and does not listen to the voice of God inside him, telling him what to do.'

'Garsfield is not expecting a blade between the ribs,' said Hay wryly. 'Even Strutt should be able to manage that – regardless of whether God does or does not think it a good idea.'

Parr grimaced at the comment but apparently knew better than to argue. 'He told me today that *you* killed Tivill. Did you?'

'No!' cried Hay, startled. 'I dispatched a pair of merchants who threatened to expose us, but that is the extent of my dabbling in such dark affairs. Besides, I would never use a stone. It would make a mess, and wigs as handsome as this one are expensive.'

'Well, someone made an end of Tivill,' said Parr. 'And it was not me, either. It is the traitor in our midst.'

'Can it be York?' asked Hay. '*He* was the one who brought Garsfield into our fold, and – as I told you earlier – my source at the Admiralty tells me there is no captain called Garsfield in the navy.'

'My instincts tell me York is not sufficiently courageous to take us on,' said the preacher thoughtfully. 'It must be someone else – someone who *used* York to bring Garsfield into our midst. Well, it will not work, because God walks at my side, and He will see this villain dance on the point of my dagger before the night is out.'

'Good,' said Hay fiercely. 'So we are agreed, then? Tonight we will tell our associates that one of them is a traitor to our cause? They will not like it.'

'We have no choice. It is the only way to flush the vermin out.'

Chaloner and a reluctant York joined the procession of cloaked men who walked silently to the east wing of Bermondsey House and down the steep steps to the cellar. Some of the conspirators carried torches, and it occurred to Chaloner that the hooded figures with the loose garments swinging about their ankles bore an uncanny resemblance to the monks whose foundation had been dissolved more than a century before. They had been processing to their prayers; Bermondsey House's guests were going to plot the end of His Majesty's government.

'You are a fool,' muttered York in Chaloner's ear as he navigated the treacherous steps. 'You heard Hay – he has killed before, and admits it freely. He thinks *I* am harmless, but you are doomed if he or the preacher see you now.'

Chaloner ignored him, not wanting to discuss the matter where they might be overheard. He took a place near the back of the crypt, York at his side, and watched other men sit on the benches in front of them. Hoods meant it was impossible to see faces, and no one spoke once they were seated. The cellar cast an instant and unsettling chill over the gathering, and York was not the only one trembling.

Hay closed the door when everyone was inside, and Chaloner watched uneasily as he sealed it with a bar. He was taking no chances of anyone coming un-announced and uninvited to the gathering – or of anyone escaping. He was the only one who did not bother with a hooded cloak.

'Gentlemen,' he said, going to stand at the front of the assembly, near the wall where the encoded letter had been left. 'You know why we are here, so I shall not waste your time with preliminaries. Does anyone have anything to report?'

'There is going to be a new tax on wool,' called a man from the front row. When he raised his head to speak, Chaloner glimpsed a long nose. 'And there is talk of it being extended to cloth – to reimburse the navy's unpaid sailors, allegedly.'

'The navy will see none of it,' sneered Preacher Parr. 'It will go towards funding the government's vice. God will strike them down for their wickedness – with a little help from us, His faithful servants.'

'I suppose we might be seen as agents of justice,' mused Long Nose thoughtfully. 'By devising ways to avoid these iniquitous taxes, we are saving dissipated ministers from themselves.'

'John White hanged himself on Sunday,' said a man who sat directly in front of Chaloner. He leaned forward as he spoke, and the spy saw fingers that were marred with small burns. He had seen such scars before, on the hands of silversmiths. 'He was taxed to death – literally.'

'We are all being bled dry·by the government,' said Hay sorrowfully. 'It is very wrong.'

'What is wrong is our government's love affair with sin,' countered Parr, using the same stentorian tones he might employ when addressing a congregation. He raised his hands, so his hood fell back and revealed his face. No one seemed surprised, and Chaloner was under the impression it had happened before. 'God is on our side, and we are right to oppose this evil regime. Long live the Commonwealth!'

There was a smattering of applause, but not nearly as much as Chaloner would have expected.

'The Commonwealth taxed us too,' remarked Hay. 'But not nearly as much as the king's men. Long live free trade and a government that does not grow fat on the toil of honest merchants.'

This time the support was considerably more enthusiastic.

'And long may we continue to move money between accounts,' called Long Nose. 'It has already saved us a fortune in revenue – by keeping it out of the government's sticky hands.'

The cellar rang with whistles, stamps and approving yells, and slowly it dawned on Chaloner that the conspirators were not aiming to overthrow the king and usher in a new Commonwealth – their main objective was devising ways to avoid paying their taxes. He almost laughed aloud, but his amusement faded when he realized that greed was a powerful compulsion, and the fact that the rebellion's aim was vaguely ridiculous did not render its instigators any less dangerous.

'And now *I* have something to report,' said Hay. 'There is evidence that we have been betrayed.'

'You mean the Archer brothers?' asked the silversmith. 'We knew they wanted to tell Spymaster Williamson about the way we manage our accounts, but you said they had thought better of it and had gone to Jamaica instead. How can they still be a problem?'

'It is not them,' replied Hay smoothly. 'They are beyond hurting us now. It is someone else.'

'But we are not doing anything wrong,' objected Long Nose, although his voice lacked conviction. 'Well, not really. We just transfer money here and there, so the government's auditors find it difficult to track – and what they cannot track, they cannot tax. It is not *our* fault the Treasury Department cannot keep up with the ways of modern commerce.'

'Hear, hear!' cried the silversmith, apparently less bothered by the ethics of the situation. 'Our plan is working perfectly, just as Hay envisioned when he first mooted the notion, and we are all the richer for it. And that being said, how could anyone want to put a stop to it? Everyone here benefits.'

Chaloner glanced at York, who raised his hands defensively. 'It would have looked suspicious if I had refused to invest in their tax-free accounts,' he whispered. 'Besides, why should I not benefit? The government takes far too big a cut of an honest man's income.'

Chaloner did not deign to answer and turned his attention back to Hay.

'A sea captain came to see me this afternoon, eager to join our ranks,' the shipping magnate was saying. 'However, I suspect his real intention is to expose us.'

'Then arrange for him to visit Jamaica,' said the silversmith with a careless shrug. 'As you did to the Archers. I do not see why a mere sailor should concern us.'

'Garsfield is not the problem,' said Parr. 'The real issue is that *someone* gave him details about our operation, and *that* man is the traitor. I suspect he is sitting among us, here in this very room.'

There was immediate consternation.

'I found this today,' said Hay, brandishing the letter he had recovered from the wall. 'It is in cipher, and addressed to Spymaster Williamson. And it is not the first, either. There have been four just like this in the past month alone.'

There was a collective gasp of horror, and then a clamour of voices as questions were yelled. Some men were on their feet, while others huddled deeper inside their hoods and appeared to be regarding their neighbours with wariness and distrust.

The silversmith's voice was louder than the others. He pointed to Parr. '*There* is our traitor. He claims he is not interested in money, only in serving God. But it is unnatural, and I do not believe it.'

'Parr would never betray us,' said Hay, although he shot the preacher an uncomfortable glance.

The silversmith folded his arms and looked triumphant. 'Then tell me why Strutt lies in a pool of blood in the corridor near my room – I almost fell over him on my way here. The answer is because *Parr* killed him! I know he is the culprit, because I saw them together just moments before.'

Hay glanced at Parr in shock. 'They were together, but—'

'It was not me!' shouted Parr, outraged both by the accusation and by the fact that people seemed rather willing to believe it. 'It must have been the real traitor—'

'*You* are the real traitor,' bellowed the silversmith.

'No!' yelled Parr. 'I am innocent, a man of God, and—'

'The traitor will be a stranger to us,' interrupted Long Nose, breaking impatiently into the altercation. 'We come here cloaked and hooded, but we all know each other, so let us end the pretence here and now. If everyone abandons his disguise, we shall see who we do not recognize.'

Chaloner began to ease towards the door. Here was an outcome he had not anticipated.

'Yes!' cried the silversmith, hauling his robe from his face. 'Here *I* am. You all know me – Jonas Evans, from Southwark.'

Chaloner shot to his feet as more hoods fell back and snatched a lamp from the wall. Immediately, hands tried to grab him, but he jigged and twisted, and no one kept hold of him for long. He hurled the torch into the niche that contained the gunpowder, then turned and raced towards the door. It was blocked by the silversmith, whose face was pale with outrage. He could not defeat Chaloner in a fight – the spy was naturally experienced in such matters – but he could delay him for vital seconds until he could be overwhelmed by others. Chaloner turned and headed for the tunnel instead, but Evans dived full length and managed to drag him to the floor. Then the flames from the torch reached the scattered gunpowder, which blazed and ignited the straw. Puzzled, Hay went to see what was happening.

'Gunpowder!' he yelled, backing away fast. 'With flames all over it! Run for your lives!'

In the event the fire did not last long enough to burn through the thick wood of the powder barrel, so there was no explosion. It was just as well, Chaloner thought as he punched his way free of the silversmith, given that the whole mansion might have collapsed had it gone off. The panic created by Hay's announcement had produced the effect the spy had wanted anyway. There was an abrupt and immediate stampede – which included Hay and York – for the stairs, and no one was very interested in lingering to lay hold of traitors. All except Parr. The preacher's face was a mask of rage, and Chaloner saw he cared little for his own safety. He did care about what he saw as his duty to God, though. He gave chase, screaming for others to help him. Evans the silversmith was the only one who obliged.

Chaloner reached the tunnel's entrance and dragged open the trap door. It was not easy ascending the narrow, cramped slope at speed, and the faster he tried to go the more he skidded and slipped. He could hear Parr gaining on him. It felt like an age before he reached the pantry and clambered out, and when he did the preacher was almost on him. He slammed the opening shut just as Parr was stretching out to grab him. Parr released a frustrated howl and began to batter the barrier with his fists. Chaloner grinned at the foul language that peppered the curses and headed for the door and freedom. He was shocked to find his way barred by Castell, who wore a hooded cloak and carried a pair of handguns.

'*You* are one of these conspirators?' he blurted, astonished that the plotters should consider admitting such a man to their ranks. A dissipated gambler was unlikely to make for a reliable ally. 'I thought you only wanted the money they paid you.'

'I despise the government,' declared Castell, staggering slightly. He was still drunk from dinner. 'Its ministers shun me at the gaming tables, and I am sick of it. Death to the lot of them, I say. Stay where you are, or I will kill you. I am not afraid to dispense a little justice.'

He aimed the weapon with a hand that was surprisingly steady for a man in his cups, and Chaloner stopped dead in his tracks. Then there was a yell of triumph from Parr – his assault on the panel was beginning to pay off, because, like the rest of the house, it was rotten and weak. It began to splinter, and Chaloner saw he was going to be caught. He took a step towards the door, tensing when Castell's finger tightened on the trigger. But the spy could see powder spilling from the pan; the weapon had been badly loaded and was more danger to its user than to its target. There was a flash, a sharp report and a brief silence. Then Castell started to scream.

Meanwhile, Parr began to emerge from the tunnel. Chaloner ran for the pantry door, and as he glanced back he saw Parr seize Castell's second gun. He suspected it was no better primed than the first, but he was unwilling to bet his life on it by lingering. He hurtled through the door and slammed it behind him. He turned left, but found himself in an unfamiliar hallway that led to a dead end. He was trapped. Parr and Evans were out of the tunnel, and he could hear them thundering towards him.

'This way,' hissed an urgent voice from behind an opening that had been cleverly concealed in the wall panels. It was Margaret. 'Do not stand there gaping. Hurry!'

With no other choice, Chaloner did as he was told. He found himself in a dark, musty room that had once been a library, judging from the number of shelves along its walls. Margaret hurried towards the fireplace, where she hauled on a lever. Chaloner closed the door and secured it by jamming a chair under the handle. Unfortunately, Parr seemed to know about the room, too, because he immediately started to hurl himself against the door, and the chair began to give way.

'Come on,' whispered Margaret, indicating with an impatient flick of her head that Chaloner was to climb through a tiny hatch she had opened. The spy baulked when he saw she held a stone in her gnarled hands. She raised it, as if readying herself to put it to good use. Suddenly something became perfectly clear.

'*You* killed Tivill! Why?'

She grimaced. 'I suspect you already know why – because he attempted blackmail.'

'But there was nothing to blackmail anyone about –

Walduck *did* kill Browne, as you know full well, given that it was you who provided me with the information to work it out.'

'That did not make Tivill any less of a nuisance, though.'

Chaloner thought aloud as he leaned on the chair, trying to brace it against Parr's furious onslaught. 'Tivill believed Walduck's protestations of innocence – although they were lies – and when his ship returned to London he came to see what he could find out. Instead of learning about the murder, he discovered what Hay and his associates were doing and threatened to tell. Am I right?'

'I dispatched him with a rock to the head and was going to drop his corpse in the fish pond. But Hay found it before I could fetch a cart. He has no idea what really happened; I suspect he thinks Parr is responsible. And speaking of Parr, are you going to go through this hole or stay and face his fury?'

Chaloner jerked backwards when a sword plunged through the worm-ridden door, missing him by no more than the width of a finger. If the preacher continued his onslaught, it would not be many moments before he was inside – and Chaloner had heard Evans offer to reload the gun in a way that would not blow off its user's hand. At such close range, Parr could not fail to hit his target, and yet the spy was loath to put himself at the mercy of the rock-wielding grandmother by climbing into what appeared to be a very small space.

'You had better hurry,' said Margaret, watching him hesitate. 'As I said earlier, Parr is a fanatic and will stop at nothing to do what he believes is right. He will kill you without a second thought.'

Chaloner indicated the stone. 'What are you going to do? Brain *me* and leave *my* body for Hay?'

The sword crashed through the door a second time,

showering him with splinters. At this rate the preacher would not need to smash the whole thing – he would be able to take aim through one of the great holes he was making.

Margaret reclaimed his attention with a sharp bark of laughter. 'Is that what you think? You could not be more wrong. My intention was to brain *Parr*.'

'Why?'

'Because he intends to bring down the government – the others are just silly men who want to evade their taxes. However, he has almost broken through that door, and I am not in the mood for dying today. So I shall escape instead.'

'Escape?' Chaloner watched her clamber into the hole with astonishing agility for one so old. It was clear she had done it many times before. He heard her voice echo eerily back to him.

'Yes, escape. Either come with me or face Parr's righteous rage. But close the panel regardless.'

When the sword jabbed through the door a third time, Chaloner abandoned it and scrambled after her, pulling shut the hatch behind him. He found himself in a narrow tunnel, so small that the only way to move forward was by crawling on his stomach. Behind him, he heard Parr's victorious yell turn to a scream of fury when he discovered the library empty. Echoes and thumps sounded as the preacher began to hunt for the secret exit. In front, Margaret was making rapid progress, scuttling along like a crab. Chaloner marvelled at her nimbleness and concluded that she was a remarkable lady. Very remarkable.

'*You* are the traitor,' he called softly. 'I assumed it was York, because he brought Browne and then me to Hay's meetings. But I was forgetting the message hidden in the wall. *You* are sending information to Spymaster Williamson.'

Margaret laughed. 'An elderly lady like me? What a thing to say!'

The tunnel forked, and she turned left, opening an iron gate to emerge in a dusty chamber that looked as though it had not been used in decades. She locked it behind them, then led the way through a maze of corridors until they reached a pleasant, comfortable room that was far nicer than anything else Chaloner had seen in Bermondsey House. The woodwork smelled of honeyed beeswax, the furniture was handsome and there was glass in every window. Margaret Castell was indeed a woman of many surprises, and Chaloner knew he had been foolish not to have seen through her sooner.

'Williamson knows a decent spy when he sees one,' he said. 'And you have been keeping him appraised ever since your grandson first started to lend Bermondsey House to plotters and rebels.'

Flattered, Margaret's eyes twinkled as she walked to a table and poured wine into two exquisite silver cups. 'Well, someone had to do it.'

'I thought Hay was a dangerous dissident, but all he is doing is cheating the Treasury.'

Margaret wagged a finger at him. 'It is still treason, and the government is partial to money.'

'Your grandson cannot know what you are doing. He believes in Hay's cause.'

'And that is what has allowed me to maintain my cover all this time. Hay assumes I will never do anything to betray the "rebels", because my grandson is a fervent member of his cabal. However, I have an arrangement with the government, and a pardon was written long ago. After all, I cannot spy without my foolish kinsman's "assistance", so it is only fair that he should be spared.'

'You said you lease your house to government ministers who want to assassinate old Cromwellians too. Do you?'

She nodded with a smile. 'Overzealous supporters can be just as dangerous as enemies, as *you* doubtless know. Do not pretend you do not understand what I am talking about. I recognize a fellow spy when I see one – just as you did with me. Why do you think I rescued you from Parr?'

'He will scour the house until he finds me, and if I am discovered here he will know you helped.'

'I do not think we should worry about that.' She sank in a chair with a sigh of contentment and gestured that he should sit opposite. 'You see, a week ago Spymaster Williamson decided that Hay's next meeting should be his last – mostly because Parr is growing too dangerous. That vile fanatic has encouraged Hay to purchase muskets and gunpowder, which takes the "rebellion" to a completely new level. I sent Williamson a message to tell him the time of the gathering, and I am expecting him and his men at any moment.'

'Unfortunately, Hay found it. Hidden in the cellar wall.'

She laughed. 'Credit me with some cunning, boy! I sent Williamson *several* notes, but the letter in the wall is actually the story of Bermondsey's ghosts, as Hay will discover when he decodes it. It will give him something to read when he is in prison, and perhaps he will blame *them* for his misfortune.'

'If Williamson is coming, then I have done you a disservice, ma'am. My actions ended the meeting sooner than expected, and some of the conspirators will have escaped before he arrives.'

Margaret grinned, rather diabolically. 'But I am quite fond of some, and do not want them imprisoned – or worse. Williamson will catch Hay and Parr, and they are the ringleaders. *I* am happy at the way matters have been resolved, though Williamson will be less pleased, I imagine. Perhaps we should not tell him your role in the affair – he can be a bit vengeful when his plans are foiled, and we do not want him thinking you did it on purpose.'

'No,' agreed Chaloner fervently. 'We do not.'

III

The unveiling of a wicked plot at Bermondsey House was written up with glee in the newsbooks and gossiped about in every tavern. Chaloner was startled to read that its ringleader was the Rector of Bermondsey, who had hanged himself before the spymaster's troops could catch him. There was no mention of Hay's involvement, though Chaloner did hear a few weeks later that the Hay's Wharf Company had offered to finance the building of new offices for the Treasury Department – the old ones, he said, were terribly cramped for the poor auditors. Despite public interest, most of the conspirators were never named. The following year, however, several wealthy Bermondsey merchants admitted to substantial losses on their annual profits.

Chaloner met Hannah at Jamaica House and told her all he had learned about Browne's murder. She listened carefully to his explanation, then nodded her acceptance of it. She was distressed to learn about the dislike her husband had engendered among his crew but vehemently denied that he would have cheated Walduck over prize money. Chaloner knew she was right, and he supposed Walduck had allowed hatred to blind him when he had grabbed the stone and brought it down on his captain's head.

'So justice *was* done when Walduck was hanged,' concluded Chaloner. 'He thought he could convince people that your husband's death was an accident due to falling masonry, but no one believed him. And those who did believe him – you and York – misjudged him. In desperation, he claimed he was in his cups, because he thought there was a chance that drunkenness might grant him a reprieve. He was wrong.'

'He was wrong,' echoed Hannah softly. She took his hand in hers. 'Thank you, Thomas. And now I have something to tell you. Captain York has asked me to marry him, and I have accepted his offer for my children's sake – I cannot let them starve, and we have no money of our own. He says he feels guilty about what happened to John and wants to make amends.'

'I see,' said Chaloner noncommittally, supposing that the offer of marriage did not also come with a confession of York's role in losing the Browne family fortune.

Hannah was lost in her own thoughts. 'He is not John, but he will suffice. Besides, he will be at sea most of the time.'

Chaloner hoped so, for both their sakes.

The following week he went to visit Margaret Castell. In recognition of her services to the king, she had been rewarded with a fine house near Winchester Palace. Further, her grandson's debts had been paid in full, on condition that he joined the navy. He had recovered from his 'accident' and was serving under York aboard *Rosebush*, where the captain taught him the proper way to load guns. Unhappily, York's attempts to educate his new lieutenant were wasted, because a few months later he drank too much dinner wine and fell off the back of the ship. His body was never recovered.

'Everything worked out very well,' said Margaret, walking with Chaloner in her new arbour. It was a fine summer day, not too hot, and the garden was pleasantly shady. 'Spymaster Williamson was annoyed not to catch a few merchants red-handed, but they were my friends, and I am grateful to you for precipitating their escape. I could not have managed that alone.'

'Right,' said Chaloner uneasily, hoping she had kept her word and left Williamson in ignorance about the role played by the Lord Chancellor's spy.

She read his thoughts. 'Do not worry – your secret will go with me to the grave. Williamson is not a man you want as an enemy – and not one I want, either, which is why I elected to accept this house and retire from intelligence work. He is too devious for his own good, and I no longer wish to work for him.'

Chaloner agreed with her assessment, but was not so rash as to denigrate one of the government's most powerful officials to a woman he barely knew. 'I am surprised Hay did not reveal your friends' identities when Williamson questioned him,' he said instead. 'He did not seem the kind of man to sacrifice himself to protect others.'

'He did betray them,' said Margaret. 'Of course he did – apparently Williamson's clerks were hard-pressed to write fast enough once he started to bleat. But there was plenty of time for me to visit my friends first and tell them the best way to extricate themselves from their predicament.'

Chaloner regarded her askance. 'What did you suggest they do?'

'Offer Williamson a percentage of their back taxes,' she replied with a grin. 'He is as corrupt as the next man where large sums of money are concerned.'

Chaloner started to say he did not believe her, but realized he was being naive. They were talking about the government, after all, an organization in which money spoke louder than justice or truth. 'What about Parr?' he asked instead. 'Did he really commit suicide?'

Margaret adopted a pious expression. 'I happened to find documents that proved he had been cheating the Treasury for years. He said he could not bear the shame of being exposed as a regular sinner, and took the easy way out.'

Chaloner frowned. 'Where are these documents now? No one has mentioned them before.'

Margaret's face was cunning and rather malevolent. 'Perhaps they never existed. But he was a wicked fellow, and I shall not lose any sleep over his demise. As I said, everything worked out very well. Very well indeed.'

hISTORICAL NOTE

Bermondsey Abbey was a victim of the Dissolution. Most of it was demolished then, although three gate-houses and sections of wall were spared, and Bermondsey House eventually rose in what was the inner courtyard. The mansion survived into the seven-teenth century, although it was in a state of serious disrepair by the 1660s and its owners were unlikely to have lived in it. They would have rented it to tenants, although its shabby condition indicates they would not have been very grand ones.

John Browne, captain of *Rosebush*, died in April 1663, and contemporary records indicate he was killed by one of his own sailors, who lobbed a stone at him while drunk. The previous year, Browne had also quarrelled with his purser, Thomas Strutt, which had resulted in Strutt leaving *Rosebush* in a huff. William Hay owned the Hay's Wharf Company, which operated on the south bank of the Thames, opposite the Tower of London. William Castell was a Bermondsey shipwright; his wife was named Margaret. Captain Richard York (died 1665) was commemorated on a tablet in Bermondsey's old church, as was the cooper Edward Walduck. Richard Parr was Bermondsey's rector in the mid-seventeenth century, famous for inflammatory sermons. Finally, Joseph Williamson was in charge of the government's intelligence network from the early 1660s and was credited with suppressing a number of rebellions, some of them small and ill-conceived, like the fictional one at Bermondsey House.

EPILOGUE

June 2004

Faces peered down from the upper decks of the red buses that ran along Tower Bridge Road, beyond the wooden hoardings that shielded the excavations from the common gaze. At one point they looked almost straight down into a large hole, the passengers unaware that they were just crossing the cloister and frater of the old priory and abbey. Around the rectangular pit, a brace of archaeologists were moodily contemplating the damage done to their earlier meticulous excavation of the vault that must have been beneath the original cellarer's building.

Edward Asprey pushed back his safety helmet and wiped the sweat from his forehead. He was a short man with a mop of black hair and a wispy beard. The summer sky was filling with ominous thunderclouds, and the oppressive afternoon was becoming too hot for comfort.

'Bloody JCB!' he muttered to his blonde assistant, Julia Masters. 'The damned place is cursed! I suppose now we'll have those officious sods from Health and Safety crawling all over us.'

She had to agree that this area of the rescue dig seemed to have a hoodoo on it. Three weeks ago, one of their student volunteers had slipped into the cellar excavation and broken a leg – and two days ago, an almost new mechanical digger had crashed into it when the end wall had unexpectedly given way. It was a miracle that the driver escaped serious injury, but all work had been halted until this morning, when a mobile crane arrived to hoist the damaged machine out.

They looked around the rest of the site, where low walls of dark stone stood exposed below ground level, like stumps of rotten teeth jutting from the brown earth and grey rubble. Built over repeatedly for almost a thousand years, the area was a confused mass of foundations from a score of previous 'developments', and only the painstaking work of the archaeologists had separated the many and varied eras of construction. Soon, a huge complex of offices, shops and apartments would rear into the sky above the remains of Bermondsey Abbey, but underneath it all would be preserved the roots of the monastic settlement that was an important part of England's heritage. But time was pressing and the cement-mixers and pile-drivers were champing impatiently, eager to put another new silhouette on London's skyline.

'Better get down there and see how much damage that digger has done,' sighed Asprey. He waved to two other assistants and a couple of graduate students from University College, who were on the other side of the hole. They all went gingerly down the laddered scaffolding and gathered on the floor which they had so laboriously cleaned of infill before the toppled machine brought down more stones and rubble. Walking to the far end they contemplated the collapsed wall, where it abutted on the side of the former chamber. Julia Masters looked dubiously at the ancient masonry.

'That looks really unsafe, now that the top courses of stone have fallen in,' she said.

'It was a lousy bit of masonry to start with,' agreed Edward Asprey.

'Must have been yet another later alteration, as the other walls have much better stonework.'

The cellar was due to be filled in level with the original ground surface before construction work began, though all the other exposed walls were to be carefully preserved underneath the huge buildings that were to be built above. Even the piles needed to support the new edifice were to be placed where they would not damage the old foundations.

The small group went closer to the place where the JCB had fallen in and picked their way through the old stones and mortar that were strewn about the floor. Julia Masters looked up at the wall and saw that most of the top half had been thrown down over a length of about five yards, leaving a large bite-like defect that came down to chin level. She made her way close to the wall, wishing the liner of her yellow helmet was not so tight, as sweat was sticking it to her head.

'Watch those stones; they look loose,' warned one of the students, pointing to the upper row of the remaining masonry. Julia carefully clambered up on to the debris at the foot of the wall, interested to see how thick it was. 'That's odd, Edward,' she called over her shoulder. 'There seems to be another wall just behind it.'

He stumbled up to where she was perched and raised himself on tiptoe to look over the edge. 'A twelfth-century cavity wall! We'll be finding polystyrene insulation here next!'

His attempt at levity was ignored as Julia, almost a head taller, peered over the upper line of stones. 'There's a good eighteen-inch space here, running right across the width of the vault,' she announced. 'Anyone got a light?'

As one of the students was dispatched to their site cabin to fetch a torch, there was a rumble of thunder and a few large spots of rain plopped down, but after a few moments it ceased, though the sky was now heavy with purple-grey clouds. When the torch arrived, Asprey handed it to Julia, who craned her head over the shattered stonework as she shone the light downwards.

'We'd better get the rest of this wall down straight away, Edward,' she said sombrely.

An hour later a mini-digger had pulled away the remaining lower courses of masonry, and the archaeologists were crowding around what was revealed at the bottom of the cavity. The group was augmented by Mary McGowan, a burly middle-aged anthropologist who had been examining the bones from burials in the adjacent cemetery.

'One male, probably under twenty-eight by the look of the inner ends of his collar bones and the edges of his pelvis,' she announced as she squatted alongside a heap of rusted metal and brittle, brown stick-like objects. 'And a young woman, almost certainly late teens.'

'What about the skulls?' asked Asprey, shaken in spite of many previous finds of skeletal remains.

'Nothing wrong with the chap's head,' said Mary. 'But the poor girl has what looks like a massive head injury.' She pointed to the skull, which lay upside down, in colour and shape like an old coconut. 'Deep depressed fracture high up above the left ear.'

'Could it not be damage that occurred long after death?' objected Julia. 'We've all seen those due to rock falls or even just a stone resting against it for years.'

Another rumble of thunder failed to drown out Mary McGowan's emphatic denial. 'Not this one, love! See that crack passing right across the base? That's a sure giveaway for a whack on the head!'

'What about those chains?' asked Asprey, pointing to the rusty links.

'That's your department, not mine, Eddie! I'd get 'em photographed straight away, before you try to move them. They'll disintegrate at a touch.'

She pointed with a pencil towards the corroded iron. 'Extraordinary! There are shackles around the lower ends of both forearm bones of the fellow, but her ribs are inside his arms ... and that other, longer chain passed under the lumbar vertebrae and pelves of both of them.'

'What does that mean, Dr McGowan?' asked one of the students respectfully.

The anthropologist rocked back on the heels of her sensible shoes.

'The bloke's wrists were chained together around the girl's back – and another chain must have gone around their waists, so that they were clamped together, face to face. She must already have been dead, with a massive skull fracture like that – but there's no reason to think he wasn't still alive!'

There was a shocked silence, broken only by a clap of thunder.

'Bloody hell!' whispered Edward. 'Walled up alive, chained to a corpse!'

Mary McGowan shrugged. 'This has to be hundreds of years old, by the state of the bones. Those loose rosary beads and that silver cross suggest it goes back at least until before the Dissolution of the Monasteries.'

'We'll have to tell the police, surely?' said Julia.

'I doubt they'll be interested in a centuries-old homicide!' snorted Mary. 'Neither will the coroner, if he considers it to be older than sixty or seventy years.'

Edward Asprey climbed to his feet. 'I'll have to tell

our director straight away and see what he says. The press will be all over this when they find out.'

Large spots of rain began to fall and there was a loud clap of thunder and a flash of lightning over towards the river.

'Let's get back to the hut and use a phone,' suggested Julia, and as the rain began to come down in torrents they hurriedly ran for shelter.

Just as they reached their Portakabin, there was a tremendous sizzling flash of lightning that almost blinded them and an almost simultaneous crash of thunder that sounded like the end of the world, as a strike lanced down into the excavation site. A smell of burning assailed them, and a wreath of smoke rose from the cellar pit, as the rain stopped as abruptly as it had begun.

When the sky cleared and they hesitantly returned to the large hole in the ground, they found that the two skeletons had been vaporized and the rusted chains were now blobs of fused, magnetized metal. All that was recognizable at the foot of the ancient wall was a scatter of amber rosary beads.

SIMON & SCHUSTER

The Medieval Murderers
Sword of Shame

Five enthralling interlinked mysteries from Michael Jecks, Susanna Gregory, Bernard Knight, Ian Morson and Philip Gooden.

Qui falsitate vivit, animam occidit. Falsus in ore, caret honore. The Latin inscription carved on the gleaming blade read: He who lives in falsehood slays his soul; he who lies, his honour. If only they had known how true those words would prove to be . . .

Lovingly crafted by a Saxon swordsmith shortly before the Norman invasion, treachery and deceit are the Sword of Shame's constant companions. From the Norman conquest of 1066 to the murder of Thomas à Becket, from an attempted coup against Richard the Lionheart to the bloodstained battle of Poitiers: at the heart of every treasonous plot, murder and betrayal lies the malign influence of the cursed sword. As it passes from owner to owner in this intriguing series of interlinked mysteries, ill fortune and disgrace befall all who wield its glittering but deadly blade.

Sword of Shame is the second series of gripping medieval mysteries from the acclaimed authors of *The Tainted Relic*.

ISBN 978-1-4165-2190-7
PRICE £6.99

SIMON & SCHUSTER

THE TAINTED RELIC

A historical mystery by Michael Jecks, Susanna Gregory, Bernard Knight, Ian Morson and Philip Gooden.

The anthology centres around a piece of the True Cross, allegedly stained with the blood of Christ, which falls into the hands of an English knight, Geoffrey Mappestone, in 1100 at the end of the First Crusade. The relic is said to be cursed and, after three inexplicable deaths, it finds its way to England in the hands of a thief.

After several decades, the relic appears in Devon where it becomes part of a story by Bernard Knight, involving his protagonist Crowner John. In Oxford, in 1269, the discovery of a decapitated monk leads Ian Morson's academic sleuth, William Falconer, to discover a link to the relic. In 1323 in Exeter, Michael Jecks' Sir Baldwin has reason to suspect its involvement in five violent deaths. Thirty years later, several suspicious deaths occur in Cambridge. As Susanna Gregory's Matthew Bartholomew and Brother Michael are to discover, the tainted relic has a crucial part to play. Finally, it's despatched to London, where Philip Gooden's Nick Revill will determiine its ultimate fate.

ISBN 978-1-4165-0213-5
PRICE £6.99